**THE COMPLETE CASEBOOK OF
CARDIGAN, VOLUME 1: 1931-32**

FREDERICK NEBEL

ILLUSTRATIONS BY
JOHN FLEMING GOULD

INTRODUCTION BY
WILL MURRAY

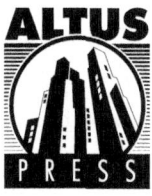

BOSTON • 2012

© 2012 Altus Press • First Edition—2012

EDITED AND DESIGNED BY
Matthew Moring

PUBLISHING HISTORY

"Introduction" appears here for the first time. Copyright © 2012 Will Murray. All Rights Reserved.

"Death Alley" originally appeared in the November, 1931 issue of *Dime Detective Magazine*. Copyright © 2012 Argosy Communications, Inc. All Rights Reserved. Reprinted by arrangement with Argosy Communications, Inc.

"Hell's Pay Check" originally appeared in the December, 1931 issue of *Dime Detective Magazine*. Copyright © 2012 Argosy Communications, Inc. All Rights Reserved. Reprinted by arrangement with Argosy Communications, Inc.

"Six Diamonds and a Dick" originally appeared in the January, 1932 issue of *Dime Detective Magazine*. Copyright © 2012 Argosy Communications, Inc. All Rights Reserved. Reprinted by arrangement with Argosy Communications, Inc.

"And There Was Murder" originally appeared in the February, 1932 issue of *Dime Detective Magazine*. Copyright © 2012 Argosy Communications, Inc. All Rights Reserved. Reprinted by arrangement with Argosy Communications, Inc.

"Phantom Fingers" originally appeared in the March, 1932 issue of *Dime Detective Magazine*. Copyright © 2012 Argosy Communications, Inc. All Rights Reserved. Reprinted by arrangement with Argosy Communications, Inc.

"Murder on the Loose" originally appeared in the April, 1932 issue of *Dime Detective Magazine*. Copyright © 2012 Argosy Communications, Inc. All Rights Reserved. Reprinted by arrangement with Argosy Communications, Inc.

"Rogues' Ransom" originally appeared in the August, 1932 issue of *Dime Detective Magazine*. Copyright © 2012 Argosy Communications, Inc. All Rights Reserved. Reprinted by arrangement with Argosy Communications, Inc.

"Lead Pearls" originally appeared in the September, 1932 issue of *Dime Detective Magazine*. Copyright © 2012 Argosy Communications, Inc. All Rights Reserved. Reprinted by arrangement with Argosy Communications, Inc.

"The Dead Don't Die" originally appeared in the October, 1932 issue of *Dime Detective Magazine*. Copyright © 2012 Argosy Communications, Inc. All Rights Reserved. Reprinted by arrangement with Argosy Communications, Inc.

"The Candy Killer" originally appeared in the November, 1932 issue of *Dime Detective Magazine*. Copyright © 2012 Argosy Communications, Inc. All Rights Reserved. Reprinted by arrangement with Argosy Communications, Inc.

"A Truck-Load of Diamonds" originally appeared in the December, 1932 issue of *Dime Detective Magazine*. Copyright © 2012 Argosy Communications, Inc. All Rights Reserved. Reprinted by arrangement with Argosy Communications, Inc.

THANKS TO
Joel Frieman, Ron Goulart, Ken McDaniel, Will Murray,
Rick Ollerman, Rob Preston & Ray Riethmeier

ALL RIGHTS RESERVED

No part of this book may be reproduced or utilized in any form or by any means, electronic or mechanical, without permission in writing from the publisher.

This edition has been marked via subtle changes, so anyone who reprints from this collection is committing a violation of copyright.

Visit altuspress.com for more books like this.

Printed in the United States of America.

TABLE OF CONTENTS

INTRODUCTION i
DEATH ALLEY 1
HELL'S PAY CHECK 35
SIX DIAMONDS AND A DICK 71
AND THERE WAS MURDER 109
PHANTOM FINGERS 143
MURDER ON THE LOOSE 179
ROGUES' RANSOM 215
LEAD PEARLS 251
THE DEAD DON'T DIE 283
THE CANDY KILLER 317
A TRUCK-LOAD OF DIAMONDS . . . 349

INTRODUCTION

WILL MURRAY

DASHIELL HAMMETT was an American original. While he had many imitators, no writer was ever his equal. When Hammett left the pages of *Black Mask* in 1930, he left a stark and gaping void.

Editor Joseph Shaw looked to one writer to fill that void. That writer was Frederick L. Nebel. In the pages of *Black Mask,* but nowhere else, Nebel was Hammett's designated successor.

True, Raymond Chandler became Hammett's heir apparent, but Chandler didn't come along until 1933, which puts him in another category altogether. And Chandler was hardly a prolific pulpster, while Nebel was one of *Black Mask's* regular star contributors.

When he was preparing his retrospective *Hard-Boiled Omnibus* for publication in 1946, Shaw wrote Nebel the following:

> Simon & Schuster have asked me to write an introduction as to what made *Black Mask* and its recognized style click. Well, that's the story of you and Dash, particularly, and Ray Chandler when he came along later. It isn't my story—I never "discovered" an author; he discovered himself. I never "made" an author. He made himself. And you and Dash made that first distinctive style.

Shaw's editorial assessment is incontrovertible. And it's interesting that he does not mention the hard-boiled pioneer Carroll John Daly, who while wildly popular was no stylist.

A high school dropout who worked on the New York docks and in Canadian farms, Nebel began writing about outdoorsy he-man types like Captain Fortune and Typhoon MacQuade for Fiction House's *Action Stories,* and assorted Mounties for *North West Stories.* For *Lariat,* he wrote of a cowboy hero he named the Driftin' Kid.

Nebel broke into *Black Mask* in 1926. Most of his early output consisted of the now-legendary Kennedy and MacBride stories and a series featuring "Tough Dick" Donohue of the Inter-State Detective Agency, who debuted in 1930. Modeled after Hammett's popular Continental Op tales, Donny Donohue functioned as a natural successor to the unnamed Op, whom Hammett retired in 1930, bowing out in the same issue of *Black Mask* that witnessed Donohue's debut.

Nebel and Hammett were good friends, but the former denied being influenced by the latter. He explained the way of it to Ron Goulart:

> The so-called *Black Mask* story was developed by a few writers who happened to be producing that particular type of fiction when Joe Shaw became editor. The only *B.M.* writers I knew well at the time were Hammett and Whitfield: we spent a lot of time together socially and I don't recall that we ever talked about Shaw's influence as an editor. We were too busy clowning around in bars to talk shop. Besides, we never read one another's published work. I did read *The Maltese Falcon*, but that was about a year after it appeared in book form....
>
> Since we were not influenced by each other's work I can only surmise that we reflected the times we lived in. Certainly we were in no way editorially influenced by Joe Shaw. For my own part I know that Shaw never told me how to write for him, or what to write, nor did he ever ask for a revision or make one himself. He was an extraordinarily enthusiastic man, warm and cooperative, and I think his most important contribution to the magazine was his ability to let a writer write in his own way....

Truthfully, Fred Nebel wrote in a cool, detached voice that was distinctively his own. His characters possessed a reservedly sentimental side that was also unique. Nebel was an original.

When Popular Publications' Harry Steeger launched *Dime Detective* in 1933, he plundered the pages of *Black Mask* for star writers around whom to build his new enterprise. Joe Shaw couldn't have been too happy, but what could he do? Nebel, Erle Stanley Gardner and others were freelancers. They could write for whoever solicited their work. And to lure them into his service, Steeger offered them a penny a word above their going *Black Mask* rates.

Fred Nebel debuted in *Dime Detective* with a knockoff of "Tough Dick" Donohue—Cardigan of the Cosmos Detective Agency. A character named Jack Cardigan had appeared in the first of Nebel's

Black Mask stories starring Captain Steve MacBride and John X. Kennedy of *The Free Press*, "Raw Law."

"A tall, lean, dark-eyed man, this Cardigan, rounding thirty years," wrote Nebel, introducing him. "Men said that he was reckless, case-hardened, and a flash with a gun. He was."

Later in the serial Nebel added:

> Something might be added; he was ruthless. As a detective, he'd been hated and feared by more crooks than perhaps any other man in the Department—inspectors, captains, lieutenants and all the rest included. Because he was hard—tough—rough on rats; rats being one of his favorite nicknames applied to a species of human being that shoots in the dark and aims for the back.

At the end of that 1928-29 serial, Detective Cardigan quits the force to start his own detective agency. Some critics have suggested that the two Cardigans are identical. That may well be. However, in his introductory story, "Death Alley," Nebel's protagonist goes by the name of Steve Cardigan. Thereafter, he's just plain Cardigan. But just a few stories along, in "Lead Pearls," his first name is inexplicably given as Jack. For this publication, we've corrected those early occurrences of "Steve" for a more pleasant reading experience.

This apparent case of an author forgetting his long-running hero's first name may not be as inexplicable as it first appears to be. In making up an issue of a magazine, pulp editors sometimes discovered they had two or three protagonists bearing the same first name among the contents! Invariably they had to change one or two. That could be the case here. In time, after avoiding the issue of Cardigan's honest name, Nebel might have reasserted his original authorial intention. According to "Six Diamonds and a Dick," Cardigan had been operating in St. Louis for three years, roughly coinciding with the time Jack Cardigan quit the force. Yet "Lead Pearls" implies that Cardigan has been with the Cosmos Detective Agency for at least seven years, not necessarily in St. Louis. Throughout the series, his attitude towards cops in general belies any sense of past fraternity. All that can be stated with certainty is that this Cardigan remains Jack for the rest of the series.

Other than George Hammerhorn, the agency's head man, only one recurring character of consequence joins Cardigan during some of his cases—Cosmos operative Patricia Seaward, who debuts in the two-part sequence comprised of "Six Diamonds and a Dick" and

"And Then There was Murder." Once in a while, she pulls his bacon out of the fire. It's suspected that Lester Dent, a Nebel fan, might have borrowed some of Patricia Seaward's fire in creating Doc Savage's cousin Patricia Savage. A ship in an early Doc novel was called the *Seaward*.

Forty-four Cardigan stories unreeled from Fred Nebel's typewriter over the next four years. They were gems. Freed from Joe Shaw's super-restrictive blue pencil, Nebel penned his Cardigan tales with an open enthusiasm absent from the darker, more grim Donohue stories. Reportedly Nebel was receiving a handsome four cents a word rate for these stories.

In fact, once Jack Cardigan got off the ground, Nebel retired Donohue. After 1933, only one more appeared in *Black Mask* and that appears to have been a rejected Cardigan story revised into a Donohue installment—Donohue is said to be working for the Cosmos agency in "Ghost of the Chance." A certain giveaway.

Just as he had with *Black Mask*, Nebel became *Dime Detective's* star contributor. A biographical page in the second issue kicked off a long series of similar author profiles. It may be significant that the first writer selected was Frederick Nebel.

He wrote:

> Writing is my business, the one and only. It's no lark but on the other hand I can think of worse jobs. I started from scratch, had some tough breaks and some good ones—and the tough ones fewer than the good. I've written almost every type of story. My first yarns were based on a pilgrimage I made to the Canadian Northwest, where my great-uncle was a pioneer. Once I shipped on a Norwegian tramp and knocked around the Caribbean. I've lived in France and in England. Was born in New York 27 years ago and spend about a month there every year. Like the city at night. There was a time where I worked on the waterfront.
>
> I react quickly to a Scotch joke or just straight scotch… Masefield, Conrad, Rupert Brook… a perfect motor… Katherine Cornell… white water… the smell of coffee boiling over a woods fire… summer fog… a dark-haired girl (my wife)… Charlie Chaplin. This could go on forever but I believe there should be a law against it.
>
> Six or seven months of the year I spend in Maine. The remainder of the year I go places and see things. Don't play tennis, bridge or marbles. Like pistol shooting but prefer the bow and arrow. Play a fair game of chess and a rotten game of poker. I can resist anything but temptation and I whistle in the bath tub.

In 1936, flushed with the success of Warner Bros.' *Smart Blonde*—the first Torchy Blaine film based on the MacBride and Kennedy stories—and breaking into slicks like *Cosmopolitan* and *Collier's*, Nebel dropped out of *Black Mask* entirely. Joe Shaw's departure was more-or-less a trigger for that.

"I cut away from the pulps completely, all at once, circa 1937," he later recalled. "The demise of the magazine was doubtless hastened by the departure, more or less at the same time, of several of those writers who had sustained it since the late Twenties. But of course the handwriting was even then appearing on the wall."

Nebel's last pulp sale was a final Cardigan case, "No Time to Kill," in the May, 1937 *Dime Detective*. He never looked back.

Like Hammett, Nebel was disinclined to allow his pulp short stories to be reprinted in hardcover. Hammett didn't mind paperback reprintings, but Nebel preferred his old pulp stuff to remain buried in magazine back issues. When in 1946 Joe Shaw selected two for possible inclusion in his pioneering *Hard-Boiled Omnibus*, Nebel balked.

"He was a little upset when I refused to let him include two of my novelettes in his anthology," Nebel later related.

At the time, he told Shaw, "The reason why I don't want to see my old *Black Mask* stuff between boards is because I think it served its purpose well when it was first published but I honestly cannot see what purpose it would serve now. These times have moved fast. The stories, published between ten and fifteen years ago, seem now to be dated. The very sense of timeliness that made them good does not, I think, make them so good now. I can work up no enthusiasm."

Because of that thinking, Nebel fell out of the public consciousness until after his death and a new generation of anthologizers began including his tales in their collections. Since the 1960s virtually every hard-boiled anthology has included a Fred Nebel story. To do otherwise smacked of sacrilege.

While several Cardigan stories have been anthologized over the years, only one collection—containing a mere six novelettes—has ever been assembled. Until now.

Here is volume 1 of *The Complete Casebook of Cardigan*. Here also is Fred Nebel at his finest. Of the 11 stories in this volume, only two have seen print since their original magazine appearances. All are sterling specimens of the Hardboiled School of pulp writing.

DEATH ALLEY

STRIKE—MOB MEETINGS—KILLERS' GUNS LURKING FOR THE WEALTHY MAGNATE WHO HAD DENIED LABOR'S DEMANDS. AND ONLY ONE MAN SUSPECTED A DIFFERENT MOTIVE BEHIND THOSE BOLD MURDER TRAPS, DARED FOLLOW HIS HUNCH DOWN A BLOOD TRAIL TO A DEADLY RENDEZVOUS OF DANGER—AND DEATH!

CHAPTER ONE

DEATH RIDE

MAX SAUL, humming "The St. Louis Blues," prodded the catch base of the Mauser's butt, drew out the magazine, slipped in eight nickel-cased bullets, jammed the magazine back into the butt and jacked a shell into the chamber.

Cardigan said, "Now for God's sake, Max, watch your step. Last week Pat O'Hara was one of us and tonight he's pushing up daisies. This client Ludwig Hartz is a nice enough old guy but he's got that going-places-and-doing-things complex. Even at a time like this."

Saul slid the flat automatic into his hip pocket.

"Once a yama-yama girl told me I'd live to a ripe old age. She said I had wonderful eyes too."

Cardigan ignored the humor, went on in a deep, blunt voice.

"If I thought Brodski was behind that kill, it would be all right. But I don't. I don't think this mill strike has a thing to do with it. Bush fell on Brodski because the dumb Polack instigated the strike and once made a crack that he'd blow Hartz's head off—and because Brodski has no alibi. But that's not enough, Max."

Saul chuckled.

"I know, I know, Jack. You've got Mrs. Hartz on the brain. And that nice-faced lounge lizard Everett."

Cardigan swore. He strode to one of the windows—a big man, a hard party, rangy in the framework and good-looking in a rough, male way. The St. Louis summer night sky was overcast. Motor cars whirred past on Lindell Boulevard.

Cardigan pivoted.

"Why the hell shouldn't I have her on the brain?" he demanded. "She's twenty years younger than Hartz. The night after Pat was killed she and Everett told Hartz they were going to see The Mikado. On

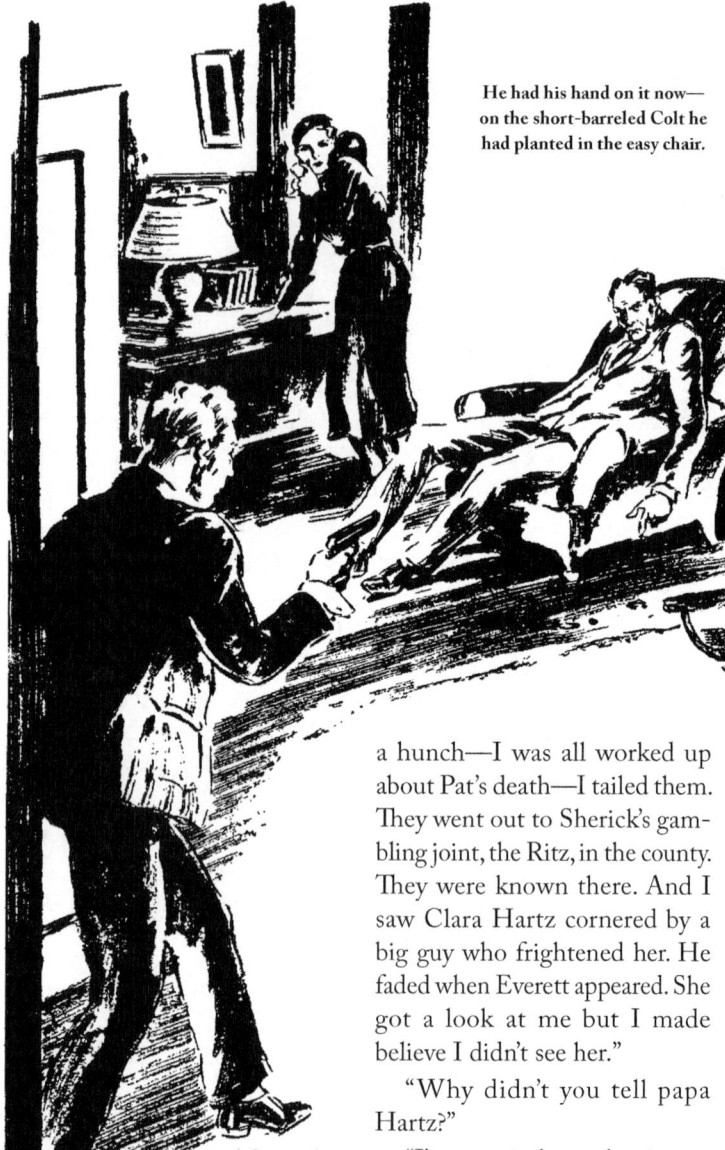

He had his hand on it now—on the short-barreled Colt he had planted in the easy chair.

a hunch—I was all worked up about Pat's death—I tailed them. They went out to Sherick's gambling joint, the Ritz, in the county. They were known there. And I saw Clara Hartz cornered by a big guy who frightened her. He faded when Everett appeared. She got a look at me but I made believe I didn't see her."

"Why didn't you tell papa Hartz?"

"I'm no snitch—unless it gets me somewhere. Hartz is dead against gambling and if he knew she went out there it would be just too bad for her. She's worried. She'll come to me. And it's damned lucky for her she wasn't out there a night later—when that machine-gun mob raided the place and got away with a hundred thousand."

Saul said, "And damned lucky, for you—the way you used a fake police badge to get in there," Saul put on his straw hat. "Well, toodle-oo, Jack."

"Watch yourself, Max."

"You know what that yama-yama girl said."

Saul went out.

Pat O'Hara was dead. Dead and shoving up daisies. He'd taken unto himself six slugs from a super .45. He must have had a flash of intuition in the limousine carrying him and Ludwig Hartz, the milk magnate, through Forest Park, that unholy night. He'd thrown Hartz to the floor of the car, yanked at his gun—and then taken the lead smack in the chest as the mystery car sped past. Brunner, the chauffeur, had jammed on brakes, smashed a mudguard against a tree—and fainted. Hartz had roared for help.

Detective-sergeant Bush had nailed Brodski, leader of the milk strike. Everybody blamed it on the strike. Everybody but Cardigan—and he was only toying with a vague idea. The Cosmos Agency had sent out Max Saul from New York to replace O'Hara, as assistant to Cardigan, the regional head. Either Cardigan or Saul had been with Hartz at all times since the murder.

Cardigan was pouring a pony of Bourbon when the telephone rang. He finished pouring, downed the drink neat and crossed the room rasping his throat.

"Hello," he said into the mouthpiece. "Oh, hello, Mrs. Hartz.... No, nothing particular.... Yes, I could. When?... All right. The northwest corner of the Hotel Case lounge. I'll walk right over."

The thumb of the hand that held the instrument pushed the hook down slowly. Cardigan replaced the receiver and chuckled grimly to himself.

A self-operated elevator took him down six floors to the lobby of the apartment house. He passed out onto a tiled terrace, strode down broad flags to the sidewalk and turned west on Lindell Boulevard.

He had gone perhaps a dozen yards when a stocky man stepped from beside one of the trees and fell in step beside him. The stocky man's right hand was in his pocket and the pocket bulged.

"Just keep walkin', sweetheart," he said.

"Where?"

"You'll see."

Cardigan's hands doubled but he kept walking. The hair stood up on the nape of his neck. Two girls and a man passed him going east. They didn't notice. The stocky man was in step with Cardigan, but a bit to the rear and to the left of him.

Ten feet further on a lank man stepped from the shadow of a parked sedan.

The stocky man muttered, "Get in that bus."

"Look here—" Cardigan began.

"Get in, get in," snarled the lank man, motionless. "You've got a date."

Cardigan looked down at the stocky man. It was a face he had seen before but for the present he couldn't place it. He was shoved into the rear of the sedan. He dropped down beside a man in shadow who smoked a cigar. The stocky man got in front beside the motionless chauffeur. The lank man climbed in beside Cardigan.

The red cigar-end moved. "Oke, Bunt."

The gear lever clicked. The big sedan moved away from the curb, swung into west-bound traffic, crossed Kings highway and hummed out along Forest Park.

"Well," said the man behind the red cigar end, "we had a long wait, *wisenheimer.*"

The stocky man in the front seat turned around.

"That's him, Gus. That's him all right."

Cardigan said, "I've seen you before."

"Honest?" mocked the stocky man. "Have you now?"

The man behind the red cigar and his lank companion suddenly frisked Cardigan of his gun.

The lank man grinned.

"Why don't you try to get out of this with your police badge?"

Cardigan started. Then he leaned back.

"Oh," he said slowly. "I see." Then his voice rushed on. "What the hell's the idea of this party?"

THE lank man jabbed a gun in his ribs. "The night before that raid at the Ritz you muscled your way in on a fake cop's shield! You were a scout for that mob! Tom Sherick remembered the shield number. You went home in a taxi. The guy drove you home remembered the address. And you paid your fare. Did a cop ever pay taxi fare? Yah! And we found out there was no such shield number on the cops!"

The car turned right into Union. Cardigan looked around at the shadowed faces.

"So help me, I had nothing to do with that." The stocky man in the front seat was the one who had let him in the Ritz. He remembered now.

"That was a fast one all right," the lank man said. "But this is gonna be a faster one."

"Ride?" Cardigan asked.

"What do you think?"

Cardigan began to perspire.

"I think," he said, "you guys are off your nut. O.K., I used a fake badge. But I'm a private dick. I was on a tail. It was the only chance I had of getting in, so I used it."

"You think up fast ones, don't you?" the lank man slurred.

The man behind the cigar laughed out loud. The man at the wheel giggled. The lank man rasped a harsh chuckle from his throat. The car sped on. It turned left into Delmar, weaved through traffic; past street cars, past traffic cops. While a gun kept pressing into Cardigan's ribs.

"Listen," said Cardigan, "I'm on the up and up. Take me to Sherick. Let me talk to him. I can square myself. I'm getting a raw deal here."

"And right in the belly," the lank man said.

Cardigan heaved in the seat. The man behind the red cigar-end moved, struck Cardigan across the head with a gun-butt. Cardigan groaned and slumped back in the seat. Through glazed eyes he saw store-windows streak by. He heard the honking of the horns, the shrill blast of traffic whistles.

Then the store windows were left behind. Sounds of the city petered out. There were occasional houses, then fewer and farther apart. The warm night wind blew against his hot face. Fields began to flow past. The big car droned on complacently, doing fifty-five on an undulating ribbon of cement. It boomed through a small settlement, left that behind in two minutes; swept past fields again and patches of dark woods.

"What is it?" Cardigan muttered. "A pitch from the St. Charles Bridge?"

"You'll see," the land man said.

"Listen," Cardigan urged. "For God's sake, listen! Give me a break. I tell you—"

"You can't tell us anything," the lank man said.

The man at the wheel, leaning out, said, "It won't be long now. Right around that bend."

There was a dark forest on the left of the wide bend, and the wind carried a dank smell of marshes.

"That path's right up here, ain't it?" the driver asked.

"Yeah," the stocky man said. "I'll say when."

Cardigan said in a thick voice, "For God's sake—"

"Lay off!" the lank man snarled; then in a quiet tone, "You and Abe go with him, Louie. We'll drive on and turn around and pick you up in ten minutes."

The car was slowing down. Presently it stopped.

"Hop out, Louie," the lank man said.

"Right," said the stocky man swinging from the front seat.

The man with the cigar threw it away and opened the rear door. Louie ran around the back and waited. The lank man prodded Cardigan with his gun and Louie and Abe hauled him out and rushed him across the road, down a path that bored into the dark, matted forest.

"So it's lights out," said Cardigan, bitterly.

Louie said, "For you, sweetheart."

They moved along the edge of a black pool on damp, soggy earth. Cardigan dragged his feet, tussled between the two. But they held him up, saying nothing, hauled him deeper and deeper into the woods.

Cardigan fell between them, dragging his knees on the wet earth. They could not walk with him that way, and they stopped. Louie cursed and struck Cardigan with his gun.

"Get up!" he snarled.

Cardigan hung a dead weight between them, breathed hoarsely, muttered, "If you heels want to give it to me, go ahead!"

Louie nodded. "Let's, Abe."

"We oughter go in further."

They redoubled their efforts, dragged Cardigan on the muddy path. His legs were straight behind him, his hands clawing at the mud.

Louie cried in a low voice. "Look out, Abe! That's water! We go left here—ain't it?"

Cardigan suddenly heaved his weight and twisted violently between them, breaking from Abe's grasp. He fell to the right, dragging Louie with him. They shot down the muddy bank, plunged into black water, while Abe clawed for a footing and Louie cried, "Help!" in a frightened voice that a mouthful of water promptly smothered.

Cardigan kicked out into the black water. He did not see Louie. He did not see Abe. It was black as pitch in those woods.

Louie cried, "Ugh—don't shoot, Abe!"

"Where the hell are you?" Abe snapped.

"Here—I'm here—gimme a hand—"

Through the black water swam Cardigan, getting rid of his coat. The voices of Louie and Abe grew fainter. Cardigan swam into gnarled roots. He grasped them, drew himself beneath them, felt his feet touch bottom. He clawed up a muddy bank and burrowed into thickets.

He did not wait to listen, but stumbled on his way, sometimes on solid ground, sometimes in knee-deep bogs. He fell and rose again and kept putting distance between himself and the two gunmen. He kept on fiercely, blindly, slushing through mud, spitting mud from his lips, choking and hacking and grunting and cursing.

He did not know it, but an hour passed before he fell headlong on a dry hump of earth. He lay gasping for breath, mud from head to foot, his brain almost bursting from the exertion. Then something inside him snapped and he relaxed with a sigh.

Gray daylight was breaking when he stumbled out on the state highway. An eastbound produce truck pulled up and gave him a lift.

The driver looked at him curiously. "You're messed up a bit, ain't you, bud?"

"I was on a wild party," Cardigan said. "I'd appreciate a butt, brother."

CHAPTER TWO

THE WIDOW TALKS

CARDIGAN DUCKED into the apartment house through the service entrance and reached his apartment without being seen. Muddy and bruised, he looked a ruin. He scuffled an envelope that had been slid under the door, picked it up and threw it on a console. He went to the bathroom and soaked himself in a hot tub. Dressed, he looked better.

He went to the console for a cigarette, lit up and then picked up the letter he had dropped there. It was apartment house stationery. A note was inside.

> A Mr. Bush of police headquarters called at 10:30 and left word you should come right down.
>
> Adams.

That was the night porter.

Cardigan scowled thoughtfully and took a drag at his butt on the way across to the telephone. He rang headquarters.

"Bush. Give me Bush if he's there.... Hello, Bush. Cardigan. I... What!... Sweet cripes!... I'll be right down."

He dived into a coat, grabbed a hat and went downstairs. He taxied to Twelfth and Clark. Bush, leaning over a flat-topped desk, looked sidewise over his right shoulder as he barged in. "Oh, you," he said.

"What the hell, Bush?"

Bush shuffled four lead slugs in the palm of his hand, then threw them dicelike on the desk and snapped thumb against fore-finger. He was a short, compact bald man. His tie was unloosed. He looked haggard from long hours.

Cardigan picked up one of the four slugs, turned it round and round, then dropped it back among the others. His wide mouth was tight, his heavy brows bent over his staring dark eyes.

Bush sighed. "Them guys sure meant business this time."

"How—how is Max Saul?"

"Was unconscious the last I seen him—three this morning."

Cardigan made a fist, looked at it narrow-eyed.

"And poor old Hartz—"

"Back of his nut all smashed in. Three times in the back of the nut. Saul took one. Brunner, the chauffeur, got one through the heart and the car smashed. They were coming home from Hamburg Hall. It happened on South Grand, near Longfellow. Why the hell couldn't you get down here before this?"

"I had a date."

"All night?"

Cardigan's lip curled.

"Keep your wisecracks under your jaw, Bush."

"Don't get hot."

"I suppose you're blaming this on Brodski too."

"Quit the razzberry. I'm going to bust this case, Cardigan. Hartz threatened to chuck every striker out of a job. In hard times like this that's a wild statement. Look here, Cardigan." He got up and shoved his pug nose almost against Cardigan's chin. "Ever since the O'Hara kill you've been giving me the razz. What the hell have you got on your mind?"

Cardigan turned and walked to the door.

"What hospital is Max Saul in?"

"You listen to me, Cardigan." Bush tramped after him, faced him again. "You get this. You've been jazzing around ever since O'Hara got bumped off. You've been acting superior and horse-laughing me every chance you got. And I don't like it. I've got more law in my little finger than you have in both hands, and if you slop around here much longer I'll fix you so you get shoved out of the city."

"What hospital—"

"You're just a wisecracking Mick that thinks the bureau's made up of a lot of hicks. I'm just as clever as you are, kid, and I'm backed up by authority. Last night Hartz and his chauffeur were rubbed out and your partner's in the hospital. It's damned funny that you shouldn't have been with Hartz on the two times he was fired at."

Cardigan darkened.

"We worked in shifts, fat-head. On alternate nights."

"That's funny, ain't it?"

"It'd be funnier if I pushed you in the mouth."

Bush glowered.

"You stay the hell out of here, Cardigan. I'll handle this case—in my way."

"O'Hara was murdered, Bush. Don't forget that Pat was the best friend I ever had. I'll get the guy that did it. I'll get him, Bush, and I'll give you the pinch—and make you like it."

A wily light came into Bush's eyes. His tone changed.

"Be a good guy, Cardigan. You've got something up your sleeve. What the hell is it? Remember, it pays to stand in good with the bureau."

"I stand in good with the bureau. I don't stand in good with you. And look at me weep over that."

"Be smart, be smart!"

"Nuts for you," Cardigan said, and went out.

At the desk downstairs he found what hospital Saul had been sent to. He taxied out, a tight feeling in his throat. Trouble was piling on his head. First O'Hara. Then Hartz and the chauffeur. And Max in the hospital.

Saul's face was pale; dark circles were under his eyes. Cardigan sat down on a chair beside the bed, laid his big brown hand on Saul's, pressed it once.

"How's it, kid?"

"I feel—you know—sort of lousy."

"Yeah."

They looked at each other.

Cardigan said, "I feel rotten about this, Max."

"Don't be a goof. I'll get over it. Let me feel rotten. It happened so fast. Six shots—and then we swerved. The car passed so close we almost scraped mudguards. We had both spotlights on. One of them swung around when we swerved. I saw a guy's face in the other car, Jack. It wasn't six feet away. He was grinning. A gold tooth flashed."

Cardigan looked at his hands. He didn't want to tell Saul about the ride. The nurse came in and told him he couldn't stay any longer.

"Let me know if you want anything, Max?" Cardigan said.

HE WENT downtown and spent three-quarters of an hour eating breakfast and reading the morning paper. Then he walked to his office in Olive Street and found Miss Gilligan, his secretary, sorting mail. She was a pop-eyed, gum-chewing girl with no looks but a great amount of vitality.

"My God!" she said. "The papers! Did you see—"

"Like a nice girl, get the boss on long distance."

He spoke with Hammerhorn in New York.

"Well, since you read it in the papers there I don't have to explain.... Max ought to pull through, the doctor said, but he'll be on his back for weeks.... Where was I? On a date.... Now don't ask foolish questions, George.... What?" He scowled at the instrument, then growled. "You're the second guy today made a crack like that. I was with Hartz night before last. Last night was Max's night.... Well, you get this, George. I don't have to take talk like that from you. Make another pass like that and you and your job can go to hell. Despite which I'll get the guy that killed my pal O'Hara.... I'm not getting hot-headed, but don't you think you can handle the St. Louis end better than I can, pull your pants out of that plush chair and come out.... Oh, well, all right, all right.... Sure, George. Good-by."

He banged the receiver into the hook and shoved away the mail Miss Gilligan had placed on his desk. He was sore. He had to admit that it looked crummy, his having been off the scene on the two occasions of murder. The ride still simmered in his brain, but he had no intention of reporting it to the police. He handled his own troubles. Besides, bigger things weighed him down. Hartz was dead. Max was out of commission. The papers were roaring with headlines.

He called a county telephone number.

"Is this you, Mr. Sherick?... Well, my name is Cardigan, the St. Louis head of the Cosmos Detective Agency. I'm the guy your sweet young things took for a ride last night. I'm back in town and O.K. Use your head, Sherick. If I wasn't a swell guy I'd turn you up. Only take a dose of something to clear your brain, look up my reputation and think over what a boner you pulled. And thank your stars I'm a swell guy. Good-by."

He hung up, felt a little better, took his hat and went out. He taxied to Longfellow Boulevard and Clara Hartz's house.

Mrs. Schmidt let him in. She had been long with the Hartz menage, as housekeeper. She steered him into the large Teutonic living room. She tried to say something but began crying instead and went out.

In a few minutes Clara Hartz came downstairs. She wore a black jacket over black pajamas. Her face was pale, angular, with a strange cool beauty. Cardigan didn't move from the shadows of the living room. His low voice said, "I'm very sorry, Mrs. Hartz."

She lifted her chin and lowered it again without saying anything. Cardigan went on. "I'm sorry I didn't show up last night."

"I waited two hours."

"You said over the telephone it was important."

She remained statuesque—cool, remote. "It was—about the Ritz the other night. I was worried. I wanted to ask you not to tell Ludwig. Or anybody. The suspense—knowing you knew—and your not saying anything—"

He crossed suddenly to her, his big brown jaw grim.

"Who do you think murdered your husband?"

She had greenish eyes, large—slightly Oriental, cool as ice.

"I wish I knew," she said in her flat voice.

"Do you think the strike caused it?"

"I don't know."

Cardigan's gray eyes glittered. Beside her smooth cool beauty he looked immense, shaggy, threatening. But her eyes never wavered.

"Remember," he muttered, "my friend Pat O'Hara was murdered first. That hits me deep and way down. I'm going to get the murderer—even if I have to cause a lot of heartache."

One of her arched eyebrows rose slightly, but otherwise not a feature changed. For some vague unknown reason Cardigan suddenly hated her. She was so cool, so collected. He was a man of blood and fire, bitter against circumstances, and her attitude touched him like a bar of ice.

"I don't suppose," she said, "that your telling anybody about Mr. Everett and me at the Ritz will gain you anything."

Cardigan scowled. "I'm not a scandal-monger."

The doorbell rang and a minute later Ralph Everett came in. He was a tall, slim man of thirty, with silky blonde hair, girlish blue eyes and pink cheeks.

"Oh, hello, Cardigan."

Cardigan grunted.

Everett said, "Dreadful—murder," and lit a cigarette. "Sorry about Saul, Cardigan."

It was an uneasy meeting. Cardigan saw no remorse here. The death of poor old Hartz did not seem to stir them. A year and a half ago Clara had married the fifty-year-old milk magnate. And for the past year Everett had been welcome in Hartz's household. Hartz had never shown any suspicion.

"Have the police got anything out of Brodski?" Everett asked.

"No. And they won't," Cardigan said bluntly. "I don't believe this strike has anything to do with it. The strike merely proved convenient for somebody else to try murder, and have it blamed on the strike."

"But Detective-sergeant Bush—"

"I know Bush," Cardigan cut in.

Everett shrugged and looked at his watch, nodded at Clara. "I have to catch a train for Cleveland."

"I wouldn't," Cardigan said.

Everett looked at him, startled. "Why not?"

"I just wouldn't. The best thing for you to do is stay right here in town."

Everett bristled. "Why?"

"Because I'm telling you. And I'm being frank with you—both of you. Stay here in town. The press is aching for news and if you pull up your stakes I'll give them a little."

Everett came closer.

"You mean about the other night?"

"Judge for yourself. And maybe if I work back I can find out about other nights."

Everett gritted, "You would like to break a scandal, wouldn't you?"

"Not unless you force me to. And don't stick your nose in the air, either, Everett."

"You as much as insinuate," Everett snapped, "that I had something to do with Mr. Hartz's death!"

Cardigan wagged a finger.

"Just stick around St. Louis."

Clara Hartz turned away, swivelling slowly on one heel. She walked out of the room and went upstairs.

Everett muttered, "You've a nerve coming here and humiliating her!"

"And you've got a nerve leaving her and trying to go to Cleveland." Cardigan picked up his hat, touched Everett's arm. "But don't," he said.

Everett paled, clenching his hands. "You're a louse—like all private detectives," he choked.

"Like Pat O'Hara, I suppose. Like O'Hara, who got in the way of a lead party to save Hartz! You lily-livered nice boy! Hartz thought you were a swell guy—the old fool! Why, you—"

He gave it up suddenly. He strode out of the room, through the large foyer, into the street, his cheeks burning. He didn't like wavy-haired nice boys and he didn't like Oriental-eyed icebergs. He had let emotion get the better of him. He felt he had acted a fool.

CHAPTER THREE

WRITTEN EVIDENCE

NO FUNERAL parlor for Ludwig Hartz, since he had not wished it that way. He lay in state in the great living room of the great brick house. Mourners came and went. Clerks, stenographers, even some of the strikers. Relatives sat about in hushed groups. Clara Hartz was in the drawing room, stunning in black, looking tragic in a cool, icy way.

Cardigan was there, standing in the foyer, a dark, shaggy-headed man, watchful though in the background.

Bush came in, his hard bald head shining. He went to the coffin, looked grim, then said some condolences to Clara and elbowed his way back toward the door. He spied Cardigan and came over.

"What are you doing here?" he grumbled.

"No law against it. I see you had to let Brodski go. You certainly paraded a lot of guys through the shadow-box this morning. Good copy, Bush."

"Be funny!"

"Any new clues?"

"You?"

"Here's a promise, Bush. I'll get you a pinch—a real, honest-to-God one. You've been nosing it around that as a dick, I'm last year's summer cold. So I'm going to get you a pinch and make you swallow those words, right on the front page."

"Baloney!"

"You're a nice guy, Bush, only you're a sorehead."

Bush swore and went out, jamming on his hat.

Everett, passing through the foyer a couple of minutes later, stopped and said tensely, "Don't you think it would be the decent thing if you went somewhere else?"

Cardigan said, "I see you didn't go to Cleveland."

Everett's lips twitched. He turned and went off stiffly.

A messenger boy appeared in the front doorway. A man-servant signed for a letter, carried it through the crowd to Clara Hartz. A minute later Clara appeared in the foyer. Cardigan saw the letter in her hand, the white look on her face. He watched her go upstairs.

His eyes narrowed. He looked around cautiously, backed up toward the stairway. He looked up, saw Clara's heels disappearing around the curve above. He turned and climbed quickly, quietly. He reached the top in time to see Clara standing in a doorway at the front of the upper hall, her back to him. Her head was bent. She was reading something. Then he heard the sudden crackle of paper as she went into the room.

He darted into the bathroom, closed the door, listened. A few minutes later he heard footsteps come down the corridor, descend the stairs. He left the bathroom, walked quickly to the front of the corridor, entered a large bedroom. He crossed to a writing-table, ran his eyes over an assortment of cards, letters, telegrams; touched nothing. There was an ivory-colored metal waste-basket beside the desk. He knelt down, saw bits of torn paper, collected them quickly, held them in his closed hand and returned to the bathroom.

On black-and-white tiles he pieced together a message written on plain white linen paper. The writing was heavy, black, oblique. It said:

> Dear Mrs. Hartz:
> My sincere sympathy. But as I said at the Ritz last Wednesday night, don't let this tragedy make you forget your obligation to me, in case you decide to leave St. Louis.
> D.D. McKimm.

Cardigan remained on one knee for a long minute, frowning at the letter. Then he gathered up the pieces, shoved them in his pocket and went downstairs.

The undertaker was closing the casket.

Cardigan went downtown in a taxi, strode into his office and said to Miss Gilligan, "Darling, call County 0606. Ask for Mr. Sherick."

He went on into his office, slapped his hat on a hook and sat down at his desk. A minute later Miss Gilligan chirped, "All right."

Cardigan pulled his telephone across the desk.

"Hello, that you, Sherick?... This is Cardigan.... Oh, I'm feeling great, but outside of that I want to see you.... No, I'm not going out there. I can't spare the taxi fare and besides I don't like that scatter of yours. I'm naming the place, Sherick, and you're going to meet me.... Now don't talk that way. Your sweet young things took me for a ride and you'll play ball with me or I'll throw you to the cops.... Never mind what I want to see you about. You come right in here and see. You know my apartment on Lindell and I'll expect you there at eight tonight—sharp.... Never mind, Sherick. You heard me. You did a dumb thing by sending your hoods after me and you'll come in or else—"

He hung up and stared hard at the telephone. He took out the bits of paper, pasted them in order to a letterhead. He read the message over and over.

"H'm," he murmured. "Obligation."

AT A quarter to eight that night he stood in the center of his living room holding a gun in either hand and looking around the room with keen speculative eyes. The gun in his left hand was a Colt automatic. The gun in his right was a special Colt revolver with an abbreviated two-inch barrel.

His eyes settled on a dull-colored mohair easy-chair and he strode toward it, sat down and shoved the revolver down between the arm and the cushion until it was concealed. With an easy upward motion of his hand the gun appeared. He shoved it back again, grunted with satisfaction and stood up. He slipped the automatic into his coat pocket.

He took a drink of Bourbon and looked at the little folding clock on the secretary. At eight o'clock he heard the elevator down the hall open, and a minute later there was a knock on his door.

Tom Sherick was a mountain of a man beneath a wide-brimmed Panama. The man beside him was small, thin, pale-faced, and he carried his hands in his pockets. They stood in the doorway.

Cardigan said, "I didn't expect the wet-nurse."

"Willie goes where I go," Sherick said heavily, his little eyes quivering with suspicion.

Cardigan stepped back and Sherick and the pale-faced man trooped in. Sherick went all the way across the room, but his companion closed the door with a kick of his heel and remained in front of it, his big wet eyes sinister.

Sherick stopped, turned, mopped his neck and face with a handkerchief. His pale eyes had fire smouldering in their depths. He gestured with his handkerchief.

"What the hell, Cardigan, what the hell? I had every reason to believe you was a scout for that mob. What do you want? Cripes, what do you want?"

Cardigan sat down on the arm of a mohair easy-chair. "Never mind the apologies. And damper down your loud mouth. I expected you alone. You had to bring along this snot and complicate things."

"Willie goes where—"

"O.K., he's here now. And you're here. And you're the guy I want to have a talk with."

"Well, talk!"

Willie drew in his lower lip and then let it fall out again, where it hung wet and shiny.

Cardigan said, "I want the lowdown on a bird named McKimm."

"Mc—who?"

"McKimm. He hung out around your place and he was known there. What's his racket?"

Sherick stopped mopping his big face. His little eyes narrowed.

"How should I know? Hell, is that what you got me in here for?"

"Just that."

Willie made spitting sounds with his lips and Cardigan looked at him. "Cut out spitting on my carpet."

Sherick started tramping up and down the room, mopping his face again.

"This is funny," he said. "This is funny as hell, Cardigan."

"Says you!" bit off Cardigan. "Don't stall around when you know you've got to come across. You spring, Sherick, or by God I'll throw you to the cops for that ride!"

Willie took three forward steps from the door. His coat pockets moved and as he stood with his head down between his narrow shoulders, a sullen glassy look was in his eyes.

Sherick threw an apprehensive look at him, licked his lips with a rapid motion of his tongue, jerked his pale harried eyes at Cardigan. Cardigan's eyes were flickering from Willie to Sherick, and the skin tightened on his jaw so that little muscles bulged beneath it.

Sherick rasped, "What the hell are you tailing McKimm for?"

"That's my business, Sherick, not yours. Yours is to tell me what his racket is and where I can call on him. I want to know that and the cheap snot over there with the two rods doesn't make me change my mind!"

Willie snarled, "For two cents—" His pale face rose, showing dark circles beneath his killer's eyes.

"Be quiet, Willie," Sherick said; then he snapped at Cardigan, "This is all a lot of crap!"

"Remember, Sherick, I was taken for a ride in the city of St. Louis. Not in the county, where you have the big shots smeared to lay off you. You'll tell me what I want to know—"

"Damn it, Tom!" rasped Willie feverishly. "This guy is askin' for a bellyache!" A sudden look of frenzy leaped into his eyes and his two guns came out of his pockets.

"Willie!" cried Sherick.

Willie panted, "The horse's neck's got it comin' to him!"

"Willie, put away those rods!"

A moan came from Willie's throat and he stood shaking and opening and closing his mouth slowly. Inch by inch his guns lowered until they hung at his sides.

Cardigan said, "Hell, Sherick, you're dumb to carry that hophead around with you."

"For God's sake, shut up!" cried Sherick.

Cardigan ran a hand across his forehead spreading cold sweat that had appeared there in shining beads.

"But you've got to tell, Sherick," he said, grimly. "I've got to know. And I want the truth—and then I want you to go out of here and keep your mouth shut."

Sherick began coughing into his handkerchief. His face was red and streaked with sweat. He looked harassed and cornered, and his jowels shook. He glared at Cardigan with hate and venom but with fear also. While Willie stood quivering like a bird dog held back, his lips wet and his eyes shining as though filled with tears.

Sherick stammered, "He—he gambles some. He used to be the silent owner of that gambling joint in East St. Louis—The Gold Casino. He went broke. Clean broke. I gave him a job, but he didn't keep it long. I don't know what he's doing. He used to come out sometimes and hang around."

"Alone?"

"Well, with a couple of pals sometimes."

"Who are they?"

Sherick groaned.

"What's it about, Cardigan? Gee, what's it about?"

"Who are the guys?"

"Oh, hell. Jack Gos and Billy Dessig."

"O.K. Now where does McKimm hang out?"

Sherick almost choked, but he got it out. "He's staying in a room over Lou Abatti's speak—down by the river. And damn your soul, Cardigan!"

Willie cried, "Tom—Tom, for cryin' out loud, let me give this punk a bellyache! You hear, Tom!"

Sherick jumped, grabbed Willie's arm.

"Willie, don't!"

He tussled with Willie, hurled him against the wall, took away the guns and thrust them in his own pocket. He held on to Willie, rushing him to the door. Willie cursed and moaned, and Cardigan opened the door.

"Remember, Sherick," he said. "Keep your mouth shut."

When he had closed the door he said, "Whew!" and stood wiping perspiration from his forehead.

CHAPTER FOUR

KILLER'S STREET

CARDIGAN CLIMBED out of a taxi at Marion and Broadway and headed toward the Mississippi. A warm river mist hung pendant in the dark streets, and infrequent street lights had needle-pointed auras of wet radiance. Cardigan's footfalls were loud, purposeful, clean-cut in the dark alleys through which he strode.

He passed a run-down billiard parlor where the curt click of balls could be heard, and the heavy voices of men. There was a boat horn braying on Old Man River somewhere beyond the house-tops. Cardigan turned a corner, passed a cigar store where a radio bleated. He turned another corner and followed a cobbled street that went slightly downgrade. Halfway down he lingered. An alley dead-ended here into the cobbled street. Fifty yards up the alley crouched a two-story red brick house with a drop light outside a door flush with a broken flag walk. Some cars were in a parking space this side of the building, and back of it was the Mississippi. Insistent was the muffled beat of a jazz band's drum.

Cardigan entered the alley. Under the drop light was a sign—black ungainly letters on white,

THE HONKYTONK

He pushed open an old wooden door painted a nightmare green. He went down worn wooden steps to a foyer where a slash-mouthed girl took his hat and gave him a check. The place was damp and hot. The old building throbbed with the beat of the jazz band. Up two steps was the dance floor. The bar was in the basement. It was a French bar—small and narrow with stools in front of it.

Cardigan pushed in. There were no bottles in sight. He ordered Bourbon straight and the barman produced it from underneath the bar. Three drunks were in a huddle arguing about the Browns and the Cardinals. The lights hanging from the ceiling quivered with the beat of the jazz band.

Cardigan drank, looking around. The Bourbon was thrice-cut. He felt his arm prodded and he turned around and looked at Sergeant Bush. The Metropolitan dick was sucking a homemade cigarette. His hard straw hat was tilted over thinned-downed eyes.

"Hello, sarge," the barman said.

"Gin," said Bush, still looking hard at Cardigan.

"You getting collegiate?" Cardigan asked.

Bush downed gin straight without taking his eyes off Cardigan. He said, "You're doing a hell of a lot of running around, Cardigan. What's on your mind?"

"Right now—a certain nosey shamus named Bush."

"Be funny!"

"Go to hell!"

Bush lowered his voice grimly.

"Listen, you. I seen Tom Sherick come out of your apartment house before. Tom and a punk of his named Willie Martin."

Cardigan scowled.

"Haven't you anything else to do but watch my place?"

"What's between you and Sherick?"

"I never saw Sherick."

"You're a liar! I was parked down the hall and saw him and the hood come out of your apartment."

Cardigan cursed under his breath. He faced Bush squarely. "You dirty flatfoot," he ground out. "Have you been tapping my wire?"

"Never mind, never mind—"

"Why the hell didn't you stop Sherick? Hadn't the guts, eh? Nah! He had his hood with him—that hophead. That's why! Bush, you're a dirty sneak. You're a disgrace to an otherwise fine detective bureau. With swell guys like Holmes and Murfee, I don't know why you were put in charge of this case."

Bush reddened and his jaw hardened.

"What did you want with Sherick, Cardigan? You better tell me, because if you don't I take a squad and go out and find out myself!"

Cardigan's lip twitched.

"You stay away from Sherick, Bush! If you go out there he'll get the idea I welched. And I've never welched on any guy."

"You got something on Sherick," Bush muttered.

"I haven't. That's just another of your weak-minded ideas."

"You got something on him and you made him come across about somebody else." Bush nodded passed Cardigan's shoulder. "Hello, McKimm."

"Hello, Bush."

Cardigan looked in the mirror back of the bar and saw the reflected image of a tall, stony-faced man who smoked a cigar. It was the man who had cornered, frightened, Clara Hartz that night at the Ritz. He went to the bar and brooded darkly over a drink.

Cardigan threw a half-dollar on the bar. He whistled, left the bar, got his hat and went outside. Bush was at his heels. Cardigan opened the door of a waiting taxi and Bush said, "I'll go with you."

Cardigan turned a withering look on him.

"Not on my money, Bush!" He climbed in and slammed the door. "Broadway," he said to the driver.

The cab swung around and got out of the alley. Looking back, Cardigan saw Bush climb in another. Cardigan leaned forward.

"Here's a two-dollar bill, kid. Drop me off up the street and then take a ride out to the north end. There's a tail back here I want to drop."

"Jake."

Cardigan looked back and saw another cab following.

"Swing left at the next street," he said. "Don't stop. I'll jump and walk to Broadway. You keep going."

"Jake."

The cab swung left sharply. Cardigan leaped off and slammed the door. He darted into an alley. He saw the second taxi shoot past, with Bush sitting on the edge of the seat.

CARDIGAN retraced his steps and entered the Honkytonk. He did not check his hat. He reentered the bar and saw McKimm still standing there, a felt hat yanked down over his eyes, his hands toying with an empty glass. The bar was crowded now with jabbering drunks, and the jazz band pounded. Cardigan ordered a drink and paid for it on the spot. Under his hat-brim he watched McKimm in the mirror back of the bar.

Five minutes later McKimm threw a couple of bills on the bar, waited for change. Cardigan turned and went into the foyer. The hat-check girl had her back to him. She was talking on the telephone. There was nobody else in the foyer. It was noisy with the sound of the music.

The swing-door from the bar opened and McKimm came out. Cardigan lifted his coat pocket. McKimm's eyes narrowed and his lips tightened hard on his cigar. Cardigan nodded toward the exit. McKimm hesitated, stony-faced. Cardigan moved his lips and went closer.

McKimm turned and went up the stairs. Cardigan crowded him outside.

There was no taxi.

"Walk fast," Cardigan said.

He drew his gun and pressed it in the small of McKimm's back.

"What's this?" McKimm growled.

"Get."

They walked through the black alley, turned up the cobbled street. Cardigan flattened McKimm against a house-wall, made him raise his hands. He frisked him, took a gun from an armpit holster while his own gun pressed hard into McKimm's stomach.

"Now walk again," Cardigan said. "Put your hands in your pockets and keep them there."

"Didn't I see you with Bush?"

"Get along, get along."

Their footfalls echoed in the quiet dark street. Four blocks further on Cardigan stopped a taxi and crowded McKimm in. Cardigan gave his address to Lindell.

McKimm started.

"What the hell's this?"

"Shut up."

They struck Broadway, turned left into Olive and bowled through the darkened business district, past the *Post-Dispatch* Building, across Twelfth Boulevard and up the hill. At Channing they left the car tracks, hit Lindell and went over the hump past the University.

Cardigan spoke to the driver.

"When you reach the address, a driveway swings through the basement garage. Take it."

McKimm sat in stony silence, his breath audible in his nostrils, his lips clamped on his cigar.

In the basement garage Cardigan backed out, covered McKimm. He thrust a couple of bills into the driver's hand. He motioned McKimm out and took him up in the service elevator.

"Listen, who the hell are you?" McKimm muttered.

"Get out," Cardigan said at the sixth floor.

He marched McKimm down the corridor, unlocked the door.

"Get in."

He followed McKimm into the apartment, which he had left lighted, and kicked shut the door.

McKimm turned and looked at him stonily. "Who the hell are you?" he asked again.

"Pat O'Hara's partner."

McKimm remained stony.

"What is that supposed to mean?"

"Sit down in the straight-backed chair, honeybunch. We're going to play school. I'm the teacher and you're the pupil."

McKimm sat down, said, "The floor is yours."

Keeping his gun and eyes trained on McKimm, Cardigan fished in a vest pocket, drew out a folded piece of paper.

"Catch it," he said.

He threw and McKimm caught it.

"Read it," Cardigan said.

McKimm unfolded the paper, squinted his eyes. Not a muscle in his face twitched. He looked up with his stony expressionless eyes and said nothing.

"Now what about it?" Cardigan said.

"What about what?"

"In your notes, there, what the hell do you mean by the word 'obligation,' McKimm?"

McKimm looked at the note again, folded it, tossed it to the open secretary.

"I don't know what you're talking about."

"I'm in a lousy mood tonight, McKimm, and I don't want wisecracks for answers. I saw you accost Mrs. Hartz at the Ritz the night before it was raided and you didn't look pleasant. And she looked scared. I'm on your tail tight as a tick."

"And you can go to hell."

Cardigan hefted his gun.

"What was the obligation?"

"Just what it said. Maybe I should have used 'debt.' A little debt. That's all."

"Debt for what?"

McKimm stood up, his lips still tight on his cigar, barely moving when he spoke.

"To hell with you!"

"Sit down!" Cardigan took three steps and punched McKimm in the chest.

McKimm sat down, his eyes hard as marbles.

Cardigan backed across the room, got hold of the telephone with one hand. He gave a number. He got a connection and asked for Mrs. Hartz.

"Hello, Mrs. Hartz. Cardigan. I want you to come over to my apartment immediately.... I'm sorry, but I'm giving orders. You'll do wise to come over, as fast as you can.... Yes. Thank you."

He hung up.

Visibly McKimm's lips didn't move, but they must have, because he was saying, "What the hell kind of a merry-go-round are you on anyway?"

"I'm reaching for the gold ring."

McKimm's eyes remained round and hard and inscrutable.

WHEN the brass knocker on the outside of the door sounded, Cardigan did not move. He called, "Mrs. Hartz?"

"Yes."

"Come in."

The door opened. Everett was there, pink-cheeked and wavy-haired. The angle of the doorway at first prohibited his seeing McKimm. He saw Cardigan, however, and the gun in Cardigan's hand.

"What's the meaning of this?" he snapped indignantly.

"I didn't expect you," Cardigan said, with a wintry smile.

"Do you think I would let Mrs. Hartz come to your place alone? Really!"

Cool and white-faced in her black cloche hat and black wrap, Clara Hartz came in first. She saw McKimm. She looked at him with her Oriental eyes, looked away. Everett closed the door. Then he saw McKimm. He seemed to grow an inch, and his white hands doubled. His blue eyes radiated sudden blue fire but he kept his mouth shut.

Cardigan said, with a touch of bitter sarcasm, "Do I have to go through with introductions?"

"What do you want?" asked Clara Hartz in her flat voice.

Cardigan pointed to the secretary. "Read that letter."

She crossed the room, picked up the piece of paper McKimm had refolded. She read the lines, shrugged, let the note slip back to the desk. One of her arched eyebrows rose.

"Well?" she said.

Everett made an exasperated sound, crossed the room, snatched up the note, read it. He flung a look at McKimm. McKimm was stony-faced, stony-eyed. Everett spun on Cardigan.

"What in God's name are you driving at?" he ripped out hotly.

Cardigan ignored him. "Mrs. Hartz, in what way are you obligated to Mr. McKimm?"

"That," she said, "is perhaps my business—and Mr. McKimm's."

"Right now it's mine too."

"On the contrary—"

"You hear!" Cardigan rasped, his face a dull red. "It's my business! It's my business to find out who murdered my partner Pat O'Hara! It's my business to know what kind of business you had with McKimm!"

"Look here, Cardigan," snapped Everett, starting toward him.

"You keep your oar out of this—and stay back!"

Everett cried, "You have no right to question Mrs. Hartz! No right at all!"

"Mrs. Hartz," said Cardigan crisply, "answer my question."

She sighed. "I suppose I'll have to. Well"—she drew in a breath—"I owe him an amount—of money. I've owed it for a little more than a year. When Mr. McKimm operated the Gold Casino, a gaming place, I played there. Rather steeply. I was foolish. He took my I.O.U.s because he knew Mr. Hartz was quite wealthy. It was unfortunate. I found out that Mr. Hartz was rigidly opposed to gambling. I never had much money to spend. Plenty of charge accounts for legitimate purchases—but no allowance. I shouldn't have, but gambling is one of my weaknesses. I couldn't get the money. The debt is still standing. That is all."

"How much?" asked Cardigan.

She let her long-held breath out. "Fifty thousand."

"What of it? What of it?" snapped Everett.

Cardigan ignored him. Cardigan's face was brown and grim with red burning beneath the brown. He was staring at McKimm. He saw the first flicker of emotion in McKimm's face. He saw McKimm's big hands gripping the sides of the chair, saw an unholy glitter growing in McKimm's eyes.

"Now I suppose," came Clara Hartz's flat, casual voice, "you'll have something else to give to the scandal sheets."

Cardigan's voice was low, ominous. "That kill's the thing, Mrs. Hartz—the murder of my partner. I tell you again I'm no scandalmonger—not just for the sake of scandal. But this goes deeper— This goes way down deep. Or I miss my bet. I miss my bet if the killer of Pat O'Hara, Ludwig Hartz and his chauffeur isn't in this room right now."

She looked at him suddenly. She saw the fierce intensity in his eyes. She followed the direction of their burning, implacable stare. Fright leaped into her eyes. She let out a stifled little cry.

McKimm raised his hand, ripped the dead cigar from his mouth. "Who the hell are you staring at, Cardigan?" he roared.

For the first time his mouth opened, his lips ripped back across his teeth. A gold eye-tooth flashed at the left corner of his mouth.

Cardigan flung at him, "I'm staring at you, McKimm! I'm staring at the guy that murdered three men and put a fourth in the hospital!"

Ignoring Clara and Everett, he took three hard steps across the carpet, his gun trained on McKimm's chest.

"Oh, my God!" breathed Clara. "No—no—no!"

"Max Saul's living, thank God," Cardigan said. "And he'll remember that gold tooth, McKimm. And you'll remember how the spotlight on Hartz's car swung around as it swerved. You used this strike as a cover-up. You're broke. You need the money. You figured to get your debt out of Hartz's legacy to his wife."

"Is this true, is this true?" cried Clara Hartz.

McKimm heaved to his feet, agony bursting on his face, guilt bare and unadorned in his eyes.

"Sit down, McKimm!" barked Cardigan.

McKimm roared, "My God, Everett—"

A gun boomed.

Cardigan felt a slam somewhere in the back and he started to pitch forward. Clara Hartz screamed. McKimm jumped and grabbed Cardigan's gun, ripped it free. He smashed Cardigan in the jaw, sent him reeling backwards and followed him, ripping his own gun from Cardigan's pocket.

Everett stood shaking and horror-stricken, a smoking automatic in his hand.

"Ralph, what have you done?" cried Clara Hartz.

Cardigan landed in the mohair easy-chair with a bang, his heels flying, his head jerking back, the chair itself tilting backwards, banging against the wall.

McKimm towered with a gun in either hand. "I'm leaving," he clipped and backed swiftly to the door.

Everett shook. "My God, McKimm, don't leave me!"

Clara Hartz pressed hands to her cheeks, stared thunderstruck at Everett. "Ralph—Ralph—"

"Shut up!" Everett screamed at her.

He shook like a man with palsy and backed up beside McKimm. "You'll—have to take me, McKimm. I just saved—you."

Cardigan snarled, "Yellow as I always thought you were! Leaving the woman to take the rap, eh?" His face was ferocious, bitter, his shaggy hair stood on end. Pain burned in his back, but he was a hard party.

CLARA'S calm was gone. She was flushed, wide-eyed, gripped with terror and wild bewilderment. She saw McKimm's gun move upward. She choked and whirled and spread her body and her arms in front of Cardigan.

"No you won't!" she panted. "I see now. I see it all. You murdered Ludwig to get that money—through me later. And you, Ralph—oh, how could you! You told him of Ludwig's movements. You urged me to divorce Ludwig. I wanted to. I didn't love him. I loved you. But you didn't want me—without his money. Oh, Ralph—Ralph!" She began sobbing hysterically.

Everett looked like a lamb shorn. His dignity, his haughty manner, were gone. He shook and looked wild and desperate.

"I gambled," she cried. "I was weak. God knows I was weak! And I have no excuse. I'm a fool—a terrible fool!"

McKimm clipped to Everett, "Come on."

McKimm opened the door, stepped into the corridor, looked up and down. Doors closed elsewhere. Voices were excited—then silent.

Glassy-eyed, Everett backed through the door, confirming his guilt, leaving the woman who had loved him. She sobbed brokenly.

Cardigan had his hand on it now, on the short-barreled Colt he had planted in the mohair easy-chair before Sherick's arrival. He whipped it up. The blunt muzzle belched flame. Everett jerked and his eyes popped wide. Then he screamed and fell backward, clutched at his chest.

McKimm bolted for the staircase.

Cardigan jumped from the chair, whipped quick words into Clara Hartz's ear.

"That door over there hides an in-a-door bed. Get in there. Close the door. Hide behind the bed. Stay there."

He ran to the corridor door, looked out. A man in a dressing-gown was standing near the elevator.

"Get a doctor," Cardigan said, indicating Everett.

He started down the staircase. Doors were opening and closing, and far below someone was blowing a police whistle. Cardigan reached the lobby as he saw McKimm bolt through the front door. He went through the door a split-second later and saw McKimm crossing Lindell.

A small crowd had gathered in front of the apartment house. Some autos had stopped. People were scattering at sight of the men with the drawn guns. McKimm began running west on Lindell. Cardigan reached the opposite sidewalk and ran after him. Pedestrians ran for shelter. McKimm looked back and fired, missed and crashed the tail light of a parked car.

Cardigan raised his gun but a darting pedestrian got in the way, yelped with fright, flung himself flat on the sidewalk. Cardigan leaped over him. McKimm turned south into Euclid, stopped, turned and waited for Cardigan to swing around the corner. His gun belched and echoes hammered.

Cardigan staggered to the curb, kept his feet, fired and saw McKimm reel but keep running. He fired again and saw McKimm swerve drunkenly. He ran after him unsteadily and McKimm turned and his gun blazed and Cardigan stopped and fell down. Half-kneeling, he raised his gun and watched McKimm jolting across the street. He fired and the bullet tumbled McKimm across the curb. But he got up and staggered on.

Cardigan got up, sweat pouring from him, pain tightening his jaw. He limped across the street. He fell down on the opposite sidewalk and saw McKimm down twenty yards further on. McKimm's gun boomed. The shot snarled against the pavement near Cardigan's head. He leaned on his elbow, looked down his gun, fired.

McKimm whipped over, tried to get up, collapsed. His gun rang as it banged down to the pavement.

Cardigan toiled to his feet, gritted his teeth, staggered toward Lindell. He drew in great breaths. He made himself walk almost steadily. He looked grim and shaggy and he could feel blood crawling beneath his clothes.

There was a crowd in front of the apartment house. He pushed through it, and people saw him and exclaimed but nobody tried to stop him. The lobby was jammed. The elevator was in use, so he took the stairway up. People were jabbering in the corridors. He barely noticed them. His feet were like gobs of lead.

He reached his floor and found a crowd there. He spotted a couple of uniformed cops. He plowed through the crowd and the cops turned and grabbed him roughly.

"Leggo," he muttered.

They tightened on him.

"You damned flatfeet, leggo!"

Bush appeared in the doorway.

"Oh, it's you, Cardigan!" Bush looked baffled and angry. "Let him go, boys."

The cops let go and Cardigan reeled into his apartment. A doctor was bending over Everett.

"I knew you were up to something tonight!" Bush growled. "Now what the hell did you do?"

"This guy on the floor shot me in the back. McKimm is lying over in Euclid near West Pine. I guess some of your cops have got him by this time."

"What'd this guy shoot you for?"

Cardigan sagged to a chair.

"McKimm killed my pal Pat O'Hara. He killed Hartz and the chauffeur. He wounded Max Saul."

"Somebody said they heard a woman scream here."

"They're nuts. It was Everett. When I cornered McKimm here Everett let me have it in the back. He was in with McKimm. He wanted to get rid of Hartz too."

"You're lying, Cardigan!"

"Go to hell, Bush! Let me alone awhile."

"There was a woman here!"

"There wasn't. I got McKimm here and then I got Everett here."

An ambulance doctor and two men with a stretcher came in. The doctor bending over Everett looked up and shook his head.

"He hasn't a chance," he said.

Cardigan, fast losing consciousness, saw the white door across the room open. He shook his head. He did not want Mrs. Hartz to come. He believed that this thing could be settled without her. He knew she had been tricked by Everett. He knew she had nothing to do with the murder of his partner. He remembered that she had put her body in front of him against the muzzles of McKimm's guns.

But she came out—statuesque and white-faced.

"So," growled Bush, with a scathing look at Cardigan.

She gasped and ran across the room. Nobody else had noticed Cardigan sagging. She reached him and put her arm around him. His eyes rolled as he looked up at her. He smiled.

"You've—got—guts," he muttered.

CARDIGAN came to a day later in a hospital room. He turned his head and saw Max Saul sitting in a wheelchair. He licked his lips. A nurse got up and looked at him.

Max Saul grinned, "He's O.K., nurse."

"Yeah," said Cardigan. "I feel like getting up and playing kick-the-wicket or something."

"I'm sore," Max joked. "You're getting all the headlines, Irish."

"How did Everett and McKimm make out?"

"They didn't. They brought McKimm here on a stretcher and identified him. Everett cleared his conscience before he went places. And cleared Clara Hartz too. It was Everett put the idea in McKimm's head that if Hartz should die Mrs. Hartz would come into a lot of money. Everett figured he would have, too—through marriage to the widow. I think I said once that guy was a lounge-lizard."

Cardigan closed his eyes. "It's tough on the woman, Max. She saved my life."

"She took it all standing up, Jack. And she's been telephoning every half hour about you. Bush started to yammer but Captain Bricknell dampered him down."

Another nurse came in with a vase of roses. Cardigan frowned. "Now who sent those?"

"Mrs. Hartz."

Cardigan relaxed and closed his eyes.

Max Saul said, "That's what I'd call a bed of roses, Irish."

A nurse wheeled him out of the room and on the way down the hall he hummed The St. Louis Blues.

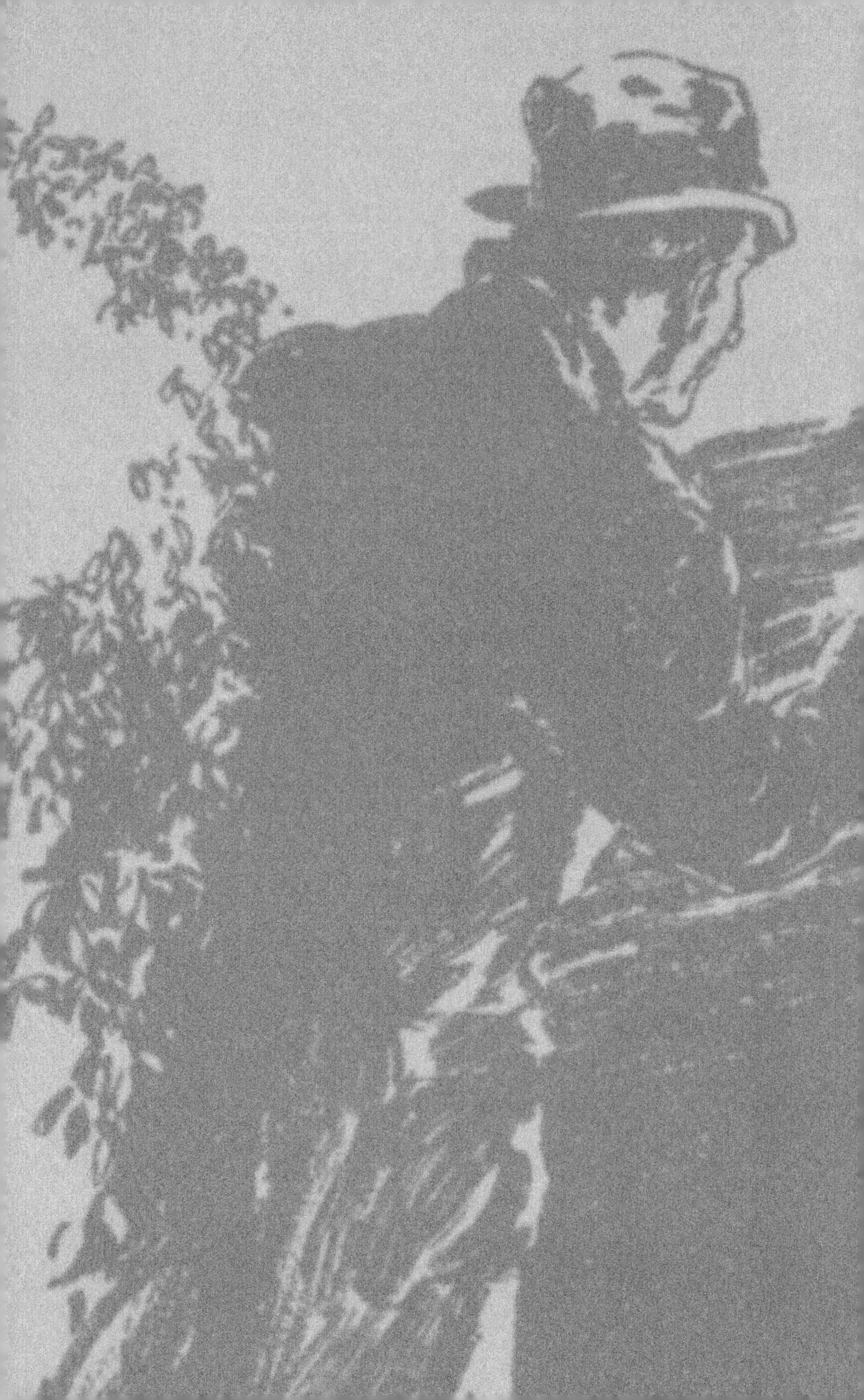

HELL'S PAY CHECK

IT WAS ONLY AN OBLONG STRIP OF PAPER BUT IT HAD BEEN DRAWN AT THE POINT OF A GUN, ENDORSED IN BLOOD. DETECTIVE CARDIGAN KNEW THAT NO MAN MUST CASH IT, THAT HE MUST FOLLOW IT TO DEATH'S CLEARING-HOUSE, CANCEL IT WITH A PEN DIPPED IN FLAMING LEAD.

CHAPTER ONE

DEATH ON ARRIVAL

THE CHANGE in the tune of the train wheels roused Cardigan. He used a broad palm to wipe steam from the rain-wet coach window. The train was crossing the Wabash River. Beyond were the lights of the city.

Cardigan bent over, dropped a magazine into an open grip, started to close it. On second thought, he drew out a .38 revolver and slipped it into his hip pocket; closed, locked the grip.

He rose, a big, shaggy-headed man with a burry outdoor look, shrugged into a wrinkled topcoat, put on a faded fedora that had seen better days. He lugged his bag to the nearest vestibule. The locomotive's bell gonged more resonantly as the train pulled into the station.

Cardigan swung down to the platform, shook his head at a barging porter, tramped heavy-footed through the waiting room. He dwarfed an average-sized man. His shoulders rocked. He slapped open a door with the flat of his hand, felt a gust of rain and raw fall wind. He moved along slowly, looking at the license plates of parked cars. Then he stopped before a large black sedan and was regarding the windshield curiously when the front door opened and a man in a chauffeur's cap stepped out.

"Mr. Cardigan?"

"Yeah."

The chauffeur saluted, pivoted and opened the rear door. He took Cardigan's bag, and Cardigan climbed in. The bag landed after him. The chauffeur climbed in front, started the motor, clicked into gear.

Cardigan leaned back, rolled a fresh cigar between his lips, nibbled off the tip, spat it through an open window. He lit up and watched wet buildings flash past. The car turned into the main drag, where trolley bells clanged, auto horns honked, and red neon lights scrawled advertisements in the rainy dark.

"Wet night," said the chauffeur.

"Lousy."

"Train was on time, though."

"Yeah. How far out is this place?"

"It ain't far. Say, you're that private dick made such a haul out in St. Louis in the summer, ain't you?"

"Better keep your eyes on the road," Cardigan said.

They shot through a railroad underpass, rolled through a tatterdemalion part of the city. The chauffeur's ears stuck out from his head. He kept wiping sweat from the inside of the windshield. Cardigan was uninterested in the scenery. He was rather fascinated by the way the chauffeur's ears stuck out.

"Much further?" he asked.

"It ain't far," the chauffeur said.

"I'm hit!" Joe gasped, and fell over a flower bed, cursing.

Cardigan squinted at the back of his head, took two long, ruminative puffs. "Stop at the next cigar store. I want to get some pipe tobacco."

"Mr. Edwards'll have plenty."

"That's all right. I said I want to get some pipe tobacco."

"All right, then, all right."

A minute later the chauffeur pulled up to the curb and Cardigan opened the door, stepped out and strode into a cigar store. The windows were opaque with steam. Cardigan slipped into a telephone booth, looked at a yellow slip of paper, made a call. Half a minute later he stepped out, picked up a tin of tobacco and went outside.

"I'll ride in front," he said. "Lucky he had my brand."

"I don't smoke a pipe," the chauffeur said, and rolled the car from the curb.

They rode in silence for a few minutes. Then Cardigan drew his gun and pressed it against the chauffeur's ribs.

"Now where the hell are you really going?" he said.

"Hey, what the—"

"Cut it out, you fat-head! Keep your hands on that wheel and don't try handing me a line."

The chauffeur was gripping the wheel hard with both hands. He didn't look at Cardigan. He stared intently through the windshield, his body tense, his shoulders hunched.

"Take the first right-hand turn," Cardigan said. "Go around the block and back to the city."

"Cripes, chief—"

"Lay off, lame-brain—lay off. The next time you try to act like a chauffeur—act like one. You've been a heel so long that you're heel-conscious." He jabbed his gun hard against the man's ribs, snapped, "Turn right!"

The man heaved on the wheel. The car skidded on the wet pavements, grazed a tree, slewed badly but held its balance. Behind, on the main street they had left, brakes ground and tires screeched. Cardigan looked back and saw a curtained touring car skidding to a stop.

"Step on!" Cardigan muttered.

"Geeze—"

"Step on it!"

The sedan gathered speed. Looking back, Cardigan saw the touring car in reverse. Then he saw it swing into the side street. The sedan swung right again, skidding, and the man at the wheel groaned and cursed.

"Right at the next," Cardigan said, "and back to the main drag."

"What a sweet spot you put me in!"

"I'm glad of that."

"They'll think I'm two-timin'!"

"Swell!"

The chauffeur snarled, "You ain't sittin' so pretty yourself!"

The rear end slewed wildly as they took the next right. The rear left wheel struck the opposite curb. The car heaved, slammed back to all fours. The chauffeur threw out the clutch, raced the motor to keep it from stalling, meshed gears again savagely and skidded on the get-away.

The beams of the touring's headlights sparkled on the rain-beaded rear window of the sedan. The chauffeur sank deep in the seat, gritting his teeth, gripping the wheel low. Cardigan twisted around and hunched down on the floor.

A gun banged in the wet dark. The rear window fell out with a crash. A hole appeared in the center of the nonshatterable windshield, with spiderweb lines radiating.

"Look!" cried the chauffeur. "Look at that!"

"To hell with that! Step on it!"

"Me—I'm gonna stop!"

Cardigan trained his gun on the man. "You stop and I'll cave in your chest!"

"Oh, Gord! They think 'm two-timin'!"

He swung left into the main drag—wildly. The wheels rasped on the wet pavement, screeched over trolley tracks. The big sedan shuddered. Miraculously it retained its balance, careened away, with the chauffeur's foot so hard on the throttle that the wheels lost traction momentarily and the rear end swung from left to right. Then the wheels gripped and the sedan shot ahead.

Another hole appeared magically in the windshield. The chauffeur choked and stared at it with horrified eyes. Then he saw a pole directly in front of him. He heaved at the wheel violently. The car slewed, skidded, turned sidewise. It swung all the way around and across the tracks—and around again. The chauffeur gripped the wheel hard, his mouth open, his eyes frozen with horror.

The right front mudguard slammed against a pole. A window fell out of the car with a crash. Guns barked and lead ripped through the sedan's body. The chauffeur screamed and heaved up and another bullet knocked him down again. The touring car roared past.

Cardigan pushed open the door, pawed glass splinters from his face. He looked once at the chauffeur's head. Another look was unnecessary. He hauled his bag out of the back of the car, ran with it across the sidewalk, back of a ramshackle house with boarded windows.

He ducked through a gap in a rotten board fence, screwing his feet into wet earth with each step to kill his footprints. He went along back of the fence, then paused in some tall grass, started to reach for his handkerchief; changed his mind. He tore off wet grass, made a pad of it, scrubbed his face and tossed the grass away. The grass and the rain were cold.

Cardigan shivered and threaded his way on back of other board fences, reached a side street and walked away from the main drag. A police siren moaned through the night. By dead reckoning Cardigan walked into the city limits, his coat collar up. The mirror of a chewing-gum slot-machine showed him that his face was not as bad as he had supposed. He sighed, whistled to himself and walked across the sidewalk into a taxi.

"Sixth and Diana," he said.

At Sixth he got off, walked north on Sixth, turned right at the first intersection and entered the Hotel Flatlands.

THE man sitting behind the enormous flat-topped desk of aged mahogany drew slowly on a large pipe shaped like an inverted question mark. He was massive himself, in keeping with the room's furnishings. Middle-aged, bald, except for offshoots of grayish hair above the ears, he had a large nose, a fighter's jaw, a broad, impressive forehead. Through black-ribboned pince-nez he gazed at the stocky youth who sat quivering on a straight-backed chair.

"Be calm, Otto," said the big man.

"Yes, sir. Y-yes, sir." The stocky youth's teeth chattered.

The big man frowned concernedly, rose and went to an eight-legged Boulle cabinet. From it he took decanter and glasses. He carried them to the desk.

"Not Napoleon, Otto, but brandy none the less."

He gave the youth a stiff jolt. Otto threw it over, choked, spluttered, grimaced. The big man chuckled, but the look in his eyes was not one of humor. Worry was there and a haunted light shimmering deep in the pupils.

Rain thrashed against the French windows.

Otto began stuttering. "I—I couldn't do anything, sir! They walked up to me—and I could see how their hands were in their pockets. They made me walk away from the car and they kept me in a touring car after one of them took my cap. They held guns against me there. Then after maybe an hour they told me to get out and walk away and say nothing. Our—your car was gone. Then they went too. I—I—"

"You could have done nothing else, Otto. Pull yourself together. That man Cardigan telephoned a second time and I thank God nothing serious has happened to him. He's on his way out."

The old negro in black livery came in. "Mr. Cardigan, suh."

A moment later Cardigan filled the doorway. He had left hat and coat with the butler and stood chafing his hands and staring keenly into the dimly lighted library. His shaggy hair stood out around his head.

The big man rose from behind the mahogany desk, held out his hand. Cardigan crossed the room, shook it, peered levelly at the pince-nez.

"This is Otto Shreiner, my chauffeur," the big man said.

Otto rose and bowed. Cardigan took him in with a piercing look, said nothing.

The man with the pince-nez said, "Leave us, Otto."

Otto went out. The grandfather's clock ticked solemnly.

"Brandy, Mr. Cardigan?"

Cardigan said: "Thanks," poured himself a tot, sniffed the aroma, then drank it. He squinted one eye at the empty glass. "Well, Mr. Edwards, what's on your mind?"

"Sit down, won't you?"

Both sat down, facing each other across the flat-topped desk. The old man took off his pince-nez, leaned back. "First," he said, "my name's not Edwards."

Cardigan, starting a fresh cigar, did not look up until he had it going smoothly. Then he spoke impersonally. "And then what?"

"I am the mayor of the city."

Cardigan maintained his impersonal stare. "Once I worked for a governor."

"I said 'Edwards,' you know, on long distance because—" He shrugged and held his palms up, then fell into a moody silence.

Cardigan studied the red end of his fresh cigar and started speaking in a low, blunt voice. "All right, then, Mr. Holmes. I expected trouble, anyhow. I always expect trouble when a client telephones long distance, offers to pay all expenses, and adds—'details on arrival.' That's all O.K. by me. It's my business. But I'll be twice damned if I like to have trouble pile on my shoulder the minute I step off a train. I'll stand for almost anything, but I hate to get mixed up in a murder before I know what all the shooting's for."

That ripped Holmes out of his moody silence. He half rose, remained that way, exclaimed: "Murder!"

"And why I'm sitting here right now, Mr. Mayor, is one of the reasons why I believe in luck, a rabbit's foot and words like abracadabra."

Holmes fell back into the chair, gripping the sides. "But—you said—murder!"

"Don't take it so hard. It happens every day. Besides, the guy that got it was a hood anyhow. He was the nice little boy that played chauffeur and started to take me places. But I had a hunch the minute we started that something was wrong. So I phoned you from that cigar store and asked what your chauffeur looked like."

Holmes squared his jaw. "Did you have to kill him, by God?"

"Me? Hell, no. His pals did it. Trailing us in another car. When I made the hood turn around his pals got sore and opened the fireworks. I ducked out and kept my mouth shut. Did you report the theft of your car to the police?"

But Holmes was still thinking of murder. "Murder—murder," he repeated in a far-away voice.

"Did you?"

"Oh— Well, Otto did. At the railway station."

"What did he tell them?"

"Just that three men had forced him away, held him prisoner for an hour, then let him go."

"Did he say he was waiting for me?"

"No."

"I've got to be sure. I've got to be sure because I want to know how I stand with the cops."

"Otto is in my confidence."

Cardigan got up and took a turn up and down the room. He stopped and looked at the mayor. "Where did you telephone me from, your office?"

"No—here. Right here."

"Any other phones in the house on this line?"

"No."

"All right. Then your wire was tapped. You'll hear about the murder soon enough, and your recovered car. Tell that chauffeur of yours to keep his mouth shut. You keep yours. Your enemies, whoever they are, know I'm working for you. That may be tough for you, but it's tougher for me. And now—" Cardigan sat down—"why am I here?"

Holmes leaned forward. "To recover a check for twenty thousand dollars that I made payable to one Roberta Callahan, a notorious woman."

"In other words, if this check gets to certain hands the notoriety won't do you any good."

"It will ruin me."

"You don't look like the kind of man would run around with a dangerous piece of fluff. Still, there was a governor—"

"I assure you I'm not," Holmes said with quiet dignity.

"Philanthropy?"

"Don't be droll. My son Edgar's a rather gay blade, and I did it for his sake. He became badly tangled with this woman and there was only one way out. I bought her off. I gave her my personal check for twenty thousand dollars two weeks ago. She immediately blossomed out in a new roadster, moved into a fine apartment—"

"You mean you want the cancelled check?"

"No—no. The check has not been through my bank. Don't you see? She cashed the check with someone—someone who is holding it against me. And I want that check."

"What makes you think some guy's holding it?"

Holmes tilted his jaw. "You know me—or of me, rather. The reform mayor. By Judas Priest, I am that! Edgar had to get himself involved with that—woman—and I, naturally being his father, had to get him out of it. Hence my check. And would a photograph of that check, printed in the daily tabloid here, help my reform platform? No—you needn't reply. The answer is obvious."

"Who would be holding that check?"

"Any number of persons. Our daily tabloid, the worst scandal sheet in the country. Or the Fusion crowd. Or Pat McHugh, the boss of the old party. Or somebody unknown to me who hopes to reap a fortune by passing it on to someone else. But there you are. There's the situation. I blundered into this because I'm not as smart-alecky as a lot of people. I'm entirely innocent. You might say that my son would come to the fore and admit the check was written to clear him. But the rest could shoot that down—and they could buy off the woman. You see?"

Cardigan had slid way down into the chair. He regarded Holmes through narrow-lidded eyes. Suddenly he knew he liked Holmes, saw his position. Cardigan, no reformer himself but a hard party down to the core, had a habit of admiring qualities which he himself did not possess.

He sat up, taking out a notebook. "All right now, Mr. Holmes. Give me all the names of persons you suspect, and addresses if possible. I don't suppose you asked the woman who cashed the check for her."

"I dare not go near her. I will pay the person who holds that check now the amount written on it—but I must have it."

"You'll get it," Cardigan said.

CHAPTER TWO

DOUGH FOR A DICK

AT MIDNIGHT Cardigan lay awake in the dark of his hotel room thinking. The rain had stopped. The sound of a crosstown trolley came up sharply out of the street.

Elections were a month hence, and old Mayor Holmes had things to think about. A reform platform is a ticklish thing to stand on. Wiseacres are always ready to accuse you of trying to kid the public, of playing the wolf in sheep's clothing. A confessed mountebank is always colorful, a good man rarely popular.

Thus thought Cardigan—until a sound at the door dismissed philosophy and snapped him to the immediate present. He reached over to the little bed-table, got his hand on his revolver and sat up with the same motion. He heard the not quite silent movement of a key in the lock, a final click. Then a pause of utter silence. Then a vertical line of light appeared where the door opened on a crack. The door swung wide slowly, silently, and three men stood there. Two of them had guns drawn while the third moved into the background. One of the armed men reached in a hand seeking the light switch.

"That's far enough," Cardigan said. "One slight move out of any of you birds and the management'll be disturbed."

The two armed men remained motionless. Then one said: "Police, Cardigan."

"Show me."

The two men turned back their lapels.

Cardigan lowered his gun. "It's damned funny that I can't get a night's sleep without you guys prowling around here like correspondence-school detectives."

The horse-faced man snapped on the lights and said, "I'm Lieutenant Strout. This is Sergeant Blake. That's Massey, the house officer. You can go, Massey."

Strout closed the door in Massey's face. He put away his gun and Blake did likewise. Blake was a chubby-cheeked fat man with a sly, smiling face. Strout was tall, muddy-eyed.

"Let's see that rod," he said.

Cardigan reversed it and Strout took it by the butt. It was a jointless solid-frame gun. Strout smelled the barrel, examined the chamber, hefted it thoughtfully, tossed it back on the bed.

"That the only one you carry?"

"Yeah."

"Look around, Blake. There's his bag."

Blake ransacked Cardigan's handbag while Cardigan stuffed a pipe and watched him with mild amusement. Strout went through Cardigan's clothes, opened the dresser drawers. Blake left Cardigan's clothes on the floor beside the bag.

Strout sat down on a chair, struck a match on the veneered frame of the wooden bed, left a long scratch there.

"What were you doing in the mayor's car tonight, Cardigan?"

"Was I in the mayor's car?"

Strout spurted smoke through his nostrils. "Don't give me the runaround."

"Well, was I?"

"You got in it at the railroad station and the chauffeur was killed twenty minutes later on Prairie Avenue."

"Says who?"

"Says me."

"Get your proof, lieutenant, and we'll continue."

"Listen, you," Blake said with his sly smile. "We've heard a lot about you."

Strout went on. "It was a stolen car. You got in and the chauffeur wasn't the mayor's chauffeur. He was all shot up when we found him and the car was busted. He was cold meat. You rode with him."

Cardigan put his bare feet on the floor, buttoned up the coat of his blue cotton pajamas, pointed his pipe stem at Strout.

"Now I'll tell you what I did. I came out of the station looking for a taxi. A guy with a chauffeur's cap on said, 'Taxi!' like that. So I thought it was an independent, and as it was raining and the car was handy I climbed in. I told him to drive to the Hotel Flatlands. After a while I began to wonder where he was going. I asked him and he said where I told him. He began to look queer to me, but I wasn't looking for trouble. So I got out at a cigar store and went in and bought some tobacco. I thought it out. I left the store and walked away. I walked back to the city and came here."

Blake laughed in a shrill, mocking tone. "That's a fast one!"

"Well, what are you going to do about it?" Cardigan said.

"What are we going to do about it?" Blake cried. "Damn you, you can't—"

"Shut up, Jake," Strout said dully and kept looking at Cardigan with his muddy, humorless eyes. "This is damned funny, Cardigan," he went on. "You were in a stolen car and the guy that drove it was murdered."

"With my gun, I suppose."

"Not with that gun there, but that don't say you didn't have another."

Cardigan laughed harshly. "And they pin medals on you guys!"

Strout blew cigarette ash to the carpet. "What did you come here for?"

"To sleep." He swung back into bed, pulled the covers up to his neck.

"I mean the city," Strout said.

"To get the hell pestered out of me by a couple of dumb clucks wearing badges."

Strout looked sullen. "None of your lousy cheap wit, Cardigan! You may have a name where you come from for being a pretty swell dick, but names are all the same to me on a police blotter."

The bed covers erupted and Cardigan was sitting up again. "Any time a client engages me it's just the same as if he engaged a lawyer. He gets my confidence and the benefit of silence."

"But there's murder in this."

"Because a heel in a stolen car starts taking me for a ride, for some reason I don't know, and I'm wide awake enough to slip out of it; and because a little later the heel is murdered with a gun that isn't mine— Listen, Strout, why the hell should I get all hot and bothered and tell you the story of my life? Do you mean to sit there in those pants and tell me I ought to get gray worrying about it? Hot dog, what school did you go to?"

Blake snapped, "This mutt is looking for a bust in the puss!"

"Yeah, and I suppose you're going to do it. Any minute now I'm going to break into convulsions!"

Strout pushed Blake back and said to Cardigan: "You come down to headquarters tomorrow."

"Like hell I will. If you want me to come to headquarters go get a warrant for my arrest. You got a lame tip somewhere, Strout, and you're trying to make me believe that it's red-hot. At your age you should know better than try that one. It was whiskered before I was born."

Strout got up, put his bony fists on his hips, regarded Cardigan with sullen eyes. "You're bright as hell, ain't you?"

Cardigan lay back in bed, pulled up the covers. "On the way out, Strout, douse the lights and lock the door."

CARDIGAN was singing deep-throated under the shower next morning, when the doorbell rang.

"Wait a minute," he yelled.

He stopped the shower, climbed out and rubbed himself down with a towel and then alcohol. He heaved into a bathrobe, kicked his feet into mules and tramped through the bedroom.

A little plump man with pomaded sandy hair and narrow shoulders stood holding a derby chest-high with both hands. Thirty-odd, he had a clerical air. He wore expensive dark clothes.

"May I come in?"

"You're a new one on me," Cardigan said, "but come on."

The man crossed the threshold and Cardigan's hands darted to his person, slapped pockets rapidly. Out of the man's left pocket he took a small, dark automatic, palmed it.

"You see," he said, "I never know," and kicked the door shut.

The little man smiled. "You're a man of parts, Mr. Cardigan. I'm sorry to have intruded so early. Be careful—the safety may not be closed."

"I find that out the minute I touch a gun. It is."

"Truly a man of parts."

Cardigan said: "Now get this. I just got up. I haven't eaten yet. I'm a lousy guy to do business with most of the time, but especially before breakfast. Cut out the drawing-room tricks and speak your piece."

"A most definite man also. My compliments." Smiling, the little man showed exquisite white teeth and crinkly red lips. "Very well. I shan't be long. Primo: what are you doing in the city?"

"Answer: none of your business."

"Of course, you are here working for the mayor."

"The words are in your mouth, not mine."

"Doubtless you came here to regain possession—for the mayor—of a piece of paper. Green, let us say. And watermarked. You know—those little wavy lines? Correct?"

"You make me sick," Cardigan growled. He extracted six .25 caliber shells from the miniature Webley, shoved the Webley in the man's pocket, turned him about and shoved him to the door. "In a word—scram!"

The man turned, smiling with his shell-like teeth. "Would five thousand dollars interest you?"

"A thousand would, but what's that to you?"

"I have a friend who would pay you five thousand dollars for that little oblong strip of green, watermarked paper."

"I work for a living," Cardigan said, "and the agency I work for has a reputation. I don't think it would go nuts about doing business with you."

"But how about you?"

Cardigan took three long strides and gripped the little man by his shirt front. "Who the hell are you?"

"Please don't get pugilistic," the little man said in a tranquil voice.

Cardigan turned about with him, hurled him across the bed. "I've been here only twelve hours," he growled, "and I'm getting fed up on a lot of people."

He straddled the man, held him down by the throat with one strong hand, used the other to go through his pockets. He pulled out a wallet, keys, some envelopes. Getting back on his feet, he said: "Now stay there," and began sifting the articles.

Presently he shrugged, tossed the lot back on the bed. "You can go," he said. "And tell that lousy tabloid you work for that they couldn't buy me for a hundred thousand! And mark me, little morning glory! If you go monkeying around here again things may happen to you. Out—and goom-by!"

The little man rose, patted down his clothes, picked his derby from the floor and bowed at the door. His shell-like teeth gleamed. He backed out saying nothing, closed the door quietly.

When Cardigan went downstairs fifteen minutes later, Massey, the house dick, headed him off.

"What did that reporter from the tab want, Cardigan?"

"A short autobiographical sketch, Mr. Massey. Something like 'From Plowboy to Mastermind.' I said mine wasn't interesting. Referred him to you."

"And for that you gave him a split lip, huh?"

"He stubbed his toe and fell against a radiator."

"Yah!"

"Goom-by!"

Cardigan ate breakfast in the coffee shop, went out carrying his topcoat under his arm. Under the facade, he looked up and down the street. Across the way, diagonally, a man stood in front of a Western Union window. Cardigan walked west, turned south into Sixth, used a store window as a mirror and saw the man follow him.

He turned around abruptly and retraced his steps, putting a cigar in his mouth. The man who had followed had no time to duck. He slowed down, however. Cardigan came up to him, stopped, said: "Got a match, brother?"

The man was young. "Sure," he said, and passed a packet.

Cardigan lit up, returned the packet, said: "Spider on you!" and struck the man's lapel lightly. Beneath the cloth he felt the hardness of a police shield.

The man looked bewildered.

"Give Lieutenant Strout my love," Cardigan said, and rolled on, puffing enthusiastically.

The plainclothesman did not follow.

CHAPTER THREE

THE GIRL IN 616

TEN MINUTES later Cardigan got out of a taxi in front of a six-story apartment house. He pounded a broad flag walk and tramped in through a broad, imposing entrance. The livery of the negro elevator boy hurt his eyes.

"How is every little thing?" Cardigan grinned.

"What floor?"

"All right, be dignified— Six, colonel."

The elevator rose in silence. Cardigan got out at the sixth floor and walked on carpets resilient as sponge rubber. He stopped, raised a bronze knocker on the black door of 616, let it fall back.

A girl with a shock of blonde hair opened it and looked at Cardigan with wide, baby-blue eyes. She had on blue pajamas and a blue peignoir trimmed with sand-colored old lace.

"Yes?" she chirped in a babyish voice.

"I have grave news for you," Cardigan said with a judicial air.

Acting fatherly, he took hold of her hand, patted it with rough tenderness, the while he worked himself through the doorway and kicked the door shut. He scaled his hat into a velours divan, grinned broadly at the girl. She shrank back, drawing her peignoir about her small, rounded body.

"What—what do you want?" she asked, fear tailing her words.

Cardigan grinned. With his ungodly shock of hair and his heavy powerful shoulders he filled the room. He indicated a love-seat.

"Sit down, Miss Callahan."

"W-what d-do you—"

He suddenly crossed the luxurious living room, looked in the bedroom, the bathroom; turned and regarded the girl across the length of the room.

"Now let's put the cards on the table, sister. I know who you are and what you are, so don't try to pull an act on me or throw a faint or in any way try to kid me into believing that you don't know what it's all about. I may look like a gorilla, but I'm not going to slam you down. All you have to do is answer a question."

The baby-faced girl swallowed. "W-what is it?"

"Who cashed that twenty-thousand dollar check for you?"

Miss Callahan sat down on the love-seat, sinking into one of its twin cushions. She gripped her knees with white hands the nails of which were lacquered in red. Her baby-blue eyes dilated. She looked innocent and hurt.

"Come on, come on," Cardigan growled, thumping across the carpet. He was big, towering, inimical in a leather-faced way.

The girl made a sound that sounded like "Eek!" and drew her knees up to her breast, gripping her ankles.

"I—I don't know what you're talking about," she cried in a tiny, breathless voice. "I—I d-don't know you. What right have you got to come in here? You b-brute!"

"For God's sake sister, don't pull a hack line like that. I tell you I know you. I know you got a check for twenty thousand. I know you cashed it—and not in a bank."

She jumped to her feet and began pacing up and down dramatically. "This is an outrage!" she cried. "I don't know you and I don't know what you're talking about. You forced your way in my apartment and if you don't leave right away I'll call the management and we'll see. Now—" she indicated the door—"get out!"

"Tone down, girlie!"

She stamped her foot. "Get out!"

He grabbed her. Her eyes popped and the flat of his hand stifled a scream. His hair stood up on his nape. He shook her.

"You fool! Pipe down!"

"Release the lady, Mr. Cardigan."

Cardigan stiffened, twisted his neck. The reporter from the tabloid stood with his back to the door holding the small Webley and smiling with his shell-like teeth.

"Naughty, naughty!" he mocked.

Cardigan released the girl. She reeled away from him, bounced into the love-seat and lay panting and choking out hysterical little sounds.

"So," grunted Cardigan, his big hands hanging at his sides, his face lowering.

"Just so, Mr. Cardigan. Observe the steadiness of this gun and act accordingly."

"Cool, ain't you?" Cardigan growled.

"As the proverbial cucumber."

"N-now who are y-you?" cried the girl.

"Your benefactor," said the little man. "I eavesdropped." He smiled politely at Cardigan. "You'll be going directly, won't you, Mr. Cardigan?"

Cardigan felt the red color of chagrin flooding his face and neck. He felt suddenly oafish in the presence of this cool little man with the gun and the steady hand. He crossed to the velours divan, picked up his hat. He kept looking at the girl and backed up toward the door. In a mirror back of the divan he could see his own and the little man's image. The little man was behind him, holding the gun, smiling.

Cardigan's right elbow shot backward and upward. It caught the little man neatly under the chin and snapped his head back violently to the tune of clicking teeth. Cardigan jumped to one side and pivoted at the same time. His fist traveled a foot and smashed against the little man's chest. The little man slammed against the wall so hard that he rebounded and ran into Cardigan's short left. That straightened him momentarily. The gun dropped from his fingers. Glassy-eyed, he went down like a balloon suddenly deflated.

Cardigan picked up the gun with one hand and with the other drew manacles from his pocket and lunged at the girl. The leveled gun cut her scream in the bud. He drew her from the divan, made her sit on the floor and manacled her to the unconscious little man.

"Now be quiet," he said huskily.

He began searching the room. He turned out all the drawers in a high, narrow secretary. He found a bank book showing a deposit of twenty thousand dollars two weeks ago. He scanned letters. He ransacked the living room and the bedroom with a vengeance. In the bedroom he knocked over a vase of flowers into a pink waste basket. Cursing his clumsiness, he picked them up, and spotted a small card and a small envelope lying in the waste basket. The card had written on it: "Just a remembrance for a favor from you know who." A plain white card such as florists supply. And on the accompanying envelope, printed in green, on the flap: "The Shelman Florist."

Cardigan pocketed card and envelope and went back into the living room. The girl was shivering.

Cardigan said: "This guy here works for the daily tabloid, so look out for him. Why the hell don't you tell me who cashed that check and get the benefit of silence? Do you want to have your name sprawled all over the papers?"

"I w-wish you'd leave."

"You little scatter-brained fool, they'll use you eventually! This guy is looking for the same information I am, but he wants to spread it in the tab."

"I—have nothing to say."

Cardigan shrugged. He bent down, unlocked the manacles and put them in his pocket. He threw the Webley on the velours divan, started for the door.

"B-but this man!" cried the girl. "What am I going to do with him?"

"Try ice bags or smelling salts. I wouldn't care."

He opened the door, went out, down the corridor. He punched the elevator button and went down with the stony-faced negro.

THE Shelman Florist Shop was in the small arcade of the Shelman Hotel. It was a small, chic cubicle with a floor of lozenge-shaped tiles. The attendant was a girl in a black jersey ensemble. She smiled brightly and Cardigan took off his hat, leaned on the black marble counter.

"If I asked you in a nice way miss, would you tell me who sent flowers to Miss Roberta Callahan, 4111 Danneford, in the last day or two?"

"Strange request, isn't it?"

"Strange as strange. How about it?"

"I don't know." She tapped her foot and kept throwing little glances at him. "It's unusual. I never had it happen before. I don't know what to say. Who are you?"

"By one look at my ugly map couldn't you tell I was a detective?"

"No."

"You're being kind. I am."

She blushed. "Wait a minute."

She went to the rear of the shop, looked through a file of carbons. In a minute she returned. "I'd like to keep my name out of this," she said.

"Sure thing."

"They were ordered by a Mr. P.K. McHugh."

Cardigan went out finding the air a sweeter thing to breathe. P.K.—Pat—McHugh, the boss of the old party. Pat McHugh sending flowers to Roberta Callahan by way of remembering a favor she had done him! Pat McHugh, arch-enemy of the reform ticket and Mayor Evan Holmes—

On his way back to the Flatlands Cardigan picked up three different newspapers, went to his room and read them. Last night's murder was front-page stuff. The dead man had finally been identified as Carl Dorshook, alias Charles Dorn, alias James Matson. His record went back to Toledo, Chillicothe, Dayton, Pittsburgh and Baltimore. According to the police, however, he could not be linked up with any local mob, though apparently he had been. Theft of the mayor's car enlarged the headlines and evoked a picture of the mayor in each paper.

Cardigan tossed the papers aside and thought things out. He knew the police were not through with him yet. He knew they couldn't hang anything on him but he also knew that they could make things uncomfortable for him. He wanted to protect himself, to steer away from any hint that he was working for the mayor.

He went out and took a high-speed train out to a suburb five miles distant. From the telegraph office at the railroad station he sent a code message to the main office in New York. Translated, the message said:

> In a jam. Send a long wire. Make it a follow up on a fake case to kid the cops. Use your own judgment.

He gave the address of the Hotel Flatlands. He suspected that Massey, the house dick, would get a copy of it, and he wanted it so. Because Massey would turn it over to Lieutenant Strout. He took the tram back to the city and at one o'clock he received a message.

> The girl may also be using the name of Sterrit. Her hair is dark red instead of brown and she was last in Cleveland, not Springfield, Ohio. She has stenographic ability and can also play on the harp. If there is any place of amusement there featuring a harpist look into it. She affects an English accent and has a complex for using big words such as amanuensis and gymnosophist. Her parents are desolated, so show results and spare no expense in obtaining same. If you feel you need the assistance of another operative let me know.
> George Hammerhorn,
> President,
> The Cosmos Detective Agency.

Cardigan appreciated the message, excepting the nonsense about the harp. Certain that the mayor's wire was being tapped, he walked six blocks to a Postal Telegraph office, wrote out a message and saw a messenger depart with it.

He was in his room at two o'clock when Otto Shreiner, the mayor's chauffeur knocked. Cardigan put him on a chair.

"You can help your boss and me in a big way," Cardigan said. "At midnight I want you to come here to my room and stay here for an hour while I'm out. The night telephone operator comes on duty at that time and she's never heard my voice. At a quarter past twelve I want you to call her and ask her the time. At twelve-thirty I want you to call the Union Station and ask the best train to St. Louis tomorrow forenoon. At a quarter to one I want you to call the operator again and ask her to call you at eight in the morning. Got that straight?"

"Yes, sir."

"Try to speak like me. You know, rough, as if you owned the place or something. Get me?"

"Yes, sir."

"You took a room here all right?"

"Yes, sir."

"What room and what name?"

"I signed Henry Josephs of Indianapolis. Room 411."

"O.K. Stay in your room and use the stairs on the way down."

"I used them on the way up."

Cardigan slapped his back. "You'll do, Otto!" Then he let the chauffeur out.

The tabloid, Cardigan knew, had no political stand, no moral stand. It had a personal grievance against Mayor Holmes dating back to a day six months ago when the mayor, in a radio speech, had called it "a filthy, depraved rag"; this because two of the tabloid's reporters had broken into the home of a woman whose daughter had been slain in a love tangle. In an effort to steal photographs and letters, they had bound the mother and precipitated a nervous breakdown. On the other hand, the *Press-Clarion* was politically definite in its stand against Holmes, carried considerable heft in the south and east ends, and obviously would jump at the opportunity to undermine the mayor's character.

Cardigan knew for certain that the tabloid was after that check. He had a strong hunch that Pat McHugh possessed the check. And he wondered if *The Press-Clarion* had a finger in the pie too. The murder of Dorshook was an accident—a bad one. It was reasonable to suppose that some mob in the extortion racket had got wind of the check, had wanted Cardigan for purposes of extracting definite information. Thus Cardigan had three distinct groups of enemies. And he was hampered by the police.

CHAPTER FOUR

STRONG-ARM STUFF

AT THREE o'clock he went down to the lobby for the afternoon editions. He was on his way across to the newsstand when he saw Strout and Blake come barging through the swing doors. He sensed trouble. A savage doggedness was in Strout's gait and manner and Blake wore a wily, bitter smile.

"Now don't give me any back talk," Strout chopped off. "Over to headquarters with you."

"What's this—another one of your bright moments?"

Blake gripped Cardigan's arm. "Ixnay on that back chat."

Cardigan looked disgusted. "Wait'll I get my hat and coat."

Blake shook him. "You come right along!"

"You go chase yourself. I get cold in the head easily."

Strout muttered: "We'll go up with you."

In his room Cardigan took his time. "What have I done now?"

"Snap on it!" Blake clipped.

Cardigan picked up Hammerhorn's wire. "Have you seen this?"

Strout read it, looked up at Cardigan with his muddy eyes, looked down at the wire again. Then he tossed it on the bed and said: "Come on."

Cardigan said: "D'you know of any place around here featuring a harpist?"

Blake took a crack at Cardigan's ribs from behind. Cardigan, whirled, cursed, his eyes blazing, but Strout grabbed him from behind. Blake snickered and went to the door, opening it, and Strout marched Cardigan out. They went to headquarters in a taxi.

In a dusty office on the second floor a uniformed cop sat in one chair and the negro elevator boy from the Danneford Avenue apartment house sat in another. His eyes got round when Cardigan looked at him and then Blake knocked Cardigan into a chair and chuckled loosely.

"Is this the guy?" Strout said to the negro.

"Yassuh."

"O.K." Strout sat on the desk, dangled one leg and turned his horse face to Cardigan. His eyes got muddier, his face dark and dour. "Now spout, big boy."

Cardigan knew it was no time for horseplay. He saw in Strout a good cop, a hard one, short on speech and not a man to be kidded when he was in deadly earnest. Blake was a wind bag, but he could be nasty too in a mean, sly way. The presence of the negro was hint enough that something had gone wrong at the apartment house. More properly, in Roberta Callahan's apartment.

"Spout about what?" Cardigan asked.

Strout indicated the negro with a nod. "This guy described you to a T. The minute he described you I knew it was you. You called on a girl named Roberta Callahan this morning. Right?"

"Tell me some more."

"All right. When you came down the elevator the boy here says you looked red and mad and mean. What the hell were you doing in Roberta Calahan's apartment."

"What proof have you I was in her apartment?"

"There are eight other apartments on that floor. We asked the occupants in those apartments if they'd had any callers. They hadn't."

"I thought the Callahan girl might have told you."

"She couldn't. She's in the hospital."

Cardigan felt a chill knife his spine. His brows bent. "Was I the only guy in her apartment?" he snapped.

"The boy says you were the only man got off at that floor before ten-thirty. She went out at ten-thirty. At two o'clock she was picked up on a road near the Wabash, unconscious. She was beaten up. She has a black eye and a fractured jaw and we don't know if she'll live."

Blake shook his fist. "By cripes, Cardigan, you can't pull off a thing like that!"

Cardigan glowered. "You horse's neck, do you think I'd beat up a woman? Outside of my personal habits in a job like that, d'you think the agency'd stand for it?"

"Listen," said Strout dully. "I don't know you except from what I've seen of you. You've been handing us the run-around since you hit the city. Now what the hell were you doing in her apartment?"

Cardigan folded his arms. "You read that wire, didn't you?"

"What of it?"

"I was on a tip that the girl I'm tailing was seen in the company of Roberta Callahan. I went there and saw the Callahan girl. She got touchy because I busted up her sleep and we had an argument. I was mad because I thought she knew something about this girl and wouldn't tell me. She finally threatened to call in the management if I didn't take the air.

"As I was about to leave a man called on her and I didn't want to make a scene, so I left."

"Who was the man?" Strout asked.

"How should I know?"

"What did he look like?"

"Kind of small, I remember. It was dim in the room and I didn't bother to look at him close enough."

Strout looked at the negro. "I thought you said he was the only man got off that floor before ten-thirty?"

"Yassuh."

Strout looked back at Cardigan. "Well?"

"Well? Well, they have a staircase in that place, haven't they?"

"Why the hell should anybody climb six flights when there's an elevator?"

"How should I know? Either the dinge is lying or the guy climbed the stairs."

"I ain't lyin'," growled the negro.

Blake chattered, "It's this guy's lying! This big bum right here! I know his kind! He can keep a straight face all he wants but he's lying! He's a lousy two-faced liar! There's only one way we can make this baby talk!"

Strout looked at Blake absently, looked back at Cardigan. Blake jumped on Cardigan where he sat, planted a knee in Cardigan's stomach and gripped his throat with both hands. Cardigan wore a cold, crooked smile.

"Spring it!" Blake rasped.

Cardigan chuckled. "Nuts."

Blake struck him across the face with an open palm. The chair creaked. Cardigan jammed his hands under Blake's armpits, rose mightily and sent Blake sprawling across the desk. The negro yelped. Blake fell to the floor, carrying a chair down with him. He came up spitting oaths and drawing his blackjack.

Cardigan was set for him. Strout turned and blocked Blake, took the blackjack away from him and shook his head. Blake cursed. Strout shook his head and shoved Blake into a chair. Strout dropped the blackjack to the desk and looked dourly at Cardigan.

A windy glitter was in Cardigan's eyes. "You pipe this, Strout! I've got a lot of power behind me and a lot of money—enough of both to make you and this whole police department take water! And as for that fat-head partner of yours, he'll get his jaw broken if he tries any rough stuff on me. I'm no heel! I'm no cheap back-alley gangster! I work for a salary and it's damned small considering what I have to put up with. And unlike you guys I get no graft."

"Shut up," said Strout.

"I'll shut up when I damned well feel like it! If you—listen, Strout—if you want to pinch me, go ahead and pinch me. You haven't got a thing on me. You know damned well I wouldn't beat up a woman. You pinch me and I'll be out inside of three hours. And what can you pinch me for? Because some heel tried to take me for a ride? Because I called on a girl who later was taken for a ride? Damn it, I've got a reputation! A big one! And not in any hick town, either! And I should throw a fit over a couple of hicks like you and Blake? You'll pinch me—yes, you will!"

Strout colored. "Can't a man ask you a question?"

"Oh, that's what you call it! That's what you call busting into my hotel room last night! That's what you call falling on me in a hotel lobby! That's what you call dragging me down here like a red-hot! Oh, what big eyes you have, grandma!"

He bent down, picked his hat off the floor, punched it back into shape and slapped it violently on his head.

"I'm going out of here," he said, "and I'd like to see you stop me. And I'd like to see you come around and bother me again. I'd just like to see you!"

He yanked open the door, shot Blake a look of scorn and banged out.

AT ELEVEN that night Cardigan walked into the Flatlands lobby, bought some tobacco at the newsstand. He asked for mail at the desk. There was no mail, but another fake wire from Hammerhorn supplementing information on the "runaway girl."

"I have to work in my room tonight," he told the clerk. "And I don't want to be disturbed by anybody."

On the way across the lobby he ran into Massey.

"I hear they had you down to headquarters," Massey said.

"Did you ever hear the story about a hotel detective who solved a great murder mystery?"

"No."

"You never will."

Cardigan went up in the elevator, checked his wrist-watch with the elevator boy's, said good night, and strode to his room. At a few minutes to twelve Otto Shreiner came in and Cardigan impressed on him the necessity of making the three telephone calls. Then he put on his coat, turned up the collar, and pulled his hat down low on his forehead.

He went downstairs by the stairway. The stairway was enclosed, with a door on each floor, and was really a fire-escape. It terminated near the side entrance of the hotel, and Cardigan left unobserved and put his head into a brisk fall wind. The city had very little night life, and what it did have was not obvious. Cardigan used darkened store windows for mirrors and walked three or four blocks to make certain he wasn't being followed.

Roberta Callahan was still unconscious. Cardigan knew who had given her that beating—or pretty nearly knew: the little man from the tabloid. What Cardigan did not know was whether the beating had served its purpose and extracted information. Lester Sisson was the little man's name. Had he given her the beating alone or had he hired strong-arm men?

Cardigan hopped in a taxi and gave a West End street corner as his destination. Ten minutes later he got out and watched the taxi speed away. The wind clapped the skirt of his overcoat smartly. The sky had a wintry look, with tattered scud driving across the moon. The wind threshed in a big sycamore tree and telephone wires hummed. Cardigan got his bearings and moved up a wide, deserted street where substantial houses stood far back from the sidewalks.

He crossed an intersection and kept on. He saw the tail-light of a parked car halfway up the block. He crossed to the other side of the street. He walked with long, purposeful strides. He looked across the street at the car because he heard its big powerful engine purring softly. There was something familiar about the car. It was a big touring, with the curtains up. He looked straight ahead. Fifty feet farther on he turned his head to the left and looked at the fieldstone house of Pat McHugh. It was dark.

Cardigan kept on, turned left into the next cross street and did some quiet and deliberate cursing. He was sure it was the car that had opened fire on him, killing Dorshook. Its presence in the street meant one of two things; either the men were friends of McHugh or had come on a mission similar to Cardigan's. If the latter, were they certain McHugh had the check or, like Cardigan, were they taking a chance?

Cardigan stopped, looked up and down the street then scaled a low stone wall. He went through shrubbery in the rear of the corner house, fell over a croquet wicket in the back yard of the next and then came to a waist-high hedge that blocked the way to McHugh's grounds. He followed the hedge to the rear of the yard, squeezed between the end of the hedge and the stone wall it met there. He went back of McHugh's double garage and peered around the corner of it at the rear windows of the house. The hatchway to the cellar was open. The garage was empty, doors open.

He had not been able to see how many men were in the car. He did not know how many were in the house. He ducked from the garage to the hedge and crept along in the shadow of it, nearer the house. He stopped, kneeling, his hand closed on the gun in his overcoat pocket. He looked at the illuminated dial of his wrist-watch. It was twelve twenty-five.

A couple minutes later he saw a shape materialize out of the hatchway. A tall man, topcoatless, dressed in dark clothes. He stood for a moment listening, a gun in his hand. Then he took hold of the open door, let it down slowly, softly.

Cardigan made the dozen feet in three long steps, jammed his gun against the small of the man's back as the latter was rising.

"Quiet!" Cardigan muttered.

The man froze in a half crouch.

Cardigan whispered, "Stick your gun straight up in the air—arm high. Quick!"

The man's arm went up. Cardigan took away his gun, put it in his own pocket.

He said: "You should have dumped that car right after you bumped off Dorshook."

He could see the man's muscles flex, heard a breath being sucked in sharply. The man started to turn around.

"No you don't!" Cardigan muttered.

"Who the hell are you?"

"A reporter from *The Press-Clarion.* Now hand it over."

"Geeze, looka here now—"

"Hand it over!"

The man whispered an oath, put a hand in his inside pocket, passed an envelope over his shoulder. Cardigan took it, put it between his teeth, drew out a smooth oblong of paper with his left hand, then shoved it and the envelope into his pocket.

"Now walk toward that garage," he said. "Along the hedge here, then across."

He kept behind the man, prodded him with the gun. He knew that if Roberta Callahan died he would have a tough time of it with the police. They had no proof against him but they could raise an unholy row, hold him if they had to and create a lot of undesirable publicity for the agency. In which event Cardigan knew he would stand a good chance of losing his job. He had to protect himself. He walked the man to the garage entrance and told him to keep walking till he reached the back wall. While the man did this Cardigan swung the doors shut, slipped on the lock, snapped it.

He heard the man jolt the doors a second later, heard him mutter fiercely: "Damn you, what you doin'?"

CHAPTER FIVE

CARDIGAN CRASHES THROUGH

CARDIGAN LOOKED at his watch. It was twelve thirty-five. He backed away toward the shadow of the hedge. He had almost reached it when he heard a twig snap. He pivoted, saw a man standing by the side of the house.

He heard "Burt!" called in a hoarse whisper. He remained silent, motionless. Again—"Burt!" A little louder, almost stronger than a whisper. And eager—anxious.

After a moment the man moved cautiously into the rear yard. He looked at the closed hatch doors, at the rear of the house. He moved again, peering hard. He was nearer the garage now.

Again he called, "Burt!" in a whisper.

The man in the garage answered in a whisper. "I'm in here! Get me out! A guy got it!"

The other tensed, went swiftly to the garage. "Got it!"

"Yeah!"

"Who?"

"A guy from *The Press-Clarion*. Cripes, get me out!"

"Sh!" the man on the outside cautioned, and stood in a tense listening attitude. Then he examined the lock. "I'm damned if I can open it."

"You gotta! You get me outa here! Here! There's no windows—only the door here—"

"Quiet—quiet, loud mouth!… Lemme think.… Hell, I can't force it—"

"Take a chance! Put a couple o' slugs through it! That egg— Listen, Louie—that egg knows I was in on that Dorshook kill. You gotta get me out. I ain't gonna fall for no rap on my lonesome. You get me out or you and Joe and—"

"O.K. Get back outa the way. I'll blow her off, then lam. Better not hang together. We'll join up at Cicero's—and don't you make any more cracks who takes a rap and who don't. O.K.—get back."

"Hey you!" Cardigan said in a low, blunt voice. "Scram!"

The man called Louis almost fell over with surprise.

"And watch that rod in your hand," Cardigan said. "You heard me—beat it!"

The pitch of his voice and the darkness made it hard for Louie to locate him. Louie began backing away.

"Louie!" cried the man in the garage. "Louie, you ain't gonna leave me here! So help me, if you lam out on me I'll shoot the whole works!"

Louie stopped. He looked over his shoulder. Another man was coming along the side of the house. He stopped and looked at the cellar hatch, then at the shape of Louie.

"Say," he whispered, "Sisson's gettin' nervous. He says we better breeze. There's a patrolman due through here any minute."

Louie backed up toward him, and the latter whispered, "Where the hell's Burt?"

"Louie!" Burt cried in a hoarse whisper.

The third man began: "What the hell—" Then Louie made a motion of his head, kept backing up.

"Come on, Joe," Louie whispered grimly.

"But Burt's in that garage! How— Say, what's the matter?"

"Come on, you fool."

"I'm gonna get Burt!" Joe lunged toward the garage.

"Scram!" Cardigan barked. "You heard what your pal said."

"Louie!" Burt pleaded.

Joe stopped in his tracks, made a half turn with his gun held low. Its muzzle whipped flame and thunder through the dark. Cardigan heard the bullet snap through the hedge. He fired the gun he had taken from Burt and the echoes barked among the houses.

Louie's gun exploded. Cardigan heard the *snick* of the bullet passing, the slap of it against the stone wall beyond. He threw a shot at the dim shape of Louie and ruined a drain pipe on the house.

Joe began yelling, "My God—my God!" and ran toward Louie. Burt hammered inside the garage.

"I'm hit!" Joe gasped. "I'm hit, Louie!"

Cardigan snapped: "You guys beat it!"

Joe, yelling, "Oh, I'm hit bad!" ran right past Louie, fell over a flower bed and squealed like a woman. Louie backed up swiftly, cursing. There was the sound of a motor roaring, of gears being meshed savagely. Joe got up out of the flower garden and looked toward the street.

He cried: "Sisson's ditchin' us, the louse!" He hefted his gun, yelled: "Hey, wait!" and staggered wildly toward the street. The touring car roared past in second, slammed into high violently.

"Hey!" screamed Joe; then— "You dirty—" Rage choked him. He raised his gun. Flame burst three times from the black muzzle.

"Good cripes!" Louie moaned. "Come on, Joe—come on!"

Rubber tires rasped on the rough pavement. The touring car slewed from left to right, blindly, like a harried animal. Then suddenly it headed for the curb. The chassis wrenched at the springs as the car hurtled over the curb. A sycamore ripped off the left rear mudguard. A low iron fence met the front tires, ripped them open. The radiator crumpled. The iron fence crumpled and the big car crashed head-on into a stone house. Glass snarled. The rear tires heaved five feet off the ground, slammed down again. The rending sound of tortured metal raked the streets for blocks.

Joe and Louie reached the sidewalk.

"Help me, Louie!" Joe gasped.

"Come on—run!"

Louie set an example but Joe found it hard to follow. He reeled along, coughing. Louie ran faster.

"Louie—lemme a hand—"

But Louie ran faster.

Joe fell down, braced himself on one arm. "Louie!!" he cried savagely. "You hear me!" He raised his gun. He fired. Louie swerved, hit a tree with such force that he bounced back and crashed down in the middle of the street.

CARDIGAN wiped off the gun he had taken from Burt and tossed it in front of the garage. He passed back of the garage, crossed the two yards, paused an instant by the stone wall and then vaulted it and landed on the sidewalk. He strode swiftly away. Stopped once to hide behind a tree and watch two cops rush past, then went on. Five minutes later he boarded a city-bound trolley. He looked at his watch. It was twelve minutes to one.

It was three minutes to one when he got off, four blocks from the Flatlands, and entered an all-night drug store. He crowded into a telephone booth, called police headquarters. He pitched his voice high.

"You guys down there—take this or leave it. There's a red-hot in the garage back of 906 Magnolia Avenue. He was one of the guys bumped off Dorshook.... Who am I? Santa Claus to you, brother."

He hung up, left the drug store and walked to the Flatlands. At one he slipped in through the side entrance, ducked to the stairway and started climbing. At two minutes past one he entered his room.

"O.K., Otto. Beat it."

"Did you get it?"

"I did," Cardigan said. "Quick. Back to your room."

He rushed Otto out. Then he whipped off his clothes, got into pajamas, rumpled his hair, grabbed a magazine and climbed in bed. He took one look at the mayor's check, chuckled, slipped it in the back of the magazine, tore the envelope to bits and dropped them in a waste basket.

He put the magazine under his pillow. He reached for his briar pipe.

The clock's hands crept around to two. The hotel was quiet. Vagrant street sounds rose sharply. No one disturbed Cardigan. He knew that headquarters must be throbbing with activity. Surely Sisson had been killed in that crash. Press wires were humming. Still the hotel remained quiet. Cardigan yawned, turned off the lights.

Strout came in with Massey bright and early next morning while Cardigan, suspenders draping his hips, was lathering his face by the bathroom mirror.

Cardigan bowed elaborately.

"Swell morning, Strout!"

"Not so swell. Say, a guy named Sisson: Massey said Sisson paid a call on you once here."

"Oh—you mean that little morning glory from the tab. Yeah, he did. He'd heard about me and wanted my picture for the tab. See that rug in there? Well, he tripped over that and busted his lip against the radiator."

Strout looked mournful. "Sisson got bumped off last night."

Cardigan stropped his razor. "Too bad."

"It was funny. Two other guys got bumped off—they bumped off each other apparently. There was a third guy locked in Party Boss McHugh's garage. It was very funny. There was a fourth guy that slopped up the other's parade. The guy in the garage said he said he was from the *Press-Clarion*."

"Reporters turning gangsters, huh?"

"That guy was no reporter."

Cardigan said: "How did the girl make out?"

"She died."

"You're here to make a collar?"

Strout shook his head. "No. Just before she died she identified the guy we found in that garage as one of the men. On the way out of the hospital the guy pulled a fast one and broke loose. We had to shoot him."

"What was all the fireworks around McHugh's house?"

Strout pawed his jaw. "Well there was one guy knows all about it. The fourth guy. And the fourth guy was the guy made a phone call to headquarters at a few minutes to one this A.M. And a gun we found was the one that did for Dorshook. Our ballistics man checked up."

"And what's that to me?"

Strout wore a bleak smile. "It's funny—how that mysterious phone tip cleared you up completely. The guy said he was Santa Claus."

"And I suppose now you're going to call me Santa Claus!"

"There are a lot of things I'd like to call you, Cardigan. But just now I'm too tired. You're in the clear now. O.K. But whatever job you are on—if I catch you in this town after tonight—"

"You knew I was leaving this morning, didn't you?"

Massey looked uneasy.

Strout turned and walked to the door. Massey opened it and went out first. Strout turned and stared sourly across the room. Cardigan, patting his face with a hot towel, grinned.

"Go ahead—grin!" growled Strout.

"Ain't I?"

"Sure."

"Grin!"

"Ain't I?"

"Damn it, laugh your head off!"

"Ho-ho! How's that?"

Strout disappeared, banging the door.

Cardigan hurled the wet towel at the door, heaved into the bathroom chafing his hands in high good humor and bursting into a lusty ballad of the levees.

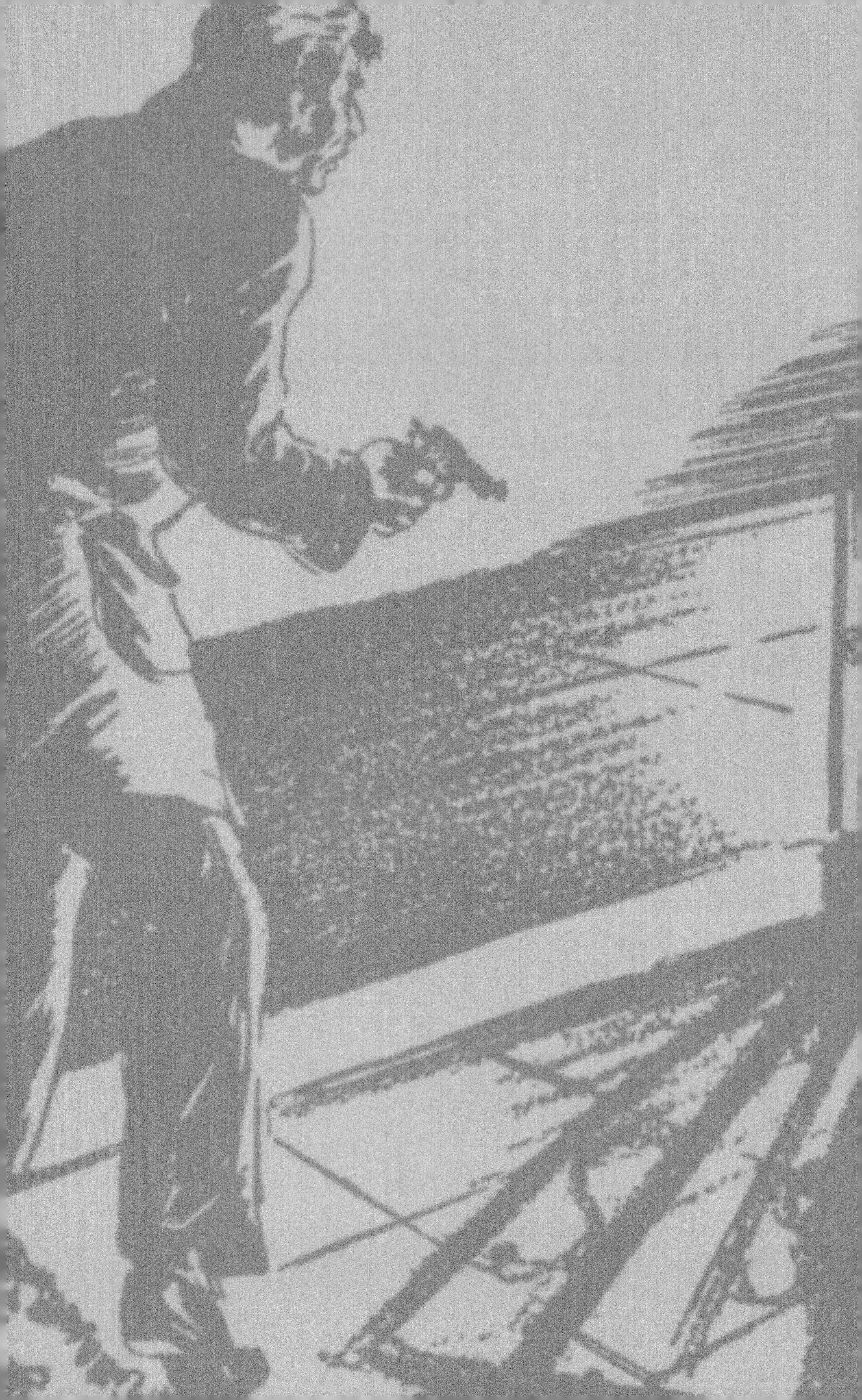

SIX DIAMONDS AND A DICK

IT WASN'T WHERE THE JEWELS WERE THAT WORRIED CARDIGAN— HE KNEW THAT ALL THE TIME. HE COULDN'T PROVE IT, THOUGH— NOT UNTIL THE CROWD AT THE CASINO GOT THEIR SPOTS CROSSED AND MIDNIGHT MURDER SHOWED UP IN THE CARDS.

CHAPTER ONE

THE BLONDE IN BLUE

THE GIRL in the slate-colored silk tights gave a fair imitation of the East Indian Nautch. The man at the bass viol plunked the strings and the trap drummer worked hard and grinned like a fool. A moving spotlight changed colors and followed the girl around the oval-shaped floor. Beyond the radius of light, sixty tables were white cases where men and women, the majority in evening clothes, took nourishment from tall glasses in which ice tinkled.

Cardigan, nursing a Corona-corona, raised his left wrist close to his face and looked at the illuminated dial of his watch. The expanse of his boiled shirt was as wide as the average man's breadth is from shoulder to shoulder. He weighed close to two hundred and his stomach was as flat as a griddle cake.

He rose and picked his way among tables to the lounge. The Dago waiter looked after him with a dark malignant stare. In the lounge high-backed gilt chairs stood against mauve-colored walls, a crystal chandelier tapered from the ceiling, carpets an inch thick muffled footfalls.

A tall man who looked like a diplomat but wasn't, took a drag on a cork-tipped cigarette and put himself in front of Cardigan. Cardigan stopped, lounged on his heels with hard easy grace.

"What's eating you, Gould?"

"I'm getting tired of this, Cardigan."

"Well, do something about it."

Gould had a thin dry-gray face, prematurely gray hair that was slicked back so tightly that his head looked like a skull. Only his eyes were dark and shiny with a surface glare that lacked depth, like lacquer. He laid long attenuated fingers lightly on Cardigan's arm.

"I mean what I say, Cardigan. You've been doing a Dracula around here for the past three hours. You haven't taken a whirl at the wheel or the tables and every now and then you take a walk around the place like you owned it."

"So now what?"

"I don't intend standing here in the lounge room arguing with you. The door is—you know where the door is." His voice was thin and quick and oddly brittle. The framework of him looked brittle.

A grin threw Cardigan's leather-brown face into many wrinkles. "I'm not ready to leave yet, Gould. I understand your overhead is ten thousand a day. Don't try to chuck me out and raise your overhead."

Gould's left eyebrow quivered. "I've got to know where we stand. I've got to know what the hell you're doing here. This is a high-class joint. I've got to be careful."

"I'm telling you, honeybunch, that what I'm doing here has nothing to do with you."

He saw the car leap into the
air. Saw it burst into flames.

"You're tailing somebody."

"Wouldn't that be a surprise!"

Gould's thin voice shook. "Who the hell are you tailing?"

At the other end of the lounge was a broad door of mirror glass overlaid with whorls and modernistic angles of bronze. Beside the door stood an attendant. In a chair a few feet from the door sat a chunky tuxedoed man with a face hard as nails. In the archway to the foyer stood another man. The three men were watching Cardigan and Gould.

Gould was saying, "I warn you—"

"You don't have to warn me. If you don't want me hanging around here then put me out. And I'd like to see you put me out. You scare me, you do, Gould. You scare hell out of me."

He went past Gould. The man at the mirrored door squinted pale eyes, opened the door. Cardigan went through.

Hum of voices, click of dice and chips, click of a small white ball in a whirring roulette wheel. Women in glittering gowns, men in evening dress. Dispassionate-eyed croupiers. A cashier with a big wallet under his arm; he appeared through a small door from time to time and went to a table where a player was checking out.

Cardigan's roving gaze fell on a burly man who was playing roulette. A Spanish-looking woman was with him. Her blue-black hair fitted her like a casque and the green gown she wore followed every undulating curve of her body. The burly man had close-clipped sandy hair. There was a scar on his forehead that glinted like a sliver of silver. The man was quite drunk.

A short, thin girl brushed against Cardigan. "A blonde—in blue. She went upstairs."

Cardigan said nothing. He moved on through the gambling rooms and came at length back to the mirrored door. He pushed out into the lounge, took the circular staircase aloft and went out on a wide veranda. Below, at the foot of the bluff, the Mississippi rolled through the night.

A girl was standing by the veranda rail, looking out into the darkness. A dimmed porch light made a faint glow on her fuzzy blonde hair. The damp river breeze ruffled her blue gown. She stood motionless, tense. Muffled was the constant throb of the jazz band below. A train went by at the river's edge, far down the bluff.

CARDIGAN took a step out onto the veranda floor. The girl whirled, her dress corkscrewing about her legs, her red mouth open. Cardigan stopped. In her hand was a glint of metal. Cardigan could see the convulsive rise and fall of her bosoms. Her face was white as a ghost's, her eyes wide and staring.

Cardigan went close to her, put his hand on the gun, twisted slowly this way and that until her fingers let go. She did not move. The fingers that had held the gun remained splayed. Her breath started to come in intermittent shudders.

Suddenly she gasped and collapsed. Cardigan caught her and let her down gently to the floor. Her mesh bag fell to his knee, slid off and fell to the floor. He let her lie. He opened the bag, ransacked it. He left bills and change, cosmetic compact. He took out a neat sheaf of white cards, thrust them in his pocket. He thrust her gun in his pocket.

Footsteps made him look around. Gould was there. And another man.

"What's this?" Gould clipped.

"Lady fainted," Cardigan said, and stood up.

The man with Gould had his gun out. He jammed it against

Cardigan's back.

Gould bent down. He lifted the woman in his arm. "Come on," he said.

The man with the gun prodded Cardigan and Cardigan followed Gould into a room where Gould laid the woman down on a divan. The sound of the jazz band throbbed in the room. The woman on the divan stirred, groaned. Gould went into a bathroom and came out with a wet towel. He patted the woman's head. He looked up at Cardigan.

"You're funny, Cardigan."

"Like a crutch, huh?"

"I'm going to see what this song and dance of yours is all about—Hello, miss. Better?"

Her eyes, open now, rolled around in their sockets; rolled slower and then stopped rolling, to steady on Gould's narrow gray face.

"I—I must have fainted," she breathed.

"What did that guy do to you?"

"Where?"

"The big boy there?"

She looked at Cardigan for a long minute.

Cardigan growled, "Don't be an airedale, Gould. I found her lying out there."

"You shut up," Gould said.

The woman passed a hand over her eyes. "I—just fainted. It was hot downstairs and I came up for some air."

"What did he say to you?"

"I don't know. I never saw him before. Just let me alone. Let me rest—please. I'll be all right."

Gould's forehead puckered. "This is funny." He got up and looked at Cardigan. "I said this is funny."

"I heard you the first time," Cardigan said. "What kind of a comeback am I supposed to make?"

Gould's left eyebrow twitched. He made a nervous, impatient gesture with both hands. "Go on. Go on, get out now.... Leave her alone in here a while, Sam. Go on, Cardigan. But by God, this is funny!" He pivoted toward the woman, biting his thin nether lip. "Are you sure this guy—"

"Please—please let me rest. I tell you I just fainted. It was hot...

and I fainted."

Gould sniffed irritably and went to the door with a nervous doggedness. He opened it. Cardigan and Sam followed him into the corridor and Gould, closing the door, shook his bony forefinger threateningly under Cardigan's nose.

"I'm getting damned tired—"

"Don't wave your mitt under my nose, Gould!" He threw Gould's hand down violently and his mouth became sullen.

Sam started to crowd him. Cardigan swung on Sam abruptly and bit him with a hot gray stare.

"And you, baby, think again before you yank that roscoe on me!"

"Says which?"

"Sh—now—sh!" muttered Gould petulantly. "Out in the hall, you saps you!" He waved to indicate the lack of privacy.

Cardigan rumbled, "Well, tie this lapdog outside then."

Gould screwed up his face into an expression that was intended to be ferocious. Cardigan chuckled. Gould blew out an exasperated breath and Cardigan passed him and rocked down the corridor. He entered the gambling rooms again, mingled with the crowd around the roulette wheel, touched the elbow of the short, thin girl. She moved her left hand and he looked down at it. In her palm was a slip of paper on which was scrawled, "$4,000." He turned and passing behind her said, "Beat it." In a minute the small, thin girl left. He was in the foyer when he saw her leave and enter a taxi. Five minutes later he got his hat and coat from the check room and was shrugging into the coat when Gould appeared. Gould stopped and regarded him narrowly.

"Goom-by," Cardigan said.

Gould didn't say anything. He kept biting his thin nether lip in nervous irritation. Perplexed indecision strained in his eyes.

AT A quarter to twelve Cardigan braked his shabby roadster in front of the Hotel Andromeda. He went through revolving doors into the lobby. There were many men and women strolling around in evening clothes. There was supper dancing in the Peacock Room off the north wing.

He sat down in a leather divan and watched the main entrance for five minutes. Then he got up and crossed the lobby to where the small, thin girl sat. He dropped down beside her.

"Any luck?" she said.

"Maybe." He took out a sheaf of small white cards and held them so she could see.

"That's the blonde, huh?"

"And not peroxide, sister. She pulled a swoon on the veranda. She had a gat—in her hand. Whether she was going to do the dutch or was getting set to go after White I don't know. I took it away from her. Who was the Spanish number?"

"Somebody called her Miss Monteclara—Nita Monteclara. But that's a lot of *braunschweiger*. Her name's Becky Steinwein. She models for underthings. The maid in the dressing room gave me the lowdown unasked. She's taking this chap White for a fare-thee-well. The blonde looked daggers at her all night—and there was murder in them blue eyes, suh."

Cardigan squinted. "And White went in the red for four thousand?"

"By his inamorata's hand. She played everything but the corners and he kept cheering her. Pardon me if I seem to yawn."

"Hit the hay, Pat. See you at the office."

Small and trim, pretty in a quiet, certain way, she went to the elevators.

Bush, the Metropolitan dick, bumped into Cardigan deliberately and said, "So that's your new operative, Cardigan?"

Bush got rid of a hollow, uncertain laugh and Cardigan left him standing in the center of the lobby.

CHAPTER TWO

THE DIAMOND TRAIL

WHEN CARDIGAN came heavily into his office next morning Miss Gilligan, his stenographer, said in her always startled voice, "Oh, Mr. Cardigan—oh, Mr. Prier of the Jewelers Cooperative Indemnity telephoned and asked—"

Cardigan, heading for his private office, said, "Call him back," and closed the connecting door behind him.

Miss Gilligan put through the call.

"Hello, Mr. Prier," Cardigan said. "We got some breaks last night…. Well, don't get excited. We just found the jane White jilted and the headache he's running around with now.... I'd rather not mention names.... Yes, White's still spending like hell. Four thousand last night up until the time I left.... Well, that's a problem. Either he fenced the stuff as soon as he came out of stir or he's living and playing on the stuff.... Yes, it's getting my strictly personal attention.... " 'Bye."

He hung up, lit his first cigar of the day, gathered together a number of sheets and went into a long room where four desks stood in a row. Three men were working over reports.

"Morning, chief," they chorused.

"Hello, gang. Blaine, that client's yelling that we're holding him up. Spend another day on that stolen radios case and if nothing breaks we'll sign off. You've covered about everything and we're not going in for cut-rates.... Hennessy, you've got to wangle a photostatic copy of the Dixon Hotel register for June 10, 1929. Don't go over fifty bucks.... Katz, I want a record of Ludlow's bank deposits during August. Drop the Flemming case. He's reconciled to his wife."

When Cardigan returned to his private office Miss Gilligan was standing in the doorway. She said, "A Mr. Ullrich to see you."

"What's he want?"

Miss Gilligan shrugged.

Cardigan dropped to his swivel chair heavily. "Well, shoot."

Mr. Ullrich almost bounded in. He was a roly-poly man with cheeks like red apples, a big-toothed grin in a small mouth, dancing blue eyes.

"Good-morning, Mr. Cardigan! Good-morning to you, sir!"

He extended a stubby arm, gripped Cardigan's hand hard. He yanked a fat cigar from his breast pocket.

"I'm smoking," Cardigan said. "Sit down."

"Yes, yes! Well, well, Mr. Cardigan, this is a grand day! A grand day to be alive!"

Cardigan eyed him curiously. "Senator Ackerman's right hand man?" he tried.

Ullrich slapped fat palms on the desk joyously. "The old eagle eye, Mr. Cardigan! Yes, sir!" He sat back in the chair facing Cardigan and rocked with laughter.

Cardigan's eyes narrowed. He said nothing. He crossed his big brown hands on his flat stomach, creaked his swivel chair gently to and fro and took slow puffs on his cigar.

"Well!" said Ullrich, getting his breath. He rubbed his fingers back and forth on the edge of the desk with a gentle, caressing motion. Back of the laughing bubbles in his eyes was a wily, speculative look. "Well, Mr. Cardigan." He looked up with his bright, dancing eyes and tongued his cigar back and forth between grinning teeth. "Senator Ackerman, you know, has his country home in Lancaster County. Lovely place, Mr. Cardigan. Ah—you were out in the county last night, were you not? Yes, yes, of course. I came here to— How is business, Mr. Cardigan?"

"Swell."

"So. So indeed! Well, well!" Ullrich took three quick puffs on his cigar, grinned into space. "Ah—Phil Gould was a bit upset. You know Phil: kind of jumpy and nervous. Since—since the Civic Service League started to percolate in the county."

Cardigan was impersonally blunt. "We're not working for the Civic Service League, Mr. Ullrich."

Ullrich's chuckle bubbled and he made vague gestures. "Of course, of course. Well, you see, out in the county, we like to keep things running nice and smooth. Phil's a good sort. Only he gets worried—and when he gets worried—"

"He runs to Senator Ackerman," nodded Cardigan. "And why? Because the senator is one of the big backers of Gould's gambling casino. So now what?"

This bluntness teetered Ullrich for a minute. Then he said, "It's just—well, Phil was worried the way you were—"

"I'm not interested in the casino," Cardigan said. "I'm not working for any civic uplift organization. Why I was there last night is my own business."

"You know, Senator Ackerman is a good man to stand in with."

"My boss is in New York and they never heard of him there."

Ullrich stood up, his face wreathed in smiles, his eyes shining. "Then that is all, Mr. Cardigan." He pulled at his breast pocket. "Do have a cigar."

"Thanks, but they look too heavy."

Ullrich shook hands violently, went out buoyantly.

Pat sauntered in saying, "Who was sunshine and happiness?"

"Don't think because you wear skirts, sister, you can bust in here an hour and a half late."

"Boo!"

"That's a nice hat you have on, Pat."

THE Shelby Arms was a nondescript apartment house on Washington Boulevard. The chemical cleaners hadn't touched the bricks in years. Cardigan entered the small, stuffy lounge, climbed three steps to a mezzanine and stopped at a chest-high desk. A fat woman sat behind it, knitting.

"Miss Carmory's apartment," Cardigan said.

"There's no switchboard. She's in 411."

The elevator was self-operated. Cardigan got in. The doors wheezed shut. He pressed a button numbered 4. The elevator wheezed upward. He opened the doors when it stopped and entered a narrow, dim corridor. He poked around in the shadows until he found a brown door with 411 on it.

The blonde opened it. There were circles under her eyes; the lids were puffy. She was pretty in a faded-flower way. She had a nice chin and wore a pepper-gray ensemble and a silk blouse of lighter gray. She regarded Cardigan with round blue eyes wide open and expressionless. But in a split minute her mouth loosened and a hurt look came into the eyes. There was something oddly harried about her but at the same time her air of passivity was definite.

"Come in." Her voice, like her shoulders, was listless.

Cardigan pushed through the doorway, took a single-room suite in with one casual glance. His hair stood out from his ears like a shaggy mop. His jaw was big, brown, heavy. A floor board creaked beneath his weight.

The girl stood looking with tired eyes at a window and said, dully, "I knew you'd come."

Cardigan looked in the bathroom, started toward the kitchenette. The girl shrugged.

"I'm alone," she said.

His "O.K." was low, resonant. He sat down on a straight-backed chair, crossed one leg over the other, closed his left hand around the ankle and sat regarding the girl with a deep, thoughtful frown. Presently she turned and looked at him.

"So you knew I'd come," his low, deep voice said.

She nodded and let herself down slowly into a divan. She rubbed her hands slowly together and said nothing.

He said, "If you were going to turn that rod on yourself last night

I'm glad I stopped you. If you were getting steamed up to turn it on Burt White—well, that's six of one and half a dozen of the other."

"Burt White?"

"Or maybe the Spanish flame that's turning him all hot-and-bothered these days."

Her lips made a round O and remained that way for a minute. Then she whispered, "Who—who are you?"

"These playboys out at the casino last night were itching to hand me a rough deal. Gould had a brain-wave and decided that I was there on a big tail. He hopped around like a hen on a hot griddle all night."

She nodded. "I know. After you left he quizzed me again. I said—well, what I said when you were there."

"Good girl."

"Well, you could have told about the gun. Thanks for helping yourself to my cards."

"Manicurist, eh?"

"Who are you?"

Cardigan put both feet on the floor, leaned forward, resting elbows on knees. "Three years ago six unset diamonds were lifted from a diamond merchant in the Hotel Midlands. Value of seventy-thousand dollars. The diamonds were insured by the Jewelers Cooperative Indemnity. Catch on?"

She said nothing in a blank-faced way.

Cardigan stood up, took three steps, jammed hands into pockets and planted himself in front of her. "Burt White was in the hotel at the time. He had a room in the rear, eighth floor, looking down on Bennington Court. All right. The diamond merchant's room was busted into, he was slugged—in the dark—and a guy got away with the diamonds. At 12:40 A.M. At 12:35 White tried to get a telephone number. Party didn't answer. He tried again at 12:43. No answer. The defense claimed that a man couldn't have got from Room 709 to 818 in three minutes. White got off on the robbery charge but just for spite they sent him up for three years for concealed weapons. A man said that at 12:45 he saw a woman hurrying out of Bennington Court. The defense proved that at midnight this man left a speakeasy plastered to the eyebrows and the clerk in the hotel where he lived said he fell in the lobby at 1:00, still plastered. So that killed that. Still the diamonds had disappeared. The indemnity company took it on the nose. Two weeks ago they engaged me to jump on the merry-go-round. You get me?"

SHE kept staring down at Cardigan's feet. "I thought you were a detective of some kind."

"How's to play ball?"

She got up slowly and walked the length of the room. She turned and looked at Cardigan and smiled wearily, shaking her head. "I'm afraid you're up the wrong tree," she said.

"No one knew who White's girl friend was. They tried to catch on through letters to him when he was in stir. There were no letters. He figured that out too. We got him lamped the minute he came out. We found out last night who his heart was. I said—*was.*"

She colored. "Burt White? Who is Burt White? I don't know him. Who is he?"

"Ask me who is Nita Monteclara."

Her color deepened. Cardigan liked the way her chin tilted. She said, "I don't know what you're talking about, please." Her voice throbbed.

Cardigan strode to her. Shaggy-headed, massive-shouldered, he towered threateningly above her, an ill wind in his eyes. "I know you're lying, Miss Carmory. You tell a lie bum as hell. I've got White figured out and I've got you figured out. I know he's chucking money away and I happen to know that when he came out of stir he was stony. We've been smack on his tail all the time and we've found that in two weeks he's spent fifteen-thousand bucks. That ice was fenced while he was in stir by his pal or he's fenced it since he got out or he's borrowing till he can fence it. You've been singing, 'Lover, Come Back to Me,' and the punk lams on you for—"

Calmly she said, "Please, you are wrong. This is all like a story to me."

"There's some dough in this for you if—"

"I work for a living." She looked at her wrist-watch. "I have an appointment at 11:00."

He searched her pallid face with glittering eyes. His wide lips tightened against his teeth. "You're White's ex. At the casino last night you watched every move he and the Monteclara flame made. You were going to do something with that gun. For God's sake don't hand me a run-around like this. White's ditched you and why you're worrying about him I can't see. You look pretty O.K. to me. That guy's a louse four ways from the jack and I've got the finger on him but I need more evidence."

She smiled gently. "I'm sorry I can't help you."

She was tranquil now—too tranquil. Back of her almost beatific calm a load of emotion was suspended by a single thread. Her face was too white, her eyes too rheumy. She moved past Cardigan and went into the little dressing room. He stared at the open door through which she had gone. No sound issued. After a minute he took a few steps and reached the doorway.

She was standing in the little cubicle. Standing with her hands clenched at her sides. Her lips puckered. Tears rolled down her face. Silent sobs ripped at her bosom and pain traced its way across her face. Her body began to shake. It trembled all over. Her legs trembled. Her mouth opened and the sobs raked out—hoarse and unimpeded now. Restraint tried to fight them back but emotion was greater. The sobs came faster and her lips quivered but she remained standing there, her heels together, her arms at her sides, her fists knotted.

"O God... O God...."

"Listen—"

"O God...."

"Please... I was kind of rough...." He made a half-hearted gesture with his hand: he ran the hand through his hair. He started toward her. He gave it up. He stood frowning not unkindly. He felt oafish and uncomfortable.

"I'm a bum," he growled.

He turned and went back into the bed-sitting room, got his hat. He went to the door, opened it and passed into the corridor. He took the stairway down. As he reached the lobby floor he saw Mr. Ullrich enter the elevator. The indicator stopped at the fourth floor.

CHAPTER THREE

CARDIGAN WALKS OUT

AT NOON Cardigan shouldered into the lobby of the Andromeda. Pat joined him and they went into the Coffee Shop for luncheon.

"Tell me a story," Cardigan said.

"I popped over to Adrienne's, the lingerie shop where the Monteclara woman models. I looked at some lingerie. I looked at it on Nita. She's neat to look at and don't think she isn't. She uses an accent that she thinks is Spanish but she goes wrong on the Spanish J. I acted dissatisfied. I mentioned a kind of lingerie they didn't have but they said they expected it any day. I asked them to send Nita to my hotel with some samples."

"So I suppose you'll buy yourself a lot of undies now and charge it up to investigation expenses. You're not a moron."

Pat winked. "You keep scowling that way and some day you're going to scare me. I reasoned that if I could get her in my room I could lay some conversational traps. If necessary"—she raised a neatly plucked eyebrow—"I could get rough—in a feminine way. Please pass the tabasco."

Cardigan nodded, frowned hard at the table top. "The Carmory woman got under my ribs. There's no buying her. She denied knowing White or anything about him—and then she busted out crying. I never saw a jane cry so hard. So I cleared out."

"Weakling."

"As I was leaving I saw Ullrich go up in the elevator. The elevator stopped at her floor. I parked across the street and Ullrich came out ten minutes later. The jane came out five minutes later and took a cab to the Congress Place Hotel. I pumped the house shamus there—Willard—and Carmory had an appointment with a dowager of the butter-and-egg trade. Manicure. She's known at the hotel—and liked. She had appointments there that carry her over till 4:00 this afternoon."

"Just a poor woiking goil."

"Don't be a damned cat. Helen Carmory's a sweet jane that's getting a raw deal but she's dope enough to keep her trap shut. The only thing I'm afraid of is that she'll bump off either White or the Monteclara—or maybe herself.

"Senator Ackerman's guts must hurt or he wouldn't be sending his mouthpiece around trying to find out what I was doing at the casino last night. This laughing jackass Ullrich would be just the guy to throw a wrench in the whole shebang."

Pat said, "By the way, when I left the office I saw Ullrich talking at the corner of Sixth and Olive with a great old friend of yours."

"Who's that?"

"Detective Sergeant Bush."

Cardigan laid down his fork and glared at Pat.

She said, "Well, why look stilettos at me?"

Cardigan cursed, took a savage poke with his fork at a chunk of meat. "He once acted as Senator Ackerman's bodyguard. They're like this." He crossed his fingers.

Pat leaned forward. "Don't look. Bush is in the lobby now looking this way."

A man's voice said, "Why, hello, Mr. Cardigan."

Cardigan stood up. "Hello, Mr. Reams… Miss Seaward, Mr. Reams."

He stood chatting for a few minutes with Reams, sat down when Reams departed and said, "Head of the Civic Service League. I once investigated a poverty case for him."

PAT left before Cardigan, and when Cardigan went into the lobby five minutes later Bush buttonholed him. Bush had two stock expressions; he could either look very hard and mean or he could assume a fixed smile brimming with suspicion. This time he wore the latter and poked Cardigan in the ribs.

"Big business, eh, Cardigan?"

"I thought there was a bad smell around here."

Bush poked Cardigan in the ribs again, stuck his blunt hard jaw close to Cardigan's chest. Cardigan jabbed him in the stomach and Bush said, "Oomp!" and made a face.

"You're soft, Bush, like dough. Why don't you drag your pants out of easy chairs once in a while?"

Bush always resented any slur against his physical condition. His face got hard as granite. "You might be on a case, big boy, that's going to get you a pain in the neck."

"You're giving me a pain right now—and not in the neck."

"Yah!"

"All right, make funny noises."

Bush took hold of Cardigan's lapel. "I could give you some good advice, Cardigan. You think you're pretty hot. You think that agency you work for is just about the most powerful in the United States. Don't—" he prodded Cardigan's chest—"think so."

Cardigan stared hard at him while taking two slow puffs on his cigar. "You get this, Bush. You tell a certain party that if anybody slams into my parade I'll start the biggest political upheaval that you or anybody else ever saw. It's damned funny that I can't go about my business around here without having you master-minding all over the place."

"I'm just telling you—"

"You could tell me that you're the swellest cop on the force and I'd believe that too. In a horse's neck I would! Go chase yourself around in circles till you get dizzy, fat-head."

Cardigan left the lobby and went through the doors like a blast of wind. For a minute he walked with a rolling, hard-heeled gait and anger crackled in every line on his weathered face. For a minute he was oblivious to the noontime crowd. His attitude toward Bush contained far more of disgust than genuine hatred. He carried a healthy contempt for Bush that a long series of petty interferences had evoked.

When he walked into his office he found Miss Gilligan blindfolded and lashed to her chair. Miss Gilligan was a spinster. Cardigan said nothing. He crossed the small office, took off the blindfold, removed the bonds.

"Oh," exhaled Miss Gilligan. For a moment she looked dazed and slightly awry. Then she said, "Whew!"

"Who did it?"

"I was inside in your office going over some files. I didn't hear anybody come in. Of course—between 12:00 and 1:00—I was the only one here. Then when I came in here that rag was pulled around my eyes. He must have been behind that bookcase. There was another one. They put me here and then I heard them going through the file cases. Then one of them came back and gripped me by the neck. He said, 'Are there any more files?' I said, 'You better go. I just pressed this button under the desk with my knee. It notifies police headquarters.' He got scared and called the other one and they went out."

The button she alluded to was once used to call her when the desk had been in Cardigan's office. Now it was out of use.

"Good girl," Cardigan said. "You didn't get a look at them?"

"No. But one of them lisped."

Cardigan made a fist, rapped the knuckles slowly on the desk. "Somebody still has a guilty conscience. Busting into my office, eh? Take a look, Miss Gilligan, and see if anything's been lifted."

Nothing had been taken.

"Do you know who they are?" Miss Gilligan asked.

"I think so."

"They ought certainly to be arrested."

Cardigan muttered, "I've got a better way."

AT 11:00 that night Cardigan was climbing into plain cotton pajamas when the telephone beside his bed rang. He crossed the room pulling up his pajama pants, knotted them at the waist as he sat down on the bed, and then picked up the telephone.

"Yeah…. When?" His face became leaden; his voice dropped to a low note when he said, "I'll be right over."

He got out of his pajamas, into undershirt and shorts. In three minutes he went down in the elevator to the basement garage, climbed in his old roadster and tooled it out. Where Lindell crosses Grand he swung right and went south on Grand, crossed the bridge and burned the wind. Five minutes later he pulled up at a dark intersection as two men were lifting a stretcher into an ambulance. A small crowd had gathered.

Cardigan climbed out of the roadster and got a look at the white face on the stretcher. He turned around and Bush and Haas were looking at him. A couple of cops kept yelling at the crowd. Bush made a spitting sound and smoke popped from his lips.

"What do you think of this, Cardigan?"

Cardigan looked back at the ambulance. His brown face was expressionless. "What happened?" he said.

A cop said, "I was up the block when I heard the shots. Three shots. I came runnin' down here and there she was layin' in the gutter. See the blood there? She was layin' there. A guy says he saw a black sedan go past the next block, only another guy says it was a blue coupe and another guy says it was a dark red convertible. So you can tie that and whaddaya got? A knot. What I mean!"

Cardigan looked at Bush. "How is she?"

"How would you be with two shots in your belly and one through your leg?"

The ambulance bell clanged. The ambulance roared away and the crowd lingered.

Bush, wearing his sly leer, said, "Want a lift, Cardigan?"

"I've got my own."

"Then we don't need a taxi. Haas and me are going your way."

They crowded into the roadster beside Cardigan. Cardigan swung the car around and headed north. Bush was in the middle. He seemed pleased with himself. Cardigan didn't say anything. He stared grimly through the windshield and exceeded the speed limit.

Bush said, "Goddard went with her. She may come to and say something but the doctor says not a chance. Me, I'm kind of interested in you."

Cardigan remained silent.

"Very," Bush added.

Cardigan looked like a man who was thinking hard. He said nothing. He seemed unaware that Bush was speaking. He reached Lindell and stopped at the corner.

"You go east," he said. "I go west."

Bush made his voice very soft, "Aren't you going to drive us to headquarters?"

"Not that I know of."

"Oh, yes you are."

Cardigan said nothing. He clicked into gear, swung right and drove east, slowly. Ten minutes later he pulled up in front of police headquarters.

"Do come in," Bush said.

Cardigan remained silent for a while, then shut off the ignition and growled, "You ought to have your head examined and find out what you use in place of a brain."

There was a neat, quiet office on the third floor. Bush closed the door after Haas and Cardigan had entered and then brushed his hands lightly together. He went to a desk and called the hospital.

"I see.... Yes, stay there anyhow, Goddard, until it's all over."

HE HUNG up, relit his dead cigar and sat on the edge of the desk, swinging one hard, stubby leg. Haas hadn't spoken yet. He watched Bush in a manner that implied he would act according to Bush's wish.

"Now what's behind it?" Bush said. He was at ease. He overdid the fact that he was at ease.

"You're the whole police department, it seems. And you ask me?"

"You knew her, Cardigan. I tailed you this morning when you went to that apartment house. I asked the woman at the desk who you went to see. She told me. I didn't think it was anything, so I left. We found her handbag tonight. The names were the same."

"You didn't see anybody else go in after me, did you?"

"I didn't hang around." Bush narrowed one eye. "Who else?"

"I don't know. I just thought somebody else might have been hanging around."

"Who bumped her off, Cardigan?"

Cardigan looked surprised. "Who bumped her off! How the hell do I know?"

Bush stuck his jaw out and came up close to Cardigan. "I want to know who put the finger on Helen Carmory."

"I don't know."

"You called on her this morning, damn you!"

"I was in her apartment about fifteen minutes. When the murder was pulled off I was home. You know that because you phoned me and I was there. Have I denied that I was at the Carmory place?"

"What were you doing there?"

"I knew Helen Carmory. I was out to Phil Gould's casino last night and Helen Carmory fainted on the veranda upstairs. I happened to be there. I picked up some things and stuck 'em in my pocket. I forgot to give them back. I gave them back this morning. Start working on that."

Bush forgot his smile. He grated, "I don't believe you."

"That doesn't knock me over."

Bush took a handful of Cardigan's vest. His face worked. "I've got enough of you, Cardigan! I've got just about enough! Since you came to this city three years ago you've been handing me a kick in the slats every chance you got! By God Almighty, this is one time when you ain't—"

Cardigan barely moved, yet he straight-armed Bush in the chest and Bush went reeling backward, knocked over a chair and landed on his back, his short legs flying. Haas looked sour and leaped in front of Cardigan with a blackjack. Red color was flooding Cardigan's face, his mouth was crooked and a little open, showing set teeth.

Bush scrambled up, his trouser legs wrinkled, the cuffs halfway up his lower legs showing his socks. His eyes popped. He had his blackjack out and his lips were sputtering wetly.

"You—you—you damned son-of-a—" he choked.

Cardigan's body engulfed Haas like a tidal wave and Haas went down. Cardigan's fist whipped in a short chopping blow. It caught Bush on the jaw and Bush slammed against the wall. Haas was up, off balance, but he took a wild swing with his blackjack and glanced a blow off Cardigan's head. Cardigan went down.

Bush rubbed his jaw and hefted his blackjack and Cardigan got up and said, "There's one word I don't like to be called."

The three of them stood breathing heavily.

The telephone rang. Bush answered it. When he hung up he said, "She just died. Never came to. Now, Cardigan—"

"Shut up!" Cardigan's voice carried a whip. "I told you I was at her apartment this morning. I told you why I went there. That's all I'm going to tell you and if you think you can hold me on that then you'll have to rewrite the criminal code."

Bush snarled, "I'll hold you over night and take a chance on that. I'll hold you over night. I'll hold you for striking an officer! Ha! How's that?"

"Fast but not fast enough," Cardigan shot back at him. "I can pull out of this. Right now! And I can make you take it through the nose!"

"Yeah?" snarled Bush.

Cardigan pointed to the phone. "Get Ullrich down here."

"Get—" Bush stopped short, gasped. The room suddenly became silent. Then Bush spluttered, "Why, dammit—"

"Get Ullrich," Cardigan hammered out. "He's not my friend. He's yours. But get him."

"To hell with you. You can't bluff me."

"I'm not bluffing. Get him. Get him or get Inspector Lewiston in here and I'll break up this little clique of yours. If you're going to pinch me because I called on Helen Carmory this morning then, by cripes, you're going to pinch Ullrich!"

"That's a stinking lie!"

"Get Inspector Lewiston and inside of half an hour he'll have Ullrich down here. I asked the woman at the apartment house what apartment Ullrich asked for. She said Helen Carmory's. In just three seconds you telephone Lewiston or I walk out that door."

When Cardigan walked out Bush looked dumbfounded.

CHAPTER FOUR

"HOW MUCH DO YOU WANT?"

IT TOOK five minutes for Cardigan to reach his office on foot. The building was dark. He turned on a light and began pacing up and down heavily. He kept combing his shaggy hair with his big brown fingers. There was a sharp, concentrated look in his eyes.

Presently he sat down and called a telephone number. After a while the operator said, "Party does not answer." He hung up and sat drumming his fingers, nibbling at his lip, staring hard into space. He made another call.

"Sorry, Pat.... Yeah. I'm down at the office. How's to run down? As soon as you can powder your nose."

Pat was one woman in a thousand. Fifteen minutes after the phone call she walked in. She looked wide awake, neat, comely. She wore a droll smile that always hinted that the world was a funny old place but all right so long as you took it as a joke.

"At this hour you get me down to your private office."

"Helen Carmory was bumped off."

She said nothing, but her smile vanished.

Cardigan slapped the desk. "Bumped off! Out on the South Side. About 11:00. She lived about half an hour. Never came to. Bush flagged me over there and then hauled me to H.Q. and began acting up."

"White, huh?"

"Says the hunch. Bush hasn't got an idea in the world that White's mixed up in it. But he may find out. There's no telling what Helen Carmory left behind. We've got to work fast. Seventy thousand in diamonds is in or has passed through White's hands. It's one of the biggest jobs I've ever had. There's ten thousand in it for the agency. It's my job to get that ice and I'll beg, bribe and coerce to get it! If Bush gets a lead, finds out White is mixed up in the murder—and gets him—we're going to be left holding the bag. With a murder rap hanging on White he'll never spring about the loot."

Under the skin Pat was all woman. "You're playing a dangerous game, chief. You've got a big political clique wondering about you. Is it worth it?"

"Sister, I like my job. The head office sent me out here because 'Boss' Hammerhorn thinks I'm a swell, elegant guy. He wired me to hang onto this job till my guts hurt. I liked the way he put it. And I'm in it—this job. Up to my neck. I'm holding good cards and—" he took a slow swing and buried fist into palm—"I don't like Bush." His teeth set and he flexed his lips over them. "That's that, sister."

Pat sighed, shrugged. "O.K."

"Now look. I rang Nita Monteclara's apartment. No answer. You run over there—take those master keys out of that drawer—you run over there, crash the place and turn it inside out. Letters. Photographs. Addresses. If you don't find anything hot wait there—hide somewhere—and if the worse goes to the worst get rough with the jane. Get Tom McWaye on the wire. His house—Jefferson 0024."

Pat telephoned and handed the instrument to Cardigan. "Hello," Cardigan said. "You, Tom? Hello, you legal lion. I might bust into trouble in the next twenty-four hours. Me or my assistant Pat Seaward. I want you to be ready to pull your legal tricks if the works get gummed.... Thanks, kid.... Goom-by."

He hung up and said, "All right, Pat, on your way."

She went to the door, turned, said, "Don't run too high a temperature, chief."

He grinned, said nothing. Pat went out.

Cardigan rolled the roadster through the night on Broadway, hummed through the South Side, crossed the River Des Peres and hit the open highway. The night wind was damp, sometimes the windshield became clouded. The road rolled up and down gently. The stars were small and far away and the countryside was empty, black, with the moon gone. Occasionally headlights burst over a rise in the road, a car went past with a vicious swish. The roadster's top clapped, hooted; the grass by the roadside looked pale in the glare of the headlights.

At a lonely crossroads Cardigan turned left and struck a dirt highway. A little farther on he veered left at a fork and followed a narrower, rougher road that went up over short, choppy hills, fell away in short, steep grades and tortuous curves, leveled off and meandered through sparse timber and broken fields.

Two stone gate-posts supported small globes of light. Beyond, in a grove of trees, loomed a large, rambling stone building with many windows lighted. Cardigan pulled up in a parking space and a uniformed attendant opened the roadster's door. About fifty cars were parked there and the muffled beat of a jazz band came from the building.

CARDIGAN walked to a white porte-cochère where half a dozen uniformed men stood around. He climbed broad stone steps, entered a large vestibule and showed a card of introduction. He was passed into the sumptuous foyer, and the louder beat of the jazz band throbbed in his ears; lovely women drifted past in alluring décolleté and the perfume of them hung pendant in the air.

He stood there and lit a cigarette. He was keyed up. He was anything but an iceberg and he could feel the blood warm and quick in his veins. One thing he had—presence, and it did not pass unnoticed by the women. He dwarfed the average man.

In a minute he moved, passed through the archway into the Louis lounge. A man sitting and a man standing by the mirrored door looked at him. The man in the chair stirred, crossed one leg over the other. The man at the door shifted his feet. Behind Cardigan was the restaurant, the throbbing jazz band, the laughter of women commingled with the tinkle of glass, the *shush-shush* of dancing feet.

Cardigan entered the gambling rooms. They were more crowded than on the night before. Smoke hung like a fog about the crystal chandeliers. The little white ball bobbed in the spinning roulette wheel. Cardigan's eyes roved. He passed on into another room.

White teeth were laughing behind carmine lips. Nita Monteclara threw dice with wild abandon. Burt White stood at her shoulder. A cigarette drooped from his thin-smiling mouth. From time to time he looked up, jerked his almost colorless eyes over the crowd.

Cardigan moved away, looked at his watch. It was half past one. Phil Gould came toward him. Gould's thin white hands were at his sides. His face was white and narrow with nervous muscles twitching near his lips. His voice was a low whisper.

"You!"

"Now, now."

"I want a word with you."

"Sure."

They went out into the lounge and Gould jerked his head, muttered, "My office."

It was the famous "armored" room: walls, floor and ceiling of reinforced concrete; the main entrance door of heavy steel, with double locks; slanted steel blinds over the windows; a small steel door that led to a passageway into the gambling rooms. Through this door money was brought, deposited in the vault against the back wall of the office. It was no great secret. Once a scribe had written it up in the Sunday magazine supplement of a newspaper.

A pale-faced youth worked over a ledger; another worked at an adding machine. There was a loud-speaker through which warning could be yelled from any part of the building.

"You've got to clear out of here tonight, Cardigan," Gould said in his quick, brittle voice. "You've got to. This is one night when you've got to get out."

The clerks were trained. They did not look up. They kept on working with smart precision.

"I'm sorry," Cardigan said. His voice was slower than usual.

Gould scratched his jaw irritably. "You've got to! Listen, this is straight: you're going out of here or you're going to get put out."

Cardigan darkened. "I'm here on a job, Gould."

"As if that's news! Maybe you thought I thought you came here to play marbles or something."

"I'm on a job. A big one."

"So then you think you're going to play cops and robbers in my place, huh? Nuts you are, Cardigan, and that's that."

"I'm not going to do a thing here. That's God's honest. What I'm going to do I'm going to do somewhere else. But the tail starts here. It's my job, Gould. It's a red-hot and you're not in any way connected with it. I know I've got a reputation as a wise-guy, but this time I'm on the level. I'm telling you the truth. I'm swearing to you that I'll pull no monkeyshines here."

"What I said stands," Gould bit off.

"I'll meet you halfway. I'm heeled. I'll leave my gun with you till I'm ready to leave. That's fair, Gould."

"There's no chance at all of meeting me halfway, Cardigan. Are you going to walk out of here like a nice guy or are you going to be taken out?"

"So you're sold on your own ideas, eh?" Cardigan's mouth tightened. "I'll tip you, Gould, that you're stepping on your own toes. I can hurt you if I want to. I've got enough stored away in my noodle to hurt you and some guys bigger than you are. You can throw me out. Of course you can, with the army of heels you've got around here, but you do it and you'll sing your swan-song."

Gould shook his head bitterly. "Tonight—you've got to clear out—that's all." Gould turned on his heel, walked to a desk, picked up some papers and studied them carefully.

CARDIGAN moved to the door. Gould dropped the papers and joined him, opening the door and eyeing Cardigan coolly. Cardigan went into the corridor and Gould followed closely and Cardigan walked slowly with his brows bent and a hint of malevolence in his eyes. He reached the foyer and the chatter of women standing in little groups. He looked distinctly unpleasant and there was a glimpse of wind rising and falling in his eyes.

"Thay, Phil—"

Cardigan stopped, turned around and saw a wavy-haired blonde youth accosting Gould. Gould muttered something and the youth shrugged and stepped back, looking at Cardigan. Cardigan suddenly went toward him.

"Did you say something?" he growled.

"I didn't thay a thing."

"Oh, you didn't *thay* a thing. You—"

Gould touched Cardigan. "He spoke to me, dope."

"Yeah. And he busted into my office at noon and took a look over my files!"

"Sh!" Gould muttered. "Keep your voice down."

"Who thaid I buthted—"

Gould hissed, "Ned, scram!" Suppressed anger bit into his words. No one ever fought in the open at the casino. No one ever argued out loud. It was that kind of place.

Cardigan rasped under his breath, "And I'm damned if I'm going to leave here till I'm good and ready!"

He pivoted and strode away from Gould. Gould did not rush him. Three hard-eyed men looked to Gould for a signal but he did not give it. Each of the three men had a hand in his pocket. But Gould was afraid—afraid of something. He was reluctant, apparently, to stage a fight in the sumptuous foyer of his elaborate casino. His face reddened and his thin fingers moved nervously in his palms. A dozen women, half a dozen men, were unaware of this taut, bitter drama.

Cardigan walked right into the lounge, turned and looked back through the archway. He could see Gould rooted to the floor. It was no effort to pick out Gould's men. He knew that at another time, in a place less public—Gould's office, for instance—he would have been jumped, manhandled, chucked out a side entrance.

The front door swung open and Detective Sergeant Bush came in. Bush did not see Cardigan. Bush's face was worried and he went directly to Gould. Cardigan stepped away from the arch. Explosive thoughts began crackling in his brain: Bush must have gone to Helen Carmory's apartment, found something there—perhaps a picture of White, or a letter, or some clue that was hot when he found it and that led him here to the casino.

Cardigan had not expected this. He hoped for at least a six-hour jump on Bush. It was open and shut that if Bush collared White for the murder the whereabouts of the diamonds would not be divulged—with any benefit to Cardigan, anyhow. White was a murderer, if Cardigan's hunch held water, and Cardigan had no intention of letting White get away with it. But on the other hand he had a job to complete, a robbery to solve, loot to regain.

A couple came out of the gambling rooms. The mirrored door swung shut. Cardigan strode toward it. The stony-faced attendant opened it and Cardigan entered the feverish gaiety. He was jostled right and left. The hour was late and many of the guests were drunk, but there was rarely any disorder at the casino.

Cardigan did not see White. He covered the three gaming rooms slowly but purposefully. Nor did he see Nita Monteclara. He returned to the lounge, walked the length of it and lingered in the entrance to the dining room. The pair weren't there. He turned and went up the staircase and stood at the top looking the length of the corridor toward the open porch doors.

He walked to the doors and looked out. The veranda appeared to be deserted. He went out and strolled along the broad rail. It was dark here. Farther on the veranda turned around the side of the building. Cardigan followed the rail around, then stopped.

Ten feet away a man and a woman were embracing. They broke, and Cardigan knew they were White and Nita Monteclara. He said nothing. He pretended he had not seen them. Turning away, he scowled into the darkness. Far down the bluff the river rolled by. His right hand rose and crossed his chest and he felt the bulge of the gun in his spring holster.

Voices and footsteps came out on to the veranda and Bush and Gould walked toward Cardigan. He took a few lazy steps toward them. They recognized him.

"What are you doing out here?" Bush growled.

"What are you?"

"I can go where I damned well please."

"So can I."

"Oh, can you?"

"As a matter of fact," Cardigan said, "I've got more of a right to be out here than you have. You're a metropolitan cop and your business ends there. You haven't an excuse in the world to be out here in the county."

HE WALKED away from them, drawing them after him, and entered the corridor. A door opened almost abreast of Cardigan and a head thrust out. The head bobbed back, its owner bumped against someone behind, there was swift confusion and the door swung open.

Cardigan got an eyeful. He saw Ullrich, the man who had bumped the other. He saw tall, lantern-jawed Senator Ackerman, a few other men. He saw half a dozen girls—young, heavily rouged. And there was a long banquet table, many bottles, many buckets of ice.

Behind Cardigan Phil Gould sucked in a breath.

No one made an attempt to close the door. Ullrich's face was a round blank moon. Ackerman was frowning. The other men quieted down. One of the girls was doing a clog to radio music.

Gould gripped Cardigan's arm. "Come on, Cardigan."

"Shut up," Cardigan grumbled.

Then Ullrich's face brightened, became wreathed in smiles. "Well, well, well, sir!"

Cardigan shrugged free of Gould, stalked into the room.

A girl cried, "O-o-o, what a big meany you look like."

Another said, "Any minute now, Gertrude, I expect to hear him growl and then see him start biting."

Ackerman half turned, muttered, "Be quiet. Go into the other room."

The girls entered an adjoining room, some of them giggling.

Cardigan leaned back against the open door. His stare was baleful. Gould came in rubbing his hands together nervously. Bush remained standing in the corridor, a fretful, bewildered look on his face.

Ackerman said, "Come in, sergeant."

Bush came in and assumed an angelic expression.

"Close that door," Ackerman said.

"I'm not staying that long," Cardigan said.

"Close it."

Cardigan moved and Ullrich closed the door.

Ackerman, a tall, bony man, crossed the room, closed the connecting door and came back to face Cardigan.

"How much do you want?" he said.

"What makes you think I want anything?"

Ackerman was blunt. "Don't beat about the bush. How much do you want for your silence?"

"If my silence were at stake, neither you nor anybody else could buy it. What the hell gave you the idea I was after a shakedown?"

"I'm not mincing words, Cardigan."

"So you think I am? Dammit, I told Ullrich today that your business didn't interest me. He didn't believe it. Two guys crashed my office and bound my stenog and looked through my files. One of them's downstairs now. Man alive, if I wanted to spring it I have enough on you to get you slammed out of the State Senate overnight. And I'm not keeping it under my hat because I like you, which I don't, but it wouldn't get me anywhere. But I'll tell you this: if there's any more hocus-pocus pulled off around me I'll get mean and low-down and land on you and your whole scatter like a ton of brick."

He whirled and reached for the doorknob. Gould blocked him and looked at Ackerman for some signal.

Ackerman droned, "Don't get hot-headed, Cardigan. Let's talk this over sensibly."

Cardigan was biting Gould with somber eyes. "Get away from that door, Gould."

"Now please, Cardigan," Ackerman said.

Cardigan grabbed Gould by the throat, flung him sidewise with terrific violence. Two men grabbed Cardigan from behind, held on grimly. Gould lay on the floor panting.

Ackerman bit off the end of a cigar. "Let him go," he said.

CHAPTER FIVE

THE CROSSED SPOT

WHEN CARDIGAN reached the lounge below he looked through the archway and saw White and Nita Monteclara leaving. He got his hat and when he passed out through the door he saw a black sedan swing around the pebbled drive. He took his time on the way to the parking space. He drove slowly through the gates and laid his gun on the seat beside him.

He doused his lights after a minute and picked his way carefully along the dirt road. From time to time he spotted the tail-light of White's sedan. When the sedan turned right on the paved road Cardigan slowed down, rolled along leisurely and then put his lights on just before he made the turn. He picked up speed gradually, saw the tail-light on a rise beyond.

In a few minutes he was aware of lights shining in his rear-view mirror. He paid no attention until he noticed that the car maintained an even pace behind. Cardigan speeded up, and as he did so the car behind followed. When Cardigan eased up on the throttle the car behind dropped back. Several times Cardigan did this and on each occasion the result was the same. It occurred to him that Bush was still watching his every move.

White's car maintained a steady speed of about forty-five. Cardigan crept up on it and the car behind crept up on Cardigan. The road made a wide turn. Cardigan looked back, cursed, and came to a decision. He stepped on the throttle and shot away. When he passed White's sedan the roadster was doing sixty. He looked back and saw the third car cutting out to pass White. He pressed harder on the throttle and the clock-like speedometer went to sixty-five, on to seventy. The wind hammered the top.

The other car was after him. When Cardigan turned, the dashlight off the needle was quivering at seventy-five. He dared not look back. He had to keep his eyes on the road. He took chances and cut corners, turned on the spotlight to see better. The roar of wind and motor was deafening; the frenzied clapping of the canvas top was enough to rattle a man's nerves. Ultimately the car's speed was eighty, but settlements a mile beyond would cut that.

Suddenly he heard a crash. Saw his spotlight go out, saw the rear of it torn open. His mouth flew open. There was a sharp *ping* of a sound. He saw a hole in his non-shatterable windshield. An oath ripped from his lips and he jammed himself far down into the seat. Lead snarled against metal somewhere behind. Cardigan flattened the accelerator against the floorboards and hung onto the wheel.

He drew away from the pursuing car. He knew now that it was not Bush. Bush was a cad and a petty nuisance but he wouldn't go in for murder. Cardigan did not look back. He blasted through a small settlement, screeched around a curve. He roared past a truck. The heat of the motor came up into his face. Filling stations flashed by. Houses grew. The open country was behind.

At three o'clock Cardigan braked his steaming car in a wide avenue, turned off the ignition. He strode quickly from the car a matter of twenty yards, then turned into a flag walk and entered a small apartment house. In the deserted lobby he paused to look in a notebook, then took a stairway up. On the fifth floor he began looking for door numbers. He stopped in front of 509, put his head close to the door.

"Pat!" he whispered. He listened a moment. "Pat, this is Cardigan!" he whispered again.

The door whipped open and a gun steadied on him.

"I just wanted to make sure," Pat said.

"Good girl," he said, and pushed in. "Lock it."

They were in the dark.

"Find anything?" he said.

"No. Isn't that jane ever coming home?"

"It's my hunch she'll be here soon—with White. Turn the lights on so I can get the lay here."

Pat switched them on and remained standing by the switch. Cardigan went to the bedroom, came out, looked in the bathroom, the closets.

"All right, kid, turn 'em off." Darkness engulfed the room. "Don't hide behind any chairs," Cardigan said. "Stand right here in the center of the room."

"I'll lock the door first."

"You take care of the jane."

"Oh, I'll take care of the jane."

TEN minutes later a key grated in the lock. The door swung open.

The man and the woman were in dim silhouette against the glow in the corridor.

The woman sauntered in. The man, directly behind her, turned the light switch and kicked the door shut with his heel.

"Reach," said Cardigan.

"Oh!" cried Nita Monteclara; and to Pat, "Why, you're—you are the—Oh!" Definite recognition added to her shock.

White kept his elbows at his sides, raising his forearms. His black felt hat was rakish over one eyebrow. He was quite a big man, with a hard pallor, colorless eyes. The scar glinted like a strip of metal on his forehead, just above his left eyebrow.

"Pinch, huh?"

"Raise 'em higher."

"This is an outrage!" cried Nita. "I weel not permeet—"

"You pipe down," Pat said quietly. "Cut out stamping the hoof and in general shut up. Sit down there."

White said, "Well, well?" to Cardigan.

Cardigan went close to him, pressed his gun firmly against White's stomach, removed White's gun and took a few steps backward. White never budged. His eyes shone like glass that has been slightly smoked.

"Well, well," said Cardigan. "I want those diamonds."

"What diamonds?"

"The Hotel Midlands job the cops failed to hang on you three years ago. Six diamonds."

"Aren't you funny?"

"Am I?" Cardigan took one step and laid the flat of his left hand across White's face.

"Oh, dear!" wailed Nita.

White stopped against the wall, lowering one hand to feel his face. "Who the hell are you?" he muttered.

"Cardigan, private snoop for the insurance company that was fall-guy over that theft. I want that ice, White. I want it and I'm going to get it. I haven't any time to spare. I'm going to get it if I have to break every bone in your body."

Nita snapped. "This is my home! You have no right—"

"You," said Pat, "had better act indifferent."

"But this is the outrage! I weel—"

"You hear me, White!" Cardigan was growling.

Cardigan's slap had left red marks on White's face. White remained standing with his back against the wall. "I don't know what the cripes you're talking about. Can't a guy come out of stir and go straight?"

"I've been keeping tabs on you for two weeks, White. I know that you've been spending jack like some big bomb and machine-gun man. You came out of the hoosegow stony. How come?"

White snapped, "You got nothing on me! I did my stretch for packing 'at pop-gun. I did it and now what's the big idea of you making cracks?"

"Where'd you get the dough to throw a party at Filone's? The dough to bust out like a rash in a new Chrysler? Where'd you get the dough to stake the dame here for whirls at the games at Phil Gould's casino? Go on—go on and tell me that your maiden aunt died."

"I got friends. I c'n borrow."

Cardigan wore a frigid smile empty of humor. "Only on good security, White. Got a job? No. Any money in the bank? No."

White's temper was rising slowly. "To hell with you! You've got no right to quiz me. You've got no right a-tall to bust in here and hold my girl and me like this—"

"You tell them, honey," Nita said, forgetting her accent.

"I'll tell 'em!" White blurted, his neck muscles bulging, his eyes striving to stare down Cardigan. He pushed his hat back. Sweat was on his forehead. Sweat made his white scar gleam. His initial coolness was ebbing fast.

"You'll tell me where that ice is, White; that's what you'll tell me," Cardigan said dully. "You dirty half-wit, I've pieced the whole puzzle together. Helen Carmory got the ice when you dropped it from your hotel window to Bennington Court. Five hours ago you bumped her off because this new heart of yours—"

"You liar!"

"Am I? Maybe you've got an alibi where you were."

"At Phil Gould's. He'll tell you."

"Will he? He'll tell me the truth because I've got enough on Gould and his bunch to send them up. He'll have to squawk to save himself. I've got him and Ackerman and the whole shebang tied in a knot. Gould can't afford to fake your alibi. I'll leave the murder pinch to the cops. I'm not after you for the murder of your former flame. I'm after the ice you chucked to her from that hotel window. You'll tip me off or you and this jane go in for the rap together."

Nita cried, "Not me!"

"Yes, you will," said Cardigan. "You'll take it right on the nose with your boy friend. Sergeant Bush has a hunch. He followed the hunch out to the casino. Gould can't stand by you because Ackerman won't let him, can't afford to. They'll chuck you to the wolves to save your hides."

White gritted, "They can't. I know too much about them."

"That's too bad. Then they'll put the cross on both of you. I'll take you out there—both of you. Come on."

"No," cried Nita in a frightened voice. "No—no!"

"I want those diamonds," Cardigan said doggedly.

WHITE moistened his lips. His breath came unsteadily. "I can't! I'm in the hole for twenty-two thousand. If I don't meet the debt—"

"I want those diamonds."

Perspiration dripped from White's chin. "How do I know you won't squawk?"

"I'm making no bargain with a killer, White. My job is to get the diamonds first. When they're in my hands I'll give you a ten-hour start, then I'll have to drop a hint to the cops."

White mopped his face. "It's no go. I'll take a chance. Gould will have to stick by us."

Nita cried, "But you heard this man say Gould—"

"Shut up, Nita," White snapped.

"I won't! You've got to keep me out of this, Burt! I had nothing to do with it."

"You tramp, you knew what was coming off. You stayed in that room at the casino so you could swear I was with you. I gave you five-thousand bucks to do it. We got to take the chance. I don't believe this guy."

"I do!" cried Nita. "Anyhow, I will not take the chance. You've got to protect me, Burt. You've got to!"

"Shut up, damn you!"

Nita stamped her foot. "I won't! You have the diamonds. You were waiting for Max Bloomberg to come back from New York so he could buy them—"

"Why, you dirty—"

Cardigan gripped him by the throat, kept his gun pressed against

White's stomach. "You're getting just what you deserve, White. Helen Carmory's death was a mistake. She looked swell to me. Are you going to fork over or are you going into a sure pinch with this jane turning color on you?"

"To hell with you!"

Nita cried, "He wears a money belt. They're in—"

"You two-timing—"

But Cardigan dropped him with a blow to the chin. White slumped to the floor and Cardigan bent down, ripped open vest and shirt, found the money belt, extracted a chamois pouch containing six diamonds.

White got to his feet, his face flushed and sullen. He rubbed his chin. His eyes were glassy. He thrust his hands into hip pockets. His face looked murderous.

"Beat it," said Cardigan, opening the door.

White moved to the threshold. He straightened up, turned and regarded Nita. His face softened. A strange smile came to his lips.

"Good luck, Nita," he said. "You were right. I was a louse. Forgive me, baby."

"Oh, Burt, I'm glad you understand."

She stumbled to the door, gripped his shoulders. "I'm only a woman, Burt. I'm not as strong as you. I couldn't stand it. Kiss me, Burt."

His hands came out of his hip pockets. There was a quick movement. Then White spun and darted away. Nita mumbled something while she swayed in the doorway. Her swaying body blocked Cardigan. He grabbed her and turned her around. Her eyes were wide. There was a jack-knife sticking in her breast. White's hands had been in his hip pockets—

"Oh—" Nita's whimper was very weak.

Cardigan felt her body relax, saw a queer fixed look in her eyes that only the near-dead wear. He let her down to the carpet, threw a look at Pat, said nothing. He lunged through the door, down the steps. He heard the front door bang.

White's car was parked in the driveway alongside the house. White must have known it would be futile to try using it. He ran up the street. He saw Cardigan's roadster and leaped for it. The key was in it, the motor was warm and started easily. He did not know it was Cardigan's car, did not know who owned it. But he meshed gears savagely and got away.

Cardigan went no farther than the lobby. From the closed vestibule he could see White getting away. And then he heard the roar of another motor. A black touring car swept by.

A minute later the sound of guns hammered in the street. Cardigan sprang to the terrace. He saw his roadster leap across the curb, across the sidewalk; heard the crash of metal as the car slammed into a stone wall; saw the car leap into the air flinging aside torn metal; saw it burst into flames—while the touring car sped on.

When Cardigan returned to the apartment five minutes later Pat said, "I phoned a doctor, but it's no use. What was all that racket?"

Cardigan stared at the dead woman. "One of fate's little jokes. A mob that thinks I know too much tried to get me on the road in from the casino. They didn't have luck. So they just tried again. Only White was in the car. They got him."

Pat spread her hands. "What a mess, chief!"

"The double cross all around. White was in deep. He could never have got out. And Gould's heels got him instead of me."

"But what a mess, chief—for us!"

Cardigan pressed her arm, then patted it. "Don't you believe it, Pat. This is easy. We didn't fire a shot. Just keep your mouth shut and let me do the talking. We had a job to do. We did it."

He crossed the room heavily, picked up the phone, said, "Police headquarters."

Waiting, he smiled at Pat. He didn't look worried.

"What a man!" she said. "What a man!"

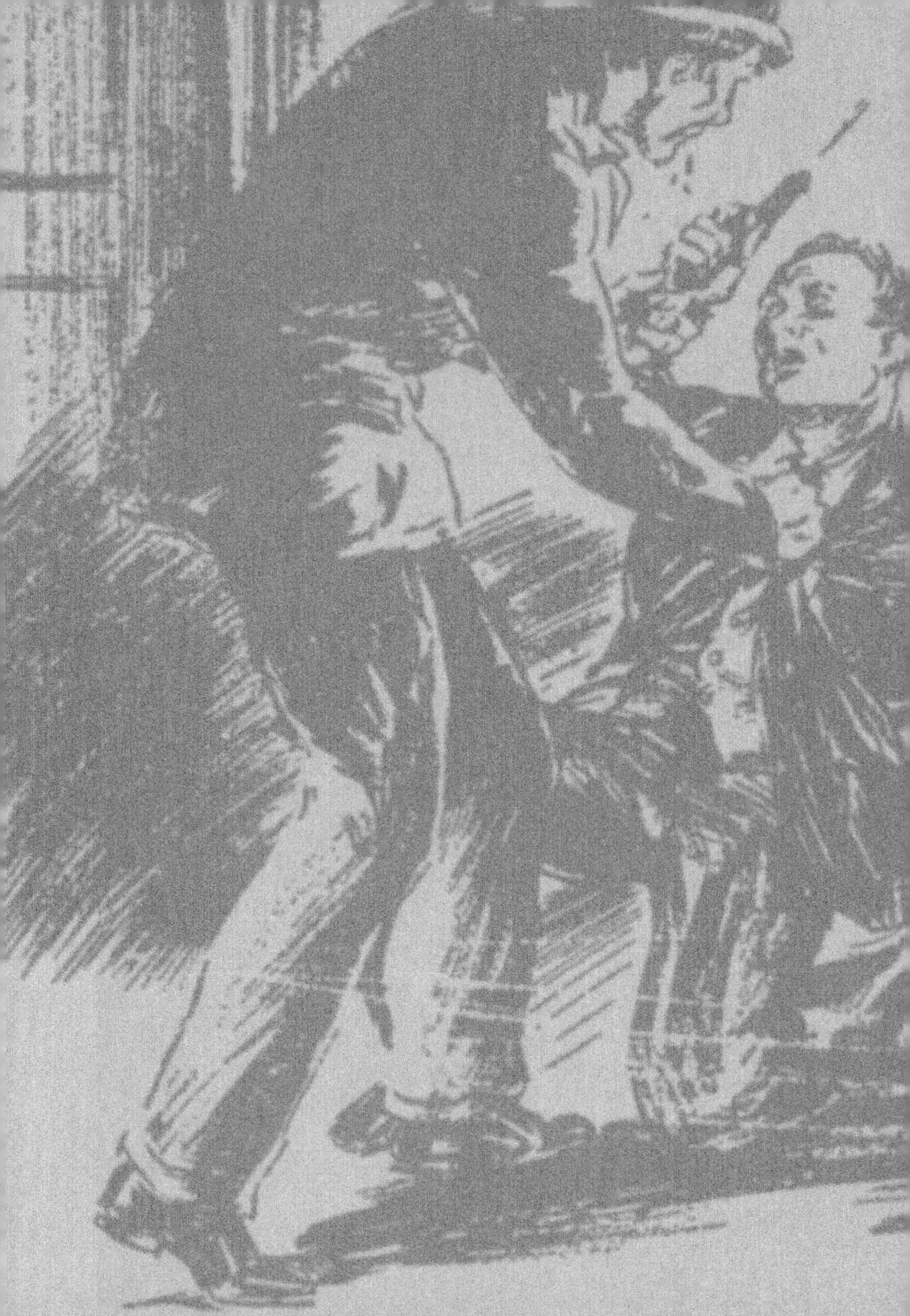

AND THERE WAS MURDER

SQUASHING POLITICAL PLUMS WASN'T CARDIGAN'S JOB. HE TRIED TO TELL THE GRAFT-GRABBERS THAT BUT THEY WOULDN'T BELIEVE HIM—NOT UNTIL THEIR OWN FINGERS GOT BURNED ON THE HOT SPOT THEY'D WARMED UP FOR THE BIG DICK.

CHAPTER ONE

FOUR BEERS AND A BODY

HIS HAIR looked shaggier: his meditative frown was deeper. His burry gray topcoat bulked at the shoulders and his shoulders were close up to his ears, his chin down and crushing his collar. Elbows leaned on the bar and a big-fingered hand moved a glass round and round and made beer sudsy, and white foam stuck to the sides. He slid the glass spinning across the wet bar.

"Roll you, Toddy."

The bartender took poker dice from the cash-register, warmed them in a black box, smacked the box down. Cardigan rolled out and the bartender rolled and beat him.

"I'll take rye," the bartender said.

The only other man in the bar drained his glass of beer. "Let me buy this round."

Cardigan didn't look up. He put seventy-five cents on the bar and caught his glass of beer as Toddy sent it skidding toward him. The man at the other end of the bar blinked uncertainly behind spectacles.

"Thanks, Akeley," Cardigan said, "but this is my last. And I never go back on the dice."

The bartender raised his rye. "Well, mud in your eye."

"*Skoal*," Cardigan said, and drained half of the glass.

Akeley looked at his fingers and found that he had plucked a cigarette to shreds. He brushed the bits off. He had a thin face with fragile cheekbones and a timid mouth. He needed a haircut. There were stains on his tie. He went down along the bar rubbing his hand on the wooden rail and stopped at Cardigan's elbow.

"Beer again, Toddy," he said. He jerked a furtive sidelong look at Cardigan, edged an inch nearer Cardigan's elbow.

Cardigan looked at him—bluntly—from beneath shaggy eyebrows.

Akeley took his fresh beer, threw back his shoulders, took a big swallow, put the glass down with assumed nonchalance.

"How about it, Cardigan?"

"Been working up to it, huh, Akeley?"

"The boss—"

"You tell your boss for me to take a nose dive."

Akeley's chest shrank and his eyes blinked. He scratched at his neck. "Aw, Cardigan, there's dough in it for you and me—"

"I don't squawk!" Cardigan growled with sudden heat; then addressed his glass in a low throaty rumble. "I take care of myself. To hell with your boss. To hell with you, Akeley. You're a nice

Cardigan grabbed Bush while McClintock fell on the senator.

enough guy—but to hell with you."

Akeley wore a pale, self-pitying look. "It'd mean a lot to me," he murmured. "I got a wife and a couple of kids and the paper's cut me ten bucks a week and times are hard and if I got a story like that I'd be on Easy Street—"

"What a swell son-of-a-so-and-so you are," Cardigan muttered. "Pulling the old hearts-and-flowers on me because I'm Irish. Dragging in the frau and the kids to make me feel like a cheap punk if I don't spring."

"Look at me—from worry. Look at my clothes." Akeley made his face look woebegone. "It means a lot to me, Cardigan. It really does!"

The phone behind the bar rang. Toddy left a toothpick sticking in his teeth and took down the receiver. "Yeah?… Yeah, he's here." He lifted the instrument across the bar, said: "For you, Cardigan."

Cardigan took it. "Hello.… Hello—hello!" He listened. He threw at Toddy, "Who was it?"

"Dunno. Jane."

"Hello—hello!" Cardigan snapped into the mouthpiece. "Hey, operator. I'm not calling any number. I've been cut off. Someone called me…. No, and I don't know the number."

He hung up.

"It was a jane all right," Toddy said.

Cardigan put his hat on. "I'm blowing, kid. If she calls again I'll be at my apartment."

"I've got to go too," Akeley said.

"I'll drop you at your paper," Cardigan said.

Cardigan pushed open a swing door; tramped down a dimly lighted corridor toward a heavier door beyond. Akeley half skipped to keep up with him. Cardigan stopped to light a cigarette and Akeley opened the heavier door and leaned against it while Cardigan rolled past him into the dark street.

The door swung too hard, jolting Akeley in the back and staggering him past Cardigan.

A brittle clatter of shots rang in the dark. A weak, pitiful "Oh God!" ached up out of the reporter's throat. Blood was suddenly on his face. He stood erect as if held up magically by an unseen hand, his arms rigid and his fingers splayed; almost on his toes he stood, with his mouth gaping. But only for a split instant. Life blew out of him abruptly like air from a burst balloon. His body wheeled toward Cardigan; stopped with a jolt against Cardigan's rooted bulk.

Shadows made a drumming sound of heels down the street. While Akeley's body slid down past Cardigan's stomach Cardigan held a gun at arm's length. Its muzzle spewed flame and echoes banged violently against the house walls. The narrow street shook under the hammerlike blow of another shot. But the shadows were far away. The drum of heels petered out in the wake of the last gun-shot echoes.

Akeley lay at Cardigan's feet.

The heavy door made a sound. A section of Toddy's face appeared there. "Cur-ripes!" he hissed.

"Yeah," muttered Cardigan.

His big brown chin was way down, his neck was a rigid column, the skin tight on the back. There was a bitter, hateful look in his eyes. Vagrant gusts of wind plucked at his burry topcoat, but Cardigan remained rooted, feet planted wide.

"Cur-ripes!" hissed Toddy again. "What in hell—is—is that Akeley?"

"Yeah."

Heavy footfalls came on the run. Cardigan looked over his shoulder, up the street. He slid his gun into his overcoat pocket and made a half turn. The houses made a ragged skyline up and down the narrow street. A few windows grated open and the blur of faces appeared and remained silent.

A cop came dodging from pole to pole.

"O.K.," Cardigan called dully. "It's all over."

The cop came out into the open and slapped his heels smartly on the pavement. "What the hell happened? Who are you?"

"This guy here got the works."

"Who's he? Who's the guy? Who are you?"

"Akeley."

"You're Akeley, are you?"

"No. The stiff's Akeley."

"And who are you?"

"Cardigan. Cosmos Agency."

"Oh, yeah? Cosmos Agency, eh? You're Cardigan, eh?"

Cardigan said: "You don't have to kill time. The guys lammed like a light."

"Don't get smart, you. Never mind now getting smart. Just answer questions: that's all you gotta do, guy. I ain't taking lip from you, see?"

"Haven't I answered 'em?"

"That's all right; just answer them and nemmine the lip."

Cardigan said, "Ah, nuts," in a low, contemptuous voice, and bent down beside Akeley.

INSPECTOR KNOBLOCK was a tall horse-faced man with soft, brown eyes and wide lips that undulated slowly when he spoke. He always kept his eyes wide open and bland and had a habit of buttoning and unbuttoning his vest absent-mindedly.

Cardigan said, "We left together. I was right behind Akeley when we went out the door. The shots came from down the street. Six of them. I think four got Akeley. One was in the cheek. He fell against me and I—and I had a time getting my gun out. I took two pot shots and missed. It was dark and there was no chance of getting the guys."

"How many were there?"

"Two—I think."

Knoblock moved a paper-weight across the desk, then moved it back, as if he were playing a game. "Did Akeley show any signs of being afraid when he was in the speakeasy?"

"I didn't notice."

"Was he drinking hard?"

"He was sober."

Knoblock looked across at Toddy. "What do you think, Toddy?"

"He on'y had four beers, and the kind o' beer we serve, no guy even with a weak stomick could get soused on ten. He was down the end o' the bar talkin' to Cardigan here and when Cardigan said he was breezin' Akeley said he'd breeze to. There was a phone call for Cardigan—"

"A phone call," Knoblock said, merely as a statement.

"Yeah," Toddy said. "I swung the phone over and I guess they got disconnected."

Knoblock said, "Know who it was, Cardigan?"

"No."

"It was on'y a jane," Toddy put in.

"What time?"

"Eleven," said Toddy. "I know because at eleven I was to take some lousy medicine for me liver and it was eleven."

Knoblock made a notation; put his gentle brown eyes on Cardigan. "Cardigan, is there any chance that Akeley was the victim of an accident?"

"I don't get you."

Knoblock smiled gently; ran his tongue along the inside of his nether lip. "I'll put it this way: Is there a possibility that the shots were intended for you?"

"Where do you get that idea?"

"I'm simply asking."

Cardigan shrugged. "There's always a possibility. I've had a finger in sending many a guy to the pen, so why shouldn't there be?"

"I mean—" Knoblock moved the paper-weight to the center of the desk—any particular possibility?"

"Nothing I could lay a finger on—right now."

Knoblock hefted the paper-weight. "You know, Cardigan, I like you. There are a few fellows in the department don't. But I do. I've watched your work. I like your guts. I'm an older man than you, Cardigan, and I've found out through experience that it's good policy to be free with ideas—not to hold them cooped up."

"Thanks," said Cardigan, straight-faced.

"This is murder. Murder of a reporter who was attached to *The Star-Dispatch*. You knew him. It's likely that he might have told you he suspected he was in danger of his life."

"I didn't know Akeley that well."

Knoblock sighed; put the paper-weight down slowly. "Very well, Cardigan. Very well."

The door opened and Detective Sergeant Bush came in. He didn't look at Cardigan. He looked straight at Knoblock.

"It was four shots, inspector," he said. "One went in one cheek and out the other. One got him in the belly. One in the left side. And one smashed his chest. Three o' the slugs were .38s and one was a .45. We looked around the neighborhood for ejected shells but didn't find none. Sergeant Stultz notified the paper and sent Goehrig out to break it to Akeley's family."

Knoblock nodded and said: "We've got to break this case, sergeant. Murder of a reporter usually raises a hell of a row. Break it—we've got to. When a reporter is killed it signifies that he knew something that might implicate someone high up. I thought—" he looked gently at Cardigan "—I thought our friend Cardigan might know, might have been told—even a hint—even the slightest hint...." His voice trailed off.

Bush kept looking straight at Knoblock.

Cardigan kept looking at Bush's stubby, hard-jawed profile. The spectre of a smile moved lightly—once—from left to right on Cardigan's lips.

"Anything else, inspector?" Bush said.

"Not right now."

Bush turned and went out, closing the door softly.

Knoblock wrote something. "What do you think of Bush, Cardigan?" he asked.

"I don't think about Bush." Cardigan said flatly.

Knoblock held his pen poised. "I always did like your guts, Cardigan."

CHAPTER TWO

MAC OF *THE STAR-DISPATCH*

WHEN CARDIGAN let himself into his apartment the lights were on. His first reaction was to reach for his gun.

But he saw Pat Seaward sitting on the divan. She was snapping shut an octagon-shaped, red vanity case. She was small and rather thin and she looked trim and pretty in a quiet, certain way.

Cardigan growled: "So now I suppose because you work for this agency you think you can hang around here."

"*B-r-r!*"

"Yeah? How'd you get in?"

"Picked the lock."

He heaved his topcoat over a chair, went to a secretary and took a bottle of Three Aces, took a stiff jolt and recorked the bottle. He scowled good-naturedly at Pat. "Well, what do you want?"

She said: "For a guy that was on the spot tonight you're pretty cocky."

"How do you know?"

"Well, I'm just a weak woman. I've been tailing you around for the past week, unbeknownst to you, kind sir. You were tailed to that speak by two men, and after you went in they concealed themselves in areaways. I was in another one. I waited a while, intending to do some shooting if trouble started. But I weakened. I hate to use a gun. So I walked to a store two blocks away and telephoned you. Something went flooey with the phone. As I came out I heard shots. I started for the speak and got to the corner and saw you on your feet. So I slipped away and reasoned this the surest place to find you."

"So you've been tailing me around, huh?"

"Forgive me, my lord."

"Cut that crap." He ran his fingers through his shock of hair, said dully: "Akeley got it. A little guy from *The Star-Dispatch*. He tried to get me to come through about Senator Ackerman. Dragged in a sob story about his wife and kids. Cripes—" he bent his shaggy brows "—feel lousy about the wife and kids."

"Yes you do."

"O.K., call me a mug." He leaned on a window-sill and looked down on Lindell Boulevard. He said: "I never liked Akeley and yet the guy accidentally saves me. He was a whining sort of guy; that's why I never liked him. He'd take advantage of you like a woman—through pity and hurt looks. I can't stomach that in a guy. And yet—" he stood up straight, turned, spread palms "—here am I and Akeley is at the morgue."

"Who did it?"

"Mobsters."

"Give me a cigarette."

Without moving he tossed her a package and said: "They were after me all right. Even Knoblock made a pass at that. I told him ixnay."

Pat lit up. "You big dope, why do you insist on holding back? Why don't you tell the cops that Senator Ackerman, Phil Gould and all that crowd are running chills and fever because of what you know? Why don't you? But no—" she shrugged "—you think you're tougher than the whole mob put together and you think it's too effeminate to run to the police."

He said, jabbing a finger toward her: "I've been marking time, sister. It wouldn't give me any swell kick to bust loose with a political scandal. You know me better than that. I've got to get something out of it."

"What you'll get will be what Akeley got."

"Horseflies! And look: I've got to prove that Ackerman sent his mob after me. I'm sure as sure myself, but what proof have I? I know—but I've got to prove it—that Senator Ackerman is the silent partner in the county gambling casino. I saw him out there on a wild party with some chorines from *Mean and Lowdown.* You know as well as I do that when White got bumped off by those guns they thought it was me. But who were the guns? And we've got to prove that they were heels from Ackerman's and Gould's scatter. I should go down to headquarters and clown around with a lot of theories? In the sweet by and by I should!"

Pat polished the nails of her right hand on the heel of her left. "To me sometimes you're a greater mystery than which-was-first-the-egg-or-the-chicken. Either you're over my head or you're just plain ga-ga. That indemnity company hired you to recover stolen ice from White. You recovered it and during the waltz-around you got mixed up in that gambling casino and they thought out there you were trying to get something on them. They try to knock you off and now you recite some bed-time fable. My, you should be cast in bronze!"

He said, patting down the air with his palm: "I just don't run to the cops because some guys take a pot-shot at me. I know what I'm doing. I—"

There was a knock at the door. Cardigan looked at the door; looked at Pat. He drew his gun, crossed the room, opened the door. A man walked into the gun.

"Don't do that, dammit!" the man rasped. "Me with a bum heart and by God I can't come here but that you play cops and robbers—"

"What do you want, McClintock?"

"I want to kiss you, darling. Well! Well! Is there a law against me coming in?… Come on, Cardigan, for noisy tears smile and show the world—"

"Get in, then," Cardigan said.

McClintock entered with gusto, said: "Greetings, Miss Seaward," went directly to the secretary and poured himself a drink.

"Hey," said Cardigan.

"Lousy rye," McClintock said.

He was a wiry, dynamic man, with a snarly mouth, sharp eyes. He wore a blue topcoat; a derby raked over one ear. His hair was pepper-colored around the ears and his nose was pointed like a knife. He sat on the arm of an easy chair and put his feet on the cushion.

"What's the straight dope on it, Cardigan?"

"Your reporter was shot and killed."

"No!" McClintock had a raucous laugh. "Listen, big fella. I was just over to headquarters and they tell me that you don't know a damned thing. As soon as I heard that I knew that you knew something. Now Akeley wasn't on any spot. I know that. These guys that did the shooting were lying on wait and Akeley got in the way. And whom were they waiting for? Ah, that is the mystery—a deep, shadowy mystery larded with many ramifications. An enigma. A startling, provocative, teeming, dirty, lousy mystery. Yeah—like hell!"

He bounded from the chair to the floor, snapped: "You know damned well, Cardigan, that those eggs were promoting your own demise! You know damned well that Akeley's croak was an accident. I don't blame you for holding out on the cops. Not at all." He dropped his voice to a hoarse, rusty mutter. "Why the good cripes should you tell the cops when we can pay you five thousand bucks for the lowdown?

Why should you?"

"You wouldn't be trying to bribe me, would you?"

"Bribe you? Dammit, I'll bribe anybody! Sure I'm trying to bribe you!"

"You're screwy," Cardigan said.

"Oh, so I'm screwy. What a belly-laugh I get out of that. Listen, Cardigan. Akeley was after you to spring some dope about some monkeyshines that took place at Gould's casino and here in the city. The killing of White was a fluke. We got a whisper that State Senator Ackerman is sugar daddy to that casino and there's one guy can confirm it. You're the guy. We like to believe that Gould's mobsters are after you because you know too much about the casino and Ackerman. We're willing to pay good money to verify it."

Cardigan took the bottle of rye and locked it up. "The trouble with you, Mac, is that you're taking a hell of a lot for granted. Akeley's been bothering hell out of me for a couple of weeks. I told him nuts—and I'm telling you nuts."

"But listen to reason, man! Why chuck over five thousand berries? You can't kid me. I know those guys had the finger on you and mobbed out Akeley by mistake. This rag I work for has dough and power and we're out to smear anybody we can. One of our men was murdered. We've got to vindicate him. We've got to make a splurge. It'll jump up our circulation."

Cardigan said, "You think you know they had the finger on me. You don't know, Mac—you don't know a damned thing. You can't bust in here and talk that way to me. It don't go."

McClintock rolled a cigar back and forth between bared teeth. His eyes glinted. "Six thousand, Cardigan."

"Go 'way."

"Seven."

"To hell with you and your rag."

McClintock cackled unpleasantly. "Or maybe you figure you can shake down Gould and Ackerman for more?"

Cardigan looked sullen. "You better go back to the city desk, Mac."

"You never were dumb, shamus."

"A punch in the kisser might do you good."

McClintock rasped: "You can't scare me, big fella! I've taken many a punch in the kisser. Dammit, I'm talking business with you! Akeley was murdered and we're going to get to the bottom of it. You're the key, Cardigan, and you'll turn or be sorry as hell."

"What can you do?"

"I'll do anything to get what I go after. Anything. And I'm after the lowdown on this song and dance and I'm going to get it. Get it, Cardigan!" He shook his fist vibrantly.

Cardigan made a half turn on his heel, walked heavily to the door, opened it. He looked somber.

McClintock bit off: "You're making an enemy of *The Star-Dispatch*, kiddo."

"Yeah. I'm making an enemy of a cheap snot of a city editor. And for two cents I'd throw him down the elevator shaft."

McClintock went to the door, his eyes narrowed, his lips bared tightly over his teeth. "I can find a way to make you strike a bargain, Cardigan."

"Nice big frame, huh?"

"I've got ideas."

"You'll have a broken jaw if you stand there much longer making faces at me."

McClintock shifted his cigar, jammed his hands into his pockets, strode through the door.

Cardigan closed it slowly and looked at Pat. "Mac's a rat," he said.

Pat said: "He'll do you dirt, chief."

CHAPTER THREE

BUSH BUTTS IN

CARDIGAN WALKED into his office at nine next morning and Miss Gilligan, his pop-eyed secretary, said, "Oh, Mr. Cardigan, another terrible, terrible murder! What's the world coming to when people—"

"Any wires from New York?"

"N-no, sir.... It says here that you missed being killed by a hair's breadth—"

"Little more than a hair. Two hairs."

"Oh, Mr. Cardigan, you joke so about death."

"Being alive, I can afford to.... By the way, if that lousy pest Schanzen calls up again about his stolen cash-register, tell him I'm not in. Tell him anything. Only tell him I'm not in. You look swell this morning, Miss Gilligan."

"Oh, thank you, sir!"

Cardigan went into his private office wearing a secret little smile, for Miss Gilligan was far from good-looking and made matters worse by using the wrong kind of rouge, the wrong kind of lipstick.

His staff came out of the adjoining room. Blaine, Hennessy and Katz.

"Ah, the three horsemen," Cardigan said, dropping into his swivel chair, shuffling the morning's mail.

Blaine said: "So it's bruited about that you've been mixed up in an exchange of lead again. *Tsk, tsk!*"

"Yeah," sighed Cardigan. "That poor little slob Akeley.... Did you ever have a dead man fall against you? Did you ever see a guy alive one minute, and then thirty seconds later dead and on his feet and leaning against you? Leaning against you dead—and sliding down you dead with his face shot to hell."

Katz droned: "You talk like a hangover."

Cardigan tore up a letter. "You're new with us, Katz. Ever seen a dead man?"

"Not yet, but I have hopes."

"That's not being hard, Katz. That's just bravado. Once you look in a dead man's eyes you'll never forget it. There's a hell of a fierce concentration in a guy's eyes just as he dies. A lot of ham writers talk about a blank stare. They're nuts. There's nothing blank about a man's eyes when he kicks off. Just like the crap I read about an express bullet whistling as it brushes the down off a guy's ear. That close, there wouldn't be a whistle at all. There'd be a distinct *snick* which is the vacuum of air closing in the bullet's wake."

"What's this a treatise on?" Blaine asked.

Hennessy said: "Was this guy Akeley on the spot? Did a wiper have the cross on him?"

"The chief's morbid this ack emma." Katz said.

Cardigan said: "I think I was the guy on the spot."

"Oh-ho!" Blaine exclaimed softly, nodding his chiseled head. "Am I to infer that certain hired hands of a state senator through a gambling-house owner tried to snuff out our illustrious boss?"

"Anyhow," Cardigan said, "Akeley got it. I went out to see his heirs this morning. A wife and two kids. One kid—three and a half—just over a double-mastoid operation. The other kid—five—in need of treatment for his eyes. Akeley was getting forty-five a week and his family living like a lot of hunkies in a lousy flat on the south side. And the wife anaemic—a little mud-gutter blonde who still can't believe her husband's dead. I tell you, gang, it got me—me of all guys."

"You don't mean to tell us you're going soft," Katz droned.

Cardigan's fist struck the desk. "Damn it to hell, Katz, don't be a smart aleck! I've had a dead guy fall in my arms. I didn't particularly like him—but he was a harmless, no-account reporter! I saw his wife and kids this morning and— You know, this is a lousy business we're in. A guy sees too much that isn't pretty. We're all wise; we're all hard. Until something gets right up close against us. You'll find that out, Katz. Or maybe I'm just a sentimental Mick—hell knows." He shuffled papers. "Go on, you eggs. Scram!"

The trio looked at one another. Blaine wore a thoughtful stare. Katz smirked and arched his eyebrows. Hennessy stroked his jaw and made a whistling mouth but didn't whistle. They went back into the large, adjoining room.

Shaggy-haired, leather-faced, Cardigan went through his mail, a hard party at odds with himself.

Miss Gilligan opened the outer office door, said, with a slight apologetic bow, "Detective Sergeant Bush, sir."

Cardigan glared. "I'm busy!"

"Yes, sir."

The door closed.

Half a minute later it opened.

"How busy?" Bush said.

Cardigan threw down a pencil, leaned back, creaked his swivel chair, folded his big hands on his hard flat stomach. "There's a law," he said, "against throwing out a cop."

Bush's hard jaw jutted as he took slow, studied steps across the floor. Haas, his partner, followed, closing the door quietly and saying nothing in a blank-faced way.

"There's lots of law," Bush grated. "There's a law that's beginning to wonder just how Akeley was bumped off last night."

Cardigan said, "By means of guns in the hands of unknown assailants. What's so tricky about that?"

"There's a trick to every trade, Cardigan. Even yours."

Cardigan stopped rocking in his chair. Two hundred pounds of him remained motionless, and his eyes steadied on Bush. "Your move again, Bush."

Bush sat down. "Maybe yours."

"I'll make one, fat-head. You've got a nerve trying to crack wise with me when I know you're friendly to Ackerman and Gould and that whole crowd in the county; when just a month ago you stood aside while Ackerman tried to bribe me to keep my mouth shut."

"This is murder, though, Cardigan," Bush said, "and I woke up this morning with a bright idea."

"Like hell you did. Somebody gave it to you. A bright idea would give you cataracts, Bush."

Bush sneered. "Where's that Seaward dame?"

"Be here any minute. Why?"

Bush grinned unpleasantly. "We're wondering about that phone call last night. It was damned funny about that. You get a call and then you take Akeley outside and he gets bumped off. Ain't that funny as hell?"

"That call was cut off."

"So you say. Who's to check up on you?"

Cardigan darkened. "You dirty—"

"How?"

Hate burned in Cardigan's eyes. "You dirty louse, you can't afford to try that on me! I didn't take Akeley out!"

"Toddy says you offered to drop him at his paper."

"But after he said he was leaving too."

Bush shook his head. "Toddy didn't hear that."

Cardigan's "Oh" was half muttered. For a long minute his brown jaw hung motionless, his eyes stared vacantly at Bush. His lips moved. "Toddy forgot, eh?"

"I didn't say that."

"I know what you said."

Bush leaned forward. "You were the only one who saw two men running away after the shots were fired. The thing is, was there two men?"

Red color began to creep over Cardigan's face. "You mean to sit there and tell me—"

"I'm not telling you anything."

"No?" roared Cardigan. "You're telling me that I put Akeley on the spot—that's what you're telling me! Why, you lousy—"

"Enough o' that!" Bush barked.

Cardigan's face was contorted. It was dull red in color, and the look in his eyes was malignant. Cords bulged on his powerful neck and red seemed to streak his eyeballs and the corners of his mouth bent downward.

Haas moved from one foot to the other and his hand strayed to his right hip and remained there. His face remained white, expressionless, doughy. Out of the corners of his eyes he watched Bush. And Bush watched Cardigan. A glassy shimmer was in Bush's eyes; his lips were pursed in a fixed, forced smile that had in it nothing of humor. His chunky neck had hard, tight rolls of fat on the nape.

Pat walked in saying, "Good-morning—" and stopped short. Then she said: "Something tells me I've walked in on a conference."

Bush looked at her. "No, lady. You're part of the conference."

Pat pursed neatly carmined lips. "How lovely!" But a wily look was in her eyes.

Cardigan rumbled: "Don't take these guys seriously, Pat."

"What we want to know," Bush said, "is about that phone call last night, Miss Seaward."

She said: "What about it, sergeant."

"Cardigan here got a call in that speak. Toddy Moore, the bartender there, said it was a woman. He gave the phone over to Cardigan and Cardigan said the party was cut off. We began to wonder about that. So we poked around the neighborhood and found a call was made at a few minutes to eleven from a cigar store a few blocks away. The guy in the store remembered a woman had made it and you were easy to describe."

Pat looked at Cardigan, then looked at Bush. "By which I am supposed to infer—what?"

"A couple of minutes after you phoned Cardigan walked out with Akeley and Akeley was rubbed out. The cops that came around didn't see you. You didn't show up at the scene of the murder, yet you made a phone call only a few blocks away."

He stopped talking, hunched his chunky shoulders up alongside his ears, locked his fingers in front of his chest and leaned hard with his elbows on the arms of the chair.

"We checked up," Bush went on. "The phone call was made from that cigar store to the speakeasy. Cardigan says he saw a couple of guys running away—but that's only what he says. Nobody can check up on him because nobody else was in the street. Why did you make that call?"

Pat said: "I wanted to have some words with him. I was cut off. I couldn't get the connection back."

"So you left the cigar store."

"Yes. I left the cigar store and started walking toward the speakeasy when I heard shots. I got far enough to see the chief standing on his feet and another man lying on the sidewalk. It was no place for me so I about-faced and left. I walked over to the Hotel Andromeda, hung around in the lobby for half an hour and then left."

"Where'd you go then?"

"Out to the chief's apartment, to see him and see what happened. I got out there about midnight."

Bush nodded slowly and wore a mocking smile. "In other words, you had plenty of time to ditch a gun on the way."

"I would have, yes, if I'd had a gun I wanted to ditch."

Cardigan growled at Bush: "Two guns did it, lame-brain. A forty-five and a thirty-eight."

"She has two hands, hasn't she?"

Pat smiled. "Isn't this all jolly!"

"So now maybe, Bush, you can tell me why we would have put Akeley on the spot," Cardigan said.

"It may take us some time to find that out, but what interests us now is the trick about the phone call and this woman leaving the scene of the murder. Cardigan fired two shots—he says at two guys—but he could have fired them as a stall. It was pretty shooting that did Akeley in, miss, and we mind the time you came down to the pistol range at headquarters and shot the eye right out of the target."

Cardigan kicked his chair back and stood up. "You're all wet, Bush. You're nuts to try pulling a stunt like this. Akeley was small change to me."

Bush stood up. "We're taking the woman to headquarters."

"You'll want me too, then," Cardigan muttered.

"No." Bush shook his head. "We want the woman first. We'll get you when we want you."

Cardigan went around the desk and gripped Bush's arm. He scowled malignantly. "You get this, you cheap gumshoe: you try any rough stuff on her and I'll beat the living hell out of you!"

"We heard," Bush said, "that Akeley was trying to get something on you for this paper. Something crooked about the recovery of them diamonds from Burt White."

"Oh…" Cardigan's voice was a hoarse whisper. "Oh, I see. I get you, Bush. So McClintock's been putting ideas in your head. Oh… I see. Sure, I thought you were acting abnormally bright this morning. I knew it couldn't be original."

Bush colored; blurted: "You can't make a monkey out o' me, Cardigan!"

"Why the hell should I pick on monkeys?"

CHAPTER FOUR

FANCY FRAME-UP

CARDIGAN CROSSED the ochre-colored tiles of the Roxbury Hotel and entered the elevator. It let him off at the eighth floor and he walked somberly down the corridor, put his hand on the doorknob of 808 and pushed the door open. He hovered in the doorway like a dark cloud that presages bad weather.

McClintock half reclined in bed, the coverlet littered with newspapers. He had on loud pajamas and the room was filled with a haze of cigar smoke. A bottle of gin and glasses stood on a small table.

"Well, as I live and breathe bad air—the old mastermind himself! Come in and try finding a chair. You'll find it stuffy in here but I was born in a stuffy room and it's said that first impressions linger. Take a drink—gin—bell-hop gin. Two drinks and bells ring in your ears and your corpuscles hop. What do you think of the Chinese situation?"

Cardigan took a slow backward kick at the door and slammed it shut. He caught hold of the back of a chair, dragged it across the room and thumped it down beside the bed. He sat down, parked his heels on the edge of the bed and thrust his hands into his topcoat pockets.

"So you go lousy on me, huh, Mac? It takes a Mick to double-cross a Mick every time."

McClintock got off a hearty, raucous laugh and tossed a paper half across the room with great gusto. "The Chinese situation is yellow with age, Cardigan. Ah! A *bon mot!* Ah—China! Land of romance! Temple bells! Do they have temples in China?"

"Lay off, Mac," Cardigan muttered. "Lay off. That was a sweet one you pulled when you put ideas in Bush's head. You want to be careful. Ideas hit Bush like bad liquor. He might even get concussion of the brain."

"Bush is a fine, upstanding policeman."

"Sure, to put over a deal like yours you'd have to pick the only rat in the department. You rats run together, don't you?"

"Language, Cardigan! Language!"

Cardigan's voice rushed out: "You can't get away with a trick like that, Mac! You can't hang that job on Pat Seaward and me!"

"But what a story!"

"You told Bush that Akeley was trying to get something on me. You know that's a stinking lie!"

McClintock sat up, squinted one bitter eye, hitched up one corner of his hard-lipped mouth. "I went to you last night, you dumb ox, and offered you seven-thousand bucks to come across with some info that would put us on the right track and give us a chance to use the biggest headlines in the plant. But no—you got up on your high horse. You were holding out in the hopes of getting a bigger slice from the guys that bumped Akeley off."

"That's a dirty lie!"

"So you pretend! I came out straight with what I was after. I tried to bribe you in a straightforward way, on the up-and-up and no ace from the bottom. And you gave me a verbal kick in the pants. All right. Now—" he shook his finger at Cardigan "—I go you one better. I'll get what I want. I'll get it for nothing! I won't pay a cent for it! I'll plaster you and the jane in the swellest frame you ever saw. I'll make you squawk to get you and the jane out—and there won't be any dough in it. I'll get a knock-out legal battery. I'll get this story and to do it I'll rake your hide over the coals till you yell 'Uncle!' I'll get the straight about the recovery of those diamonds. I'll get the straight about Ackerman and his affiliations with Gould and that gambling crowd. That's what I'll do, my dear sweet Mr. Cardigan—you bum!"

"You'll drag in Bush. He didn't buy that new Lincoln on a cop's salary."

"To hell with Bush. I'll use him till I squeeze him dry and then to hell with him. Bush means nothing to me. You mean nothing to me. The jane means nothing to me. The only thing that matters a damn is whether or not I get that story. And, big fella, I'll get it! So help me God, I'll get it!"

Cardigan dropped his heels from the bed, reached over and yanked sheets and blankets to the floor. McClintock twisted. His hand shot beneath the pillow, came out gripping a heavy automatic. His lips snarled over his teeth and he cackled raucously.

"No you don't!" he rasped. "Get back, big fella, or I'll blow you to hell!"

Cardigan hung poised over the bed, scowling. "I guess you would, Mac."

"Sure. Why not? You broke into my room. 'Famous city editor kills private detective in self-defense.' A big stick on the right and the good old name of McClintock prominent in every paragraph. To make it more dramatic I'll say you pulled a gun on me. What a story that would be! And I'd like to make it one, Cardigan—I'd like to make it one. Make a grab at this gun—and give me a break."

Cardigan straightened, his jaw red and heavy, dull hatred smouldering in his eyes. "I'd like to meet you in a dark alley some night, Mac."

"So would I. I'd plug you in the back and make a big story out of that too."

Cardigan went to the door, put his hand on the knob. "Be seeing you again, Mac."

"Swell!"

Cardigan walked heavily down the corridor. He cursed and kept cursing deep in his throat till the elevator doors opened.

He went across to police headquarters and found Pat downstairs in one of two detention rooms. The room was clean and bright. Down the corridor were the women's cell blocks. A matron left Cardigan at the door and Cardigan entered the room.

"Didn't you bring flowers, chief?"

"Hello, Pat." Cardigan sat down on a chair, put his big hands on his knees and looked at her. "Good kid," he murmured.

"So this is McClintock's doing."

Cardigan nodded his shaggy head. "The rat.... What happened, kid?"

"Nothing much. I took your advice and didn't take Bush seriously. I kidded the ears off him. He got all hot and bothered and now he's waiting for Inspector Knoblock to show up. What should I say?"

"Stick to your story till I look around. This guy McClintock burns me up and I'm going to hurt him. I've got to get these guys red-hot that bumped Akeley off. This is no time to spring names at random. After all I've only got suspicions—no facts. That bum McClintock will never get this story—never. He's framed us and I'll pay him back with interest. How do you feel?"

"Fine and dandy."

"You're a brick, Pat. You're the berries. Give me till tonight to crash this frame. You'll never spend the night here, kid."

She said: "Bush wasn't so dumb. He didn't want you because he knows you. He knows he wouldn't get a murmur out of you. But he thinks I'll weaken. And he knows that if they make this case seem bad enough for me—you'll be Irish and bust down and—"

"That's correct up till there, Pat. But Bush really thinks he'll nail us for this job because that great brain McClintock talked him into believing it. Bush'll work his head off—what head he has. McClintock's the brains in this. Bush is just a babe in his hands. McClintock engineered this."

"Don't worry about me, chief. Only if I have to stay here you'll have to run over to my hotel and get me a nightie."

He stood up. "You won't stay here, kid."

He walked to his hotel, entered the writing room, sat down and wrote three pages of dark, crisp script. He addressed the envelope to himself at the agency office and took it down to the post office. He sent it by registered mail and slipped the receipt into his vest pocket.

MR. ULLRICH, Senator Ackerman's right-hand man, was a rolypoly fat man with cheeks like red apples and bubbling, twinkling eyes. He had a big-toothed grin in a small mouth and tried to minimize the impression of avoirdupois by bounding around on his toes. The impression one got, however, was that Mr. Ullrich was an overanimated elephant.

"Well, well, well, Mr. Cardigan! How do you do, how do you do, how—"

"How do you do," said Cardigan.

Ullrich's office was paneled in dark wood. The desk was a massive, carved piece out of some museum. Ullrich had bounced and bobbed from the desk and gripped Cardigan's hand. Cardigan shook it, but not with enthusiasm. He had a dark, steady eye on Ullrich and the set of his face was not pleasant.

"This is a lovely day, Mr. Cardigan! It's wonderful to be alive on a day like this, to see and feel the sun—"

"Akeley's family, for instance."

"I beg pardon?"

"I suppose Akeley's wife is just doing a dance and raving about the beauties of nature too."

"Akeley.... Oh, yes! Oh, my yes! Oh, you mean that poor chap who was murdered last night. Horrible!"

"Any minute I suppose you'll bust out and cry."

Ullrich affected a hurt look. "My dear Mr. Cardigan—"

"My dear Mr. Cardigan my dear sweet aunt's eye! I didn't come here to have you pull a burlesque on me! You're Senator Ackerman's mouthpiece. You be his ears too. And listen." His voice dropped. "Listen, Mr. Ullrich."

"Yes?"

Cardigan's voice dropped another note. "You know as well as I do that I was the one who was supposed to have got bumped off last night. Me. I was tailed to that speakeasy. The rats didn't have the guts to come in after me. They waited out in the street, probably all hopped up, and when I came out—and when Akeley stumbled and got in the way—those guys' hands were so hot on their rods they had to let go. Me they wanted. Akeley they got—a skinny little no-account newshawk. You hear!"

Ullrich stepped back, putting his hand to his chest, looking shocked and innocent. "But my dear Mr. Cardigan, my sympathy is all with the family of the deceased. It is, truly. But yet I cannot fathom out why you burst in here—"

"For the love of God," Cardigan's deep voice throbbed, "don't go in for the old run around! Don't!" He chopped his fist through the air. "You know me. I know you. Standing orders from my boss in New York are never to break a political scandal. Never. Unless it's the last resort. Phil Gould—and you—and Ackerman—you're all in a dirty big puddle. I could make a fortune springing what I know about you. I've turned down a bribe already. I never went out of my way to find these things out about you guys. It just happened. Yet, by cripes, all of you have done your damnedest to silence me. First by bribery—which I turned down. Then guns. Then guns again—last night—and another blunder. I was willing to play the lone wolf. I never run to the cops crying for help. I was ready to snoop out these heels of yours and shoot it out with them. But it's off now. It's no go. Somebody has to take the rap for the murder of Akeley. Somebody—" his voice grated "—in your own back yard."

Ullrich pulled a silk handkerchief from his breast pocket, patted his forehead, his cheeks, raised his chin and patted his throat.

"I will say, Mr. Cardigan, that you gave me a start. Indeed, sir, you gave me a start. Indeed you did!"

"You can't laugh it off, Ullrich. I promise you, you can't laugh it off."

Ullrich folded his handkerchief carefully, slipped it into his breast pocket, patted the pocket. "Now, Mr. Cardigan—my dear Mr. Cardigan. You assume too great a public spirit—and the weight of it may one day bear you down—"

"It's not public spirit, Ullrich. It's just that some guys have gone into a huddle and come to the conclusion that my aide Miss Seaward gave Akeley the works."

"How atrocious!"

"To me, it's just lousy. And there's only one thing to do about it. The night, one month ago, when Burt White was murdered while in my car, it was forgotten quickly because White himself was a heel. I'd recovered stolen diamonds from him and he'd shot his girl friend, run out, jumped in my car. A murder car got him—thinking it was me. That was easy to forget. But this time a reporter was bumped off. That's bad. So there's only one thing to do. I want the guys that did Akeley in."

Ullrich put his head on one side. "I see you are in deadly earnest, Mr. Cardigan."

"It's got to be swan-song for somebody—and not for Miss Seaward or me."

"You are an uncommonly hard man to handle, Mr. Cardigan."

"You and your mob have tried like hell to get rid of me, Ullrich. I'm hard to get rid of. In the beginning I never knew one tenth as much about you as you thought I did. But now I know a lot. Ordinarily I'd shut up. But you guys forced this. Get started doing something. Miss Seaward's in the holdover and she's got to be out by night."

Ullrich tried to look cheerful through a sheen of perspiration that had formed on his face. "Sit down, Mr. Cardigan. Please sit down."

He bobbed to the desk, rubbed his hands together, took a deep breath, reached for the telephone.

Cardigan said: "And no clowning."

CHAPTER FIVE

SCAREHEAD STUFF

SENATOR ACKERMAN was a lantern-jawed tall man with steely eyes weakened by dark half-moons beneath them. He closed the heavy office door quietly, flexed his lips against his teeth and put fists into the pockets of his dark blue coat. He made his stare hard and straight on Cardigan.

Ullrich said, bounding from one foot to the other: "Mr. Cardigan has a grievance."

"I like how you put it," Cardigan chuckled harshly.

Ackerman's voice was blunt. "Now see here, Cardigan; I've had enough of your interference."

"I'm not interfering. I'm here to get the guys that bumped off Akeley. I've not been engaged by anybody to get them. But headquarters has got Miss Seaward in for questioning and there's influence that will hang the kill on us."

Ackerman scowled. "What makes you think we know anything about the murder?"

"It's not the first time your mobsters tried to get me, senator. But it's the last. Miss Seaward got onto the tail of two guys that were tailing me last night. When I went in that speak they waited outside. She tried to warn me by telephone but the connection was cut off. Akeley got in the way—and Akeley got killed instead of me. There's only one guy would want to see me silenced. And you're the guy. I'm banking on that."

"You cannot prove that, Cardigan."

"Does Miss Seaward stay in the holdover tonight? Am I going to be hauled in on a framed charge, cost myself and my agency a lot of money? Or are you going to turn over the guys that killed Akeley?"

Ackerman's eyes were frigid. "I—am—going—to—do—nothing, Cardigan."

"You've got the most guts of anybody in your scatter," Cardigan said, "but that's not enough. Your reputation's at stake. I see your point of view. You'll brazen it out." He shook his head. "But you'll never make it. I can give what I know to *The Star-Dispatch,* but for spite I haven't so far. I can, though. I hate McClintock and his whole tribe but I can forget that. I want the guys that did the killing."

He strode to the desk, put his hand on the telephone.

"Who made the pinch of your aide?"

"Bush."

Ackerman cursed. "Give me that phone." He called headquarters, spoke with Bush tartly, told him to come over. "And right now!" he finished hotly.

When Bush arrived he was quite out of breath.

Ackerman said coldly: "Bush, Cardigan tells me that you pinched Miss Seaward on suspicion for the Akeley murder."

"Yes," Bush said, scowling at Cardigan, "and before night we're going to clamp on this guy too."

Ackerman's voice grew colder. "Why did you pick the woman up, Bush?"

"We had a right to. She was around the scene of the murder. She made a telephone call to Cardigan from a store a couple o' blocks away. Then Cardigan takes Akeley out. Then Akeley's bumped off and the woman never shows her mug."

Ackerman scowled. "Why the hell didn't you tell me something about this?"

"I wanted to surprise you. It's a red-hot, Senator. Akeley was trying for a couple o' weeks to get something on Cardigan about the recovery of that ice from Burt White—"

"Who told you that?"

Bush colored, swallowed. "A—a guy on *The Star-Dispatch.*"

Cardigan growled: "McClintock put that bug in his brain."

"McClintock!" Ackerman got up, his face darkening. "You fat-head, what right have you to go into cahoots with McClintock?"

Bush looked scared. "I ain't in cahoots. But it was hot—it was red-hot. He was sure the woman did it and he gave me lots of reasons for it."

"I don't give a damn what he thought!" Ackerman bellowed. "You half-witted idiot! McClintock—of all men, McClintock!"

Bush gaped. "But why?"

"I'll tell you why," Cardigan said. "And it's a scream. Mac's one of your great enemies, senator. And he's one of mine. I hate him like nobody's business. And here he is playing us one against the other. The bum tried to pay me seven-thousand bucks to break him some dope about you and Gould's casino and some other things I'm supposed to know about you. I kicked him out. Because I hate his guts and because I never take a bribe. I'd always have to be living it down. So he comes back at me through Bush. He gets Bush all steamed up about Miss Seaward and Bush falls for it. Why? Because Bush hates me like poison. Because he'd like to see me take a long rap. And because he's dumb—or wise, and if wise, he's taking a slice of graft from *The Star-Dispatch*."

Bush shook with rage. Spluttering made his lips wet. "That's all one of your dirty lies, Cardigan. It's—"

"Shut up," Ackerman cut in icily.

The room fell silent.

"Oh," ground out Ackerman, "you unmitigated fool! You idiot! You hopeless blockhead!"

"Good gracious!" breathed Ullrich.

Bush stuttered, "B-but—"

"Enough!" chopped off Ackerman. "I see it all. I see McClintock's line of thought. No, you wouldn't. But it's got to stop, Bush! McClintock will throw you to the wolves when he's used you. You've got to take water. You've got to let that woman go, that's all."

Bush went white. "Let her go! By God, I can't. It's slated for the evening papers. Inspector Knoblock's working on the case too, now, and—God, I can't take water! I can't explain. If I let McClintock down—"

"Who's your friend, Bush," Ackerman said, "McClintock or me? Who's the man who put you where you are today?"

"But don't you see—"

"I see either one of two things. Either you're dumber than I ever thought you were, or you're double-crossing me."

Bush raised a shaking hand, shook his head violently. "No—no, I'm not double-crossing anybody—"

"Me, you're trying to," Cardigan said.

"You—you!" Bush bellowed. "You are always razzing me! Ever since you came here—"

"Quiet," Ackerman said. "This guy Cardigan is after us. You'll have to drop this case against him. You'll have to tell Knoblock and the chief anything you want—but this case must be dropped. We can't afford it."

Bush made a sound something like a moan. "I didn't mean wrong, senator. Honest to God, I didn't!"

Ackerman was cold. "You made the wrong move, Bush. You've got to straighten it out."

The words ached out of Bush's throat: "But I can't!"

"My dear senator," said Ullrich, fluttering, "let us pause to consider, to reason things out."

"There's nothing to reason out," snapped Ackerman.

Cardigan said: "I'll say there isn't," and stood up, a lowering look in his eyes. "The whole trouble here is that all of you guys are in the mud. You want to throw Bush for the fall-guy now. But that won't end things. I'm tightening down. I'm after material evidence—and the best material evidence will be the two guys that bumped off Akeley. And that's what I want."

Ackerman, his face livid now, crossed the room and faced Cardigan. "I warn you to damper down, Cardigan."

Cardigan reached out and laid his hand on the telephone. "I warn you, senator."

Bush began raving like a man gone mad. "I won't be no fall-guy! I got the jane and this guy to rights. I can hang this kill—"

"You rat," Cardigan muttered.

Bush held his hand out. "I'll take your gun, Cardigan."

"You will?" Cardigan showed his teeth. "I'll show you something you won't forget, gumshoe. I'll show—" He slipped his hand beneath the left lapel of his coat.

Ullrich, his eyes shimmering, moved on his heel. A gun leaped in his hand. Exploded.

Cardigan turned half around, looking at Ullrich with shocked eyes. Cardigan wheeled against the desk, bounced away from it, hit a chair and crashed down to the floor, taking the chair with him. His head banged against a radiator.

Ullrich wore a pop-eyed smile. His voice leaped from his lips. "This does it, my dear senator! He tried to draw a gun on a police officer! Assault with intent to kill!"

Bush spluttered, "He—he—"

"Shut up, Bush!" Ullrich cried. "You saw him! You, senator—you saw him! It's the only way out—it's the only out! Indeed—indeed it is!"

Ackerman stood rigid, rooted to his feet, his eyes staring at Ullrich. "By George!" he whispered hoarsely. "You've hit upon it! I always knew you could be relied upon—in a pinch!"

Cardigan lay panting, half propped against the radiator, his hands spread-fingered on the floor.

Ullrich took two bobbing steps, moistened his lips, gripped his gun hard. He looked at Ackerman.

He whispered, showing his teeth in a queer smile, "It would be doubly certain if he were exterminated completely. We hang suspended by a single cord." His wide, bubbling eyes turned on Cardigan. His gun came up.

Cardigan's voice rushed out. "Do it and weep, Ullrich! I'm no fool! Not all fool! Before I came here I wrote out the highlights in the dirt against you. I sent it to myself—registered mail—care of my office. It's in the mails now—where you can't get it, where, by God, you can't bargain with me to get it! Pull that rod, you wiper—pull it!"

Ullrich almost stumbled. His fat hand began to shake. His eyes did not bubble. His fat face became contorted and his lower lip popped out with a slight sound, hung loose and shining.

Bush put a hand to his eyes, moaned. Veins stood out on Ackerman's temples.

Outside the door, suddenly, there were sounds of a scuffle, a hoarse cry. The door whipped open violently and McClintock, his derby smashed in, his tie half undone, barged in, slammed the door shut, locked it.

"This is the lousiest, damnedest place to get into I ever saw!" he rasped.

THROATY, rattle-voiced, Ackerman said: "There has been a little unpleasantness here."

"Now isn't that news! By cripes, I've been parked half an hour on my pants downstairs trying to get up here. The longest I've ever waited for anybody—two presidents and a bootlegger included. So I heard the boom-boom... and was it a close race to the door with your secretary? Boy, did I sock him?" He became suddenly sky-eyed. "Well, senator?"

Ackerman nodded to Cardigan. "This fellow came in here. You know him, I believe. Detective Sergeant Bush came here after him—to take him to headquarters for questioning. He resented by attempting to draw a gun."

Ullrich nodded politely, saying: "I did my best to protect an officer of the law."

Cardigan got up slowly and leaned against the radiator. He took off his topcoat, suit coat and vest; took a handful of his shirt and ripped it off; ripped off his undershirt. He twisted his neck and looked down at his right side, where blood flowed slowly. He made a face.

"This is going to be a story," McClintock said. "A lalapaloosa! Did you shoot him from behind, Ullrich, or was he looking at you? How'd he do it, Cardigan, you big bum?"

Ullrich said: "Cardigan went for his gun. He shoved his hand inside his lapel—"

"Oh, yeah?" Cardigan said. "When my gun is—" he drew it from his hip-pocket "—here!"

Ullrich stared. "You said—"

"I said I was going to show Bush something he'd never forget." He took from his upper left-hand pocket of his vest a small slip of paper. "This. The receipt for that registered letter. The letter that's in the mails now!"

Bush swung on McClintock. "You said you were sure Cardigan and the woman had a deal in that Akeley kill. Tell him! When I tried to pinch—when I asked him in a nice way for his gun—"

"You damned liar!" Cardigan roared. "You're all liars! I had you all tied up. Only Ullrich saw a way out—when you went meshuga and asked me for my gun. Only Ullrich—and the fat slob yanked his gun and let me have it. Let me have it—because he had two witnesses to say I pulled a rod! *Pulled it from an armpit holster!* When you see—now—and even McClintock sees that it was on my hip. And I've got you all tied up now."

He lunged to the desk, grabbed up the phone. Ackerman jumped and got him from behind, around the neck. Yanked him away and sent him spinning against the wall. The phone banged to the desk. Drops of blood flew from Cardigan's wound.

"Let me at that phone!" Cardigan bellowed.

Ackerman said: "Listen—a minute," and got in Cardigan's path.

Cardigan hit him on the jaw and sent him against Ullrich, and

Ullrich fell down. But Ackerman stayed up and flung himself between Cardigan and the desk.

"Let me—get Knoblock!" Cardigan snarled.

McClintock grabbed up the phone and snapped into it: "Get me *The Star-Dispatch!*"

Ullrich knocked him down and McClintock, hanging on grimly, tore the telephone wires from the box.

Ullrich panted: "Please, sir—"

"Please me—will you!" McClintock cried, scrambling to his feet.

He hurled the instrument at Ullrich.

Bush, looking horrified, turned and fled. Fled to the door. Got his hand on the knob and was turning the key when Cardigan came plowing across the room, grabbed him by the neck, swung him around and hurled him across the room. Bush recovered and tried again.

"Let me out of here!" he cried. "I ain't done nothing! I want to get—"

"Stay back!" muttered Cardigan savagely. "You heel, you're a disgrace to the shield you wear!"

But Bush was crazed. "So help me Cardigan—" His gun was in his hand.

Cardigan crowded him, grabbed Bush's gun hand. The gun boomed.

A gash appeared in the dark wood of the wall and Cardigan, dripping blood and sweat, twisted Bush to the floor, twisted the gun from his hand, left Bush moaning and grovelling.

Ullrich fell into a chair, a glazed stare in his eyes.

Ackerman took two steps, ripped the gun from Ullrich's hand, turned it on himself. McClintock fell on him—but as the gun exploded. Ackerman went down to his knees, fell forward on his face.

The room was a shambles when a dozen men broke down the door and rushed in.

"Listen, Cardigan," McClintock barked. "What the hell's the use of bleeding to death? Why don't you let me bind you up?"

"You sure think the world of me, don't you?"

"Yeah—a world of dirty names. But I like your style, big fella. And—say—what a story!"

THE room was still a shambles ten minutes later. It was filled with blue-coated policemen. There were an ambulance doctor, another doctor. Knoblock was there.

Ackerman lay on a stretcher. "We all went mad," he murmured. "Things happened so fast. There was no time—to talk—explain. I was in—deep. I knew I was in deep. Cardigan was after us. There was no shaking him off—no bargaining with him."

"You fool," Knoblock said, sadly.

"I know. And it was—pretty bad—knowing he knew something—and not knowing just how much he knew. I took the chance. I sent two men after him. To end—the suspense. They bungled. And then—there was nothing to do—but bargain—and he wouldn't—he wouldn't listen—to—anything. Give Ullrich—and Bush—a break."

His head fell to one side and one of the doctors said: "That's all. That's the end."

Knoblock turned a clouded face toward Ullrich. "There'll be two men we want. He said—two."

Ullrich did not smile. His voice was like a ghost's. "Yes, my dear inspector. I can give you the names."

Downstairs, Cardigan was sitting in an ambulance, smoking a cigarette.

"Should you ask me," McClintock said, "I wouldn't hang around here."

Cardigan said: "That's an idea," and climbed out.

McClintock hailed a cab, handed Cardigan in and followed.

"Listen," Cardigan said, "I don't need you for a nurse. Go on. Beat it."

"Say—I'll get you a nurse that'll knock your eye out. Not because I like you, Irish. But because I like your style. You're the first real, honest-to-cripes opposition I've had in years. You're a pick-me-up after about a ten-year hangover."

"Baloney!"

McClintock laughed raucously. "And how I slice it!"

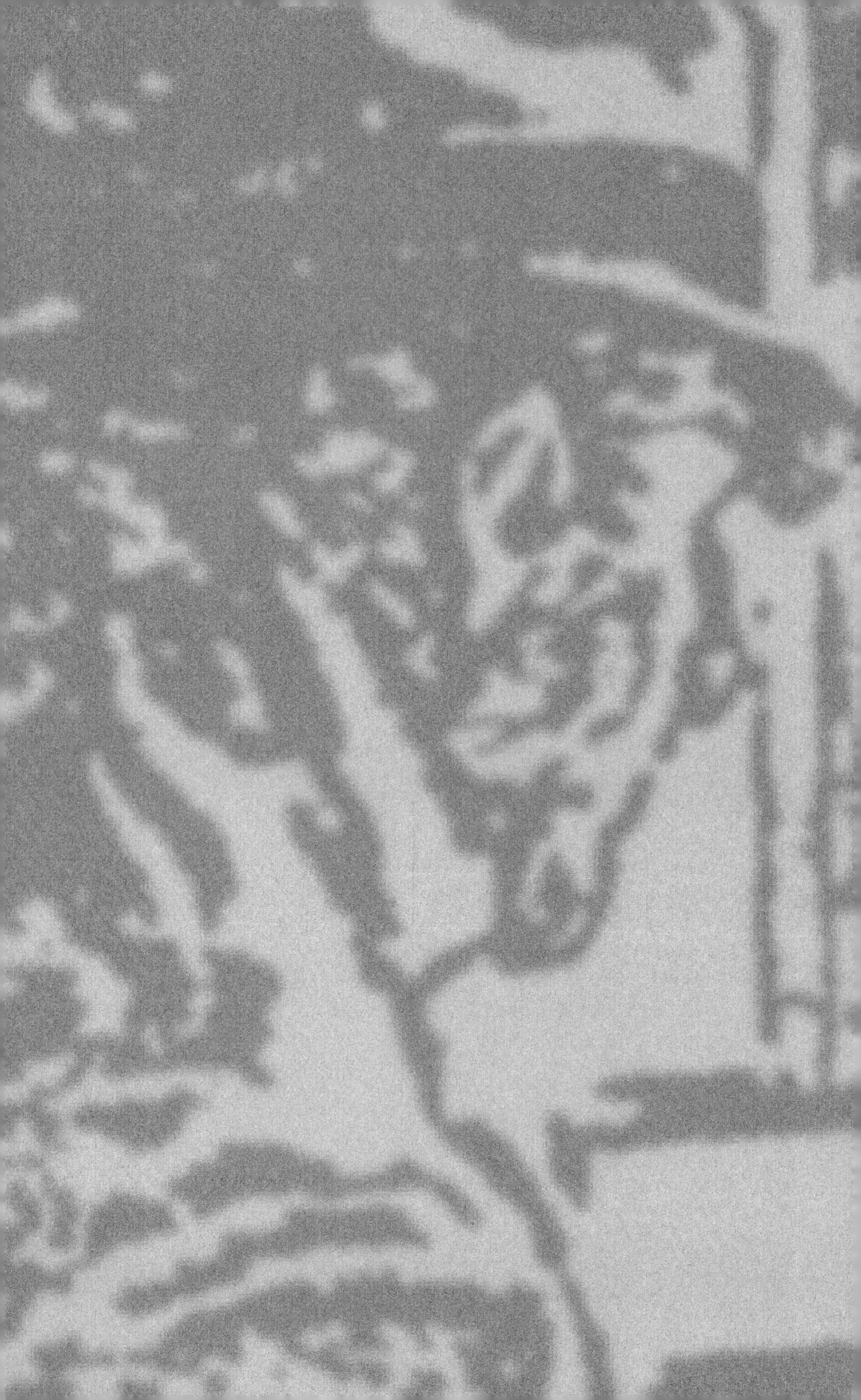

PHANTOM FINGERS

THREE TIMES THOSE LIVID PRINTS HAD BEEN FOUND ON DEAD MEN'S THROATS—THREE TIMES THE MYSTERIOUS WIDOW HAD MADE HER KILL. AND NOW, A GRIM AVENGER, DETECTIVE CARDIGAN SETS OUT TO RIP AWAY THOSE MOURNING WEEDS THAT VEIL MURDER.

CHAPTER ONE

MR. BARTLES OF 303

PAT SEAWARD was locking the office door from the outside and Cardigan was halfway toward the elevators when the telephone rang. Pat looked after Cardigan, called: "Phone, chief. Should I let it slide?"

"Yeah, let it slide."

"Well, maybe I'd better answer it."

"O.K. Answer it."

Cardigan stopped and leaned against the wall, his faded fedora battered down over one eye, shaggy gobs of hair sticking out around his ears.

Pat reappeared. "For you, chief."

Cardigan growled: "I thought my day was done," and went slowly, heavy-footed, toward the office.

Pat sang, lightly: "When day is done and evening shadows—"

"All right, brat, all right. Let that slide too."

"Arf! Arf!"

He entered the outer office, swept up the telephone. "Hello.... Yes, this is Cardigan.... Just a minute." He put the phone on the desk, leaned down, collected pencil and pad. "Spell it, please.... Yeah, I've got it.... *Uhunh*—Westminster." He looked up at Pat, looked down at the pad again, wrote scattered notes. "Well, it's five-thirty now.... Well, if it's important I could.... *Uhunh*. O.K., then.... I get you. Sure.... Good-by."

He depressed the hook with his right hand, hefted the receiver in his left for a moment and then slapped it into the hook. He tore a sheet off the pad, regarded it, regarded Pat quizzically.

"This is funny," he said. "A guy named Bartles out in the Western

Arms is having a jane call on him at six and wants a private detective out there to sit through the interview. Details—" he stroked his jaw—"when I get there."

"So what?"

"He's sick a-bed."

"Maybe he wants you to hold his hand or something."

Cardigan folded the slip of paper, tucked it into a vest pocket, grabbed Pat by the arm and hustled her out. "For two cents I'd slap you down. Get along, you."

"But first I must lock the *casa, señor*."

Cardigan went on to the elevators, caught a downbound car and held it while Pat came skipping down the corridor. Below in the lobby Cardigan said: "If you promise to shut up I'll drop you at your hotel."

"Promise," she said, with a flash of long eyelashes.

They rode west on Olive, turned right at Twelfth and stopped in front of the Hotel Andromeda. Cardigan got out, handed out Pat and said: "Dinner at eight and omit the mascara."

"Oh, you big, strong silent man!"

"Scram!"

Cardigan saw it was not the man whose picture had been on the handbill.

Chuckling, he climbed back into the cab, gave a number on Westminster. The cab went up Locust past double-decker busses. At

Channing it swung into Lindell and went over the hump past the big Masonic building. The rush of air through the open windows was cold and Cardigan held his hat between his hands and let the wind tousel his shaggy crop of black hair. The cab made a right turn into Vandeventer, caught a green light at McPherson and took the next left into Westminster.

The Western Arms was not pretentious, but it raised six stories of red brick which the chemical cleaners had recently gone over. It had a green lawn out front and a narrow cement terrace with six wicker armchairs in a row. The lobby was clean, cool and deserted. There was no desk—no elevator.

Cardigan climbed three flights of stairs, walked toward the front of the building until he came to a door marked 303. This door was made of horizontal blinds and when he opened it there was another, regular door of dark wood. He knocked on this, then turned the knob, opened it.

"Mr. Bartles."

The living room was dark because the blinds were half drawn. Bartles had said over the phone that he should walk right in. Cardigan, having closed the door, said again: "Mr. Bartles."

The living room was stuffy. Objects began to make themselves apparent as Cardigan's eyes became accustomed to the dim room. He went toward a partly open door, but turned back when he saw it led to a bathroom. He espied another door across the room and walked toward it, wearing a wrinkled frown.

The door was open and Cardigan saw first the foot of a brass bed and next the shape of a body beneath a white coverlet.

"Mr. Bartles."

Westminster was a quiet street and there was no sound of traffic. A clock was ticking in the room. The shades were drawn all the way down. The shape on the bed remained motionless.

Cardigan took a few steps into the room, moved nearer to the side of the bed. His hand went out and he turned on a small reading lamp that stood on a table beside the bed.

He muttered: "Oh," quietly.

His hand shot in beneath a blue pajama coat, remained there while his eyes regarded a twisted, discolored face. He stood up again and put his fists on his hips. There was a slip of paper lying on the little bed-table. On it had been scrawled hastily the name of his agency, the address, and then across one corner his own name.

"*Um,*" he muttered.

HE DID not disturb the paper. His lips felt dry and he moistened them with his tongue. He looked at the alarm clock on the table. It was ten to six.

There was a green ash tray with the stub of a cigarette resting in one of three niches. Cardigan bent closer. There was a hint of red color on the end of the cigarette that had been between two lips. Rouge....

Cardigan looked at the clock again. Beside it was a telephone. He picked up the telephone and said: "Police Headquarters." He glanced around the dim room with thoughtful eyes. "Headquarters?... This is Cardigan, the Cosmos head. Say, there's a guy dead in apartment 303 at number—Westminster.... Where am I? In the apartment.... Oh, I just walked in. I had a date.... Bartles.... Well, strangulation.... Sure, I'll stay here."

He hung up and put the phone back on the table, gently.

Bartles was a small man—skinny. Even alive he must have been a dry and twisted clinker of a man, standing perhaps five feet five, weighing perhaps a hundred and ten. His fingers were like bones. His chest was bony. His body didn't make much of a lump in the big brass bed. Pitiful body, all wasted and bone-ridden.

"*Um,*" said Cardigan with a vast, heavy sigh.

He turned on more lights. He opened a closet door and looked at clothes hanging there. A black alpaca suit—a tan linen suit—a dark blue suit of serge, of fair but not excellent quality—a soiled shirt hanging on a hook. On the floor of the closet—a suitcase of worn, cracked leather and a smaller handbag—a drab gray overcoat. Marks on the clothing showed where labels had been ripped out. Shoes on the floor—a black pair and a tan pair, both pairs old with soles curving upward.

Cardigan went back to the bed-table, rapped the sides. He found a small drawer, opened it and found a worn pin-seal wallet. Bills were packed neatly into one of the folds: five hundred and twenty dollars. Otherwise the wallet contained nothing. He returned it to the drawer, bent down to look at a pair of worn slippers.

Beneath the head of the bed, where wall met floor, he saw an automatic pistol. He reached under and got it. It was a .30 caliber

Luger. He smelled the muzzle, put the gun down beside the telephone.

He stood looking abstractedly at the door leading to the living room, then strode toward it and entered the room, looking for a light switch. He heard a scraping sound. In a split second the dim form of a man crowded him and Cardigan felt the hard muzzle of a gun pressing against his stomach.

An instant later there was a man behind him. Wedged between two guns, Cardigan let his hand slide away from his hip.

"Git 'em up!" muttered the big man facing Cardigan.

When Cardigan's hands rose the man behind him took the gun off his hip and said: "Got his gat."

The big man had on a tremendous overcoat, the collar turned up. A floppy hat he wore was yanked down far over his eyes. His face was nothing more than a shadow which emitted harsh, deep-voiced sounds.

"Now them other things, bo—them other things," he grated.

"Them what?" Cardigan said.

"Ah-r-r!" rasped the man behind, jabbing his gun hard against the small of Cardigan's back. "Lay off that, lay off that!" The big man menaced: "You hear, bo—you hear!"

"You birds cripples? Search me."

"Arnie," the big man growled, "frisk him. If he moves I let him have it."

CARDIGAN felt small, nervous hands ransack his pockets. He peered hard and tried to make out the features of the man he faced. It was impossible. Darkness had fallen rapidly. The room was quite dark now. Way behind him was the bar of light coming from the bedroom.

"Remember, Arnie—six o' them."

Arnie gave up. "They ain't on him. He musta bunked them."

The big man muttered in a deep, passionate voice: "Bo, we ain't foolin'! We want 'em! Six o' them!"

"You frisked me, didn't you?"

"We frisked you and they wasn't there! You killed Bartles for them—"

"If I had them they'd be on me, wouldn't they?"

The big man grated: "I ain't askin' you for questions, bo! By God, I mean what I say! You got 'em. You gotta have 'em! Six, bo—six. And they don't take up much room and they're worth enough as I'd blow your belly out to get 'em. You hear me! I ain't lettin' eighty thousand in emeralds git away from us! There's been too much double-crossin' goin' on and— Listen, bo, maybe you ain't got me right. I'm a killer."

The wail of a siren came up from the street. The big man stiffened.

"What the hell's that?" he growled.

The small man cat-footed to a window. "Cops!" he gasped, whirling.

"Stoppin' here?"

"Out front!"

The big man seemed to bulge in his overcoat. The small man was a shadow scampering to the door.

"On the lam, 'Beef'!" he hissed.

The big man towered, swayed. Suddenly he swore. His gun whipped up, chopped down. It ran against Cardigan's head. Cardigan muttered: *"Unh,"* staggered back a step, reached out a hand blindly, felt the wall and held himself up with a great effort.

The big man followed the small man through the door.

Cardigan felt his way along the wall, snapped on the light switch. He looked at himself in a mirror, took off his hat, punched out the dent the blow had left, replaced the hat on his head. He saw his gun lying on a divan where the small man had tossed it. He recovered it and put it back in his pocket. He looked at himself again in the mirror. There was no blood. Only a throbbing pain on the top of his head.

Making a face, he stood with clenched fists and muttered a stream of oaths in a low, vindictive voice. Then he stopped swearing and rolled a thought off his tongue: "Six emeralds… eighty thousand bucks." Savageness had fled from his eyes and his eyes narrowed and a tightness came to his lips.

Flying glances hit and stopped on a low, thin-legged desk. He lunged to it, sent fingers probing rapidly into pigeon-holes. Dusty pigeon-holes. Nothing there. He yanked open a drawer and found two pint bottles of Bourbon lying side by side. Nothing else.

He turned and went lunging into the bathroom, searched the cabinet over the wash-basin. He let out a short oath as pain beat harder through his head. Finally he left the bathroom with long, swift strides, as if he were headed for a definite point. He stopped in the middle of the floor and looked exasperated.

A small portable gramophone stood on a low end-table by the

divan. He went to it, picked it up, shook it. *Body and Soul* fell off, rolled across the floor. Cardigan put the gramophone down, straightened, listened.

He went back into the bedroom, took his handkerchief and unscrewed the brass knobs on the bed-posts. He shook the knobs and listened and then screwed them back on. The pain throbbed harder again and he closed his eyes and winced and when the pain lessened he cursed and tramped back into the living room.

His eye dropped on the record that had rolled off the gramophone. He picked it up and carried it back to the end-table. He looked round and round the room intently, looked for something he might have overlooked.

"Six emeralds," he muttered. "Eighty thousand bucks."

He dropped to the divan, stretched out his legs, lit a cigarette. He heard the clatter of heels coming up the stairway. The door opened and a man stood there.

"Hello, Cardigan."

"Hello, Fitz."

CHAPTER TWO

GREEN ICE

SOME UNIFORMED cops remained in the hall. Some came into the apartment and looked around. Lieutenant Fitz, plain-clothes, followed Cardigan's gesture and went into the bedroom. Dumpy Sergeant Conkey made eyes at Cardigan, grinned, made mysterious gestures with pudgy hands. He grinned eternally. He looked over his shoulder at Cardigan as he followed Fitz into the bedroom. His moon face beamed like an idiot's.

"Hey, Cardigan." That was Fitz—lantern-jawed, lean-boned, somber-eyed.

Cardigan went across the room and leaned in the connecting doorway.

"When'd you find him?" Fitz rapped impersonally.

"Ten to six."

"How come?"

"When I was leaving the office the phone rang and this guy asked me to come right out. Said a jane was calling on him and he wanted me here. Said he'd explain when I got here. I thought I might pick up twenty-five bucks—and it was on my way home."

"What's his name?"

"Bartles. He'd told me to walk right in. He said he was sick in bed. So I walked in. Found him—this way. The gun there was lying on the floor, so don't throw a fit if you find my print on it. I picked it up. It hadn't been fired recently. There's a wallet in the table drawer containing five hundred and twenty bucks."

"Couldn't you leave things alone?" Fitz snapped.

"You know how it is."

Fitz took out the wallet, counted the money. He examined the gun. It was fully loaded. Fitz looked at the dead man. He chewed on his lip and his eyes scowled. Conkey pried into the closet, tossed out the clothes. The coroner's man came in and made a superficial examination while carrying on a spirited conversation with Fitz about the stock market.

A cop marched a baffled-looking man into the bedroom and the man almost took a header when he saw the body.

Fitz scowled. "Who're you?"

"He's the manager or something here," the cop said.

Fitz pointed. "This guy's dead. He was choked to death between five-thirty and ten to six. How long's he lived here?"

"Only—a week. He paid a month in advance."

"Know anything about him?"

"No, sir. I didn't see him from the day he took it."

"Took what?"

"Why—the—this apartment."

Fitz settled on his heels, tossed off shortly: "Get in anybody living in apartments around and above and below this one. And you come back too."

Conkey was happily tearing apart the clothing on the floor.

Fitz jabbed Cardigan with a frank stare. "Are you sure this guy didn't tell you anything else?"

"Sure."

Fitz dropped his voice, dropped a glance toward the body. "Happen to know him?"

"Never saw him before."

"Why do you suppose he wanted you here?"

Cardigan shrugged. "You've got me, Fitz. I guess he was afraid of the dame."

"He didn't give her name?"

"No."

Conkey said cheerfully, "No labels in these duds, Fitz. There was though, once." He got up and went over and looked down at the twisted face. "Nope. I don't know him, either. Hey, here's a watch under his pillow."

He held up a big gold watch by a chain. He pried open the back of it and something fell out and fluttered to the floor. Conkey bent down and retrieved the picture of a girl. Patiently it had been sheared down, rounded to fit the back of the watch.

"Not bad-looking," Conkey said. "Huh, Fitz?" He held it up and Fitz scowled at it.

CARDIGAN went into the room and looked innocently over Fitz's shoulder. Fitz glanced around at him.

"What makes you interested, Cardigan?"

"Conkey said she was good-looking."

Conkey said, beaming: "That picture ain't been in there long. It's new. You can see it's new." His mouth was wide open, grinning. His big pop-eyes sparkled.

There were voices in the living room and a cop said that some people had come in with the manager. Fitz strode briskly from the bedroom, struck at each new face with a swift, bitter glance.

He said: "There was a murder committed here between five-thirty and ten to six. Anybody hear anything?"

No one had. Fitz seemed angry. He whirled suddenly and drove a kick to the seat of a man who was training a camera through the bedroom doorway. The man turned around, grinned and tipped his hat.

"Sorry, lieutenant."

"Get the hell out!" Fitz bit off.

The news photographer went out with mincing steps.

Fitz turned back to the group. "Well, then, did anybody see anybody in the halls, or hear anybody about that time going up or down? Speak! Don't look scared, dammit—I'm not going to bite you!"

"Well," ventured a spinsterish little lady and paused to make a gentle curtsey.

"Well, madam?" said Fitz stonily.

"Well, I live directly beneath this apartment. I was coming in at about twenty to six. It was rather dark in the hall. So I had a time finding the keyhole and when I finally found it I saw a woman come down from this floor and go on down toward the lobby."

"What'd she look like?"

"Well, sir, the only thing I know was she was wearing mourning. There was half a veil hanging from her hat, and she was kind of tall, I would say. I mind I listened, rather fascinated, to the way her steps were going down the stairs—slow and measured kind of. I felt sorry for her, sir."

"You didn't see her face?"

"No, sir."

Fitz snapped: "Anybody else see this woman?"

There were negative movements of heads.

"You may go," Fitz clipped.

When they had gone Fitz said to the cop stationed at the door: "Close it—and if that photographer shows up again kick him in the face."

Cardigan buttoned his topcoat. "You know where to find me, Fitz, in case you want me."

Fitz chewed on his lip. "What do you think of this?"

"I'd say, offhand, that there's a killing widow loose in town."

Fitz said: "Mind if we look you over?"

Cardigan chuckled good-naturedly and held his arms out. Fitz searched his pockets, read the notation Cardigan had made in his office. Cardigan kept smiling down at Fitz's bony face. Fitz stepped back and eyed him levelly.

"O.K. I just wanted to make sure. It's funny as hell, the way this happened, the way you happened to be the first on the scene."

Conkey was grinning, showing most of his teeth clamped on a cigar. Cardigan looked from Conkey back to Fitz, chuckled briefly deep in his throat and strode to the door. He opened it and passed into the hall and went down the stairs slowly.

Halfway down, a fierce breath gushed out of his mouth and he raised a hand to his head, dropped the hand hopelessly. He covered the remainder of the steps with a savage, reckless gait; reached the cement terrace and stood for a moment in the blustering wind, looking up and down the dark street. He lit a cigarette and sloped to the sidewalk, caught a taxi at Vandeventer.

PAT leaned back against the door and laughed softly, gently—eyes twinkling. Cardigan glowered from the mohair divan in his apartment and said over a glass of rye and White Rock: "Clown around now, clown around."

"But you do look a perfect scream, chief."

There was a turkish towel rapped around his head. In the hidden folds of the towel was a quantity of chipped ice, to freeze away the pain. He looked quaintly oriental.

"Run into something?" Pat asked.

Back of the droll humor in her eyes was a spark of concern. Another woman might have exclaimed, run to him with tender hands. But Pat knew her men, knew, particularly, Cardigan. He was a hard party, hated to be fussed over.

"Maybe," he said, took a swallow, added: "Pardon me if I don't get up and kiss your little hand, madame. I might get the ice down my neck.... Well, some big bruiser—I couldn't figure him out—he took a swing at me."

He gave her the details. She sat on the edge of the divan, looked at empty dinner dishes on a card-table, and listened. Occasionally she said: *"M-m-m!"* or "My!" or used her lips or eyebrows to register surprise, concern.

"So that," Cardigan said, "is why we didn't dine and dance tonight. I walked into something all right."

"But don't you think you should have told Fitz about those two men?"

"Sure I should have. I should do a lot of things. But I didn't. Besides, those two guys didn't kill Bartles. Besides—" his eyelids lowered— "there's eighty thousand dollars worth of green ice floating around this man's town. Stolen, you can bet. Well, they pay rewards for stolen jools, Calamity Jane. And papa needs new shoes and a vacation from this lousy business and maybe he could salvage some of his stocks."

"Sure. But the home office might get peeved."

Cardigan said: "This is private business."

"O.K.," Pat said, shrugged. "You'd have your own way anyhow. And with that—" she indicated his head—"you're off to a swell start, I might add cattily."

"Maybe I'd give you a bauble or a gadget or something."

"Greeks bearing gifts."

Cardigan chuckled lazily. "Good little woiking goil."

"Another forward pass like that and I'll smack you!"

Cardigan finished his drink, spread himself in a rousing grunt of satisfaction, and said: "Mind you, kid, keep what I've told you under your hat. There's a few guys in the office who'd break their necks to tattle-tale to the home office in the hopes of getting my job. The business is getting too big. Too many operatives. Too much—envy."

Pat made a little jaw. "I certainly know one—" She stopped short and sat silently.

"Huh?"

"Nothing."

"Tell papa."

"I'll mention no names."

Admiration lay drowsily in his eyes. "You're a natural, Pat," he said. "You're sure a natural."

POP-EYED Miss Gilligan was all of atwitter when Cardigan pushed into the office next morning.

"Oh, Mr. Cardigan, you f-figured in a m-murder again, oh!"

Cardigan mocked the magisterial. "Please don't put it that way, Miss Gilligan."

"Did the p-poor man suf-suffer?"

Miss Gilligan was not ordinarily a stammerer, but headlines invariably knocked her askew. She was a good-hearted, unlovely, faithful secretary.

"Any wires?" Cardigan said.

"N-no, sir."

He entered his private office, taking off his big overcoat, hung it with his battered hat on a costumer in the corner. Morris Katz came and stood in the doorway leading to the operatives' room. He was tall, dark, with sliding hazel eyes, polished ebony hair, and arresting clothes.

"Greetings or condolences?" he droned languidly.

Cardigan said: "Good morning, Katz," and sat down at his desk.

"Who was this Bartles?"

"Bartles—that's all."

"What's all this crap in the papers about a mysterious widow?"

Cardigan said: "Just what it says," and became absorbed in the morning mail. His back was to Katz. His hair, so black, thick and bushy, hid the bump on his head.

Katz remained leaning in the doorway, a striking figure of a man in his dark, polished hardness. The agency used him a lot at formal dances, dinner parties and big social and political functions.

"Was there really a widow?"

"There was a widow," Cardigan said, "in the building at the time. A woman in mourning."

"Talkative, aren't you, this morning?"

Cardigan turned down a letter. "Aren't you on that Willis job, Katz?"

"Sort of."

"Then get the hell on it. There's no special privileges around here."

"I get you. Only concerning the *femme*, huh?"

Cardigan rose, turned and crossed the room and regarded Katz with candid malevolence. "Watch that tongue of yours."

Katz showed even white teeth in a crooked brazen smile. "You wouldn't be getting tough, would you?"

"I happen to be running this shebang. Get on the job."

Katz shrugged, dropped his sliding eyes and went back into the big room. He came out wearing a tan polo coat and a secret little smirk. He walked quietly on soft leather soles. From the back he had an athlete's build. Vanishing, he left an aromatic odor of Turkish tobacco.

At ten Miss Gilligan announced that Sergeant Conkey was calling, and a moment later Conkey's round face appeared in the doorway—beaming as usual, with eyebrows halfway up his forehead, eyes bursting with bright wonder, and mouth grinning and pushing up fat cheeks into bloated red balls. He came toward the desk in a bunch like a bear's, palms pressed to his sides; then he shot one hand outward as if executing a rare trick in magic.

"Good morning to you, Cardigan!"

Always a little baffled by this man's hocus-pocus, Cardigan shook hands casually and said, "To you, sergeant."

"Ah!" Conkey exclaimed as if receiving a great favor. His voice was no voice at all but a rushing hoarse whisper which he somehow managed to freight with wonder and mystery.

Cardigan hooked a heel on an open drawer of his desk and watched Conkey sit down opposite.

CHAPTER THREE

BIG MAN—LITTLE MAN

CONKEY SAID: "Fitz thought I ought to drop in and see if anything turned up since last night." Eyes shimmered, mouth grinned in eager anticipation.

"Not a thing, Conkey."

Conkey aimed a finger joyously at Cardigan. "Who do you think Bartles was?" He raised his hand, put thumb against second finger and held the forefinger rigidly straight.

"Dunno, Conkey."

Conkey snapped his fingers. "No sooner was his picture in the papers this morning than a gent named Hardin calls up from Cleverly Hotel and says Bartles looked like one of four guys that held up his jewelry store in Indianapolis two months ago. We get Hardin over at the morgue and he says Bartles not only looks like the guy but is the guy."

"There's a break for you," Cardigan said.

Conkey exclaimed: "Ain't it!"

"Sure is."

Conkey rubbed his hands together slowly and put shining, merry eyes on Cardigan. "And so a guy who lives in a house back of the Western Arms calls up and says about six last night he was putting his car in his garage. He seen two guys come out the basement door o' the Western Arms. One's little and one's big. Big, little—see? And these guys stand for a couple minutes and then go away. So, reading in the paper this morning about the murder, he calls up."

"That's interesting."

"Ain't it!" His eyes bubbled. "Fitz was wondering, since you got there before six, Fitz was wondering didn't you maybe scare away two guys."

Cardigan leaned back, clasped hands behind his head. "If I did, I didn't see them."

Conkey looked almost ridiculously coy. "Fitz thought maybe you saw them but didn't link it up with anything."

"No."

Conkey darted out a finger. "That's what I said! I told Fitz that if you saw them, you'd sure as hell tell us; you wouldn't let a thing like that slip your mind. That's what I told Fitz. I said, 'Hell, Fitz, Cardigan wouldn't forget a thing like that.' That's what I said."

The way he leaned forward, with mouth and eyes eager, gave the impression that he was hard of hearing and trying to read lips.

"How about that widow?" Cardigan asked.

"Great possibility! 'Sure,' Allison from *The Globe-Herald* said, 'Make it a widow. Better headlines, better story. Go ahead, you guys, make it a widow.' But finding now this Mr. Hardin from Indianapolis and the guy that says he saw—"

A door banged. The inner connecting door burst open and Pat came in, flushed and out of breath. The presence of another in the office besides Cardigan whipped her up short. She appeared like a flame suddenly blown tall and thin and congealed and her teeth bit into her lip and the red color of her face deepened. Something struggled valiantly in her eyes and her lips started to twitch as she felt she had to say something and didn't quite know what.

So she said, breathless: "How—how is your hurt head this morning?"

The fleeting look on Cardigan's face gave the impression that he felt like a man with a bridge suddenly giving way beneath him.

But he said. "Swell.... Now I don't want to have you busting in here late every day, but if you keep on running to work like that something'll happen to you."

She gasped: "I—I'm sorry."

Cardigan became gruffly formal. "That's O.K. Don't let it happen again. And don't try to wash things up by asking about my health. I'm busy. Please...." He nodded toward the big operatives' room.

She made a meek little bow and disappeared.

Cardigan, frowning, moved about some objects on his desk and said: "Women, women, Conkey—especially in this kind of a business."

All of Conkey's face was toned down to a shallow, softly radiating expression of mirth and bafflement. He looked at the door Pat had closed behind her. He looked at the ceiling, at the wall, at various objects in the room. Then his face went blank—like a light snuffed out—and an instant later was beaming again, joyous and cheerful and buoyant.

"Hope you weren't hurt too bad, Cardigan."

Cardigan said: "When people build doorways high enough for guys like me, I guess I'll stop cracking the old dome."

Conkey bounced to his feet like a heavy rubber ball, put his palms on his sides and then shot his right hand forward. "Well, been a pleasant little call, Cardigan."

"Any time, sergeant," Cardigan said, rising and shaking hands.

"You know Fitz, always shooting me around to bother folks. Hope I ain't bothered you. Fitz is all right, but you know Fitz. Come around for pinochle sometimes, Cardigan."

He swivelled like a squat turret and went out with a heavy, bounding tread, humming an air of *Pagliacci*. He left behind him in that room a weird admixture of carnival mirth, side-show cunning, that left Cardigan high and dry as to what it was all about.

Cardigan clipped a short, exasperated oath between teeth that clicked. He turned and looked at the closed door leading to the big room. He went to the other door and opened it and saw Miss Gilligan in violent combat with the typewriter. He closed the door, crossed the room and sat on the desk.

"Pat," he called.

MUCH of the flush had gone from her face when she reappeared. There was evidence that she had touched up with puff and lipstick. A black hat with a pert little brim was raked becomingly over one ear.

"So I pulled a boner," she said.

"Outside of that, what did you pull?" He flipped open a plain cedarwood box. "Smoke?"

"Never before breakfast and toothbrush."

"Been out all night?"

She dropped to a chair and wagged her head. "And was it a night, milord—was it a night! Look at my shoes. I walked."

"Serves you right."

"What a big help you are to come home to. I feel as if I want to put my head on your shoulder and weep—and tell all."

"Cut out the clowning."

She settled back and looked gravely at him. "When I left you last night I walked out of your apartment house and heard footsteps coming down the front walk back of me. When I turned a chap took me by the arm. I said, 'Pul-lease!' and he said, quite to the point: 'You got a date, sister.' I said: 'With you?' He said: 'No. With this gat in my pocket—if you try any shenanigans.' So I went along with him and we were joined by a big fellow and then we all hopped in a car and I was blindfolded and we drove off. Miles. At least it felt like miles."

Cardigan didn't exclaim. He kept regarding her with intense, narrowed eyes.

She said: "I was hustled into a house, into a room. The blindfold was removed—and there I was! In a beastly room, all smelly and simply frightful. And there were the two chaps, the big one and the little one. I was so mad I forgot to be frightened.

"It seems they'd tailed you to your apartment when you left the scene of the murder. The little one hid in the linen room obliquely across from your door. The other one waited at the car. The little one had hoped you'd come out again. Instead, I went in—he saw me—and he saw me come out half an hour later and took it into his head that I was your moll and tailed me. What I get for knowing folks like you."

"They hurt you?"

She pulled up a sleeve, showed some black and blue marks. "Only these—some very crude arm-twisting—and I'll tell you I'll bet I kicked holes in their shins."

"The mutts," he growled.

"So they swore high up and low down that you killed Bartles, that I was your moll and that they'd kill you if I didn't tell all. Whereupon, I said: 'First you'll have to find him.' Well, that brought the house down and brought on the arm-twisting. A little later—it really hurt—I passed out."

Cardigan smacked fist into palm.

"But wait," Pat said. "When I came to, the room was deserted. The door was locked. I was up three stories, couldn't jump. I tried the lock with a hairpin. No go. I turned up the mattress, forced one of the little circular springs from the bed-spring, twisted it to a shape I wanted and tried the lock again. It took me ten minutes to open the door and I used the back of my little nail file to take four screws from the snap lock on the hall door. And so out."

A glimmer of admiration in Cardigan's eyes was followed by: "Swell, kid—Swell!"

"I got the number of the house and when I got to the first corner I got the name of the street. 205 Ellsworth. By this time dawn was breaking. There were no taxis, no street cars. So I began walking and then I got sick and sat down in a doorway and like a fool I began crying. An old Italian woman opened the door and she made me come in and gave me a drink and I was dizzy and sick and went to sleep. So when I woke up I walked again and found a street car and got off when I saw the first taxi and took it and here I am."

Cardigan grumbled: "Poor kid," and regarding her gravely, his thatchlike eyebrows shadowing his eyes.

"That was Sergeant Conkey, wasn't it?" she asked.

"Yeah."

"I'm sorry, chief."

"Forget it. Only Conkey has something up his sleeve. He put on a fine act here. He gets me, that guy does. I always expect him to pull rabbits or something out of his hat. They know who Bartles is—or was. It was a jewel-store stick-up in Indianapolis."

"Really!"

Cardigan nodded and went dejectedly to the window where he stood, spread-legged, staring down into Olive Street. A scowl began to overshadow his face, his lips tightened and then curled in a wintry, sardonic smile.

Conkey and Morris Katz were standing on the corner, talking.

CARDIGAN lunched in the Clevely Coffee Shop, then climbed into a taxi and said: "Ellsworth and Hale," and settled back with a dappled cigar. The sky was overcast, the air muggy and motionless. Sounds reechoed with a dull, heavy clarity, as in a fog. Street cars slam-banged over switches and trucks came up like thunder out of side streets. Neon lights scrawled red script in the gloom.

Far over on the South Side Hale Street crossed Ellsworth and Cardigan got out and stood on the corner watching the taxi disappear. A block north an old brewery reared forlornly. Squat, dumpy houses crowded each other in a galaxy of colors, heights and stages of decay.

Cardigan turned down Ellsworth. The street was shoddy, quiet. A rusty garbage can, overturned and empty, gave the impression that everybody in the street had packed up and gone away. 205 Ellsworth was a narrow frame house with a door flush with the cracked sidewalk. The windows of its three stories were shattered.

Cardigan used a gloved hand to try the knob and miraculously the door swung open. Something scraped on the floor. It was the black snap lock that Pat had unscrewed. Cardigan closed the door and stood for a moment in the dim, musty hallway. Presently he groped his way till he found the staircase. He climbed slowly, a step at a time, and paused on the first landing. Hearing no sound, he moved and found the second staircase and climbed to the top.

There was a door slightly ajar. He drew his gun and swung the door open. Light filtered in from a dirty window. The room was empty. The mattress of a bed had been removed to the floor. Obviously this was the room in which Pat had been detained. He retired quietly and moved down the hall. In another room, a larger one, he found six five-gallon crocks of mash. In another room he found a still. A third room was empty of anything but dust.

He went down the staircase to the second floor and stood for a moment in perplexed indecision. Then he moved and his groping hand found a door, groped until it found a knob which he turned slowly. The door gave. A glow of wan daylight hung outside the horizontal blinds of dark shutters but did not penetrate the room.

His knee struck something and there was a slight metallic squeak. A bed-spring. He pulled a match from his pocket, struck it on a thumb nail and watched the glow spread to a wide-eyed face on the bed. He blew the match out abruptly and breathed quickly once or twice. He moved and swung his arm in an arc above his head, over and over, until a chain rattled against glass. He pulled the chain and light flooded the room.

There were two beds in the room. On each bed lay a dead man. One was big, burly, the contour of his head and shoulders was similar to that of the big man who had cracked him in Bartles' apartment. The smaller man's mouth was slack showing broken teeth. On each man's throat were fingermarks.

Cardigan's heavy brown features froze in a grimace that lasted a long minute. He put his hands in his overcoat pockets and stood looking vaguely around the room. Presently he crossed to an old roll-top desk. There was a sheet of paper on which figures had been scrawled, added at the bottom making a total of $243.50. In a pigeon-hole was a batch of papers: advertisements of various kinds of malt, flavoring, a Burlington time-table, a clipping from a magazine setting forth the advantages of Wildflower Hair Tonic and another advertising a full set of false teeth—former price twenty-five dollars, reduced to nineteen-fifty. A pamphlet entitled, *How to Win the Girl of Your Dreams,* a speakeasy address in Columbus, Ohio, a magazine picture of Clara Bow, a pink handbill, slightly yellow, advertising *The Vagabond Road Show,* on the lower half of which were photographs of a man and a girl: Vantura & Arline, Famous Acrobats.

"*Um,*" mumbled Cardigan.

Arline was the same girl whose picture Conkey had found in the back of Bartles' watch.

Cardigan folded the handbill and stuffed it into his pocket, returned the other papers to the pigeon-hole. He pivoted and regarded the two dead men on the bed. He took slow steps across the room and stopped short when he heard a sound from the hallway. His right hand plunged into his pocket, came out gripping his gun.

He watched the half-open door. He saw a hand holding a gun come into the shaft of light that escaped the room. He moved to one side and his jaw hardened.

"Hello, chief," Katz said and lowered his gun.

CHAPTER FOUR

KATZ CUTS IN—AND OUT

CARDIGAN WENT to the doorway and stood looking stonily at Katz. Katz put his hands in his pocket and stood rocking easily on his heels and waving the skirt of his long tan polo coat.

"Thought you might need help, chief."

Cardigan put away his gun and lifted his hard brown jaw, opened the door wide and said: "How's your stomach, Katz?"

Katz saw the dead men on the bed and drew a secret little smirk across his lips, leaving his handsome white teeth bared.

"Dead, I take it."

"Smart, you are," Cardigan said. "Smart-alecky."

Katz acknowledged this with a raised eyebrow, sauntered into the room, looked icily at each of the dead men and then glanced negligently about the room. He walked to a chair, sat down and hung a long leg over one knee.

"Cute," he said.

Cardigan muttered: "What's on your mind?"

"Fifty per cent."

"I thought maybe you'd want eighty."

"No use being sarcastic, Cardigan."

Cardigan snapped: "You dirty cake-eater, you can go to hell!"

"Can I?" droned Katz, smiling. "You wouldn't be talking out of turn, would you?" He folded his arms, revealing a strap-watch held to his wrist by gold links. "You can't waltz me around, chief. There's dough in this and I'm going to horn in for a cozy slice of it."

"Yeah… and where's the dough?"

"That, mastermind, I leave to you."

"I see. I go around taking the chances, maybe get it, maybe not—and if I do, you get fifty-fifty."

"Precisely."

"What a belly laugh I get out o' that!" Cardigan put his hands on his stomach, then took them away, made fists and jammed the fists into his pockets. His face became overshadowed and lowering and a dull, malignant fire glowed in his eyes. "You heard me, you cheap tinhorn. You heard me. Ixnay. Nix." He opened one fist and sliced his hand through the air. "Nix!"

Katz stood up, tall and lean and smoothly hard, his satin-dark jaw gleaming. His voice droned: "You thick Irish tramp, if you have to report this to the cops, they'll wonder how come you happened to find these guys. Just as how come you found Bartles. They'll know these mugs."

"Who," Cardigan intoned dully, "says I have to report this to the cops?"

Katz tapped his own chest. "I do—me. I do unless I get a fifty per cent rake-off. By God, there's dough in this and you're not going to hog it!"

"This is not an agency job, Katz. The agency has to stay out of it. I stumbled into this and I'm not asking anybody to take chances with me. It's a rough go. There've been three murders inside of twenty-four hours and—"

"I'm not taking chances, Cardigan—not me. I'm standing by, marking time. You're taking the chances. I'm not even going to get my feet wet. I'm going to watch you."

Cardigan said, scarce above a whisper: "What a sweet stinking rat you turned out to be. Well—" his voice banged suddenly—"to hell with you!"

"To hell with me—and I wise the cops. They'll find these stiffs before the day's out—but I'll wise them beforehand who found them."

"I said—to hell with you."

Katz warned: "Conkey's no fool. I told Conkey I'd keep an eye on you."

"You heard what I said."

Katz inhaled, walked to the desk and picked up the telephone. He held it before him reluctant to raise the receiver. "Think it over, Cardigan. Think fast. We can get a big rake-off out of this. There's fifteen per cent of eighty thousand for the guy that gets those emeralds. Half an' half of that, Cardigan—"

"Half and half of hell! What I said stands!"

"Thick, stubborn and Irish, eh?"

"Thick, stubborn and Irish," Cardigan said.

Katz said: "O.K.," and took off the receiver.

IRRITABLE, moody-eyed, Fitz entered the room with quick, short steps, looked at the bodies on the bed and went to the closer of the two. Conkey bounded heavily through the doorway, threw his stomach out, sneezed violently. Fitz half turned and scowled irritably.

"Pepper," Conkey said, and winked.

Fitz rasped matter-of-factly: "Same thing as Bartles. Choked."

Uniformed policemen circulated and the coroner's man came in jauntily, said: *"Tsk! Tsk!"* and pranced over beside Fitz.

Fitz stood up and his face jerked into tight, sarcastic lines. "It's beginning to be a source of wonder to me, Cardigan, how the living hell you manage to be first on the scene of every murder in this town."

Conkey exclaimed: " 'S marvelous, ain't it!" and beamed.

"Shut up," Fitz clipped shortly.

The coroner's man said: "Simple strangulation. No! I think chloroform was used first. Indeed! But not—not on the other fellow. You know—what's his name—Bottles."

"Bartles," Conkey said.

"Oh, yes—oh, yes—Bartley."

"Well?" snapped Fitz, looking hard and bitter at Cardigan.

Cardigan stirred. "Well, here it is: Miss Seaward, my operative, was kidnaped last night when she left my apartment. I didn't know it until she turned up in my office this morning. She said two men had waylaid her, blindfolded her and taken her away. She was beaten; she fainted. When she came to she pried her way out of the room on the top floor, pried her way out of the hall door below—at about dawn. She was sick and didn't get back to the office until late. She remembered the address. I came out here to get tough and found these bodies. Katz, here, thinking I was going into danger, covered me."

"How long did it take you to make up that story?" Fitz asked.

"About a minute—since you came in here."

"Don't be funny."

"I'm not. What the hell do you want me to do, break down and get dramatic?"

Conkey chirped, gleefully: "These are the guys all right! Arnie Oldham and George Beef Cunarko! That's three! Then there's the jane and a guy named Doke. Bless my soul—"

"All right, all right," Fitz cut in irritably.

A cop poked in, said: "There's mash and a still upstairs."

Conkey dived down between the two beds like a hippo and came up, staggering but beaming, and holding a charred cigarette. "See! Rouge on it, too! Holy Moses, I'd hate to have a jane like that!"

Fitz took the butt from him, examined it beneath the light, then tucked it away in his wallet and bent exasperated eyes on Cardigan.

"This crime links up with the Bartles one. It's queer as hell how you happened to be on both."

"I explained, didn't I?"

"What did they kidnap the woman for?"

"She didn't stay long enough to find out. I imagine they wanted her as hostage, hoping to get out of me some information. Maybe they thought Bartles had engaged me already and I knew a lot. Something like that, anyhow."

Conkey exploded in an uproar of mirth. "How's the hurt on your head, Cardigan?"

"Swell."

Conkey pawed gleefully at Fitz's sleeve and bubbled: "Yeah, Cardigan's got a hurt on his head. He said—ho! ho!—it was a door! Bless my soul!"

Katz looked askance at Cardigan and Fitz crossed the room and stopped very close to Cardigan.

Fitz said crisply: "I don't like monkeyshines, Cardigan."

"I never liked them myself—"

"Cut it!"

Cardigan knew good metal when he saw it. He knew Fitz. This lean, moody, rasp-voiced man was nobody's fool.

Cardigan said: "I told you what, Fitz. Whether you take it or leave it there's nothing you can do about it. Maybe you think I know who murdered Bartles and these two guys. I don't. I swear by God that—right now—I don't know. Conkey—bless my soul—thinks a bump on my head means something. And what about that?... I came here to bust two guys who gave Miss Seaward a rough deal. I found them dead."

Fitz looked at Katz. "What about you?"

"I covered him up."

Cardigan glanced quizzically at Katz and Conkey rocked hugely on his heels and pawed happily at his jowls.

The coroner's man said: "These men have been dead about twelve hours or so."

Fitz, swallowing, looked bitterly at Cardigan and said: "I'd like to do something to you, Cardigan."

"Only call your shots, Fitz. That badge you wear don't make you God."

"You can't lone-wolf it in this man's town."

"When I can't," Cardigan said, "tell me."

"I'm telling you now!"

Cardigan smiled. "You ought to know by this time, Fitz, that I'm no pushover."

HE BUTTONED his coat, yanked his hat lower and strode to the door. He plunged down the stairs and walked up Ellsworth. When he was nearing Hale he heard footfalls and saw Katz following. He stopped at the corner and kept baleful eyes on Katz while the latter drew nearer.

"You smell, Katz. You play both ends against the middle—you and me against Conkey and Fitz, or you and Conkey against Fitz."

"Any means toward an end. Dough in my pocket is as good as it is in yours."

"Only it won't ever be in yours."

"So says you."

"You don't rate, Katz. You're small change and you're all spent. If I catch you on my tail again I'll cave in those pretty teeth of yours."

He pivoted and strode off.

When he barged into his office carrying three newspapers Miss Gillian fluttered.

"Oh, I'm g-glad you're back safe."

"What now?"

"Oh, I just had a f-feeling."

He grinned, said: "That's a nice dress you have on," and went on into his private office.

Pat said: "I found out finally that that Maloney girl has been robbing the till at that restaurant for three months to support a drunken brother."

"O.K.," Cardigan said. "Write the report out in full and I'll sign it and shoot it to our client…. Well, there's been another murder—two."

"Where?"

"Where you spent the night."

"Oh-oh."

"The two guys who kidnaped you. And Katz—well, Katz is trying to bust into big time. The dirty louse tried to bargain with me and I told him where to get off."

"How were they killed?"

Cardigan held up his hands and looked at her.

She said: "Doesn't this put you in a tough spot?"

"Kind of—but I like it. Go ahead and make that report up. I'm busy."

She left the room, regarding him over her shoulder. He began turning sheets of one paper, scanning the columns closely. He finished with it and started on the second, turning sheet after sheet until finally his forefinger settled on an advertisement. He took shears from a drawer, made two slices upward, one across, lifting a column a foot long. He cut off ten inches of this, retained the smaller portion, leaned back and studied it reflectively, then slipped it into his vest pocket.

For five minutes he sat motionless, his fingers interlocked, stormy shadows moving in his eyes. Then he slapped a palm on the desk and called: "Miss Gilligan!"

She appeared in the doorway with a notebook.

"Take a letter."

"Oh, yes, sir."

"Address it to me, the Cosmos Agency, and so forth, dear sir. All right. 'Dear Sir: I hereby tender my resignation, under the above date. Trusting you will accept, I remain.' That's all. Draw a check to Morris Katz for—" he figured on a pad "—twenty-seven-fifty. I'll sign it."

"That's all?"

"That's all."

When Katz sauntered in, an hour later, Cardigan pointed and said, offhand: "Sign that."

Katz leaned on his arms, read the letter, looked, at Cardigan. "Funny, aren't you?"

"Sign it or I'll fire you."

"Like hell I'll sign it."

Cardigan reached over, removed the clip which attached the check to the letter and slapped the check down. "O.K. Have it your way. You're fired."

"Now just a minute, big boy—"

"Shut up!" Cardigan rose ominously, pointed to the check. "Take that and get to hell out of my office before I throw you out!"

"Why you lousy Irish—"

Cardigan's fist arced briefly, hit Katz on the jaw, drove him reeling across the room. Katz struck the connecting door. The square glass panel fell out with a crash and Miss Gilligan yelped from the outer office. As Katz rose Cardigan crowded him.

"Now get, you poaching, two-timing punk."

Katz straightened, brushed glass splinters from his sleeve, adjusted his hat. His eyes glittered and his lips were drawn lightly across his teeth.

"O.K.," he breathed, turned, went out.

Cardigan said: "Miss Gilligan, write out a new check and deduct two-fifty for the glass panel Mr. Katz broke."

"Y-y-yes, sir."

"And mail to his hotel."

Pat, standing in the other door, said: "You weren't by any chance steamed up, were you?"

"Was I!"

CHAPTER FIVE

THE KILLING WIDOW

A WARM autumn rain fell, more like a mist, making a shimmering halo around street lights. Auto lights drove long beams down wet macadam and rubber tires made a sucking, swishing sound. People scurried like leaves before a fall wind.

Halfway down a narrow, gloomy street electric bulbs blinked their announcement on and off.

B
U
R
L
E
S
Q
U
E

The usual crowd hung around the lobby: down-at-the heel clerks, red-faced laborers, very young men and very old, sly-eyed men and self-conscious men.

Cardigan pushed through, ignored the ticket window, said to the man at the inner entrance: "I want to see Finkleberg."

"Way up and—"

"I know."

He climbed two flights of stairs and went down a narrow corridor toward a door marked 'Manager.' He knocked and pushed in. A fat, white, flabby-eared man sat reflecting over a cigar.

"Hello, Barney."

"Hello, Cardigan. How's business?"

"Jake."

"With me it's lousy. Don't sit down, the chair's dusty."

Cardigan grinned. "Say, Barney, O.K. if I go backstage tonight?"

Barney smirked. "I didn't think you went in for them dames."

"I'm funny that way."

"But don't say I didn't warn you."

Cardigan said: "What kind of a show is this?"

"Terrible! *Ach, du lieber!* The comedians; the gels are like elephants only not so goot; and the only thing worth admission is a couple of ackerbats.... I'll phone back you're the King of England!"

Cardigan went downstairs to the foyer, walked down a side aisle, back of a box and climbed three steps to a narrow door. Backstage the property manager shook hands limply and wandered away mournfully.

Faded girls stood in groups and chattered. A magician stood alone and aloof like a man in a trance. Two comedians kept calling each other vile names. A singer got temperamental with the orchestra leader and kicked him, and the orchestra leader made a pass at her and was stopped by a blackface. A director appeared and swore violently and the chorus got into formation.

The show started.

Then Cardigan saw the girl—tall, slim, muscular. The man with her was not quite as tall, but pale. He was not the man whose picture Cardigan had seen on the handbill. They did their turn about half an hour after the show started. The stage was dark but a spotlight followed them. It was marvelous the way the girl tossed the man about. She had strong arms. The audience cheered and the pair did an encore, took two more bows and then went backstage where they stood with arms folded. They did not mingle with the others. The girl never smiled; she was almost pretty.

Cardigan hung around till the show was almost over, then slipped out the stage entrance and waited. Ten minutes later the crowd surged out. The lights went out. Then the first of the performers appeared; in a few minutes, the girl. Her partner was with her and the girl did not wear mourning.

Cardigan followed. A couple of blocks farther on the pair stopped, conversed in low tones. The man turned right and disappeared and the girl kept on. The street was dark and deserted. Cardigan's legs moved faster, and soon he was close behind the girl, then abreast of her.

"Keep walking, sister."

She looked sidewise, startled.

"Keep walking. There's a gun in my pocket."

She looked straight ahead and kept walking.

Cardigan said: "To your hotel, to your room."

"What is this?" she breathed hoarsely.

"Keep walking and keep shut and take the stairway when we reach your hotel. One move and it will be too bad."

A BLOCK farther on she turned into the lobby of a run-down hotel. Cardigan held her arm and walked very close to her. She kept looking straight ahead and they climbed a staircase together. Climbed four flights and went down a hallway where floorboards creaked. Past a red fire-exit light to a brown door with cracked paint on it.

The girl took a key from her purse. He watched her hand and saw how white and smooth and strong it looked. She inserted the key in the lock and Cardigan got close behind her.

"I don't get you," she said.

"You will."

She opened the door and there was a light burning in the room. She stamped her foot.

A man stirred on a bed, blinked open his eyes, muttered: *"Huh?"*

Cardigan gave the woman a push in the back and sent her staggering. He covered the man on the bed. The man's eyes gaped and he rose to his elbows. He was dressed in pants and an athletic undershirt. He was slim but muscles rippled in his arms.

"What the hell!"

The woman stood stockstill, white-faced. Not a muscle twitched. She seemed cool as ice.

Cardigan closed the door.

The man was wide awake now. "Who's this?"

"How should I know?" the woman said tonelessly.

"I'm bad news," Cardigan said. "You," he snapped, as the woman moved, "stay where you are!"

It was awkward for the man on the bed to rest on his elbows so he lay back again, the head of the bed propping his head forward. His face was white naturally, the skin seemed transparent over the framework and the eyes were large and moist.

"Now, then," Cardigan said, dangling manacles. "You, Arline, raise your right hand." He got behind her, watching the man on the bed, and clipped one of the bracelets on her wrist, he prodded her to the head of the bed and said: "Now stick that arm between two of those vertical bars. O.K. Now you, mister, clamp that empty bracelet to your right wrist."

"Say—"

"Clamp it!"

Cardigan watched the bracelet enclose the wrist, then made sure that the manacles were locked. He stepped back and regarded the man and the woman. Neither could move from the bed. He went to the door and locked it and pulled down the window shades.

The man on the bed snarled: "Say—"

"Shut up."

Cardigan crossed to a closet, began tossing out clothes and presently appeared holding a black hat with veil attached and a dress of deep mourning.

"Bartles, Oldham and Cunarko," he said significantly and flung the widow's weeds on a chair. "You have nice strong hands, Arline. Who was Vantura?"

"My husb—" She stopped and tightened her hueless lips.

"So—your husband. Once of the team of Arline and Vantura of The Vagabond Road Show. Died—when?"

The man on the bed said: "What is this, what is this?" in a snarly, petulant voice.

Cardigan pointed. "And you... Doke?"

The woman gasped; the man's face blanched.

Cardigan said heavily, and yet playfully: "Just before Bartles was murdered a woman in mourning was seen leaving the house where he lived. In the back of his watch police found a picture of you—Arline."

"Me!"

"Little you. In the house where Oldham and Cunarko were found murdered was also found an old handbill showing pictures of you and your late team-mate—and husband. Two and two equals—something. Emeralds. Lifted in Indianapolis two months ago. At the scene of each murder was found a smoked cigarette with lip rouge on it. I'm pleased to meet the killing widow."

He put his gun in his pocket, crossed to a bureau and pulled out all the drawers. He rifled clothes, boxes. He ransacked all the clothes he had taken from the closet. He lit into a wardrobe trunk and turned it into a shambles. He opened and searched a valise and two handbags.

STANDING finally amid the chaos he said: "Maybe you get the idea that I want those emeralds."

The man cried: "You're crazy! Who are you?"

"I'm not crazy and I'm a private shamus to you. And I want those emeralds. They were stolen from Bartles. He was murdered. Cunarko and Oldham were murdered because they had a share in the loot. You don't turn them over and I'll sic the cops on you. Turn 'em over and I'll spring one of you but I've got to have one to chuck to the cops. Come on—start figuring. You, Arline, did the job but maybe Doke here is a big-hearted guy and will take the rap. Come, Doke, how's to?"

"I'll take no rap! You can go to hell!"

"No? O.K. Then it's the jane. Act fast. Come on. Where the hell are those emeralds?"

The man's mouth began working.

He choked: "In the bathroom—buried in a jar of cold cream."

Cardigan went around the foot of the bed, into the bathroom. When he reappeared he held six emeralds, smeared with cold cream, in his hand.

The man cried: "Come on, you! Come on, lemme go now!"

"You can't," the woman told Cardigan. "Because I have an alibi. I was rehearsing the afternoon Bartles was killed. Thirty people can prove it. Doke killed Bartles and Oldham and Cunarko. He wore my weeds. Bartles trusted me but nobody else, but I didn't think a hell of a lot of him. He was supposed to have an 'in' with a good fence but the guy was out of town. The other guys got the idea he was trying to frame them because he didn't turn the deal. But he was waiting. Doke here was most impatient of all. Bartles went down with the grippe and got scared and wouldn't let any of them in. Doke's a ventriloquist. He telephoned Bartles, imitated my voice and wanted to see Bartles about his grippe. Bartles always had a crush on me but not me on him. Doke knew it. So Bartles fell for it and Doke dressed in my weeds while I was out and went. I'd stopped wearing them three days before that but Bartles didn't know it. So Doke went and did him in.

"I threw a fit when I heard of it but Doke promised me fifty-fifty and I was tired of this two-a-day and fell for that. So then he finished off Oldham and Cunarko. I had no hand in it."

Cardigan said: "But Bartles made a phone call to me."

"That was Doke trying to make it seem more certain that a woman did it. You can't spring him, mister. And you're not going to spring me, either. I'll take it on the button but I can get in the clear. I'll stay right here. So will Doke—the rat!"

"Listen, you!" Doke cried to Cardigan. "Lemme go! You gotta lemme go!"

Cardigan said, bluntly: "I can't. And if I'm ratting on you it's the first time I've ever ratted on any guy. But I don't think I'm ratting. You'll have to fight it out with the court between you—"

Winded and moaning, Doke relaxed.

Cardigan went to the telephone and said, when police headquarters answered: "Send a couple of dicks over to the Rice Hotel, room 509…. Cardigan…. The guy that killed Bartles and Cunarko and Oldham."

"O God!" Doke moaned.

"Oh, hell," the woman said, "shut up!"

Cardigan made another call. "Hello, Pat…. Cut out yawning…. Baubles and gadgets and things…. Yeah, happy ending. Tell you tomorrow. Goom-by."

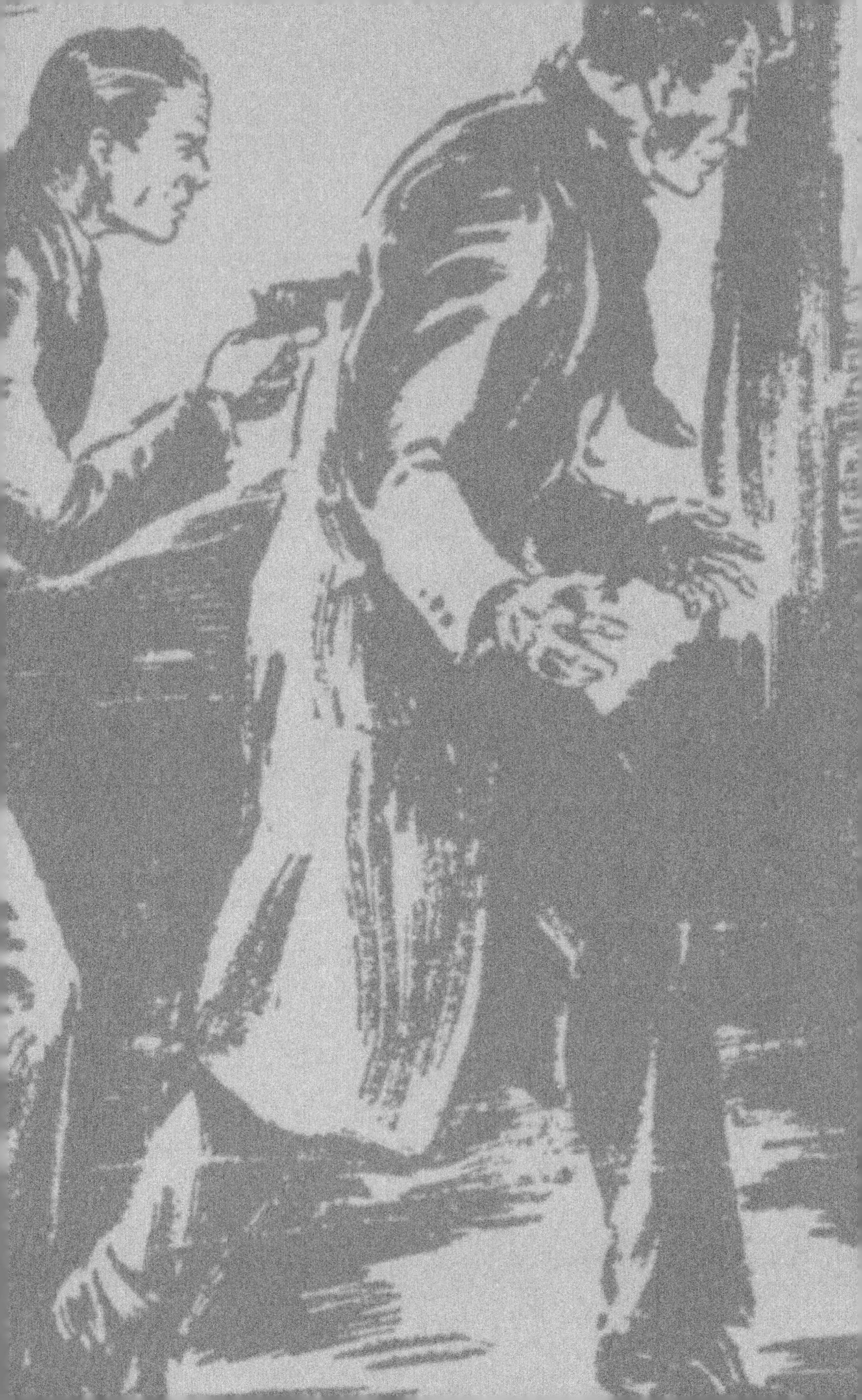

MURDER ON THE LOOSE

It wasn't an agency job and Cardigan had orders to leave it alone. But a dirk-stabbed body on the floor of his own hotel room wasn't the sort of thing he could ignore. Even when mixing in meant his job—and the taste of buckle and tongue in a fancy torture trap.

CHAPTER ONE

MYSTERY BLADE

CARDIGAN SAT in the depths of the wing-chair, absent-mindedly tinkling cracked ice in a drink composed of Scotch, seltzer and a slice of fresh lime. The twelfth-story room was moderately cooled by a breeze that puffed in from the East River, four blocks away; with it came the sound of an elevated train slamming south on Third Avenue and the lesser but nearer racket of a Lexington Avenue street car.

Dr. Korn said, "H-m-m… it must have been instantaneous. Yes, I'd say it was instantaneous."

Cardigan took a drink.

Fogel, the house dick, broad as a church door, mashed a handkerchief between sweaty palms and hitched a fat white neck uncomfortably in a hard collar. "Cripes," he said. "Cripes."

"Distressing," said Ownes, the night manager, rolling his eyes and pressing his palms piously together.

The man on the floor said nothing. He was dead. Stabbed through the heart.

Cardigan took another drink, untangled his legs, got up, strode to the little white pantry. Korn and Ownes looked at each other and heard the clear-cut chink of ice against glass, the fizz of a siphon. Cardigan reappeared carrying a fresh drink and saying, "Help yourself, gentlemen. The makings are all in there." He made a semicircular detour around the body on the floor and resumed his seat in the wing-chair.

Ownes said righteously, "This is murder, Mr. Cardigan!"

"Sure. A guy busts into my room and another guy who was already in here or came in afterward gave him the works. What am I supposed to do?"

Ownes made a hopeless gesture, and Fogel, shoving out his cleft chin, said, "This sure is funny, this is."

Cardigan looked at him. "You wouldn't be making any cracks, would you?"

Dr. Korn's interest was purely clinical. "An expert thrust, a very expert thrust—just one." He held up a finger. "Once."

Cardigan was still looking at Fogel. Fogel buttoned his coat, slid his gaze slantwise away from Cardigan, went to a window and regarded the cool spire of the Chrysler Building. Cardigan looked at the folds in the back of his thick white neck and consumed a quarter of the drink.

There was a rap on the door. Ownes started, turned. Fogel turned

"This isn't going to get you anywhere," Bradshaw said patiently.

from the window, threw Ownes a look and then thumped his flat feet across the carpet and opened the door.

"H'lo, Fogel," Lieutenant Bone said.

"Hello, Abe. Hello, Frank."

"Hello, Gus," Sergeant Raush said.

Hatchet-faced Abe Bone dropped a dour gaze on the dead man, lifted it to Dr. Korn, moved it to Ownes, moved it on to Cardigan.

"Oh," he muttered. "You."

Cardigan saluted with his glass. *"Skoal."*

Bone said impersonally, "I thought you were in St. Louis."

"I was. For several years. I'm back."

"Yeah, I see. How come you're in this room?"

"I live here."

Bone showed no surprise. "Who's the stiff?"

"I don't know. I walked in my room twenty minutes ago and fell over him. I called the desk downstairs, and Fogel and Mr. Ownes came up and brought Dr. Korn with them."

Bone looked at Dr. Korn. "Dead when you got here?"

"Oh, yes. Quite. Dead for several hours, I'd say."

BONE'S slab-cheeked face remained expressionless. He knelt beside the dead man, studied the wound, studied the face. His own expression never changed. His hard, bony hands probed pockets and brought forth odds and ends which he laid on the carpet. He rose suddenly and crossed to Cardigan.

"When did you come in here?"

"Eleven-ten."

"Did you touch the body?"

"Felt it—the pulse—that's all."

"Who is the guy?"

"I don't know."

"Was your door open or locked when you came in?"

"Locked. It locks automatically when you go out."

"What's your theory?"

"A guy was in here or came in while this egg was frisking my room and let him have it."

Bone said, "What would this guy or the other guy be after?"

"Haven't the slightest idea."

"Miss anything?"

"No. The room's just as I found it, except that door to the in-a-door bed was open. One or the other of the guys didn't have time to complete a frisk."

"Find a gun?"

"There's one under the stiff."

Bone drew a handkerchief and pulled the gun out by the barrel. It was a .32 Webley automatic, fully loaded. He wrapped it in his handkerchief and thrust into his pocket. He looked at Cardigan with hard, sour eyes.

Cardigan drained his glass, rose and carried it to the little pantry. He reappeared empty-handed and said to Ownes, "Of course I'll want my room changed."

Bone said dismally, "If this guy broke into your room, he must have been after something."

"Sure. Most crooks that break into rooms are after something."

"Never mind that. There was another guy after something, too."

Fogel put in, "So he says."

"You keep your oar out of this!" Cardigan snapped.

"Never mind him," Bone chopped in. "I'm talking to you."

Cardigan looked at Bone. "I've told you."

"You haven't told me enough."

"Then that's just too bad, and what do you think you can do about it?"

Bone was bleak. "I can pinch you—"

"In a horse's neck you can. Dr. Korn told you the guy's been dead several hours. My key was on the rack downstairs. I got it at eleven-ten and came right up."

"Two guys were after something," Bone said. "Each on his lonesome. They crossed, and one of them got rubbed out. One guy might have been on an ordinary break, but not two, Cardigan—not two. What did the one guy get?"

"Nothing."

"What was he after?"

"I don't know."

"What might he have been after?"

"I don't know."

Fogel said, "Hell, Abe, he'd never tell you, he wouldn't. I know him, I do."

Cardigan said, "Just one more burp out of you, you cheap keyhole artist, and I'll take a swing at you."

"I told you never mind him," Bone cut in.

And Cardigan swung on Bone saying, "There's a dead man. I found him in my room when I came in. I don't know him. I don't know what he was after. I notified the desk a couple of minutes after I found him. I got the doctor up. I acted according to law in every respect. So now try using your head instead of your mouth for a change and figure it out for yourself!"

His expression changeless, Bone said, "I'm figuring it out, Cardigan. I know you. Any time you think you can pull the wool over my eyes—"

"I'd hold him, Abe," Fogel suggested. "I'd hold him. I'd make him tell."

Cardigan pivoted, took one step and a swing at Fogel. Fogel sat down on the floor, and Bone and Raush jumped and caught hold of Cardigan's arms.

Bone snapped, "Now cut it out, Cardigan."

"All right, then tell this crackpot to keep his mouth shut. Leggo!"

Bone and Raush stepped back and Cardigan said, darkly, "I'm moving to another room. Try any rough stuff and see where it gets you. Just see."

DAYLIGHT was filtering through drawn green shades when the telephone bell jangled. Bedcovers erupted, and out of them appeared Cardigan's tangled shock of hair. A long arm slewed outward; a big hand picked up the instrument from the bed table and drew it to the bed.

"Hello.... Well, what the hell's the idea of waking me up so early?... Oh, it is? Well, now *I* think that eight o'clock is too early—... All right, George, all right. What's on your mind?... You did? Big headlines 'n everything, huh? Swell.... Didn't know the guy from Eve's daddy.... Yeah, Bone was there, sour-mugged as ever. And Fogel.... You know the guy you canned three years ago. And is he sore? Uhn-uhn!... I'll tell you when I get down the office, George.... Goom-by."

He hung up, swung out of bed and plowed into the bathroom, clearing his throat raucously. He took a cold shower, cursed it, rubbed down with alcohol, dressed and went down to the coffee shop. He drank half a pint of tomato juice, ate three eggs, four rolls and drank two cups of coffee. It was nine o'clock when he came out on Lexington Avenue and said 'hello' to the *chasseur*.

He walked north to Thirty-ninth Street, stopped and looked backward. He didn't see anyone tailing him. He walked on north to Forty-second Street, turned west. At a stand in front of Grand Central Terminal he bought a newspaper, saw his name mentioned twice, got the gist of the story and walked west to Fifth Avenue. He boarded a taxi and gave an address.

Fifteen minutes later he got off at the corner of Seventy-fifth Street and West End Avenue. He walked north for several blocks, passed the Whitestone Hotel, stopped at the next corner to light a cigarette and look around, then turned back and entered the Whitestone. From one of three house phones in the lobby he called suite 708, then took an elevator and got off at the seventh floor.

A man with carroty hair and freckles on a sun-tanned face opened the door.

"Well," Cardigan said, "so it's started."

The man was in pajamas and dressing gown. His voice shook, but his mouth remained firm. "Yes, I read it. Come in."

Cardigan tramped into the living room, scaled his battered fedora onto a divan, toed an ottoman out of the way and dropped into a mohair armchair.

"Drink?"

"Not till the eggs get down," Cardigan said.

The man had locked the door. He was tall, broad-shouldered, had a muscular jaw and steady blue gaze. He dropped to the divan with a faint outburst of breath, shrugged and slapped his palms to his knees.

"I'm sorry, old bohunk." He leaned back. "What did he look like?"

"Tall, thin, yellow hair—about forty."

"That would be Tracy. He must have tried to lone-wolf it."

"Then who got him?"

"Bradshaw, Sterns—or the woman."

"Leave the woman out. Bradshaw or Sterns."

A brindle bull walked in from the bedroom, flopped down and stared at Cardigan.

Cardigan said, looking at the dog, "Charley Wheeler, I don't know what you're going to do."

The carroty-haired man shrugged. "I came back for Mary. I'm not leaving this man's burg till she's well enough to pull out with me. I don't like the way those guys have turned on you, though."

"You worry about yourself, Charley. Don't think that the cops or these heels or anybody else is worrying me. Not me. I like it. It's not often I get the chance to work for an old pal."

Wheeler said, reflecting, "She ought to be O.K. in a week. Anyhow, we're booked on the *Gigantic* for Southampton next Tuesday. What do the cops think?"

"Nothing worth a damn. Abe Bone is on it—and Abe's hard as nails and twice as nasty. I gave him the run-around last night, but he didn't fall like a tree."

"They can't hang anything on you, can they?"

Cardigan laughed shortly. "I should say not. They might try, but—" he rose and raised palms toward Wheeler—"they'll wish they hadn't."

Wheeler stood up and looked grimly at Cardigan. "I hope to God we can make that boat, Mary and me. If there was any chance in the world of me sliding out by telling the cops, I'd tell 'em."

"They'd never recognize you, Charley. That plastic surgeon did a swell job, and your hair's a knockout."

Wheeler held up his hands. "They have my fingerprints. They'd find out. The papers'd get it and spring it: 'Big-Time Charley Wheeler, Former Beer Baron—'" He shook his head. "I'd never stand a chance, old bohunk."

Cardigan came over and towered close to Wheeler. He laid a big hand on Wheeler's shoulder. "You'll make that boat with Mary, Charley. You had the guts to come back and get her. I always said you had guts. You'll get her."

The brindle bull, scarred and battered, got up and went back into the bedroom.

CHAPTER TWO

ON THE LOOSE

WHEN CARDIGAN tramped into the inner sanctum of the Cosmos Agency, George Hammerhorn, the brass hat, lifted a leonine blonde head and said, rusty-voiced, "Now what the sweet hell have you gone and got yourself into again?"

Cardigan said, "Morning, George," and went to an ice-water cooler, drew and drank two glasses of water while Hammerhorn regarded him with agate-colored eyes.

"I said, by cripes—"

"I heard what you said," Cardigan cut in. "Now keep your pants on and don't get loud-mouthed, for, after all, I'm only working for you, and for two cents I'd start an agency of my own."

"Who said anything about starting an agency?"

"I did."

"Piffle, piffle, piffle!"

"All right, piffle all you want, but get over the underfed idea that you can land on me like a ton of brick and make me like it. I had eggs for breakfast and they haven't settled yet. Now lay off."

He walked around the room, and Hammerhorn, no weak sister himself, followed Cardigan with a glacial squint until by a circuitous route Cardigan reached the chair on the other side of the desk. Cardigan remained standing. He looked somberly at Hammerhorn for a long minute, and finally Hammerhorn, breaking a tight, hard smile, said offhand, "You're getting temperamental as a chorus girl. Unload your feet, big boy. Sit down."

Cardigan did not sit down. He placed palms on the desk, locked his arms at the elbows and leaned on his braced arms. "Did you ever have a friend that got in a tight spot?"

"Make it short and sweet, will you?"

"There's a friend of mine in a tight spot. He's in town under an assumed name. Three years ago he was a pretty big shakes in the beer trade, but he bailed out and skipped the country. He was through. He had the lousy racket up to the gills, and he was through. A lot of guys figured out beforehand that he was making to slide and told him he'd get the hot grease, if he tried to lam. He called their bluff and lammed.

"He went to Europe, had his face made over, dyed his hair. He went to Algiers and lived there. He met a doctor—a half-cracked old guy—and they became friends. One night a stranger busted into the doctor's quarters with his belly all shot to hell. The doctor did what he could for him, but the guy died. It was an incident, and for a month it was over. Then one night the doctor was stabbed and died. He left a crazy will. He left a signet ring, an old empty jewel box, his instruments, and a bulldog to this friend of mine.

"A couple of days later a guy approached this friend of mine and talked about the doctor. He wound up by pulling a rod on this friend and demanding to see what the doctor had left him. He saw. But he wasn't satisfied. He wanted five diamonds that he claimed the doctor must have taken from the guy he attended a month before. This friend got mad, and in the tussle took the gun away from the heel.

"He left a few days later for Paris. He was still in love with a jane in New York. He's a guy like that. He took a ship and came here and found the jane recovering from an operation. He asked her to marry him, and she said O.K., but they're waiting another week till she can navigate. Then they're going to Europe.

"Now who should turn up but the guy that pulled a rod on him in Algiers. He's got two pals with him and a jane. They're still after those five diamonds. This friend gets in touch with me to ask me what to do. I tell him to sit tight. They must have seen me come out of his apartment, and they make a stab at my room. One must have tried to double-cross the others. He got knifed in my room.

"Now—this friend of mine is in a tough spot. He's innocent, but if he gets tangled up in this, the cops'll find out who he really is. Word will spread, and the mob he ran with, the guys that threatened to rub him out, will get on his tail.

"That's why I'm in this. That's why I clowned around with Bone last night."

"And what, I might ask, do you intend doing?"

Cardigan straightened. "See that this pal of mine makes that boat with his frau."

"How much is in it?"

"Nothing. It's not an agency job."

Hammerhorn stood up. "Drop it. I'm not going to get mixed up with the cops. We can't afford to."

"Are you asking for my resignation?"

"I'm telling you not to be a damned fool."

"I'm not dropping it."

Hammerhorn had a glacial squint. "I still happen to run this agency, you know."

"I still happen to have an inclination to quit."

Their eyes measured each other.

Hammerhorn said flatly, "You're the best man I have. You ran the St. Louis branch swell for a number of years until you antagonized the wrong people out there."

"I antagonized a lot of cheap political grafters, and they broke my license in the State of Missouri. I'll get that license back again inside of six months. If your guts aren't equal to pressure of that kind, to hell with you and your agency."

Hammerhorn came around the desk. "Don't talk like that, Cardigan. I'm just trying to tell a thick-head Mick something for his own good. I'm telling you that you can't waltz these cops around and get away with it."

"You're telling me to leave this pal of mine in the lurch and I'm telling you, George, to go to hell for your pains. I'm strictly kosher. Nobody has anything on me. Bone doesn't worry me. None of them worries me. I didn't know the guy who was found dead in my room and I told Bone that. I had an idea, but I should go around ladling out ideas. Yes, I should!"

"Do you know now?"

"Yes."

"Then tell Bone before he gets really nasty and makes things hot for you."

Cardigan mouthed a corrosive laugh. "You're getting plain gaga now, George."

"Oh, yeah?" Hammerhorn pivoted and went back to his chair, sat down and stuck a cigarette in one corner of his mouth.

Cardigan darkened and leaned on the desk. "If you so much as make one crack to the cops about what I've just told you, I'll cave in your jaw."

"Says you."

"What I told you I told in strictest confidence. Break that confidence, sweetheart, and you'll be an ambulance case."

Hammerhorn snapped a spurt of smoke through his nostrils and regarded Cardigan blandly. "We're both saying things we don't mean, Irish."

"I mean what I say."

"As much as I do."

"I mean what I say."

"All right, all right, I know what you mean. If you think I'd welch on you, you're just a case of arrested development. I'm just trying to tell you. I see it does no good. But I'm not Santa Claus. I've built up a good agency here, and I'm not going to take the chance. Resign now, and if you get clear in this mess, we'll tear up the resignation."

They measured each other evenly.

Cardigan said, "Sure. Thanks. Thanks for being a great big-hearted son-of-a-so-and-so. Only there's one thing wrong with your statement, honeybunch."

"Yeah?"

"Yeah. This resignation is permanent."

"You're a fool, Irish."

"You're a louse."

"O.K."

"O.K."

ONE OF Cardigan's favorite hangouts was Andre's, in West Fortieth Street near Eighth Avenue. You got good steak and mushrooms there, coffee in a glass and Three-Star Hennessy straight off the French boats. There was a small quiet bar and a dining room in the rear and also three tables against the wall facing the bar. Cardigan sat at one of these tables pouring French dressing over imported endive. He had four dry Martinis under his belt, a bottle of Chablis at his elbow and a ruminative scowl on his forehead. A drunk was sitting on a high stool at the bar telling the story of his life, and an ingenue from a current Broadway success was trying to keep her eyes open while nodding mechanically at regular intervals. Emil, the barman, wore an expression of polite inattentiveness. It was a cheerful, homey bar, unlike the rowdy joints in the hinterland of Greenwich Village, miles south.

Abe Bone came in with his hands in his pockets, his Homburg sliced over one ear and his horsey face long and gloomy. He came straight to Cardigan's table, pulled out a chair, slapped it down and seated himself. He removed his hat, hung it on a prong above the table, blew his nose, and all the while kept his dark, cavernous eyes on Cardigan. Cardigan went on crunching crisp endive between long strong teeth and disfavoring Bone with intermittent glances.

"Mind if I try some of your white wine?"

"Yes."

Bone said, "Thanks," poured a glassful, raised the glass and added, "Whatever they say in French."

"Could you by any chance be at the wrong table?"

"I could, but I ain't."

A waiter swooped down. "Monsieur?"

"I'll have," said Bone tonelessly, "a pair of lamb chops, well done, some of those trick thin potatoes, some spinach and that's all."

The waiter vanished, and Cardigan said, "Don't you ever go home to your wife?"

"I haven't got a wife."

"Maybe janes aren't wise nowadays, huh?"

Bone spread a napkin, then reached for the wine. Cardigan put his hand on the bottle. "This stuff is six bucks a bottle, little boy, and times are hard."

"You don't like me, do you?"

"Oh, you're all right—in your place."

Bone said to the bar, "Bottle of that Canadian ale." He returned to Cardigan, saying, "My place happens to be smack on your tail,

Cardigan."

"Yeah, I saw that keyhole artist, Fogel, tail me from the hotel. Using him for a stool pigeon nowanights?"

"I'll use anybody, Cardigan. Who was that guy?"

"Who?"

"The stiff."

Cardigan put knife and fork together crosswise on his plate and said, "It's pretty tough when I can't enjoy Andre's swell food without having you planting your ugly mug opposite me."

"Pulling a waltz-me-around-again-Willie isn't going to get you anywhere, Cardigan."

"I'm not going anywhere, Bone, so now what?"

"You're a nice enough guy, so why don't you play along with the right people? What's one job going to get your agency when you run up against us?"

"I'm not working for any agency."

Bone looked at him. The waiter arrived with the chops and went away, and Bone was still looking at Cardigan.

"You're not what?" Bone growled.

"I'm on the loose. Out of a job. Temporarily. Until I start an agency of my own…. You don't believe me? O.K., call up George Hammerhorn. I've resigned."

"What you resign for?"

"Found the Cosmos too confining for my unusual talent."

BONE balanced three *pommes frites* on his fork, swallowed them and kept his gloomy eyes on Cardigan. "I've got a good mind to haul you over to the house and beat a little truth out of you, smart aleck."

"You'd better have your mind examined then, Bone."

Cardigan had drained his glass of coffee. He said to the waiter, "I'll take my brandy at the bar," and stood up. Bone kept looking gloomy-eyed at him. Cardigan turned his back on Bone. The drunk at the bar fell to the floor. Cardigan picked him up and helped him back onto the stool. The drunk went right on with the story of his life, and his ingenue friend seemed unaware of the fact that he had fallen. She had a rare glow.

Cardigan drank brandy and Benedictine, half-and-half, and Emil read him the latest race results. Bone finished his meal and two bottles of ale and came up to the bar for a pony of Scotch.

Cardigan called to the girl at the cigar counter, "Check, mademoiselle," and finished his drink.

He paid up and started down the corridor, and Bone was behind him. One of the waiters unlocked the front door and let them out. Cardigan reached the curb and bent his head to light a cigarette.

"Hold it," Bone said.

Cardigan held the light, and Bone got a cigar going. "Be sensible, Cardigan. You know damned well I'm going to find out who that guy was."

Cardigan tossed the match into the street and headed east past the newspaper sheds where trucks were loading up. Bone walked along beside him. They reached the whirlpool of Times Square and wedged through the eight o'clock theatre crowd. Cardigan ducked into the Times Building, went through the lunch room and took the staircase down to the subway. A northbound train was at the platform. Cardigan jumped and stopped a door from closing. Bone bumped into him.

Cardigan said, "All right, get in."

Bone hopped in. Cardigan stepped back and let the door close. Bone, in the vestibule, tried to stop it, but was too late. Cardigan tipped his hat and watched the train pull out with Bone, sour-faced, in the vestibule. Cardigan climbed the stairs and took the Broadway exit out.

At eight-twenty Cardigan tramped into the lobby of his hotel on Lexington Avenue, went past the desk and turned left toward the lounge. In the small connecting corridor there were two house phones on the right and two high-backed Italian chairs on the left. The place was very quiet.

Cardigan sat down on one of the chairs, looked at his watch, spread a newspaper and held it up before his face. Whenever he heard anyone at the phones he looked over the top of the paper and listened. At eight-thirty he heard a woman's voice say, "Mr. Cardigan, please."

He looked over the top of the paper and saw a tall, well-dressed girl in profile. She had on beige stockings of a weave called waffle, a modified Eugenie hat made of straw, and a blouselike jacket of transparent blue velvet with a skirt to match. When she hung up and turned away Cardigan raised the paper in front of his face. A moment later he was aware of another presence and, looking around a corner of the paper, saw the girl walking into the lounge with a large, bull-necked man. They disappeared around an L, and Cardigan lowered his paper and smiled to himself.

He rose, went into the lobby and caught an elevator up. He barged into his room—1115—and swung up the in-a-door bed which a maid had let down. Two doors closed and hid the bed in its compartment. The room was large, mannish and well furnished. He opened a window facing east. The night was bright, and he could see near the river the tall stacks of the New York Edison Company and the lights of Tudor City.

The telephone rang from a misplaced end table near a lowboy. "Hello," Cardigan said. "Yes, sure…. Come right up."

He hung up, and his right hand slapped a gun's bulge on his hip. His heavy eyebrows met each other over his nose in hurried thought. His eyes glittered in deep sockets. He heaved out of his coat, put on a shaggy dressing gown. He sat down, took off his shoes and put on slippers. From the desk he took a small Colt automatic, slipped it into one of the shoes. He placed the shoes neatly beneath an armchair. He went to a south window facing an open court and looked up two stories at the rail of the solarium on the roof. He pulled the shade all the way down.

When the brass knocker on the door sounded Cardigan slushed his loose slippers across the carpet and opened the door. The tall girl stood there smiling.

"Come in," he said.

"Thank you."

He looked down at her as she sauntered past, then closed the door which locked itself automatically.

CHAPTER THREE

RUSSIAN LALLAPAZZA

THE GIRL was an almost-platinum blonde who apparently knew the virtues of cosmetics. Her eyebrows were penciled black; her lips wore a rouge that was very dark. Worth or Patou or someone equally as chic must have sponsored the ensemble of dark blue velvet.

"I called at eight-thirty," she said. "You weren't in."

"I was taking a turn up on the roof and forgot the time. If I'd known you were such a knockout, I'd have been hours early. Smoke?"

She took a cigarette, and he struck a match. Her fingernails were lacquered red. "I'm Lorraine Valhoff," she said.

He was lighting his own cigarette. "You came alone, I suppose."

"Why, of course."

He smiled. "That's very swell." He sat down and dropped his chin to his chest. His shaggy mop of hair flopped down over his forehead. "So now what, Miss Valhoff?"

"Well, I was desperate when I telephoned you this afternoon. I am alone in the world, and a woman alone finds it difficult to fight men. Especially when something big is at stake. You were good to grant me an interview."

"Not at all. It's my business."

She nodded. "That's what I had hoped. And I want to ask you again, Mr. Cardigan: can I be certain that whatever passes between us will remain a secret?"

"Miss Valhoff, I'll be as aboveboard with you as you are with me."

"Yes. Yes, of course— These diamonds over which the man was killed are mine."

"No!"

"Yes. Yes, they are mine. They were stolen from me in Cairo six months ago—five of them. They're of the first water. My husband, when he died, left them to me. He was a diamond merchant in South Africa. They're worth approximately ninety thousand dollars."

"Why didn't you go to the police?"

"If the diamonds are brought to light through the usual channels, I shall have to pay a heavy duty on them. I do not live in America. My home is in Paris. If I could get back these diamonds I would find a way of getting them back into France. That is why I came to you."

Cardigan said, "You probably know that a client's engaged me to protect him from a clique that thinks he has those diamonds."

She said, "I know the man who brought those diamonds to this country."

"Yeah? Who?"

"Charles Wheeler."

He leaned an elbow on one knee. "Go ahead."

"The man who took those diamonds from me was named Carl Uhl. He escaped from Cairo, went to Rome and then went to Algiers. There he was attacked by another man who was also after these diamonds. He escaped, but badly wounded, and was taken in by an expatriate England doctor. He died there. It is certain that this doctor took those diamonds, because other effects of Carl Uhl's were found in his possession. He was killed by the man who killed Carl Uhl, but this man found no diamonds, nor was there any report of diamonds having been found. But Charles Wheeler was intimate with the doctor, and directly after the doctor was killed Wheeler fled to Paris. These events I have pieced together. I am now alone against Wheeler and against a clique that is against both Wheeler and me."

Cardigan leaned back. "So then I'm supposed to get these diamonds for you."

"You would be returning them to the rightful owner."

"And how about the client I'm working for now?"

She sighed wistfully. "I am a woman—a woman alone—of gentle birth and breeding and unaccustomed to dramatics such as have been going on since Cairo. I don't know what to do. My people were exterminated during the revolution in Russia, and I fled with what jewels I could gather on short notice. These diamonds mean a lot to me. My livelihood!"

He said, "How much would I get out of it?"

"I thought—perhaps—ten per cent. Is that not usual?"

"Nothing is usual in this business, Miss Valhoff. We try to get as much as we can."

"Perhaps even—well—twelve thousand—"

He took a long time to grind out his cigarette. "My client tells me that he hasn't got the diamonds, that he never has had them and that if he did have them, he'd give them up."

She quivered. "That is a lie!"

Cardigan stood up and jammed his hands into the pockets of his dressing robe. "Who was the guy bumped off Tracy?"

She started. "I— One of the clique, I suppose. I tell you that I am all of atwitter over these goings-on and hardly know who is who any more. Please, Mr. Cardigan—"

"Now, hold on. If you expect me to fall head over heels, you're ahead of yourself, Miss Valhoff. I'm working for a client and you want me to double-cross him."

"But I am in the right! The diamonds belong to *me!*"

"How am I to know that?"

"Because I am telling you! Because it is the truth!"

"Have you any proof?"

She rose dramatically. "In those days of turmoil when I fled from Russia, how could I take proof? I was only a little child. I fled with my uncle who later was assassinated in the streets of Constantinople." Her voice shook— "Don't you believe me, Mr. Cardigan?"

SLIGHTLY exasperated, Cardigan stood on wide-spread feet, his fists jammed against his hips. She came across to him, her eyes and lips pleading. Her long attenuated fingers gripped the lapels of his dressing gown. There was about her a faint breath of attar of roses. Back of the irises of her eyes was a translucent green shimmer.

Her voice was a throaty purr. "You are so big and strong. You would not deny a woman alone who is incapable of combating the wickedness of adventurers. Would you?"

Her hands rose and were cool against his jaw. He remained rooted to the floor, rocklike, and his eyes seemed to recede farther into their sockets until they were mere horizontal glints.

He said, "Pretty cute."

She pressed closer to him.

He said, "Before your name was Valhoff, what was it?"

She said nothing, but kept pressing her pliant body closer and staring at him with her shimmering green eyes.

"I've had many a racket pulled on me," he said, "but this is a lallapazza. I could fall for you any day, sister, if Wheeler didn't happen to be an old pal of mine. I like 'em tall like you, and good-looking—like you—but those eyes, sister, they spell trouble." He stepped back and laughed good-humoredly. "Scram while I still take it as a joke."

She recoiled and stood like a tall quivering flame. Color rushed over her face, and her hands clenched. "I did not come here to be insulted!" she exclaimed.

"You came here to try to make me one way or another, and I'm telling you to take the air. You can't sell me a damned thing. Now take it before I get nasty."

There was a sharp rap on the door.

Cardigan's hand slapped his hip-pocket. "Who's there?"

"Me—Bone."

He looked at the woman. He went close to her, muttered, "Sit down there and say nothing."

Then he went to the door and opened it, and Bone stood there with Fogel, the house dick.

Cardigan said, "Haven't you got any kind of a home? A room of your own somewhere?"

Bone's face was dull. "What the hell did you mean by giving me the slip in the subway?"

"I meant it as hint that I don't care to have you shadow-boxing all over the city after me."

Bone pushed in, and Fogel came after him. But Cardigan pushed Fogel in the chest. "No you don't."

"I'm coming in here!" Fogel snapped.

"You're not coming in!" Cardigan laid the flat of his hand against Fogel's face and sent the house dick careening into the corridor. He slammed the door and spun on Bone. "I'm getting tired of this, Abe! It's come to a swell pass when I can't eat or enjoy the comforts of home without having you master-minding on my neck all the time!"

Bone was looking at the woman. "You know what I'm after, Cardigan, and you know blamed well that I'm a hound for punishment. I hang to a thing till I bleed."

Cardigan said, "Just now I happen to be entertaining. Miss Valhoff, this is Lieutenant Bone, one of our great modern detectives. He read Sherlock Holmes at a tender age, and it had a bad effect on his brain. He stops perfect strangers on the street and springs questions like, 'Where were you at 9:36 on the night of January such-and-such a date?' So don't pay any attention to him."

Unimpressed, gloomy-eyed Bone regarded the woman. "I'm glad to meet you, Miss Valhoff."

The woman sat stiffly in the chair, breath bated and a puzzled half-frightened look in her eyes. "How—how do you do, lieutenant."

Bone looked wearily at Cardigan. "I suppose Miss Valhoff is another client."

"Once," Cardigan said, "I tailed a Mexican hairless of hers into the fleshpots of Hoboken and brought him back. Since then we've been friends."

"Still funny, ain't you?"

Cardigan did not look so. He looked dark and mean, and his steady gaze bordered on the malignant. "When you bust into my place like this you can expect goofy answers to anything you ask."

Bone looked at the woman. "Are you here as a client, Miss Valhoff, or as—"

Cardigan stepped in front of Bone. "Listen to me, Abe. Get this. Get it straight and remember it. I don't care a hoot who you are or what you are. I wouldn't care a hoot if you were the commissioner himself, which thank God you'll never be. But get me, baby—get me. You've no right in here. You've no right to ask anybody any questions in here. You get the hell out of my place and stay out."

Bone raised his knobby chin, but his eyes remained gloomy, his face changeless. "Yeah?" he asked tonelessly.

"And don't think that strong-silent-man crap goes over big, either."

Bone said, "You had a date tonight, Cardigan—such an important one that you were in a hurry to shake me."

"I had an appointment with Miss Valhoff."

"I see that. I want to find out what it's all about."

"You've found out. Good cripes almighty, can't I even have a nice sociable date any more?"

Bone stepped to one side and looked at the woman. "Miss Valhoff, why did you come here tonight?"

She was poised again, almost languid. "To pay a friendly call on Mr. Cardigan for what you call old times' sake. If I am intruding—" she shrugged— "of course, it will be better that I leave."

Cardigan got in front of Bone again. "I mean it, Abe—by God I mean it! Get out!" His voice was low, throaty, with a subdued fierceness. "You don't get out right now, and I'll go down to the commissioner tomorrow and put up such a hot smell that you'll get kicked out into the sticks. As a private citizen I've got certain rights. You might be able to pull this noise on some punk, but I'm damned if you can pull it on me!"

Bone's voice was dull. "You're rubbing me the wrong way, Cardigan."

"As if I care whether I rub you up, down or across. You're not God Almighty! Now slide out of here, shamus—slide out!"

Bone flexed his lips once, clipped, "Have it your way, then, wiseacre," and went to the door, opened it and, going out, bumped into Fogel who had been listening at the keyhole. Cardigan booted the door shut. It banged. He barged into the little serving pantry and hove into the living room a minute later carrying a drink.

Miss Valhoff was smiling. "It is obvious, Mr. Cardigan, that you would be an uncommonly bad man to antagonize."

"Take that as a lesson then, Miss Valhoff."

"It was very good of you to conceal from the lieutenant that I came here as a potential client."

"It wasn't for your—" He stopped short, took a drink. A flush of red undermined the brown of his big face.

She said, "I am sorry you will not champion my cause. I would be very grateful. In the Midi I have a charming villa." Her eyes became seductive. "You would like the Midi." She rose, purring, "I like a man like you—dark, stormy, capable and unafraid."

He dipped his head. "Thank you. I don't blame you."

"And one who is rather—conceited. I like conceit when it is violent and healthy."

"Thanks again. But I never mix business with pleasure—especially where a woman is concerned. It took me ten years to learn that, Miss Valhoff—and sometimes I still weaken. But not tonight. You'd better watch out that Bone doesn't follow you. Change cabs at least three times on your way home."

"This, I suppose, is dismissal?"

He made a mock bow. "Much to my sorrow."

She shrugged and sauntered to the door. With her hand on the knob she turned and said curiously, "It was very strange, the way you tried to conceal from the lieutenant that I did not come here as a client."

He said nothing. She smiled, turned the knob, opened the door, sauntered out. The door clicked shut.

CARDIGAN kicked off his slippers, took the gun from one of his shoes, replaced it in the desk. In a minute he was dressed. He caught the freight elevator down and ducked out the service entrance into the street. Reaching the corner of Lexington Avenue, he saw Miss Valhoff and the bull-necked man walking north. He crossed the street and walked north also. The woman and the man crossed and headed west into Thirty-ninth Street. Cardigan stopped on the corner of Thirty-eighth and looked around. He did not see Bone.

He turned west into Thirty-eighth and walked fast to Park Avenue, reaching it in time to see the woman and the man going north past the Princeton Club. Cardigan went north on the east side of the street and did not cross till he saw Miss Valhoff and her escort turn west into Fortieth. He tailed them across Madison and Fifth, past the back of the library toward Sixth Avenue. At Sixth Avenue they entered a taxi, and Cardigan jumped one coming east on Fortieth, at the corner.

"See that yellow starting off? Tail it."

An elevated train thrashed by overhead and stopped at Forty-second Street. The yellow turned east and then south on Fifth. Turned east again on Fortieth and turned north to take the Park Avenue ramp around Grand Central Terminal. It struck out north past the new Waldorf. At Forty-seventh Street the man and the woman switched taxis.

"Pass 'em," Cardigan said, and switched cabs himself at Forty-eighth. Once in the second cab, he said, "That blue one that just passed, tail it."

Another change was made at Fiftieth and Lexington. Cardigan changed, too, and followed them west on Fifty-first street, north on Madison. At the corner of Fifty-fourth and Madison the man and the woman got out. It was a traffic stop, and Cardigan sat in his cab while paying up and saw the two head east on Fifty-fourth. He got out and reached the corner. He got behind three men walking east and saw the man and the woman climb steps to a brownstone front.

He stopped. After a minute he crossed the street and looked up at the face of the house. Lighted windows showed on the first and third floors. He waited. Presently he saw two windows on the fourth floor, at the left, light up. He caught a glimpse of the woman as she drew down the shades.

He turned and saw a familiar figure coming along in the shadows. He recognized the dumpy walk as Fogel's. As he turned, Fogel ducked into an areaway. Cardigan cursed silently for a long minute. Then his jaw tightened. He crossed the street and mounted the steps of a house two doors from the one which the Valhoff woman and the man had entered.

He pressed a button at random and after a moment the door clicked open and the lock kept clicking as he entered a large, dimly lighted corridor. He took a packet of matches from his pocket and jammed it at the bottom of the door so that it would not close completely.

Then he hid in the dark stair well. He heard a door open above, heard footsteps. After a minute the footsteps receded, and a door closed. Two minutes later Cardigan saw Fogel slip into the hallway, heard the door close gently. Fogel walked on tiptoes, reached the foot of the staircase, listened, then began climbing.

Cardigan crept from beneath the stair well, flattened against the wall on the way to the door, reached the door and slipped out. He ran diagonally across the street, went down an areaway into a speakeasy and piled into a telephone booth. He called the nearest police station.

He said, "There's a strange man prowling around the halls in a house at number —— East Fifty-fourth Street."

Five minutes later he stood in the street in front of the speakeasy and watched two cops roughhouse Fogel down the steps diagonally opposite and march him eastward toward the Fifty-first Street station. Cardigan lit a cigarette, tossed the match away with an air of complete satisfaction and headed toward Madison Avenue.

CHAPTER FOUR

POOCH AD

WEELER LET him into the suite on West End Avenue, and Cardigan said, "Well, I hope I'm rid of Fogel for a while. He's going to have a hell of a time explaining what he was doing in a strange house in Fifty-fourth Street tonight."

Wheeler looked worn and haggard and in no mood for levity. His eyes searched Cardigan's face. "What about the woman?"

"She claims the ice is hers and tried to pull the sweetest story ever told. Only I happened to know that she didn't come alone. There was a big guy waiting for her in the lobby."

"That ought to be Bradshaw. I saw him with the woman once."

"You never saw this jane before you hit Paris?"

"No. I'm sure they connected there."

Cardigan was eyeing him keenly. "You're sure, Charley, that you're not giving me the run-around?"

Wheeler's mouth hardened. "What do you mean?"

"That you never had anything to do with that ice."

"As far as I'm concerned there never was any ice. What the hell are you driving at?"

"O.K., O.K., Charley. How's the little woman?"

"She'll be ready to sail—unless these lousy heels take a crack at me. What about the cops?"

"Bone's still doing a hop-skip-and-jump on my heels, but he can't touch me. You'll sail, Charley."

"What does your boss think?"

Cardigan smiled. "He's O.K.—a swell guy."

There was a knock on the door.

Cardigan stiffened, put a finger to his lips and slipped into the bedroom. After a moment Wheeler called him out.

"It was only a bell-hop. I had him take the pooch out for an airing, and the pooch broke the leash and beat it. He asked me if I wanted to put an ad in the paper."

"No, you don't," Cardigan said.

"Why not? Damn it, I've come to like the homely mongrel."

Cardigan pointed. "You keep out of the papers, kid. You always were a sentimental egg, but you're taking orders now—if you expect to bail out of this man's town. These heels may see the ad and trace you through it."

Wheeler shrugged. "Oh, all right."

Cardigan looked hard at him. "I mean it, Charley. Don't think you can put an ad in on the sly, because I'll be watching the papers. They traced you to your first address and got a line on me, too. They're trying like hell to trace you to this one."

"All right, old bohunk, all right. But the old doc was a swell guy, and the pooch—"

"Now lay off." Cardigan put on his hat and strode to the door. "So I'll be seeing you."

IT WAS eleven o'clock when Cardigan dropped from a taxi at Madison Avenue and Fifty-fourth Street. Walking east, he became aware of heels keeping time with his own. He looked around and saw a figure walking behind in the shadows. He slowed down, and the dim shape behind turned into a hall door. Cardigan went on, and a moment later turned his head about and saw the dim shape again walking. Cardigan looked up at the brownstone front and saw that the fourth floor, left, was dark. He went on until he reached Park Avenue, stopped and, looking back, saw the dim shape come to a pause. Cardigan turned south, walking fast, and when he reached Fifty-third Street saw the man idly following. Cardigan turned west and walked faster. When he reached Madison again he had dropped the dim shape. He turned north and again entered Fifty-fourth Street.

He dodged into the vestibule of the brownstone. He got the hall door open with a master key and climbed to the fourth floor. He stood in the corridor for a moment getting his bearings, then went toward a door he was certain led to the Valhoff woman's apartment. He knocked several times and listened intently. There was no answer, nor did he hear any sounds inside. He tried his master key and several others, but none worked.

He went to the rear of the hall—it was not long—and opened a solitary window there. He leaned out and saw a fire-escape platform. He climbed out, closed the window and squatted for a minute on the metal platform. He leaned way out and saw that one of the adjoining windows was open a couple of inches. He swung closer to the building, got his left hand on the ledge, stretched farther and got hold of the bottom of the open window. Holding it hard, he clung to the frame of the fire-escape with his right hand while working his left foot over to the window ledge. For a brief moment he remained spread-eagled, then kicked out with his right foot, swayed and came to his knees on the ledge, gripping the bottom of the open window with both hands. Bit by bit he raised the window, stepped into a darkened room and remained motionless, but breathing heavily.

After a few moments he began moving. From his vest pocket he drew a flashlight the size of a fountain pen. Its meager glow showed him a bedroom. He entered another bedroom and then went straight ahead into a living room. Before him were the front windows of the apartment. He cruised the living room without finding anything of consequence. Then he entered the middle bedroom, closed the connecting door and turned on the lights.

The bed had not been slept in that day. Half-packed bags were on the floor, and a man's clothes hung in a closet. Gradually Cardigan became aware of the fact that they were the clothes of two men; the suits varied in size. He plowed into a steamer trunk that appeared not to have been unpacked. Stenciled on it were the initials L.S. Apparently they stood for Sterns. In the bottom of the trunk he found an assortment of knives—five in all—of varied construction, thickness of steel and length. One he knew was a Malay *kris;* another was a stiletto; another a broad-bladed dagger with a mottled agatelike grip. All the knives were clean. He replaced them and, disappointed, closed the trunk.

The rear room was obviously the woman's. Only two dresses hung in the closet. Most of her things were packed. Cardigan went back into the middle room, searched beneath the pillows and the mattress. He flung the mattress down again, straightened, turned, and found himself looking at a man standing in the living room doorway. The man held a gun. He was the bull-necked man, and he wasn't smiling.

"**CAREFUL,** Cardigan. I believe it's Cardigan." Over his shoulder he said, "Lights." Lights in the living room sprang on, and beyond the bull-necked man Cardigan saw the woman and a tall, emaciated thin man. Cardigan removed his hat and fanned himself.

"Bradshaw," he said. "I believe it's Bradshaw."

The bull-necked man said, "We are glad to meet, I'm sure."

"It's a pleasure," said Cardigan.

"For me," said Bradshaw bluntly.

The thin man, impeccably dressed, strode past Bradshaw and stood regarding Cardigan with a withering glance.

Cardigan said, "And Mr. Sterns, of course."

"And what about it?" snapped the thin man.

Cardigan said, looking past him, "And Miss Valhoff. I see, Miss Valhoff, that you've stopped being a woman alone."

"Enough out of you!" Sterns ripped out. "What the hell are you doing here?"

Cardigan's smile was not genuine. He must have known he was in a tough spot, but he said, "Imagine your surprise."

Sterns took two jerky steps and laid the flat of his hand across Cardigan's cheek. Cardigan did not budge. Only his head moved to one side, snapped back straight again while his eyes shone with a frigid smile.

Bradshaw said, "Cut it out, Lester," in a tone that indicated such an act was child's play.

The woman remained in the living room taking slow drags on a cigarette.

Bradshaw said, "What are you looking for, Cardigan?"

Cardigan was honest. "Some hint as to which one of you birds bumped off Tracy in my room."

"And you found the hint?"

"Of course. Sterns did it."

The woman laughed mockingly.

Bradshaw came into the room saying, "Lester, take away his gun.

Get behind him and take it."

Sterns got behind Cardigan and removed the gun from Cardigan's hip-pocket. He moved to one side and released the safety.

Bradshaw said patiently, "Lester, close that safety and give the gun to me."

"Why?"

"I am not going to have you monkeying around with a gun."

Cardigan put in, "Sure, when his game is knives."

"That's enough out of you," Bradshaw said. "You are going to talk, but not in a light vein. You are going to tell us where Wheeler is located. We are going to get those diamonds. Each and every one of them."

"You're screwy," Cardigan said.

Bradshaw said, "Tracy tried to double-cross us, you know. He hadn't the brains, though. Tracy was the one who located Wheeler, but did not tell us. But we were watching Tracy. Get in the living room."

Cardigan did not move. Sterns kicked his shins, and Cardigan grunted and stumbled forward. He went into the living room and found the woman regarding him maliciously with her green eyes.

He said, "I suppose you're waiting to see the Irish take water, huh, sister?"

She smiled. "With pleasure!"

"Go to hell," he growled.

Sterns kicked him in the spine, and Cardigan whirled, but Bradshaw was there solidly with his gun. "Nix, Cardigan," he said patiently.

Then he said to the woman, "Lorraine, turn on the radio—rather loud."

CHAPTER FIVE

IRISH BLOOD

THE WOMAN went to a cabinet and turned a knob. A Harlem jazz band cut loose. Bradshaw made Cardigan sit down in an armchair, then spoke to Sterns. Sterns went into one of the rooms and reappeared carrying two heavy leather luggage straps. He buckled one end to the other, then threw the strap across Cardigan's stomach, put the ends through the arms of the chair and buckled the strap behind the chair.

Bradshaw sat down on another chair with his gun, and Sterns leaned over Cardigan and said close to his ear, "Now where is Wheeler staying?"

"You want him," Cardigan said. "You go find him."

Sterns whipped his fist into Cardigan's face. Blood trickled from Cardigan's lip, but his head snapped back to an erect position, and he pressed his lips tightly together.

"Where is he?" Sterns snarled.

"The trouble with you guys," Cardigan said, "is that you're all nutty. He hasn't got the diamonds."

"If he hasn't got the diamonds, why didn't he report to the police? Why didn't you?"

"He didn't want to make trouble."

"No. He didn't report because he has those diamonds, and he knows that if he reports, that will be the end of them!"

Cardigan said, "He hasn't got the diamonds."

"Where is he staying?"

"You'll have to find that out for yourself."

"I intend to."

He kicked Cardigan's shins and kept kicking them until Cardigan lashed out with his foot, caught Sterns in the pit of the stomach and sent him smashing into a chair ten feet away. Chair and Sterns went down to the floor, Sterns moaning and rolling back and forth on his stomach.

The woman disappeared and came back quickly, her green eyes shimmering. She carried a razor strop. She whanged it across Cardigan's face while Sterns still groaned in agony on the floor. Bradshaw took a clinical interest in the proceedings.

The woman laughed hysterically. "How do you like that, eh?"

"I'm not crazy about it," Cardigan said.

"What is that address now?"

"I told you once to go to hell; that stands."

Whang!

The buckle went clear around the back of his neck and opened his right eyebrow.

The green-eyed woman shook with rage. "You regret insulting me today now, don't you?"

Pain kept Cardigan's lips shut.

Bradshaw got up and came over and leaned close to his ear while the radio jazz band thundered. "Don't be a fool, Cardigan. We're going to get that address."

Cardigan's sneer was freighted with contempt.

Sterns got up with oaths bubbling and fizzing on his lips. He grabbed a poker from the fireplace and rushed madly toward Cardigan. Bradshaw caught the descending arm, wrenched it, and the poker fell to the floor. "Not that," he said. "We want information out of this guy, Lester." He was patient. "Now don't be an idiot."

"I'll kill him!" Sterns grated.

The woman cut loose with the strop again, and Cardigan grunted. He heaved up, lugging the armchair with him, and broke the straps with his body and arms. Fury burned red in his eyes and as the woman struck out again Cardigan gave her the flat of his hand across her mouth. She yelped and fell down, spat out a tooth.

He whirled with his fist knotted and moving uncorked it into Sterns' face, lifted Sterns off his feet and dropped him into a divan where Sterns bounced like a rubber ball and then lay chattering.

But Bradshaw stuck his gun in the small of Cardigan's back and said patiently, "This isn't going to get you anywhere."

The woman was emitting crazy chirping sounds.

The jazz band had stopped.

A voice was saying, "Late news dispatches. Here's a good one. The only one hundred thousand dollar bulldog ever found. And dead at that. An unidentified brindle bull was run over at ten tonight at Ninety-second Street and Broadway by a Broadway street car. Killed instantly. Patrolman Swenson took charge of the body and in lifting the dog noticed something fall from one of the wounds. It was a diamond. On closer inspection it was found that four other diamonds were imbedded in the dog's flesh. It appears that these diamonds had been placed in an incision, whereupon the incision had been sewn up. A doctor claimed that it looked like an expert job, probably the work of a surgeon. A cursory examination of the diamonds by an expert indicates that these diamonds are worth about a hundred thousand dollars. Some dog, folks—"

The woman had stopped mumbling. Sterns had stopped gibbering. Cardigan looked at the radio, transfixed, and Bradshaw said, "By God," dully.

The woman yelped, "Wheeler had a bulldog! The doctor's bulldog! The fool didn't know—we didn't know. Oh, what utter fools!"

Sterns said, "The diamonds are in the hands of the police!" as though making a revelation.

"Of course," Bradshaw said. He looked stunned, but he kept his gun hard against the small of Cardigan's back.

Cardigan said, "I told you. I told you Wheeler didn't know anything about those damned diamonds."

Sterns crept from the divan and stood on shaking legs. His voice was clotted. "But that doesn't let you out. You know too much. Too much."

The woman sprang up. "Too much indeed."

Cardigan said, "Tracy was a heel like the rest of you. His death doesn't mean anything to me. The case is over. Believe it or not, this will never get to the police."

"Take him out," the woman said. "Kill him somewhere. Meantime I will pack the bags."

Sterns said, "I'll wash my face first." He went into the bathroom.

Blood streaked Cardigan's face. "I'll break even on this, so help me."

"We can't take the chance," Bradshaw said. "You know too much. Start packing, Lorraine."

Sterns reappeared, carrying a slender stiletto. "This is the thing. No noise. We'll gag him in the car. Should I go and get the car?"

Bradshaw said, "Yes, get it and wait down the block. I'll bring him. Get in the bathroom, Cardigan, so Lester can wash that blood off your face." He pushed Cardigan into the bathroom, and Sterns washed Cardigan's face with mocking tenderness.

"You guys'll regret this."

Bradshaw said, "We've got to do it."

STERNS dried Cardigan's face, and Bradshaw marched him back into the living room. Harlem was again on the air. And there was another sound. Someone was knocking. Sterns looked at Bradshaw, and Bradshaw looked at Cardigan.

Cardigan said, "There's only one guy could be out there."

"Who?" Bradshaw asked.

"The cop that met Miss Valhoff at my place this evening—Lieutenant Bone. If you think you can shoot it out with him, you're crazy. He's a wizard with a gun."

Bradshaw set his jaw, and Sterns began to get panicky.

Cardigan muttered. "I said we'd break even. Turn the lights down. I'll sit in that armchair. You, Bradshaw, sit in that one. Tell Sterns and the woman to go in the back and close that connecting door. You and I are friends. Act that way. It's your only out—so take it—and quick."

"I don't believe him!" Sterns said in a whisper. "As soon as the cop comes in he'll tell. No—no!"

"So help me," Cardigan promised.

"No—no!" cried Sterns.

"What'll you do?" Bradshaw asked.

"Tie two bed sheets together and let myself down to the fire-escape. It slants beneath the rear window."

"How about Lorraine and me?"

"I'm going," Sterns said. "You and Lorraine can make it, too. Come on."

"How about this guy?"

Sterns said, "For some reason or other this guy is just as much afraid of the cops as we are. We'll make him go, too, and get rid of him on the East Side. Come on."

"No," Bradshaw said. "Get in that room, close the door and keep Lorraine in there."

The knocking was louder.

"You hear me!" Bradshaw growled. "You bungled one job, and you're not going to bungle another. We can take care of Cardigan later. Get in there!"

Sterns winced, turned and went into the other room. He closed the door. Bradshaw turned all the lights out but a bridge lamp. He motioned Cardigan to a chair. He put his gun in his pocket.

"Remember," he said. "No tricks."

He turned the radio off and went to the door. He unlocked it, turned the knob and pulled the door open.

"Put 'em up, you!"

Bradshaw stepped back and raised his hands. Cardigan jumped up, leaped across the room and threw the bolt on the connecting door. He heard Sterns' fists pummel it. He pivoted and saw Bradshaw backing into the room.

George Hammerhorn said, "Come on, Irish."

Cardigan came up behind Bradshaw, reached into Bradshaw's pocket and took out the gun Sterns had taken from him. He crossed the room and picked up his hat, put it on. Bradshaw was speechless, dumbfounded. Cardigan walked to the door and stood beside Hammerhorn.

He said, "All right, Bradshaw. I'll give you till nine tomorrow morning to get out of town."

Bradshaw, red-faced, growled, "This man is not Lieutenant Bone!"

"I'm as surprised as you are," Cardigan said. "Remember, Bradshaw. Out of town by nine tomorrow morning.... O.K., George."

They backed out into the hall side by side, Cardigan with his left hand on the knob, his right holding his gun on Bradshaw. He closed the door.

"Go ahead, George."

Hammerhorn walked to the stairs, and Cardigan backed toward them, watching the door. The door did not open. They went down the staircase, out the front door and into the street.

"There's a speak across the street, George. Let's."

"Swell. God, but you're a goof."

"You've got a hell of a nerve tailing me around."

"Have I?"

"Yeah," Cardigan said. "And I like it."

"You're leaving on a job in Buffalo tomorrow."

"Oh, yeah?"

"What the hell do you think I got you out of that tough spot for, because I like you?"

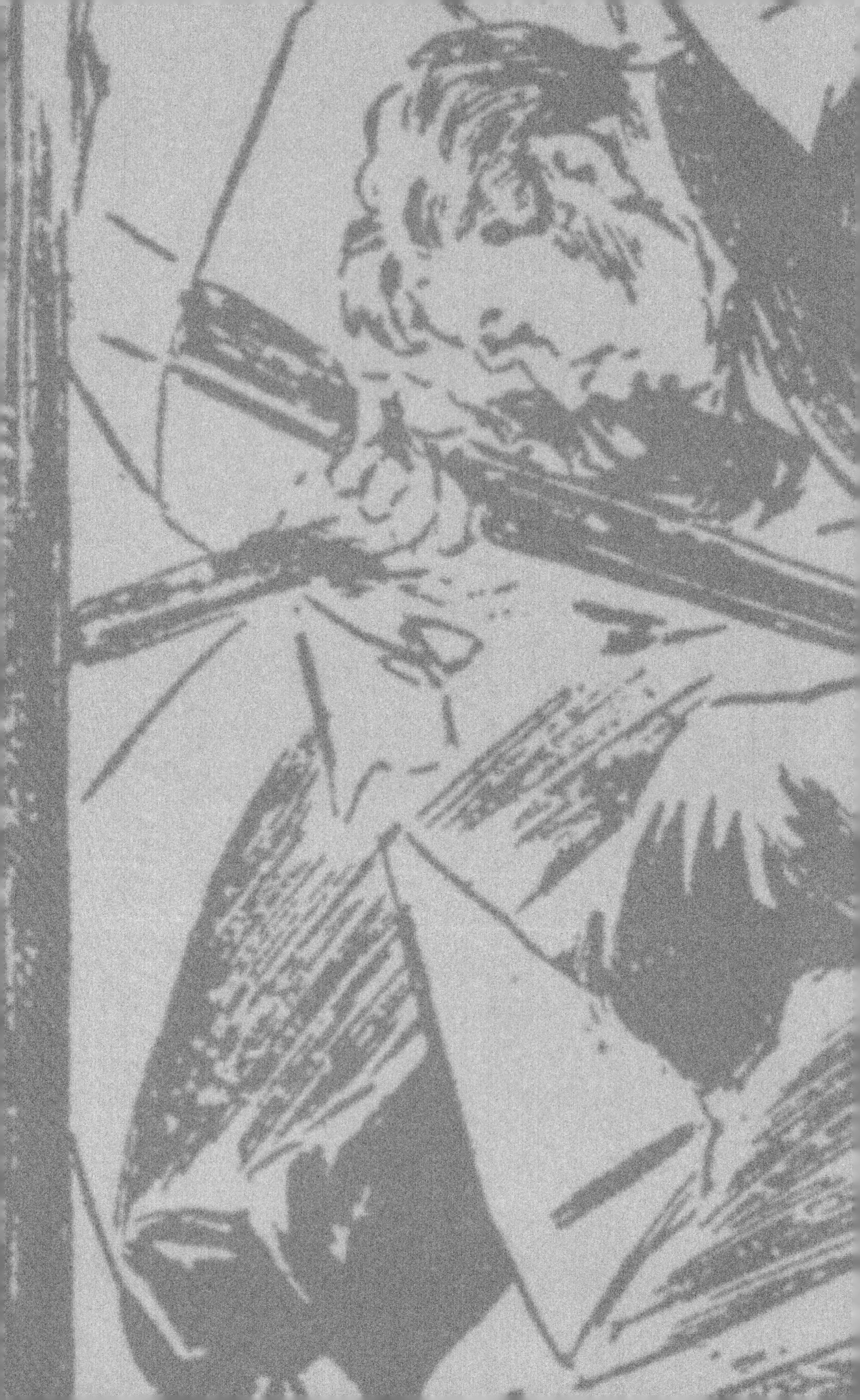

ROGUES' RANSOM

IT'S BAD ENOUGH TO HAVE TO HANDLE LAWYERS, CROOKS AND FRANTIC PARENTS IN A SNATCH-GANG SET-UP. BUT ALL THAT DIDN'T FAZE CARDIGAN. IT WASN'T UNTIL A LOT OF JOB-MINDED COPS STARTED IN TO GUM THE WORKS THAT HE REALLY BEGAN TO WORRY. THEN IT WAS RED RAGE AND FLAMING LEAD IN THE FASTEST CLEAN-UP OF HIS THRILL-PACKED CAREER.

CHAPTER ONE

SNATCH-RACKET STUFF

THE TOLL-BRIDGE made a black fret-work against the setting sun. The wheels of the train clicked more leisurely and the Pullmans had a lazy side-to-side heave. The hills beyond the Ohio were burned brown and the river itself was flat and copperish.

"Wheelburgh!" intoned the porter.

Cardigan needed a shave and a clean shirt. The ride had been hot. His shaggy crop of hair was damp; it looped wetly around his ears, down his forehead. He shoved it back with his left hand, used his right to yank on a faded gray fedora. As he rose, towering, the porter came along with a whiskbroom.

"Nix," Cardigan said, and flipped him a quarter.

He had a brown Gladstone that was new years ago. He picked it up and went down the aisle, reached the vestibule and pushed on into the next Pullman. Halfway down the aisle, a girl sitting alone dropped a handkerchief. Cardigan stooped, picked it up and thrust it into her outstretched hand.

He muttered: "Not too close, Pat."

"O.K.," she said.

He rolled on to the next vestibule, set down his bag and drew a packet of cigarettes from his pocket. They were damp and crumpled and he lit one and it didn't taste good. The Pullman sloughed over switches. The *bong-bong* of the loco's bell was more resonant as the train moved past outlying freight sheds. A porter hauled bags into the vestibule, raised the metal leaf in the platform and opened the door. The train slid into the station and stopped.

Cardigan swung down the steps, barged through a flock of red-caps and lugged his bag up the platform. Going into the waiting-room, a newsboy shouted in his face: "Read all the latest news about big kidnaping!"

"Here, kid."

He bought a paper, dropped his bag, snapped the paper open and down with a loud report.

POLICE FOLLOW NEW CLUES IN MILBRAY CASE

"Cardigan, ain't you?"

Cardigan looked over the top of his paper; saw first the baggy knees of black alpaca trousers; next, the tarnished buckle of a broad belt that girded a generous paunch. The black alpaca coat was open and Cardigan followed the plain white shirt up to a black bow tie; then to a hard round chin, a humorless mouth, a scraggly mustache, a nose like a twist of rope—and China-blue eyes, steady, probing.

He said: "Selling something?"

"Advice, maybe."

Cardigan regarded him for a brief moment, then bent down, scooped up his bag and started past. A big freckled hand closed on his left arm. He looked at the hand and then at the man's China-blue eyes.

He said: "Take your advice and that hand, stranger, and go places."

The man didn't say anything. He smiled humorously and turned back the lapel of his coat.

"Badge 'n' everything, huh?" Cardigan said.

"And the name's Michaels." He lifted his thumb. "There's an empty office down there. I want to talk to you."

Over Michaels' head Cardigan saw Pat Seaward. She was standing just inside the platform entry holding a black patent-leather suitcase and watching him with a cool, quiet look. He made no gesture.

"Sure," he said to Michaels.

THEY went down past the baggage room and entered a small cubicle of an office furnished with two chairs and a roll-top. The office was hot as an oven and smelled of coal dust. Michaels closed the door, turned sluggishly, took off his hard straw hat and mopped the sweatband with a handkerchief. His hair was dry, thick, reddish; it bunched down over a low forehead, overlapped the back of his collar. He fanned himself with his hat.

"Now get this, Cardigan," he said. "We know all about you. We know you're an A-1 dick. But we don't need you here. We don't want

Cardigan grabbed the shotgun— leaped through the window.

you clowning around Wheelburgh." He spoke in a throaty monotone, thick and harsh. "That train east is a nice one. Grab it and give New York a break. We don't need you."

"Is that all?"

"That's all."

Cardigan picked up his bag again and started toward the door. Michaels put his broad bulk between.

"Where you going?"

"Hotel," Cardigan said. "Bath, shave, drink, meditation."

"You can do all that on that train."

Cardigan dropped his bag and jammed his fists against his hips.

"Copper, I'm going to a hotel. For a few days I'm going to live in your lousy city, not because I like it, but because I've got a job here. All this bright conversation on your part is just a lot of bushwa."

"It's worth its weight in gold, Cardigan."

"I'm off the gold standard." He picked up his bag and walked around Michaels.

Michaels grabbed him. Suddenly his big freckled hands slapped Cardigan's pockets.

"Cut it!" Cardigan snapped.

Michaels grabbed his wrists. "Where is it?"

"What?"

"Your rod."

"Fat-head, the Cosmos Agency has a license to operate in this state!"

"The license don't say anything about packing a gun."

Cardigan's eyes drooped. "Right away you're getting lousy, huh?"

"Where is it?" Michaels nodded to the Gladstone. "Open that."

Cardigan eyed him darkly. Then he swore. Then he took a ring of keys from his pocket, selected one and opened the bag. He shoved his hand down beneath his linen, drew out a gun and hefted it in his palm.

"I'll take it," Michaels said.

"O.K.," Cardigan said.

He half-turned, hurled the gun. It smashed a window pane and went outside into the yard.

Michaels reddened. "Tricks, eh?"

"You started it."

Michaels had his gun out. "Come on. We'll get it."

"You want it. You go get it."

"Get outside, Cardigan!"

Cardigan sat down. "Waving that rod don't kid me, Michaels. You want my gun. You go out and get it. I know a frame when I see it and you're trying to frame me."

Michaels went to the door, looked out. He called: "Hey, Brady!"

A uniformed cop came down from the waiting room and Michaels said: "Watch this guy, Brady. He's funny."

"O.K.," the cop said, and twirled his nightstick.

Michaels went on down the corridor, found a door near the end and shoved out into the yard. His heavy shoes crunched cinders. He reached the broken window, looked in and saw Cardigan sitting on the chair. Then he swung around and his eyes swept back and forth across the cinders. He saw no gun and he saw that there was no place where it might be concealed. The cinder field was flat and stretched to the nearest rails, fifty feet beyond. He cursed. He turned and saw Cardigan leaning in the window. He reddened. Then he crunched around on his heel and reentered the building, reentered the office.

"Things get funnier," he said, husky-voiced. Some of the red color of his face seemed to have gone to his eyes.

Cardigan picked up his bag. "Well, I'll be going."

Michaels' face looked bloated. He stepped in front of Cardigan.

"Get out, get out," Cardigan said.

Michaels stepped aside. The cop took this as a hint and lowered his nightstick. Cardigan swung out of the office and went hard-heeled toward the waiting room. He didn't pause once. He went straight to the sidewalk and climbed into a taxicab.

"The Wheelburgh," he said.

THE room was big, on the fifth floor. The hotel was on a grade. The fifth-floor window overlooked smoke-grimed roofs; and beyond these were warehouses, freight yards, and beyond all, the copperish river. There was a red haze in the air, the wake of a sun gone down. The hills made a bowl and in the center of the bowl lay the city; hot, smoky, unlovely.

Cardigan had shaved and put on a fresh white shirt, but it made him look no less shaggy. He was good to look at in a hard male way. He was cramming a pipe when a knock sounded on the door.

"Who's it?"

"Me, chief."

He let Pat Seaward in, closed the door, took her arm and led her to the window. He bowed, nodded: "Beautiful Ohio. Am I right or am I?"

"Here's your gun."

"What a pal, what a pal!"

She took a flat black automatic from the sleeve of her light-weight blue coat and slid it into his palm.

"How'd you know?" he said.

"Well, I saw him take you in the office so I went around outside and crept up beneath the window. Incidentally, when you chucked the gun out, kind sir, you almost beaned me…. So I took it and said 'abracadabra' and—lo!—I vanished."

He muttered: "Little wonderful!"

She began fanning herself with a newspaper, and stared blank-eyed at the Ohio. "What was the matter with that dick?"

"Professional jealousy—maybe." He bent his wiry brows, warped his mouth. "Or something screwy. He burned me up, that baby!"

"Hear from Blaine and Stope?"

"They got in on the 4:30 bus from Harrisburg. They're in 209 awaiting orders. What are you in?"

"One floor down—412. The dick tailed you here. I tailed him. He got your room number from the desk and then went away."

"O.K. Now you go down to your room, wash the coal dust off your face and catch up on your reading till you hear from me. I've got to see Milbray. Scoot, chile!"

She smiled—that bright, certain smile he liked. Then she turned and went out, trim from white nape to bright patent-leather heels.

He put on a hat and a coat and caught an elevator down. Twilight was in the hilly streets, and the air hung motionless like a warm invisible cloud. He walked around the block, looking over his shoulder at each turn. Then he hopped a taxi and gave an address.

The cab climbed out of the heart of the city. The street lights were turned on and presently a broad avenue opened before the cab. It followed this for a quarter mile, turned right and followed a winding road past large, pretentious houses. It stopped before a stone gateway across which a heavy chain had been stretched. Cardigan got out, paid up, and went toward the chain. A short, leather-faced man appeared there.

"Who are you?"

"I'm Cardigan. Mr. Milbray's expecting me."

"Oh, yeah. I'm the gardener." He unhooked the chain. "Just follow the driveway."

It was a hundred yards to the broad veranda of the big white house. A dumpy old woman in a black dress and an Eton collar opened the door.

"My name's Cardigan."

"Oh, thank goodness you got here!"

He entered and she took his hat and steered him across a foyer, through a music room to the entry of a library. A lean man with white hair and a drawn face rose from a divan, drew shut the folds of a silk dressing gown and knotted a rope at his waist. Cardigan crossed the soft carpet with his right hand extended. They shook and stood for a moment looking at each other in silence. The old woman backed out, closed the door quietly, and the white-haired man sat down, sighed, laid a hand on either knee and stared morosely at the carpet.

"Please sit down," he said.

Cardigan turned, walked several paces, picked up a straight-backed chair and brought it over to face the divan. He sat down.

"Let's have it," he said in a low voice.

MILBRAY straightened, then leaned back in the divan and thrust his hands into his robe pockets. "She was abducted a week ago today. Right out of the garden."

"How old is she?"

"Three. At four o'clock Mrs. Floom, the woman who let you in, called the nursemaid from the garden. My wife is ill. Her fever was high then and she'd fallen out of the bed and it took her nurse, Mrs. Floom and the nursemaid to get her back. Little hysterical, you understand. When the nursemaid returned to the garden, ten minutes later, Gloria was gone. There was a note in the carriage. It said: 'Don't tell the police. You'll get a letter tomorrow.' But the women were all upset. Mrs. Floom called the police. I wasn't here, at the time. In Pittsburgh on business."

"Any of the help see anybody in the garden—before or afterwards?"

"No. There are woods behind the house. Whoever kidnaped Gloria could have gone that way, easily, and not been detected. So the police came, and the newspapers, and at nine there was an extra on the streets. I got home at midnight. The police were still here, droves of them, and the newspapermen—all asking questions. I was shown the note the kidnaper left. I—I told the police to get out. I—you understand, I wanted to get my baby back!"

"Naturally."

Milbray ground the heel of his hand on his knee, stared hard into space. "Next day—the letter. Twenty-five thousand dollars and instructions where to put it at nine that night. The police came again. The reporters again. It was like a madhouse. They wanted to know what arrangements had been made. I told them I would not tell them. The child was mine, the money mine, and all of it no affair of theirs.

"Well, this is the fourth kidnaping in Wheelburgh in five months and the three others were successful. The administration has been booed from all quarters and the police are desperate. They're determined to get the criminals in this case—even, I believe, at the risk of sacrificing my child. You see?" he cried out suddenly, shaking.

"Go on."

"Yes—yes of course. Well, I kept the letter secret. I managed to get twenty-five thousand cash. I was instructed to take it to the abandoned Marsh farm on the Hillside Road and to place it under the right side of the front porch. An hour later I was to receive Gloria. The letter explained that she would be left in some doorway with a note pinned to her dress explaining that the finder should notify me.

"Well, I started out for the Marsh farm. I placed the money under the porch and drove away. I came home. I was barely in the house when the telephone rang. A man's voice said: 'Not this time, Milbray. You might just as well go back and get that money. We told you not to bring the cops along. The ante is up another ten thousand. You'll get a letter in a day or so.' So I drove back there and sure enough the money was under the porch. As I took it out half a dozen plainclothesmen jumped on me. They apologized. Imagine!" he cried. "Apologized!"

Cardigan grunted. "I've had an example of this burg's gumshoe," he said. "The example was terrible…. So now what?"

"The kidnapers have got bolder. They instructed me to engage an agent to act as intermediary. They have named an attorney to act as their representative. You probably know what procedure to go through. You will meet their agent, talk with him and arrange matters. I have the cash on hand."

"Who's the shyster?"

"His name is Aaron Steinfarb. He has an office in the Metals Building. But, remember—this is in strict confidence. The police seem to have acquired a grudge against me simply because I refuse to take them into my confidence." He thumped his chest and his voice was clogged. "After all, my child is—my child!"

Cardigan stood up. "Been bothered today?"

"All day. If it's not the police it's the newsmen. Driving up. Ringing bells. Taking pictures."

"O.K.," Cardigan grunted and held his hands out, palms down. "I've got two men assistants and a woman along. We'll keep these grounds clean. I'll see Steinfarb."

They shook and Cardigan strode into the foyer. Old Mrs. Floom got him his hat.

"You'll try your best, sir?" she pleaded.

"Madam—yes."

She opened the door and there was a man standing there. "I'm Casey of *The Morning Trib* and—"

"Oh, yeah?" Cardigan said.

He moved. He caught Casey by the nape with one hand, by the seat of the pants with the other. He heaved once and Casey never touched a step on the way down. Cardigan walked down the steps and reached the gravel as Casey was rising.

"You fell," Cardigan said, unpleasantly. "It breaks my heart."

"What the hell's the idea—"

"Blow, sweetheart, blow!"

CHAPTER TWO

THIRTY-FIVE GRAND

THE METALS BUILDING was two squares west of the hotel. It was old. The elevator was old and looked like a tarnished brass cage. It wheezed up three flights and Cardigan got out. Night lights were burning in the corridor and down at the end glowed a frosted square of light that was a glass-paneled door. There were black letters on it saying: Aaron Steinfarb, Counsellor at Law.

"Phooey," muttered Cardigan.

He knocked and a voice said: "Come in."

"I thought I might have to look up your home address," Cardigan said, kicking the door shut behind him.

"Who are you?"

"Calm, counsellor."

Cardigan tipped back his hat and eyed the small, chubby-cheeked man behind a battered flat-top. "You're Steinfarb, huh?"

"Can't you read?"

"Now is that nice?"

Steinfarb took a couple of quick drags on a tremendous cigar. He stood up. He was a very small man, far below medium height. He was all white and chunky and looked like a flyweight boxer gone to soft weight and too much electric light. His black hair was combed back flat, but through it his scalp was visible.

"Spiel it," he said. "And be quick. I was just about to leave. Get it off your chest. Come on, come on!" He threw his hands up irritably. "You think I've got all night?"

Cardigan said: "I'm representing Mr. Milbray. You're representing the quantity known as X."

Steinfarb blinked, screwed up his white fat nose. "Oh, you're—then you're the rep—"

"Cardigan.... Please sit down, counsellor. You give me the heebie-jeebies ducking around like that."

"Well, well, of course, of course. Ah, yes, Mr. Cardigan." He smacked his white hands together, beamed, sat down in the swivel chair. "It is really lamentable that—"

"Quit it, Steinfarb. I'm no babe in arms. Quit the preliminaries. All I want from you is the dope on how we can put this deal through. I understand that these heels that snatched the Milbray kid engaged you as counsel. All right. Now just what is what?"

Steinfarb got up, went to the door, opened it and peered into the corridor. Closing the door, he locked it and returned to his swivel chair.

His voice, his manner, ceased to be theatrical. His eyes took on an oblique slant, evading Cardigan's. His mouth jerked: "Well, the price is thirty-five thousand. It was twenty-five but the cops got childish and my clients upped it ten grand. They've got the kid. The kid's unharmed, well and happy. If there's another fluke it'll be swan song."

"Have you seen the kid?"

"No."

"How do you know she's well and happy?"

Steinfarb's fingers drummed, his shoulders twitched. "I was told. When a guy walks in here with a proposition like that he's bound to tell the truth."

"How do I know the kid's not dead?"

"I'm telling you."

"And you were told by somebody else. How do you know the guy who walked in here and propositioned you wasn't some wise bunny that didn't kidnap the kid at all but is just muscling in on general principles?"

Steinfarb made a sour face. "Are you telling me my business?"

"No. I'm working for Milbray. You're working for these kid-snatchers. It's my job to have my client's interest at heart and I've got to be sure of where this dough goes. It's not my job to pinch these guys. I'm interested only in getting the kid back. I've got to have proof that this client of yours has the kid."

STEINFARB drew on his cigar, rose and went to one of the windows. The shade was down, but he drew it gently aside and peered down into the street. In a minute he turned, came back to the desk and sat down. His eyes narrowed. He picked up a pencil, held it erect—then tossed it aside and laughed harshly.

"You can't talk to me, mister," he snarled. "I'm sitting on dynamite and I've got to be careful."

"What's eating you?"

Steinfarb nodded to the window. "Instead of leaving Lieutenant Michaels down under that street light, why didn't you bring him up with you?"

"Michaels?"

"Michaels!" Steinfarb barked. He picked up the pencil and threw it down again. "Michaels! Michaels!"

Cardigan got up and started for the window.

Steinfarb snarled: "Stay away from there!"

Cardigan turned and found Steinfarb holding a gun. Cardigan raised his shoulders. "You've got me."

"I just don't want Michaels to see where you are."

"O.K. Put that gun down."

The storm passed as quickly as it had risen. Steinfarb slipped the gun into his desk drawer and chewed petulantly on his big cigar.

Cardigan said: "Don't be a goof, Steinfarb. The bum ran into me as I got off the train today. He tried to make me take another train back east. I thought I'd ducked him but he must have picked me up again. I represent Milbray—not the cops. The cops want these heels. I want the kid."

"All right, all right. I got excited. I just got excited." He looked at the ragged end of his cigar. "The kid's all right. Safe. Sound. All I can do is carry on negotiations. You give me thirty-five thousand dollars. I give it—minus my commission—to my clients. The baby will be returned—automatically."

"Fair enough. But first—first, counsellor, I've got to be sure your clients have the baby."

Steinfarb flared up. "My God, do you think I can take you to these guys!"

"No. Take this." He pulled a small vest-pocket camera from his coat. "Have your clients take all exposures on this of the kid in various positions."

"Why?"

"So we'll know she's alive."

Steinfarb leaned back, drew one eye shut. He smiled—a bleak, warped smile. "You think of things, don't you?"

"I'm in 517 at The Wheelburgh."

"I'll see."

Cardigan turned and went to the door. "Is there a back way out?"

"Yeah. Downstairs, turn left after you get out of the elevator. At the end of the lobby there's a door. That leads down a flight of stairs to a garage. Go out that way."

CARDIGAN ignored the elevator in The Wheelburgh. He walked all the way around the lobby, stopped at the cigar stand, bought a paper and some pipe tobacco and used the mirror behind the counter to watch the lobby. Then he took the stairway to the second floor and knocked on 209. Blaine let him in and Stope lay on the bed in an undershirt kicking his heels up and laughing.

Cardigan shot Blaine a dark sidelong look and Blaine said: "What the hell, he said he was going out only for a paper."

Cardigan went over to the bed, drew a blackjack and smacked Stope on the soles. Stope's body vibrated as though an electric current had shot through it. He sat up, half laughing, half snarling: "What do you think—"

Cardigan laid the flat of his hand against Stope's cheek and knocked him spinning across the bed. Stope put his face in his hands and went into a crying jag. Cardigan crossed the room to a lowboy and picked up two pint flasks. They were unlabeled and contained a smoky white fluid. Cardigan uncorked them, sniffed.

"You try this, Blaine?"

"I've got kids to support."

Cardigan took both bottles into the bathroom and emptied them. He dropped the empties into a wicker linen hamper, reentered the bedroom rubbing his hands slowly together. Stope was sitting up, cross-legged like an Indian. He wore a silly grin and kept hiccupping regularly. Cardigan suddenly shot across the room, grabbed Stope by the throat and shook him violently.

"Listen to me, you dirty bum! What the hell do you think you are, a traveling salesman?"

"Jus' little drinky—"

"By cripes, you're working for a tough agency, Stope. You got kicked off the cops for boozing. I don't care how much you drink when you're not on the road with me, but when you're out with me—*Ah-r-r*, you sap!" He flung him across the bed. Then he began tearing Stope's clothes off.

"Come on, Blaine. We'll sober him."

They stripped him and held him under an ice-cold shower. He moaned, groaned, prayed. They turned the shower off, hauled him out of the tub. Cardigan threw him a towel and motioned Blaine into the bedroom.

He said: "You and Stope go out to the Milbray place pronto. Bum's-rush anybody who doesn't belong there. Leave your rods here. The cops in this burg are funny that way. Ask Milbray for a room. Let this honk-out sleep a couple of hours, then you catch shut-eye—and so on, alternating."

"O.K., chief."

"Now open the door and see if anybody's in the hall."

Blaine looked, said: "O.K."

Cardigan went out and climbed to 412. Pat had on black pajamas and a mandarin coat.

He began: "I'd climb the highest mountain and swim the broadest river—"

"Be your profession. I hate mountain climbers. Always make me think of yodeling."

He spun his hat on a forefinger. "Milbray's all broken up. It must be tough on a guy when they snatch his kid.... Well, look. You be down in the lobby bright and early in the morning. I figure Michaels still might try to pick me up for packing a gun. You pack my gun. You follow me wherever I go and if I get in a jam, pass me the gun and then get to hell out of the way. Savvy?"

"Little Chinee girl savvy."

He raised his hand. "Stop that!" And grinned. He turned and said: "Take a look in the hall."

She opened the door, looked out, stepped back in. "Scur-ram!" she said.

"Happy dreams!"

IN A minute he was in his room. Five minutes later he was in blue cotton pajamas, his big feet thrust into worn-down slippers. He crammed an ancient briar and opened both windows wide. Night brought fewer sounds, but each of these was clear, resonant; the drawn-out rattle of a trolley crossing switches, the toll of a freight engine in the railroad yards, the sad hoot of a river boat. He drew on his pipe, cuddling the smoke behind his lips in the manner of the true pipe-smoker. Darkness had a way of making the unlovely city romantic—and of making him feel acutely lonely.

He chuckled to himself: "Sentimental Mick!"

Knuckles rapped his door. He scowled at it, his face a hard network of shadows. He crossed and put his ear to the panel.

"Yeah?"

"Cardigan, this is Kittles, city editor of *The Trib.*"

"I'm not interested in subscribing."

"Listen, Cardigan, I've got news for you!" the voice hissed.

Cardigan let him in, eyed him with a calloused stare. The man was scrawny, wore spectacles that looked like thick magnifying glasses. He had a confidential air, rolling eyebrows, dry wrinkled lips. He started off by tapping Cardigan's chest.

"Now don't do that," Cardigan said. "It makes me fidgety."

"Of course, of course," Kittles' low voice raked on in a cracked whisper; and his eyebrows rolled. "Cardigan, we're glad to see you're here. I, personally, am glad to see you here. Oh, I've heard of you. Remember the time you were head of the St. Louis branch? Yes, yes, indeed! Ah, yes. Great work, great work!... Can I send you up a case of nice liquor, the real McCoy?"

"Thanks—no. You can tell me what you want, though."

He huddled close to Cardigan. "We'd just like to know, old man, what progress you've made since you came here. What transpired between you and Milbray? Have you made contact with the kidnapers? When do you expect to have the child back? Just a few words, old man—just a hint, here and there."

Cardigan rolled a harsh laugh between closed teeth.

Kittles raised a finger. "Oh, of course, we expect to make you a little present. Little pin-money. Five hundred, say."

Cardigan repeated the laugh, raked Kittles from head to foot with a sardonic smile, turned and crossed to one of the windows. Kittles blinked, looked at the ceiling, at the floor, then at Cardigan's back. Then he crossed the room, moistening his lips.

"Of course, old man—"

Cardigan swiveled. "Of course, old man!" he growled. He tossed his thumb. "I don't like your groceries. Blow!"

Kittles wore a quaint, hurt expression. "But, gosh, old man—"

"Yeah, a swell chance Milbray has of getting his kid back when you newspaper guys and the cops clown all over the city. What about those other three kidnapings? What good are they? You print a lot of crap in the papers. You scare the heels. You're no help and you're a lot of nuisance. Now get out of here. And stay away from Milbray's place. And don't bother me. And go to hell."

Kittles pouted. He turned and scuffled to the door. He paused to blink at Cardigan through his heavy glasses. Then he scowled petulantly and went out, slamming the door.

CHAPTER THREE

KICK-THE-WICKET

CARDIGAN WENT downstairs at eight next morning and had breakfast in the coffee shop. The headlines went far toward spoiling his appetite. They made him curse; made him glare at the waitress, through her, beyond her; until she began blushing and backing away.

"Baked apple," he said. "And eggs, three, three minutes. Rolls. Coffee."

"Y-yes, sir."

He crackled the paper and glared at it.

POLICE PROMISE ARREST IN MILBRAY CASE

"Horsefeathers!" he muttered.

New Clues Indicate Early Arrest of Baby Milbray Kidnapers

He tossed the paper to one end of the table, ran his hand across his cheek, up around the back of his neck. He rushed through his breakfast, ate too rapidly, and left the table with a stuffed, unpleasant feeling. And in this condition he ran into Michaels, in the lobby. Michaels had a couple of boys with him. At the same time Cardigan saw Pat watching him from the depths of a leather chair.

Michaels took his arm. "We wanted to wait till you ate, Cardigan. Come along."

"Where?"

"Headquarters."

"What for now, pitching pennies?"

Michaels moved his head. "Come on. No use stalling."

"What for?"

"Little talk."

Cardigan shook his head. His voice was low, quiet, but dynamite was in the background. "I'm busy, Michaels. I can't go." He put his left hand on Michaels' right and wrenched it from his arm. "Grow up, copper." His dark eyes were steady, sultry.

"Now wait, Cardigan," Michaels said, blocking him. "We're going to have a talk with you. There's three of us and if you start to get rough we'll jump you and beat hell out of you and fix you for a three-months' spree in jail. Use your head. Use your head. Come on before we get sloppy."

Cardigan looked at the other two men. They were big, bigger than Michaels, and looked like hard parties. He shrugged. "O.K., let's go."

THEY went outside. The street was already hot, the air motionless and soggy, the sun hidden behind a dull haze but nonetheless felt in the narrow street. The two bruisers walked beside Cardigan and Michaels walked in front, led the way around the corner to a parked sedan. They got in and one of the bruisers took the wheel.

After five minutes Cardigan said: "Headquarters, huh?"

"Sit tight," Michaels said.

Cardigan turned and punched him in the jaw. "You crummy bum,

I know where headquarters is!"

The bruiser on his right grabbed him and then Michaels had his gun out. "Easy, Cardigan." His face looked red and bloated and somehow desperate.

Cardigan put his hands on his knees and stared straight ahead. The car left the suburbs and went down the other side of the mountain. It passed a glass factory; went on downward toward the coal mines; cruised along the outside of a husky settlement drenched in coal dust, sooty and tatterdemalion. It entered a clump of trees and stopped before a board-and-batten shack. A gaunt man with one eye missing came out and unleashed a slow tobacco shot.

The two bruisers hustled Cardigan inside. The place smelled of raw corn liquor. He got one arm free and took a smack at the nearer face and then Michaels came in and helped crowd him into a chair.

"Now use your head, Cardigan."

Cardigan hit Michaels in the stomach, rose wheeling the chair with him and let it fly. It missed both bruisers but stopped the one-eyed man in the doorway. It was a heavy chair. It knocked the man cold. Cardigan had a stone jug in his hand by this time, but Michaels clipped him with a blackjack and Cardigan leaned against the wall, shaking his head. They shoved him into another chair.

"Be your age!" Michaels cried hoarsely. "We don't want to kill you, dope!"

Cardigan walked across the room and sat down heavily, his arms hanging, fingers touching the floor. He addressed Michaels in colorful if unprintable idiom.

"That won't get you anywhere," Michaels said. He planted a chair in front of Cardigan and sat down solidly. He looked serious, worried, desperate. "I've got to know how things stand," he said. "I'm going to break this case. I've got to. I've got to get this kid-snatching crowd. I've got to. There's no halfway measure about it. Get me, Cardigan. I mean it. There's no out for me. None. I either crash this case or I'm all washed up. All washed up."

"Good. I hope you get all washed up."

"Cardigan—" Michaels leaned forward. His stomach bunched, overlapping his tight belt. He looked red hot, sweaty, and there was a fierce glow way back in his China-blue eyes. "There's been a kidnap gang systematically working this city for six months. Three times they got away from me. I'm on the carpet now. If I flop this one, I'm out—out. Broke. Out on my pants! I can't afford it." He made a fist, looked at it, then laid it on his thick knee.

Cardigan said: "You'll flop this like you flopped the others. Why? Because you're dumb. Because you're the kind of cop that went out of style when I wore diapers. Because you're a louse. You couldn't even get a job sweeping out our agency's office."

"Cardigan, I am going to get the lowdown on this. Milbray won't even talk to me. He's talked to you. You've made contact. You were in the Metals Building last night. Who'd you see?"

"That's my business."

"That building is full of lawyers. You saw a lawyer. Who is he?"

"Again—my business."

Michaels thumped his knee. "I'm telling you I'm serious. There's nothing going to stop me. I'm going to get these heels. Where are they? When is the money to be turned over—and where?"

Cardigan said: "My job is to get the kid."

"Mine is to get the gang."

"Even if it costs the kid's life?"

"I tell you, Cardigan—I've got to break this, one way or another, and I don't care who pays."

CARDIGAN raised his foot, planted it on Michaels' chest and toppled him to the floor. The two bruisers grabbed Cardigan as he rose and slammed him down again. They held him locked in the chair. Michaels got up, replaced his hat and jammed his hands into the pockets of his alpaca coat. Red color swam in his eyes and sweat poured down his face.

He said: "You may as well come clean, Cardigan, because if you don't you'll stay here till you rot. You'll be no good to Milbray or anybody else."

Cardigan shook his head. "I'd rot before I'd tell you anything."

Michaels hitched his shoulders. "Give it to him."

The two bruisers landed on Cardigan and spent five minutes tossing him around the shack. In the end, he sat in the middle of the floor, tie and collar gone and a stupid look in his eyes. Then very quietly, as though no one were watching him, he got on his hands and knees and began crawling toward the door. One of the bruisers took half a dozen easy steps, braced himself in the doorway, and when Cardigan arrived reached down and cracked him between the eyes. Cardigan fell flat and lay very quiet.

The bruisers looked worried. One said: "Hell, we might kill this guy."

"No fear," Michaels said. "But we've got to make him talk."

The one-eyed man came to and sat up. Michaels got him a drink and the man said: "What hit me?"

"A chair. There it is. Now sit on it till you feel better."

Cardigan began coughing. He rolled over on his back.

"Be sensible," Michaels said.

"Nuts," Cardigan said.

A voice screamed from the woods: "Help! Police! Help!"

Michaels started. "What's that?"

"A woman," one of the bruisers said.

"Oh-o-o-o! Help!"

Michaels snapped at the one-eyed man. "You all right, Jake?"

"Sure, I'm all right."

Michaels took down a shotgun from a rack on the wall, thrust it into the one-eyed man's hands. "Watch this guy!... Come on, boys. We'll see—"

"Help!"

The three men barged out and Jake stood up gripping the shotgun and peering after them. Gradually his gaze lowered to Cardigan. He saw Cardigan's mouth fall open. He saw a fixed, wide-open stare. He shuddered, moved a step closer.

"Hey," he croaked.

He saw that not a muscle twitched. He saw that Cardigan's chest was motionless. And the eyes stared at the ceiling, the mouth was lax, deathly.

"Jeepers!" he croaked. He started for the door.

Cardigan heaved and floored him. Jake hit hard and his head bounced against the floor. A blow ripped to his jaw and moved his entire body several inches across the boards. Cardigan grabbed the shotgun, went out through a back window and lunged along the woods road. A figure leaped from the bushes. Cardigan almost struck.

"How was that?" Pat asked.

"Little wonderful—step on it!"

She had a gun of her own—and his gun. She thrust it into his hand and he tossed the shotgun away. They reached the hill road and there was a taxi parked a few yards away. He bundled her into it.

"I fixed their car," she said.

"What'd you do?"

"Broke their carburetor."

The taxi was speeding past the Hunky settlement. Dust billowed in white clouds behind.

Cardigan looked at her. "Do you know what Michaels is?"

"Don't," she said. "I hate language."

CARDIGAN entered the hotel by way of the garage. He found an open unattended service elevator. He ran it up to the fourth floor and left it there. Pat's key was in his hand and he went to her room. Five minutes later she came in with some packages. She opened them and displayed absorbent cotton, salve, antiseptics.

"Sit on that chair by the window," she said.

"Yes, mama."

"And don't be funny."

She had small hands, white hands, neatly pointed at the tips. She washed his face with a soft sponge, did some cauterizing.

"Ouch!" he said.

"Don't be a baby."

She washed and cleansed a broken welt on his back where a hard shoe had torn his flesh.

"Boy oh boy," he said, gazing out of the window, "what names I could call Michaels!"

"Don't." She sighed. "Some day you're going to discover that while you're a pretty hard hombre you can't lick more than double your weight. Sometimes I think you're a case of arrested development."

"A few more cracks like that I'll recommend your discharge."

"Yes, you will!... There milord, except for five tiny bits of tape on the face, you look presentable."

He shook her hand. "Thanks, trainer."

"What now?"

"Well, for the time being I think Michaels will lay off me. I've several calls to make. You stay here, right at the telephone, until further notice. I'll go up to my room and put on a shirt and tie."

"Wait till I brush your suit."

She whiskbroomed it thoroughly. Then she looked into the corridor, nodded, and he went out and climbed to his room. He put on a white shirt and a blue tie, looked at himself in the mirror, said, "Humph!" and left the hotel.

AARON STEINFARB was dictating to a gum-chewing stenographer when Cardigan looked in. The lawyer shooed the girl into her own little office and waved a tremendous cigar. It said 11:25 by the clock on Steinfarb's desk.

"I phoned you this morning," Steinfarb said.

"I wasn't in."

"No."

"I took a ride out to the mines to see some country. I fell in some broken glass."

"It's tough, falling in broken glass."

"Yeah. Well?" Cardigan said, lifting an eyebrow.

Steinfarb reached into his desk, brought out the little camera. "There. All exposures made. You can get 'em developed."

"Thanks."

Steinfarb screwed up his white pudgy face. "Listen…." He chewed one corner of his lower lip, scowled sidewise at a blank wall. "Listen, Cardigan. I think I ought to tell you. It's going to be tough getting that kid."

"Why?"

Steinfarb made a sour face. "Oh, the cops. Not all the cops. Some. One or two or three. They're sore. They hate private dicks in this town. They hate anybody who tries to butt into their bowl of cherries. Just be careful."

"Thanks. Is everything set?"

"Thirty-five thousand bucks."

Cardigan said: "C.O.D."

"Huh?"

"I've got a girl with me. She'll go with you. She'll carry thirty-five thousand dollars. The cops don't know her. They don't know she's with me. She'll take the thirty-five thousand and she'll turn it over on receipt of the baby. If," he added, "these pictures satisfy me."

"*B-r-r!* They'll shy at that."

"Listen, Steinfarb. I'm on the level. If I'd been hired to get these guys, I'd get them. But I've been hired to get that child. This mug of mine, well—" he shrugged— "some cops tried to play kick-the-wicket with me. But they don't know this girl. She's an agency operative. Do you know why the cops kicked me around?"

"No."

Cardigan pointed. "They wanted to know who I came to see last night in this building."

"Oh," Steinfarb nodded. "Oh, I see."

Cardigan walked to the door. "Get in touch with these kid-snatchers and talk turkey. I'll be seeing you."

CHAPTER FOUR

PLATE GLASS—AND A PUNK

THE ROLL of film gave up four good exposures. The others were blurred or blanks. Cardigan got the pictures at 3:30 that afternoon and hopped a cab. Blaine was on the Milbray grounds.

"Where's Stope?" Cardigan said.

"Snoozing."

Cardigan went on through the grounds and Mrs. Floom let him in. Milbray was fully dressed. He looked not as depressed as he had on Cardigan's first meeting with him. He had a grip on himself, chin up, jaw tight.

"Well?"

Cardigan took the four snapshots from an envelope. "That her?"

"Yes! But where—how—"

"I don't know where, yet. I made Steinfarb get pictures of her. She's alive—"

"Thank God!"

Cardigan tapped the pictures. "You can see. Here she's looking scared. Here she's smiling. Here she's looking down and here she's looking to one side. That's swell."

"This is a great load off my mind, my heart. But I say—your face!"

"Slipped getting out of the bathtub this morning. Now—" Cardigan dropped his voice— "the money. Have it ready at a moment's notice."

Milbray's chest swelled. "Your confidence, sir, makes me feel that the worst is past!"

"Good! It is, I'm sure." He looked around. "Where is Mr. Stope's room?"

"Up that stairway—at the rear of the corridor."

Cardigan climbed the staircase, strode down the upper corridor, knocked. He opened the door and found the room empty. His lips tightened. He went downstairs again and into the kitchen. No one there had seen Mr. Stope. He returned to the library.

"I ought to be back about five," he said.

He went out like a blast of wind and found Blaine at the gate. He gripped Blaine's arm. "Stope's not there."

"Oh-oh."

Cardigan made knots of his fists. "Sure you didn't see him outside?"

"Left him in the room, last."

"When?"

"Hour ago." Blaine began swearing, then stopped and said: "Do you think he slipped out for a drink?"

Cardigan turned on Blaine and yelled at him: "I told Hammerhorn he should never have sent that booze hound with us! I told him! You heard me tell him!"

"Well, why take my head off?"

Cardigan shrugged. "Sorry, fella.... O.K., you stay here. If he turns up, phone Pat and I'll connect with her later. That bum!"

AARON STEINFARB lit a large cigar and whipped smoke out of one corner of his mouth. "Jake, Cardigan. It's all set. You get the dough and give it to the jane and the jane and I will go and meet my clients. There's four of them, Cardigan, and I'll be frank with you—two of them are real hot hoods. So don't double the cross."

"I'm no gofor."

"I don't think you are. I just said that—well, to convince you that only the up-and-up will get that kid. You may think I'm a louse for representing these guys. Maybe I am. Only if I didn't they'd have got someone else. And besides, louse or not, I'm being partially instrumental in the attempt to get the kid back. Don't get me wrong—I'm not grabbing any glory. Don't want it."

Cardigan said: "You don't have to alibi your motives."

"Am I? Excuse me!"

"That was no crack, Steinfarb."

Steinfarb cackled. "O.K., boy, O.K.!" He picked up a pencil, twirled it. "Pictures good, eh?"

"Swell."

"I'll meet the jane at Windsor and Pellman—northeast corner—at nine tonight. And for crying out loud, don't let Michaels or anybody else see you with her or they'll catch on. Michaels will crab this if he can. He's got a lot at stake."

Cardigan said: "The girl will have the dough when she meets you. Stand on the corner whistling something—say, *Sweet and Lovely*. Know it?"

"Yeah."

"Goom-by!"

CARDIGAN entered Pat Seaward's room at 8:30. He took from his pocket a long flat package wrapped in brown paper and bound with ordinary twine. She was sitting in an easy chair reading a magazine which she lowered when the package struck her lap.

"Thirty-five thousand," Cardigan said.

She hefted it but didn't say anything. Cardigan sat on the edge of the bed. He looked at her a few times in silence and then looked at the floor. He was chewing on his lip. He looked dark and worried.

"Penny for your thoughts."

He said: "They're worth thousands, little wonderful." He scowled down at his wrist watch, still wore the scowl when he looked at Pat. "No word about Stope, huh?"

"No."

He rose, smacked fist lazily into palm and took a few exasperated turns up and down the room. Then he stopped and extended a hand toward her. "Can you imagine a guy like that?"

"Do you suppose he's on a drunk?"

"Of course."

"Well, that ought to make him harmless."

He growled, paced the length of the room, stopped and said: "Do you think I like having that drunk wandering around town on a night like this? Anything can happen. He might take a pass at some guy and get pinched. Then what? Then they'll find his identification in the station house. Then what? Well, if Michaels happens to be around…." He swore under his breath and heaved his shoulders.

"What does Steinfarb look like?"

"Little guy. Dark clothes. Derby. Very white face—sort of too white. You'll know him by the song."

"Should I carry a gun?"

"You'd better."

She stood up and stretched her arms. "Well, here's hoping."

"If we win, Pat, hike the kid right to home. Don't bother phoning me until you've got the kid home. Only—" a shadow passed his eyes and his mouth hardened— "if that bum Stope were only where I could lay my hands on him!"

She smiled. She had a rather soft smile at times. "Don't get all steamed up, chief. You might get rash."

He muttered: "Better get started, Pat."

She made a trim figure on her way through the lobby, ten minutes later. She had a smart, straight-legged walk and a fine eyes-front way about her. She looked white and cool and clean in the hot street. Lobby loungers looked after her.

The street climbed upward here. No matter their original state, the buildings, one and all, were made dusky brothers by the everlasting coal dust. Neon lights looked red and swollen in the warm night haze. Pat reached the top and flicked a glance at the signpost there. She went on past the bleat and blare of a radio store. Corner loafers whistled at her. One wise guy tried to take her arm. She gave a backward kick, expertly, and the man fell down huddling his shins. She went on.

A block behind, on the other side of the street, Cardigan drifted past shop windows, took a passing interest in their contents, followed with intermittent glances the progress of Pat. On the next corner was a large weighing scale surmounted by a large mirror. He stopped before it and in the mirror he was able to see a block ahead. Remaining there, he saw Pat cross the street, saw her linger on the corner and, after a moment, turn toward a small man. Cardigan kept his gaze fixed on the mirror. He saw Pat and Steinfarb start walking.

"Gain any weight?"

Cardigan knew the voice. He didn't turn. "I've all the weight I need, Michaels. I suppose it'll get to the point where I won't be able to take a bath without having you pop in. How do you like my face?"

"What happened to you?"

Cardigan turned slowly and made a sarcastic grimace.

Farther up the street there was the sound of glass crashing. Pedestrians stopped, turned. A police whistle blew.

Cardigan stiffened.

MICHAELS raised his chin, started off on the run and Cardigan followed at a fast walk, joining the crowd. Then he too broke into a run. People began shouting and, beyond the next corner, a crowd was gathering, bunching on the sidewalk. Cardigan elbowed his way ahead roughly. In a minute he saw what had caused the sound. A plate-glass window had been smashed. Heels were grinding glass to powder on the sidewalk and a cop's red face was working.

Michaels broke through. "What's up, Finn?"

Cardigan saw the cop holding Stope by one arm. Stope was drunk. His hat was on the back of his head and his hair was in tatters down on his forehead. He was swaying on his feet and complaining.

Steinfarb was holding Pat. He was saying: "The guy's drunk. I didn't strike him. He tried to get smart."

Stope said: "F'r Gawd's sake, ossifer, I tell you I know the lady. Old pals. Yeah… I jus' said hello and wanna shake hands and she high-hats me. And the bozo shoves me and this here glass window kind of bends out and smacks me and breaks. 'S 'onest trut'."

Pat was white-faced. "I'm sorry, officer. I never saw this man before. He must be mistaken."

"What's your name?" Michaels butted in.

Steinfarb said: "My name'll do. The lady's a friend of mine. Pinch this punk if you want to. He took a swing at me, missed and struck the window."

"Stay there," Michaels rapped out; spun on Stope. "What's your name?"

"Harvey M. S-Stope."

"Where do you live?"

"N' York."

"What are you doing here?"

"Sh! Mustn't tell, commissioner! 'S trut'—hic—I'm private detective. Like you—only ver' private. I—I—"

Cardigan came through, glitter-eyed. "I'll take him, Michaels. The fat-head works for me. We'll settle for the window."

"Oh, yeah?"

Cardigan grabbed Stope by the throat. "For two cents, I'd push in your mug. Stand up! What's the idea of insulting strange women on the streets? Every woman you meet you think you've met before. Stand up!"

"See here, Cardigan," Michaels broke in.

But Cardigan thrust him aside, said to Pat: "I'm sorry, madam, my friend did this. He's drunk. I'm sorry. I'll fix it for this window."

"O.K.," Steinfarb said.

He turned Pat around and marched her off. Michaels looked after them. He started to say something several times. His face reddened. Then he turned to Cardigan.

"All right. Beat it. Take this guy home."

The storekeeper cried: "But what about my window?"

Cardigan thrust an agency card into his hand. "Send your bill there, mister."

He wheeled Stope across the street, and when he looked around he saw Michaels stretching his legs up the street. Cardigan stopped, watched him for a split-minute, then shook Stope violently.

"Listen, you. Go back to the hotel—" It was useless. Stope couldn't stand up. Cardigan walked him to a taxicab, opened the door and pushed him in. He gave the driver a dollar. "Take this stew to The Wheelburgh and drop him in the lobby."

"O.K."

Cardigan stepped back, turned, and went sloping up the street. He saw Michaels climb into a taxi beneath a corner street light a block beyond. He ran a hundred yards, caught another taxi making the turn. He flagged it and climbed in.

"Follow that white cab."

CHAPTER FIVE

BLONDE PICCANINNY

THE WHITE cab jounced over broken pavement. Sparks showered from Steinfarb's cigar to the floor. He stamped them out.

"That chump Michaels," he said, irritably.

Pat said: "Stope, you mean!"

"You used your head, little girl." He reached over and patted her hand. "I could go for you in a big way."

"Pul-lease."

"Honest, I could—"

"Stop that!" She bit off and threw his hand back across his lap. "Keep your mind on your business, Mr. Steinfarb."

He chuckled and leaned back in his corner, drew reflectively on his big cigar. The cab struck smoother pavement and rushed on through the dark streets. Presently Steinfarb leaned forward and tapped the connecting window, pointed ahead. The cab stopped at the next corner. Steinfarb got out, paid up, took Pat's arm and walked her down a narrow, deserted street.

They walked two blocks, turned into a main drag. It was a narrow, noisy street, lined with cheap novelty shops, cheap burlesque houses, open-faced soda-pop stands, sidewalk shooting galleries alive with the flat metallic rattle of .22 caliber rifles and revolvers. High-yellow girls sauntered with strutting black sheiks. Cheap perfume clogged the soggy air. Tough whites stood on street corners and cops traveled in pairs.

Steinfarb stopped Pat before the Old West Shooting Gallery. Twelve rifles and six revolvers lay on the platform. Behind it stood a mulatto in a ten-gallon hat and a lavender bandana. He looked at Steinfarb. Steinfarb nodded, then the mulatto nodded and went to the rear, disappearing behind a curtain.

"How's your eye, Miss Seaward?" Steinfarb smiled.

She picked up a nine-shot .22 revolver and knocked down eight moving ducks.

"Whew!" whistled Steinfarb.

"It's a cheap gun," she commented.

"As if you needed an alibi!"

The mulatto reappeared and jerked his thumb. Steinfarb took Pat's arm and guided her into a hallway. They climbed a narrow wooden staircase in which yellow gas light wavered. A man opened a door and looked at them with eyes that were yellow in the yellow gas light. They entered a drab sitting room and a second man stood leaning against the wall with his hand in his coat pocket. He had some nervous affliction and his lips, his nose, his brows kept twitching.

He said: "Happy to thee you. Thit down."

The man who had opened the door now closed it and shot a bolt home. His yellow hair was fine and shiny like corn silk, his neck rugged.

He said: "You got it?"

"I've got it," Pat said. She held up the brown paper package.

"Open it."

She opened it and thumbed the thick sheaf of bills. The yellow-haired man came toward her. She stepped back.

"C.O.D.," she said.

The man scowled.

Steinfarb said: "Don't get fresh now. Everything is on the up-and-up. Get the kid."

The lisper did not move from the wall. The yellow-haired man turned on his heel and went into another room, closing the door. When the door reopened a large black woman came out carrying a black child.

Pat frowned. "What's that?"

The black woman grinned. She drew down one of the child's stockings, showing white flesh. Only the arms and the face had been stained and there was a black knitted cap drawn tightly over the head. She lifted this, showing golden curls.

THE yellow-haired man came in and said: "There she is. We had a hell of a time getting that stain off to get those pictures. It was easier getting it back again." His eyes were hard as they moved from Steinfarb to Pat. "The nigger'll take the baby out. She'll walk two blocks down to Ennis Street with the kid. You watch her from the front window. You'll give us the dough and you'll stay in here till we go out. We'll go up the street. You can watch us. When you see us turn a corner you come out. Not before. If you run out right after us, the kid gets it. Right now we've got two guys stationed down the street. If something starts, these guys let the kid and the nigger have it."

Pat started.

The yellow-haired man said: "The nigger's deaf."

The negress kept grinning like a fool.

Pat threw the money on the table and the yellow-haired man scooped it up, counted it. He peeled off several bills and gave them to Steinfarb. Steinfarb pocketed them. Pat went into the darkened front room. The bay-windows were large. She had a full view of the street, both ways. She came back into the lighted room.

The yellow-haired man was telling the negress things with his fingers. She nodded and went over to the door. The yellow-haired man opened it and the negress went out. They all moved into the front room and stood by the windows.

They could not see Michaels. He was down leaning against the counter of the shooting gallery.

"A little guy," he was saying, "and a neat-looking jane. They came down this street and I lost track of 'em. Did you see 'em? Come on. I'm asking you!"

The mulatto looked innocent. "No, boss, I ain't seen 'em."

"You're lying!"

"Me lie? Shucks, I wouldn't lie!"

Michaels gnawed his lip. "They came down on this side of the street. You—"

He stopped and turned. A man had cursed out loud. Stope had reeled into the man. The man had shoved him and Stope had fallen down. Now he rose.

"Ah!" he said, spotting Michaels.

He started forward and began losing his balance. He came fast. Michaels, scowling, stepped aside and Stope hit the counter, bounced off, reeled on and collided with the negress as she came out of the door. Both went down. The negress yelped, clutching the child tightly as she rolled over. The black knitted cap fell off and gold curls burst into view.

"M' Gawd!" exclaimed Stope. "A blonde piccaninny!"

Michaels' teeth clamped shut and he leaped forward.

Upstairs, Pat was the first to sense things. Her gun was in her hand and she whirled on the lisper and the yellow-haired man. "Beat it!" she said. "Get out the back way and run. The woman fell and there's a drunk and a cop down there!"

The yellow-haired man snarled: "A frame!"

"Get," Pat said. "I could hold you boys, but get while you've got time. We've been double-crossed! Go on, fools!"

Steinfarb said: "You heard her. Do you think I'd risk getting in a jam like this? It's a tough break. You dopes, scram!"

The two men turned. Pat was at their heels with her gun. She saw them through a rear window and watched them scamper down a fire-escape. She spun and Steinfarb was glowering.

He snapped: "That drunk didn't go home!"

"You're telling me!"

SHE flew across the room, out into the hall, down the stairway. She reached the sidewalk to find Michaels trying to tear the child from the negress's arms. Michaels struck with his gun and the black woman tottered, her arms loosened. Pat leaped and the force of her body staggered Michaels. She caught the child as it fell, as the negress went down.

Cardigan came bounding across the street, caught Michaels' arm as Michaels swung on Pat. He twisted Michaels all the way around.

"Michaels, beat it!" he rasped. "This is a hot spot!"

Pedestrians, loungers, began running away.

"Leggo!" Michaels roared.

The roar of a car gathering speed rose above the tumult in the street. Pat clasped the child and ran toward the open hall door. The black woman was up, wild-eyed, reeling about. Stope was up, teetering.

Pat flung a terrified look over her shoulder as she saw the car swing in toward the curb, speeding. She fell over the threshold, into the hallway. Guns banged and a bullet splintered wood near her head. She crowded her small body against the baby, protecting it. The guns banged again. Stope, staggering around, suddenly stiffened. He was directly in front of the door, in front of Pat and the child. His body stopped four bullets and then he turned around twice, sat down, coughed, and straightened out.

Pat couldn't seem to get up. Cardigan flung away from Michaels, leaped to the door, laid his big hands on Pat's shoulder.

"I'm all feet," she panted.

"Shot?"

"No—no."

Bang! Bang! Bang! The gunflame was red, spurting from the darkened tonneau of the car as it whipped past. One shot broke a window, one chipped pavement, the third hit Cardigan somewhere above the waist, behind, and he cursed and fell down. But he was up in a second, wheeling around, drawing his own gun.

"Put 'em up, you!" Michaels screamed, his gun leveled.

"Me? You fool, why don't you get that car?"

"Put 'em up or I'll— Put 'em up, Cardigan!" yelled Michaels. He was red-faced. In his voice, in the blaze of his eyes, was madness.

The negress lolled against the counter, her eyes rolling. She looked mad, too, but in a dazed, dumb way. Her big black hands fell on two revolvers. She gripped them. They were .22s, nine shots each. She swiveled hugely and began pumping.

Michaels turned on her, his eyes widening as the small slugs drove into him. He fired. His gun shook in his hand and the negress went down to her knees; and while she knelt she kept on pulling both triggers. She cut Michaels down. They were all hits. His gun fell before he did. Then he fell on top of it. And then the negress fell, for Michaels' one shot had been well aimed.

The street was suddenly quiet. There was no one nearby. For two blocks, either way, the street was empty. Until a squad of cops came running on the double.

Cardigan ran a hand across his eyes, grunted and sat down in the doorway. Pat was sitting beside him. She held the child in her arms, rocking it gently saying, "Sh—sh; don't cry, don't cry, honey."

Then she put one arm around Cardigan's neck. "Steady, chief. Steady!"

"I'll be all right, little wonderful."

He woke up in a hospital several hours later.

Pat was sitting beside the bed.

He said: "I'd climb the highest mountain—"

"Please," she said, half smiling, and patted his hand. "Please, chief, don't yodel."

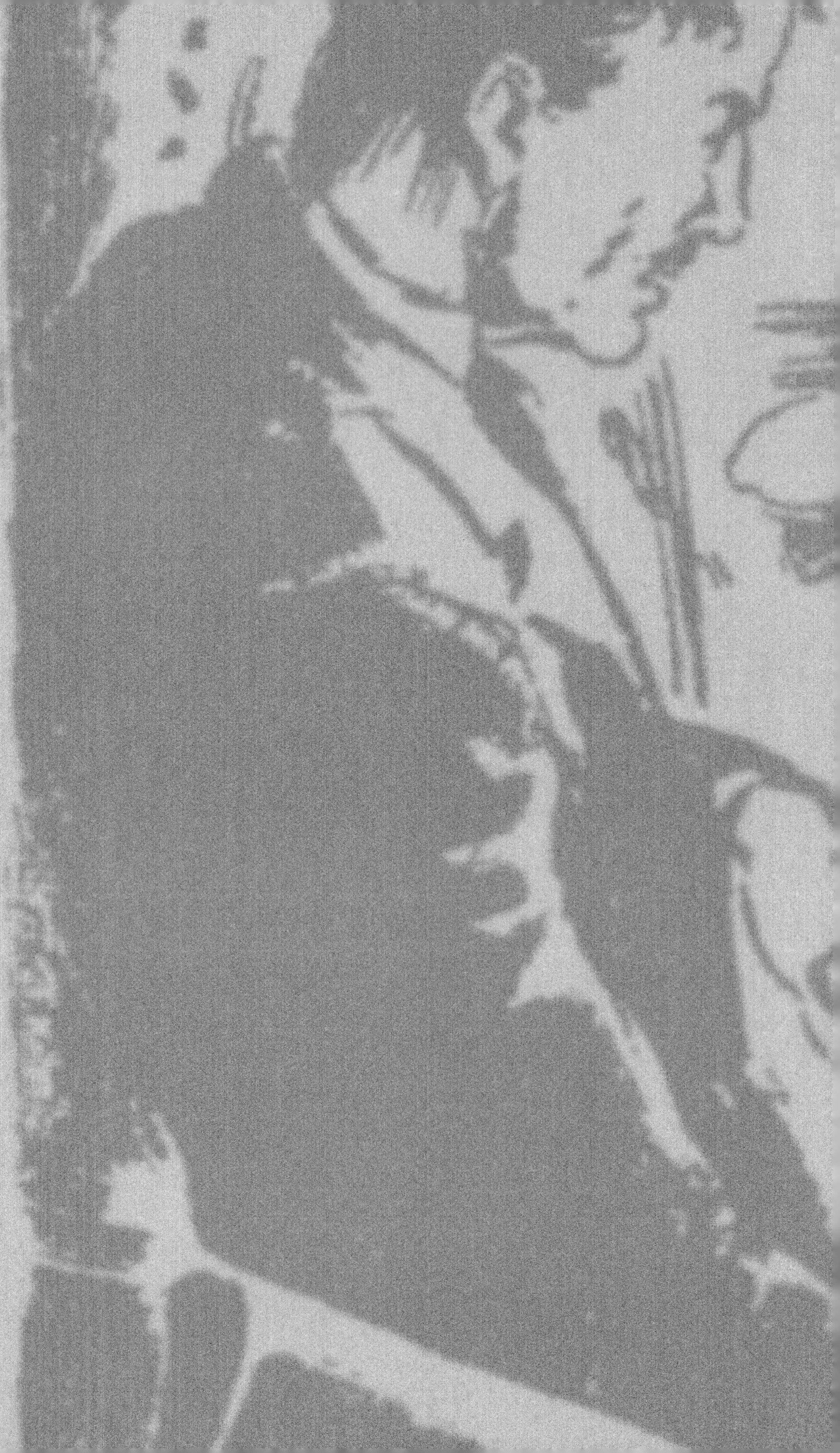

LEAD PEARLS

It all started with murder—nothing new to that big dick Cardigan. The motive was what mattered. That and the bloodstained string of pearls which belonged around the Kemmerich woman's throat.

CHAPTER ONE

"—AS A HOUNDS TOOTH"

L**ILY KEMMERICH** moved onto the tiled terrace twenty stories above the East River. The drone of voices was behind her, in the big living room. She was in evening clothes—pale ice-blue against the creamy whiteness of her skin. Her hair was blonde, parted in the middle and drawn tight to a doughnut over each ear. She leaned over the railing and looked down. She shuddered, turned away and pressed hot, moist palms together. A pulse in her throat throbbed.

The butler lay face upward on the living-room carpet. He had lain face downward until the arrival of Sayer, the medical-office man. The carpet was mouse-colored, and there was a large blotch of darker color near the butler's head.

A couple of uniformed cops stood near the corridor entry. Detective Dirago stood with hands on hips trying to make sense out of a futuristic water color on the wall. Lieutenant McCartney came down the short corridor from the bedrooms. Behind him came fat Leopold Kemmerich.

"This is a lulu," said McCartney, irritably.

Dirago turned a swart, handsome face. "Hahn?"

"Nix," McCartney growled. "The place is all busted up and nothing's been h'isted. This guy's been beaned to death and there ain't even a penny missing. Tie that!"

Kemmerich sat down heavily and said, *"Ach, du lieber,"* wearily.

Sayer, the medical-office man, looked at his hat. "Well, I'm all set, lieutenant. I'll breeze. Got a date. This is murder."

"You're telling me?" McCartney said.

He looked at his watch. "Ain't that guy come yet?"

He was an angular man, with one shoulder higher than the other and a warped, sour face.

Sayer went to the door and had his hand on the knob when a knock sounded. He opened the door and Cardigan stood there hat in hand, his shaggy mop of hair shadowing his forehead. He nodded to Sayer and came in.

Sayer said: "Well, be seeing you," to McCartney, and went out, closing the door softly.

"Hello, Cardigan," McCartney said.

Cardigan stared at the body on the floor. "What's this?"

"What's it look like?"

Cardigan tossed his hat to a divan, crossed to the body, stood over it and after a moment lifted his eyes to McCartney. "Brained, huh?"

His eyes left McCartney and settled on Lily Kemmerich who stood now in the terrace entry, one hand held against her throat. She dropped her glance sidewise, entered quietly and took a chair in the shadows. He swung his eyes back to McCartney.

"Where do I come in?"

McCartney raked a short laugh between his teeth. "I understand your agency's working for the indemnity company that handled Mrs. Kemmerich's necklace—the one that was stolen a week ago."

"Sure."

McCartney poked a finger toward the body. "I just thought you might be interested in this. Mr. and Mrs. Kemmerich came in here half an hour ago and found the butler conked out. He was socked on the dome with a blunt instrument and rubbed out. Sayer said about two hours ago. Find any dope about that necklace yet?"

"No."

"You wouldn't by any chance ever take it into your nut to crash this apartment to see if the necklace was really stolen, would you?"

Cardigan narrowed one eye. "Clear that up, Mac."

"I mean, suppose you figgered that the necklace might still be here."

"Nonsense!" cried Leopold Kemmerich.

McCartney raised a hand toward him, said to Cardigan: "How about it?"

Cardigan sighed. "I thought it'd be something screwy like this. I was in bed, Mac. Where'd you birth that idea, anyhow?"

"Nothing's been taken," McCartney said. "Mrs. Kemmerich's bedroom was turned upside down but there wasn't a thing h'isted. Not a thing. Jewels are layin' around, dough, lots of things. It wasn't

Coal dust and crockery showered down.

an ordinary house break. There's a fluke somewhere. That room was dressed down by a guy who knew his groceries, but there wasn't a thing—not a thing—lifted. I ask you, now."

Cardigan was looking at the shadowed Lily Kemmerich. "You're sure of that, Mrs. Kemmerich?"

"I'm sure," she said in a throaty whisper.

Fat Leopold Kemmerich was annoyed. "My wife has said she is sure. I am sure. That is finished. Find the killer, lieutenant!"

SITTING in the shadows, Lily Kemmerich kept her hands pressed tightly together, her chin up, her breath bated. She moved her eyes from one to another of the men in the room; she did not drop them to the dead man on the floor.

Irritable, whiny-voiced, McCartney came up close to Cardigan. "I'm trying to think that this here murder's got something to do with that stolen necklace. That necklace was worth thirty thousand bucks. It was stolen from Mrs. Kemmerich last Wednesday night in the theatre crowd in front of the Dorado on Forty-fourth Street. That's her story. It's possible, ain't it, that you might have doubted it was stolen?"

"Don't be an egg, Mac."

Kemmerich was on his feet. "You're calling my wife a liar?"

"Now, now," McCartney whined, shaking his hands, "don't get me wrong, Mr. Kemmerich. I've got a job to do. I'm just wondering about Cardigan here."

Lily got up and left the room, swiftly, quietly.

Cardigan was glowering at McCartney. "You don't have to wonder about me, Mac. I'd sure be a sap to crash this apartment. Give me a little credit, anyhow."

"All right, then. What ideas have you got on the stolen necklace?"

"Just that—it was stolen, fat-head. We're working on it and we've got a good chance of getting it back."

McCartney's eyes widened. "Oh, you have! Good! Been getting some good leads, eh? Well, I'm glad to hear that!"

"Yes, you are!"

Cardigan turned on his heel, crossed the room and scooped his hat up from the divan.

McCartney looked worried. He flopped his arms up and down in a nettled, jointless fashion and yammered: "Don't get all steamed up now, Cardigan. You don't have to get all steamed up now, do you?"

Cardigan turned on him. "Oh, I don't, don't I? I should maybe thank you for getting me out of bed and over here on some half-baked idea! Goom-by, sweetheart!"

He yanked open the door. Looking beyond McCartney, he saw that Lily had returned to the living-room entry. She was tall and beautiful against the low light of the inner corridor and her hand was against her throat again; her face was unnaturally white.

Kemmerich began complaining gutturally: "All these stupid questions about the necklace, when what you police should be doing is sending out alarms for the murderer!"

"On what?" moaned McCartney, shaking his arms. "On what? When nobody saw the guy. When not even the elevator boy saw the guy. On what, I ask you?"

Cardigan was saying to one of the cops: "If you think hard, it might occur to you that I want to get through this door."

"Should I, lieutenant?"

McCartney came over wearing a pained expression. "I don't want to hold you, Cardigan. I'm a white man. I had no idea of holding you. I—"

"You just want me to sit down and tell you how I know about that necklace job. Christmas is five months away, Mac, and you don't notice me wearing a white beard."

McCartney looked crestfallen. He waved his hand loosely. "Let him go, Abel—let him go or he'll get nasty."

Cardigan went out.

PAT SEAWARD was small, trim, neat. She had a one-room suite on West End Avenue, high enough to overlook the Riverside Drive houses and catch a glimpse of the river and the Jersey shore. It was late. She wore black pajamas and a mandarin coat and she sat curled up on a divan buffing her nails when the buzzer sounded.

She got up and opened the door and Cardigan squinted at her. "At this hour," she said.

"Detectiving is the curse of the leisure classes, little home girl."

She shrugged, kicked the door shut when he had entered and stood with her back to it, buffing her nails industriously. He scaled his hat across the room into a chair, dropped to the divan and smacked his knees, stared hard across the room at nothing.

"The Kemmerich butler got it," he said.

"Got what?"

"A look at back of beyond." He sighed. "Croaked. Bumped off. Finished."

"Oh!" she said, softly, and stared at him for a full minute.

He nodded. "McCartney woke me up and got me over to the Kemmerich *casa*. Crime in the stronghold of the *élite* always seems out of place."

Worry masked her eyes. "Oh, chief, you didn't—"

"Now you're going to start that," he growled; shook his head, saying: "No, I had nothing to do with it. McCartney thought he had an idea that this murder was in connection with that necklace job—a house break. The butler must have poked in and the guy took a haul at him. You should see him."

"Thanks, no." She shuddered.

He said: "Pat, there's something on the low-and-low about the necklace business. When I hit that apartment tonight Lily Kemmerich looked like a ghost. Like a very beautiful ghost. I heard her speak once. Her voice sounded—you know—clogged. She's worried about something."

"What do you think?"

"I don't know."

"Do you think it was really stolen?"

He looked at her. "Yes, I'm sure it was stolen. It was lifted in the street, on the sidewalk. It was on her neck when she walked through the lobby. Her coat was open and six people saw it. She lost it between the lobby and the curb—in the crowd."

"What did they get tonight?"

"Nothing. That's the funny part about it. The apartment was crashed; McCartney said Lily's room was knocked apart—but nothing was taken. She said nothing was taken."

"Then why was she frightened?"

He stood up. "Listen, little wonderful. Get out bright and early tomorrow morning. Get on her tail. No matter where she goes, tail her. See what kind of people she meets. Stick with her till she gets back home. That clear?"

"Perfectly. What's on your mind?"

"I'd like to know why she looked so white tonight."

Pat sighed. "Listen, chief. Why get mixed up in this killing? Leave it to the cops. You've got a pretty good steer on who snatched that necklace. You've got two men tailing 'Packy' Daskas and if they tail him long enough—"

"I know, I know," he broke in. "Packy was in Forty-fourth Street that night and we know snatching necklaces is his business. But do as I tell you. Tail Lily Kemmerich."

She shrugged. "O.K., iron man."

He went to the door, opened it and turned to smile at her. "You look nice in black, Pat."

She was back at her nails. "You should see my grandmother," she said.

HE WENT downstairs and grabbed a cab. West End Avenue was dead as a country lane and he leaned back, crammed an old briar and lit up. He'd got the tip about Packy Daskas from a barman in a Forty-fourth Street walk-up speakeasy. The barman was a cop hater but on the other hand he had no use for Packy Daskas. He liked Cardigan, and when Cardigan had dropped in a few nights after the robbery the barman had told him about Packy.

"See that front window?" he had said. "Well, Packy was in here for an hour before the show let out. And three or four times he went to that window and looked across at the Dorado. He left here about ten minutes before the show was out."

Two agency men, working through stoolies, had landed on Packy's tail. They'd frisked his room on Seventh Avenue, found nothing. He wouldn't be fool enough to carry thirty thousand dollars worth of pearls in his pocket. The natural assumption was that he had fenced them, and the agency had the two men still on his tail in hopes of finding Packy's connections.

The cabman was taking corners rapidly.

"What's the hurry?" Cardigan asked.

The driver said: "I don't know for sure, buddy, but I got an idea you're bein' follered. There's been a checker takin' all these turns with me. I'm headin' for the bright lights and then you give a guy a break and get out. I got a wife and kids and I ain't figgerin' on gettin' me or the buggy shot up."

Cardigan looked around. Then he turned front and said: "Thanks. Here's half a buck. I'll take the next corner on the hop."

"Am I relieved!"

Cardigan opened the door, and when the driver slowed for a southbound turn he swung off and went bounding to the shelter of the corner building. He crowded it and watched the checkered cab take the turn. The tonneau was dark, but he had a feeling that a face inside was turned toward him. He shrank back. The checker loafed south, stopped at the next block. Cardigan, standing now on the curb, saw a figure leave it and duck down a side street. He knocked out his pipe, walked east as far as the park and boarded another cab.

When he reached his apartment hotel on Lexington Avenue he went straight to the telephone and called Pat.

"I was tailed," he said, "from your hotel. So watch your step.... I don't know who it was. May be one of McCartney's men trying to be bright or it might be somebody else. But keep your ears pulled in, little girl."

He hung up and then called his boss, George Hammerhorn. He said: "Listen, George. The Kemmerich butler was killed tonight during a house break. McCartney's on it. Thinks it has some connection with the necklace. The police department may be camped in your office when you get down in the morning, so act innocent.... I'm clean as a hound's tooth.... That's all."

He pronged the receiver, jacked a chair against the door, undressed and piled into bed. He drank a stiff nightcap straight from the neck of a flask he kept in the bed-table drawer. Elevated trains slammed up and down on Third Avenue, but he went to sleep in a few minutes.

CHAPTER TWO

SOL FEITELBERG ENTERTAINS

IT WAS nine-thirty when Cardigan entered the outer office of the agency on Madison Avenue. Miss Goff, the stenographer, had a handkerchief to her face and above it Cardigan saw that her eyes were wet. He closed the door softly.

"Man trouble?" he said.

She shook her head, made a face, started to say something and then began crying harder. He shrugged, crossed the little office and pushed in the glass-paneled door that led to the sanctum of his boss.

George Hammerhorn sat at his big flat-topped desk. His hands were palms-down on it, the arms at full length. His bulk was motionless. His big face was a mask and his eyes stared out through an open window. In an instant he was aware of Cardigan's presence, and he made a sound in his throat, blinked his eyes, and began moving things aimlessly around on his desk.

"Well, Jack...."

Cardigan was scowling.

Hammerhorn looked up at him. "Fogarty got it."

"What!"

"Two A.M. this ack emma."

"Fogarty!"

"Fogarty was killed at two this morning in West Tenth Street, near Sheridan Square. Two shots—both in the back of the neck. He wasn't carrying any identification, so they didn't find out who he was until an hour ago."

Cardigan ripped out, "Packy Daskas—"

But Hammerhorn raised a hand. "Don't get hot. Sit down a minute. Don't go off half cocked."

Cardigan looked brown and ugly. "If that Greek so-and-so—"

"Sit down, sit down, sit down."

"If that Greek so-and-so gave Fogarty the heat I'll bust more than his schnozzle!"

Hammerhorn slammed the desk. "Sit down! I tell you, sit down, Irish!"

Cardigan rolled to an iced cooler and drew a glass of water. He slopped half of it on the floor, downed the rest. He planked the glass back in the metal container, gave all indications of an impending explosion, then suddenly relaxed and walked quietly to a chair, sat down, put chin in palm.

"Poor old Fogarty," he sighed, heavily.

Hammerhorn blinked wistfully. "He was my first operative."

"Where was Goehrig?"

"Goehrig covered the tail till midnight. Fogarty picked it up then and Goehrig lammed home to get some shut-eye."

"Who found Fogarty?"

"A cook in an all-night restaurant—on his way home."

"I mean the cops."

"A patrolman—Ferraro. He busted over from Sheridan Square and found poor old Fogarty in the gutter. He got nervous and took a swing at the cook with the locust. So the cook passed out for two hours and everything was balled up. The cop called an ambulance and the ambulance hit a drunken driver in Hudson Street and that tied things up too."

Cardigan made a jaw. "O.K. I'll go out and find me this yap Daskas. Or have the cops got him?"

Hammerhorn passed a cold palm across his forehead. "No. I didn't tell the cops. You know how I feel about Fogarty. I know how you feel. That's all very jake. But you've got a job to do. We've got to recover that necklace. If we stick the cops on Daskas that'll end things. If Daskas did lift that necklace, we'll never get it if the cops slap him in jail. There'll be a big commission for us if we get it—and a nice slice for poor old Fogarty's wife. We've got to think of that too. Fogarty—you know—didn't carry any insurance. We've got to—well—look out for his wife." He made a few awkward gestures. "It's the only right—kind of—thing. You know?"

"I get you, boss." Cardigan stood up, made a fist with his right hand and eyed it; then snapped the fingers open toward Hammerhorn and sighted down along them. "But I'm going to make contact with this Greek."

Hammerhorn hardened. "I don't want you clowning around just for the sake of a grudge."

"I know what I'm doing."

Still hard, Hammerhorn said: "Remember, it was on your say-so that we put the tail on Daskas. You haven't got a thing on him. You don't know that he lifted that necklace. After all, I'm running a detective agency here, not a crap table. And I'll be damned if I'm going to have you run this Greek punk against the wall and load his belly with lead! Not while I'm in these pants! If you want to play the role of avenger, we're quits. You may be Irish, but I'm Dutch."

Cardigan let the echoes die, meanwhile regarding the ceiling. Then he lowered his gaze and said in a tranquil voice: "I stuck Pat on the Kemmerich woman."

"Why?"

Cardigan told him, then added: "Pat'll be glue on that lady's heels and we may find something. Lily Kemmerich's got something up her pretty sleeve and I don't mean her shapely arm."

Hammerhorn stood up and got his hat, cleared his throat. "Well—I'm going to run up and see what I can do for Fogarty's wife."

CARDIGAN was marking time in the office when Pat rang in a little before noon.

He said: "O.K., sugar. I'll run right over."

He hung up and was reaching for his hat when McCartney came in chewing the stub of a cigar to shreds. Everything about the bony lieutenant was shapeless—his hat, his coat, his shoulders, his worried, irritable face. When he took his hat off his slabby hair was partless and ragged. He took it off to scratch his head. He was not a bad man;

he was a fair cop but he had a reputation for a busybody and by some he was called "Old Woman McCartney."

"Sorry," Cardigan said. "I was just about to leave."

"Cardigan, Cardigan…." McCartney's head shook like the head of a loose-jointed marionette. He yanked at his loose pants and ran the back of his hand across his sour, worried lips. "Look at this now, Cardigan. Here your man Fogarty is bumped off only a few hours after the Kemmerich butler gets slammed out. Cardigan, now listen—"

"Mac, I've got a lunch date."

McCartney wobbled his loose arms and stamped one foot like a child being deprived of candy. Half embarrassed, half petulant, he also seemed on the verge of tears.

"Honest, Cardigan, I can't help believing this kill of the butler has some connection with the necklace. You say it's your job to get that necklace. O.K., and luck to you. But it's my job to get the guy who knocked over the butler. You must have a suspicion. Give me a break."

Cardigan slapped on his hat, nodded toward the door. "Going down?" He did not wait for an answer but headed out, reached the corridor and drifted to the elevator bank.

McCartney was at his heels, plucking at his elbow. "Here I am a good guy, always giving other guys breaks, living a straight home life and taking no more graft than I need—and everybody takes advantage of me."

"Going down!" sang out the elevator boy.

Cardigan bowed. "Before me, Mac."

McCartney stamped into the car, jerked at his tie, made irritable sounds in his throat until they reached the lobby. Out in the street, Cardigan turned and gripped the lieutenant's arm.

"You made a few cracks about me last night I didn't like, Mac," he said, then shook his head, adding, "but I'm not holding that against you. Fogarty was the best-liked man in this agency. I liked him especially. The old boy broke me in. Seven years ago he took a bullet in the gut to save me. Now I'll tell you—and it's on the up-and-up, strictly kosher—that I don't know who bumped him off. I don't know if there's any connection between that and the rubbing out of the Kemmerich butler. I don't know anything that would be worth a damn to you. I have suspicions, but I learned long ago that they're worse than dynamite to handle. Now for crying out loud, don't hang to my tail. Scram."

He turned sharply on his heel and strode down Madison Avenue. A little farther on, he hopped a cab and sat back while it tussled with traffic down and across town to Grand Central. He got off at the Forty-second Street entrance and found Pat waiting for him inside, near the bootblack stand. She had never looked more trim. They walked down to the oyster bar and climbed onto high stools, ordered Blue Points on the half-shell.

"So what?" Cardigan said.

"She came out of the apartment at nine-thirty. She didn't ride in the family chariot. Took a cab at Third Avenue and I, therefore, into a second cab. No, I don't use Tabasco."

"McCartney turned up. Good old McCartney. He said—"

"I thought you wanted to hear my story."

"I do, keed."

"So I followed her, with the old female eagle eyes. Directly to a pawnshop on Eighth Avenue. Here's the address. I popped into a drug store across the street and ordered a milk shake. I don't like milk shakes, so I was able to make it last longer than any other drink I could think of. She was in there half an hour. When she came out she walked a block and got into another taxi. I followed her to a hairdresser on Fifth Avenue. Probably she stopped in for an appointment, because she came right out and then I followed her to a modiste in Fifty-seventh Street, east. She was in there half an hour. When she came out she took another cab and so to home. I spoke with Miss Goff before. What's poor Fogarty's wife going to do?"

"George'll find a way." He laid down the oyster fork and looked Pat square in the eye. "Fogarty must have got pretty close. So close that the heel let him have it. There might be something doing down around Sheridan Square."

"I don't like the way you say that."

"Why?"

"The tone seems to indicate that you might revert to the sod and do something crazy."

He picked up the oyster fork. "What do you suppose Lily was doing in that pawnshop?"

"Buying a doohickey, maybe."

They both looked at each other and then Cardigan said, "I can imagine. S. Feitelberg, *huhn?* Pawnshop—Eighth Avenue. All right, Pat—back you go to watch Lily. Watch every move she makes."

Pat said, "Swell," and slid a morning paper across the counter. "That item I checked off there. It probably means nothing, but just the same everything concerning Kemmerich ought to interest you. Heinrich Van Damm, the Holland gem expert, is arriving on the S.S. *Oberstadt* today and is to be entertained by Leopold Kemmerich, his boyhood friend. With butlers being killed, cops, private and city, horseplaying around the Kemmerich bailiwick, I imagine Mynheer Van Damm will find the entertainment gorgeous. No, thanks; no dessert. The old waistline, governor!"

"Watch Lily, little wonderful."

"I'd stare my eyes out even if I didn't know her. She knows how to wear clothes."

HE STOOD for a while outside, in front of the sporting-goods store, getting a cigar started after Pat had walked east. He had watched the smart, rhythmic swing of her bright, trim heels. He had given a bum a quarter.

Presently he walked down the broad sidewalk and pushed into a taxicab. It hauled him westward across town through a stubborn honeycomb of traffic and deposited him on Eighth Avenue. By this time the cigar was half smoked. He walked south. He had the lunging walk of a big man.

Sol Feitelberg's pawnshop was bigger than most, but fundamentally it was the same inside—so dark that Cardigan, coming in from the harsh sunlight, stood for a moment blinking his eyes. Then he was aware of a head bent toward him over a small counter between a high brass mesh and a high showcase.

"Feitelberg?"

"No, I'm the clerk."

"Where's Feitelberg?"

The temporary blind-staggers left Cardigan. Out of the mist came the face of the clerk, clear now in its pale thinness. And the too-large glasses, the black alpaca coat with elbows out, the cuffs ragged.

"You want to see Mr. Feitelberg?"

"Of course," Cardigan said.

The clerk disappeared behind the counter. When a door in the rear opened, Cardigan heard voices, but they stopped immediately—and then the door closed behind the clerk. But in a moment it opened, and there weren't any voices.

The clerk and a small, chubby man came out. The chubby man was bald and very white. There was not a hair on face or head. He had owlish eyes that attempted to be so frank that you got the opposite impression.

"Yes?"

"I want to talk to you alone a minute," Cardigan said.

"Me?"

"Mr. Feitelberg."

"Who are you, please?"

"Just now I'm representing the Odegard Indemnity Company."

"Come around back."

The office behind the store was small, dusty, cluttered, and had another door in the rear. There was an ash tray on the desk with a cigarette still smoldering. Cardigan took out his leather cigarette case.

"Smoke?"

"I don't smoke, thanks," the chubby man said.

Cardigan crushed out the smoldering cigarette and Feitelberg made a nervous gesture with his hands. Cardigan saw the gesture, but did not let on. He sat down.

He said: "You do a good business, don't you?"

"Good—yes, sometimes."

"High-class trade?"

Feitelberg shrugged. "I never ask. A man comes in. He buys something or he pawns something, but I never ask."

"Or a woman."

"Eh?"

"Or a woman comes in."

"Yes, yes, sometimes a woman."

Cardigan looked at his hands, said toward the floor: "What was the biggest loan you ever made?"

Feitelberg knew his rights. He was polite, saying: "That of course is something I am not obliged to give out. Just what do you want here, mister?"

"I'm looking for the lost Kemmerich pearls—a necklace valued at thirty thousand bucks."

IT WAS a blunt statement, and it sent the chubby man back a few paces. But he straightened against the wall. He laughed, nervously.

"That is simple. I can tell you I know nothing about it. It was stolen last week, wasn't it, was it not? Ah, yes—now I remember. It was in the papers. Yes, I read all about it." He seemed suddenly cheerful, his owlish eyes sparkling. "It was a big piece in the papers about it—"

"Know Mrs. Kemmerich?"

"I have not the pleasure."

"What name does the lady go under who spent half an hour in here this morning?"

"There were a number of ladies in here this morning."

"One about ten o'clock."

Feitelberg bent his hairless brows studiously. "I do not seem to remember. I mean I do not associate any particular lady with any particular time."

Cardigan stood up. "You're a liar."

Feitelberg recoiled against the wall. "I hope I am not going to be insulted in my own place of business."

"I said you're a liar!"

Feitelberg leveled an arm. "Get out! Get out of my place of business!"

"Mrs. Kemmerich was in here this morning. She spent half an hour here. Her butler was killed last night. One of our agency men was killed shortly after midnight. There's a hook-up somewhere."

Feitelberg got excited and knocked over a chair. He cried out in astonishment. The door leading to the store opened and the big-spectacled clerk stood there with a gun in his hand. He was young and scrawny but he was also cool.

"Trouble, Mr. Feitelberg?"

The chubby man was panicky. He picked up the chair and promptly stumbled over it again. But he reached the phone, and though his chin had the shakes there was a white grimness about it.

He panted: "Now get out, get out or I call the police! This is my place of business and I will not be insulted in it!"

The hand of the clerk was very steady and that made the gun he held doubly menacing. Cardigan scowled at it, scowled at the clerk, scowled at Feitelberg. He said nothing. He turned and walked into the store, out into the street.

He doubled around the block, scaled a board fence and worked his way into an alley that terminated in a small yard behind the pawnshop. He made his way to the door. Looking down, he saw three cigarette butts on the cement apron in front of the door. One was still smoldering.

Cardigan began backing away. He returned into the maw of the alley between two brick buildings, found another way to the street without scaling the board fence. There he slowed down, took up a position in the recessed doorway of a store placarded with *For Rent* signs.

Ten minutes later he saw a man come down the alley. The man walked rapidly, with head down. He was neatly dressed though his pants looked too tight and he wore patent-leather shoes. He appeared wiry, quick, and there was something definitely hard and sleek about the way the short-brimmed gray fedora was yanked down over one eyebrow.

The man was Packy Daskas.

CHAPTER THREE

P. & O. PUNK

CARDIGAN LINED out after him, taking his time, taking it easy. Packy flagged a cab on Seventh Avenue and it headed south. Cardigan caught one and passed a two-dollar bill through the window with brief instructions. At Fourteenth Street the cabs shot west and then south on Hudson Street. The tail wound up at Sheridan Square. Packy stood on the corner of West Fourth and Grove long enough to light a cigarette. Cardigan stood on Christopher near the subway entrance and let Packy get a start.

Packy went down Grove Street and slipped down into an areaway speak short of Bedford. Cardigan walked as far as Bedford, turned, killed a couple of minutes watching the areaway, then went toward it, down into it and pushed open an iron gate.

The bar was long with a lot of colored lights behind it. A couple of heavy afternoon drinkers stood at one end of the bar; a looking-glass drinker stood alone in the center hiccuping, and Packy stood at the other end nursing a drink between his hands and looking absorbed in thought. Cardigan went to the opposite end where there wasn't much light and ordered a gin rickey. A cop came in, got a pint, shoved it under his coat and went out whistling. Between mixing drinks, the barman read an account of a love-nest murder and made clicking, disapproving sounds with his tongue. It looked like a clean, orderly and law-abiding place.

After a while a man came in, looked around and then went slowly to a place at the bar beside Packy. Their elbows almost touched. Their heads went down, eyes shaded by hat brims, and the barman mixed two drinks. The man who had just come in looked older than Packy. He had a brown face, lined, and a black mustache and broad shoulders. He wore a Homburg and looked like an actor or a gambler or like a good imitation of either. His air was one of faded elegance and he looked dissipated. He also looked haggard and he addressed Packy with a nervous, sidewise twitching of his mouth which he half concealed by a restless hand.

The two drank up; the older man paid and both went out. Cardigan planked a half-dollar piece on the bar and went out a minute later. He saw them walking toward Sheridan Square and followed them to West Tenth Street. They entered a narrow red brick house and when Cardigan slipped in he heard them walking frontward in the hallway above. Then he heard them mounting a second flight of stairs and he was up on the first landing by the time they reached the second. He heard keys jangling and catfooted up the second flight. His head came level with the hall floor and he saw through the railing that they entered a door at the rear of the hall.

He went downstairs, into the street and started walking east. He stood on the corner and watched the red brick house. An hour later the two men came out and headed west. When they had disappeared Cardigan strode to the house, entered the hall door and climbed to the second floor.

It took him three minutes to work his way through the lock. There was dirty chintz on two rear windows of a square, old-fashioned room. In the center stood a large brass bed. There was a cheap bureau. Under the bed was a battered steamer trunk which Cardigan dragged out. It was locked. He went through the bureau drawers and through the single closet, found nothing except indications that only one person occupied the room. It took him ten minutes to get the trunk open.

He found a couple of Luger automatics. There were cord breeches and boots, flannel shirts, canvas coats, and lots of white duck. In the bottom he found a large photograph of a woman. On the back was inscribed "To my husband, forever. Lily." He whipped the photograph into better light.

It was Lily Kemmerich—Lily Kemmerich maybe ten, twelve years before. In the lower right hand corner were the name and address of the photographer—Lundmann, Cape Town.

Cardigan repacked the trunk, relocked it. But he did not replace the photograph of Lily Kemmerich. He had to fold it to get it into his inside coat pocket. He searched the room again, replacing meanwhile everything as he had found it. Then he stood in the center of the room, his back to the foot of the bed, and looked around.

Finally, satisfied, he moved toward the door, but before his hand settled on the knob a light knock on the oaken panel stopped him in his tracks. His shaggy brows bent—all his body went into quick, steel tension. Pivoting quietly, he went to the rear windows. There was no fire-escape, no way out. He swung around and then moved so that he would not be in silhouette and at the same time his hand slid beneath his left lapel, came out gripping a flat black automatic.

HE SAW the knob turn. Saw the door open, slowly at first, then more rapidly. And because the room was dim due to the thick, dirty chintz on the windows, Lily Kemmerich did not see him at first. He lowered his gun. He saw she was alone, plainly dressed in something dark blue and tailored with an oval-shaped hat of dark straw quite concealing her blonde hair.

Then she said, "Oh!" in a soft, strangled whisper.

"Quiet," his low voice warned.

"You!"

"Quiet!"

She swayed once, a little forward. He crossed the room, closed the door and stood with his back to it. She was a tall woman, but Cardigan dwarfed her. The top of his hat was on a level with the top of the door. His face was brown, lined heavily, almost malignant now because, perhaps, he was thinking of poor Fogarty who had been killed only half a block up the street.

Sarcasm touched his words— "From the swank east side to the dumps of the west side, Mrs. Kemmerich. This is not so sweet and lovely."

She moved backward, not smoothly, but with wooden-kneed steps, until she touched the brass rail of the bed. She leaned against this, and in the dimness her pale face was beautiful, almost exotic.

He growled: "Why did you come here?"

Her lips opened, but a visible pounding in her throat seemed to gag her. She made a short, inarticulate sound, and then suddenly tears made bright-shining pools of her eyes.

"Oh," she murmured. "Oh, God."

"Talk to me. Not God."

"Oh, please—please!" she sobbed. She staggered sidewise.

He took a quick step. He was Irish, with the quick moods, good or bad, of the Irish.

This time he said: "Take it easy, Mrs. Kemmerich. Steady does it. For crying out loud, don't pass out."

She sat down on the edge of the bed and stared white-faced at the soiled chintz curtains. Her lips quivered and there were little sounds fighting one another in her throat.

Cardigan growled: "Say something."

"What shall I say?"

"Who lives here?"

"A man."

He chided with—"Honest?"

"Don't—don't ridicule me."

"What did you come here for?"

"I can't tell you." She said it desperately, her hands clenched, her jaw firm.

"What were you doing at Sol Feitelberg's this morning?"

She was on her feet. The move was so abrupt and accompanied such a look of terror that the momentum carried her to the wall and she flattened against it, her eyes wide.

"No—no!" she cried.

His voice hardened. "A man of mine was killed in this street early this morning. He was following a man named Packy Daskas. Packy Daskas was in this room a short while ago with a man you know—the man who lives here, the man you came in to see. Our man was murdered because he was too close to something. He was murdered by either Daskas or the man you came to see. Where are the pearls?"

"I don't know."

"You lie. It was a frame-up on the insurance company. You pretended they were stolen so that you'd get dough from the insurance company and also dough from a fence. Those pearls were turned over to Feitelberg."

She shook her head, cried passionately, "No—no! You're wrong! Oh God, you're so, so wrong! Please—" She straightened and started for the door. "Let me go! Please let me out of here!"

"It was all arranged. Those pearls were turned over to Packy Daskas. You unhooked them yourself and in the crowd you moved so that it would be easy for him to receive them. Get back!"

He gripped her by both arms and his big, scowling face was close to hers. "Remember," he gritted, "that an old friend of mine was killed. Remember that."

She looked cold white. Her broken voice said: "You're stronger than I am. You can break my arms—do anything. But I had nothing to do with killing your friend."

"Then tell me what you know."

"I can't."

"You will!"

"I can't! I can't! Let—let me go!"

SHE tussled with him. She heaved and squirmed and he stood rock-still on his feet, holding her with both hands until she should become exhausted. But suddenly she went limp and with a little, hopeless cry she slumped. He let her down to the floor and saw how white her face was. He grimaced. He looked angry and chagrined and bewildered and for a moment he did nothing but stand there and look down at her.

Then he bent down, lifted her in his arms and moved toward the bed. The door opened and a voice said: "All right, lay her down and then watch your hands."

He did not drop her. He looked over his shoulder and saw the haggard man kick the door shut. There was a gun in his hand. Cardigan laid Lily Kemmerich on the bed, straightened and turned to face the man.

"Watch those hands, you!"

"You watch 'em," Cardigan muttered.

"What the hell are you doing here?"

"What the hell do you think?"

"I wouldn't get fresh, funny face."

"Nuts for you."

"And pretty soon a load of lead in the belly for you. How do you like that?"

"No more than my friend Fogarty did."

The man was running sweat. He looked at the bed and snapped, "She brought you here, *huhn?*"

"I find my own way about."

"That's crap. Nobody knew about this but Lily. She brought you here, the two-timing slob."

"She never looked like a slob to me. Was she out of her mind when she married you?"

"Oh, she told you that, too!" His mustache twitched and his dark eyes burned across the room. "Well, it isn't going to do you any good. She married me when I was in the jack. When I traveled the ocean liners and the P. & O. boats taking suckers for a ride on the spotted pasteboards. The first jam I got in she lammed on me, the bum. I was a big shot in those days—"

"I don't give a damn what you were. Right now you're a small-time punk. Get down to business. If you'll let me, I'll put some water in her face."

"To hell with her! Don't you move or I'll let you have it!"

Cardigan grunted. He slid a glance down at the unconscious woman and a shadow passed across his face as though suddenly he regretted having been so harsh with her.

"Just stand there," the man said, as he flung a quick glance at his strap watch.

Fifteen minutes later the door opened and Packy Daskas came in. He stopped, took a few drags at a cigarette while running quick eyes over the scene.

He clipped: "What's this—a rehearsal?"

"It's her," the haggard man said, "and another one of those private dicks. She came here with him to fan the place."

Packy had better nerves than the other. He relaxed, tossed his butt to the floor and stamped it out. "This ain't the berries," he said. "Something's got to be done about it." He was flippant, cold as an icicle.

The haggard man's voice shook. "How about that other thing?"

Packy glared at him. "Clean. Do I have to keep telling you all the time?" He took off his hat and ran a hand over his lacquered dark hair, nodded toward Cardigan and spoke to the haggard man in a matter of fact tone. "This egg knows too much. It's no good. Something's got to be done about it. When it gets dark."

"And her too?"

"Sure."

Cardigan said: "She came here alone. I came here first, you saps. I crashed the place and after a while she came in. There's no hook-up."

Lily came to, turned her head from side to side. Finally her eyes settled on the haggard man and she said, weakly, "Harry."

"To hell with you!" the haggard man said.

"Harry. I—please—"

"To hell with you!"

CHAPTER FOUR

THE CRIMSON NECKLACE

MAYBE IT was the sight of Lily, so beautiful, that gushed fresh rage through Harry's body. He talked as if things had been pent up for a long time—while Packy Daskas stood slim and cold, his gun now in his hand and leveled toward Cardigan. Harry struck the brass rail of the bed with his fists, and his lips became wet and red with frenzy.

"Lammed on me," he cried, "when I got in that jam in Algiers! Bailed out! Left me flat! And now you come here with this dick to my room! And what did you find? Nothing!"

She said, subdued: "I came here alone, to plead with you."

The hushed tranquility of her voice seemed to enrage him. He came around the bed and slapped her face and Cardigan, bitter-lipped, kicked him in the back. Harry spun away from the bed, arching his back, crying out in pain, and Packy came closer with a white, icy look in his face and his gun closer to Cardigan's stomach.

But he spoke to Harry— "Lay off, Harry. Keep your head. We've got to keep our heads. Lay off now and don't go meshuga over a dame. It's the bunk."

"He kicked me," Harry panted.

Cardigan said: "I'd like to put my foot down your throat," without emphasis, in a voice hard and brittle.

It was getting dark. Daylight was fading rapidly beyond the chintz curtains.

Lily sat up. "I must go home."

Harry laughed hysterically. "You're never going home, Lily!"

Packy was matter of fact again. "Never, Lily. You brought this dick here and neither you or him are ever going home. Take that and try to like it."

"She didn't bring me here," Cardigan said, bluntly.

Her eyes widened as though now for the first time she was becoming aware of her predicament. Her hand moved up to her breast and beyond to her throat. The men in the room were becoming vague blurs because of the thickening twilight, but each was made a distinct personality by his voice.

Harry whined: "You left me flat, Lily, and now you brought a dick here to my room."

Her voice was far away—"I didn't leave you, as you say, flat. I met you in Africa and I was young and didn't know men. After a week of it I knew I was all wrong. You changed. Or you didn't change but were your real self and not the man I met on shipboard. When I met you first you acted the part of a world traveler. But I married you and how quickly you showed your real self. And I loathed you. And myself. And then I felt that love was done with me. You left me for six months, and not a word from you, and then I met you in Algiers and took pity on you and then the very next night you were caught. And then I left you."

"Cut this. Cut this," Packy said coldly. Then his voice hardened with finality. "Harry, we've got to lam. We can't hang around here all night. The car's gassed and all set and we've got to blow while the blowin's good. Turn on the lights."

Harry turned on the lights and these made the room more drab and bare and Harry's face looked more haggard, more sallow and haunted. Ghosts were in his fevered eyes but Packy remained cold and hard and certain.

He said: "The gas."

"Huhn?" Harry said.

"The gas—for both of them. Take this guy."

Cardigan moved—got his broad back against the wall. "I tell you, she came here alone."

Harry yammered: "Being brave, hey? Spare the gal and—"

"I'm not being brave, louse. I'm trying to tell you something."

"Take him, Harry," came Packy's crisp, cold voice.

Lily was off the bed—on her feet. She cried passionately: "If I've done anything—anything—my life's yours to do with as you please. Everything is ruined. This will ruin everything. I'm done for. I tried to begin all over again, but there was no use. But I've done nothing wrong—nothing."

HARRY struck Cardigan. The blackjack came miraculously from somewhere in his clothes and Cardigan was off guard because his eyes, wondering and curious, were on the woman. The blow sent him sliding along the wall. He reached the washstand and braced an arm against it. He looked stupidly down at the white bowl there. Harry came behind and let him have it again.

The woman moaned and Packy said: "Shut your trap, sister."

Harry, striking Cardigan, cried in a hoarse whisper: "I'll give you the same as I gave your partner! He got in here too! He found those pearls and he was taking them out but I got him! And you the same—I'll get you!"

Cardigan muttered: "So it was you got poor old Fogarty—"

Rage must have suddenly overcome him. His foot swung and hit Harry and Harry reeled across the room and landed on the bed. Packy jumped and slammed his gun against Cardigan's stomach.

"One more crack like that, guy, and you get it quick!"

Lily sprang to the door and got it open and cried, "Help!"

Packy choked and spun and Cardigan, drunk with pain and half blind, made a pass at him but only succeeded in getting him off balance.

"Help! Help!" Lily screamed in the hallway.

Harry, off the bed, made a vicious lunge for Lily, but suddenly there was a new tangle in the doorway and out of it Pat came. There was a small Colt automatic in her hand. Harry stopped against its muzzle.

She said: "Stop, you!"

But Harry, wild-eyed, struck at her and she reeled away. He plunged through the door. That scream of Lily's had turned matters. There seemed in Harry's actions only a frantic desire to get out of the room.

Packy, white as death, heard the blast of a police whistle somewhere below. He moved like something shot from a spring. As he reached the hall there was a blinding flash. He ducked. But the flash had nothing to do with him. Lily was falling and Harry was backing away, his gun smoking, his mouth wide open in dumb awe.

Packy still had nerves. "Scram!"

Harry whipped toward the stairway but Packy snapped: "We can't make it that way, dope! Up—the roof!"

Pat choked in the doorway: "I should have got him, chief. I couldn't. I couldn't—kill anybody."

"You did enough, little wonderful," he muttered. "See about Lily Kemmerich—"

Plunging into the hallway, he saw Lily settling on the floor, her face stricken and her head shaking from side to side as though she were saying: "This didn't happen—this didn't happen."

His lips tightened and a raw oath ripped from his throat. He slammed his way along the hallway and looking upward saw the heels of Packy disappearing through the door to the roof. The door slammed. In a split minute Cardigan was up at it. He almost carried it from its hinges. Then he was in starlight and the cool summer night, among the chimney pots.

Red flame split the shadows of the next roof. Lead tore through a rusty ventilator against which Cardigan's arm brushed. He dropped and then heaved to one side and then shot forward around a chimney and his gun banged. The echoes walloped across the roof, and commingled with them was a short cry. But the two shapes were still running, dodging, scaling the dividing walls between the roofs.

But one began to lag during the next minute. He half turned and fired but he was wide of the mark and wrecked a skylight. Glass exploded and fell with a harsh, rasping noise. Cardigan's gun boomed for the second time and the one lagged, stumbled forward, turned all the way around. But he was late. A third shot slammed him down and his gun bounced six feet across the roof.

It was Packy, panting: "Don't finish me—"

"Now where's your ice-cold nerve?"

"Don't! Here—" Out of his pocket came a pearl necklace. "Take it, but don't—"

Cardigan snatched it from his hand and thrust it into his pocket. He jumped over Packy and slipped down along the front of the roof. He heard a roof door bang. He plunged past a chimney, reached the door, listened. Heels were clattering down a stairway. Cardigan yanked the door open and a gun belched from the bottom of the stairway. He fired off balance, missed. Harry ducked. Cardigan lunged downward and only when he reached the bottom of the staircase did he realize that his face ached. His cheek had been burned open by the bullet. Blood was flowing.

A fat woman opened a door, saw his bloody face, screamed and banged the door shut. Harry was down the next flight. Doors were banging all over the house, and women were screaming. Harry went through a door, knocking a woman clear across the room. Cardigan reached the door as Harry crashed into a coal range. The stove pipe broke loose from the wall and coal dust showered downward. Harry fired blindly and his shot smashed crockery on a shelf above Cardigan's head.

Cardigan snapped: "Drop it, Harry!"

But Harry was too far gone to reason things out. Cardigan had to let him have it. The shot pinned Harry against the wall behind the stove for a brief second, and then he sank, slack-jawed.

Cardigan walked across the room, reached down and with little effort took the gun from Harry's hand. The old woman was sitting on the floor, rocking from side to side and moaning. Cardigan lifted her, piloted her to a rocking chair and eased her into it.

"You're all right," he said. "Just be calm."

He turned and saw a cop standing in the doorway holding a gun. "Lift 'em, fella," the cop said.

"I'm O.K.," Cardigan said. "I'm Cardigan, of the Cosmos Agency."

"Who's this?"

"His name's Harry. There's a guy named Packy Daskas on the roof."

"No he ain't."

"Huhn?"

"He pitched to the sidewalk. We been looking for him. Him and another guy stuck up a pawnshop on Eighth Avenue this afternoon. We sure been looking for him. The owner was killed."

Cardigan's left hand was tight on the pearls in his pocket. He headed for the door and the cop stepped aside and Cardigan went down into the street. He walked to the red brick house. The riot squad was there. He recognized Flamm, a precinct dick. Then an ambulance pulled up.

"Did you get Packy?" Flamm said.

"I guess so."

"Some guys get all the breaks."

"Oh, you think so?"

Pat came down out of the hall door. She held a handkerchief to her face and Cardigan pushed through the crowd and took hold of her arm.

"Hurt, kid?" he said.

"No. Just"—she grimaced—"sick. She died. They won't need the ambulance. Poor thing—poor thing."

"Chin up, Pat."

"I know, I know."

Cardigan turned to Flamm. "This is Miss Seaward, one of our operatives. I'll get her out of this and then come back."

"Sure—sure thing," Flamm said.

More cops were arriving. Windows were open and hall doors were jammed with wide-eyed people. Traffic was being diverted from this block. Cardigan walked Pat to the next corner and found a cab. They got in.

"Still sick, kid?"

"It was terrible, chief. She was so beautiful."

The taxi gathered speed.

Cardigan said: "She say anything?"

"Yes. She said Harry Pritchard was her husband, once. She got a divorce and only two months ago he turned up, after nine years. He used to be a gambler. He was down and out and he threatened to tell of her former marriage if she didn't help him. She pawned that necklace, got a paste one to match it and wore that and her husband never knew. He was proud of the necklace. There'd been bits in the paper about it.

"Then this jewel expert Van Damm was coming. She got panicky. She hadn't the money to get the real one out of hock and she knew Van Damm would know the one she wore was a fake. She went to Harry and told him. She was desperate. She had to lose that necklace, have it stolen. All that was arranged. But she wouldn't tell him where she had pawned the real one.

"He was hooked up with Packy. She let Packy steal the fake. Then Packy and her former husband decided to get the real one. How? Well, she had the pawn ticket. Packy crashed the apartment and got it and that's why she said nothing had been stolen. The pawn ticket showed them where she'd pawned the necklace. They destroyed the fake one."

Cardigan said: "And they had to bump Feitelberg off to get the real one."

She lay back in the cab, closed her eyes. "She was a good girl, chief. You've got to believe that. She did her best. She could never have stood it if Van Damm had seen the necklace she wore was paste."

He drew the pearls from his pocket.

They were stained crimson. They had got that way from Packy's hand.

THE DEAD DON'T DIE

GILES JACLAND LAY STABBED IN ROOM 904 WELTERING IN A POOL OF CRIMSON. AND ONLY CARDIGAN HAD SENSE ENOUGH TO SPOT THE SINGLE CLUE TO MURDER, HAD GALL ENOUGH TO LIFT THAT PAPER FROM UNDER THE VERY NOSES OF THE COPS AND READ BETWEEN THE LINES.

CHAPTER ONE

CURTAIN COLUMN

THE HOTEL grapevine vibrated with the news. The telephone operator going off duty at 8:00 A.M. gave it to the red-head coming on. The page-boy, on his way through overheard it and, scooting out of the little office, he passed the word on to the bell captain. The bell captain slipped it sotto voce to his favorite hop, and the hop, headed downstairs to get a pressed suit for 900, gave it to the valet, the head porter and the engineer. The head porter passed it on to the housekeeper, but she'd already heard. The red-head who had relieved the night operator plugged in a surreptitious call to a newshawk friend on the daily tab.

Her voice was a dramatic whisper. "Listen, Hank. Get this on the nose and don't ever tell me I'm not your pal. Giles Jacland is dead in his apartment here…. Go on now, ask me a lot of dumb questions! Ain't I told you enough?" She plugged out, plugged in, lilting, "Good-morning-sir-Hotel-Saxony!"

M. Broéue, the Swiss managing director, got it from the fourth assistant manager at breakfast and dropped his half-eaten croissant into the coffee. "But no!" he exclaimed.

"The police," said the fourth assistant manager, "are here."

"And Strout, the house officer?"

"He is there representing the management."

"The press?"

"No one knows of this but you, the housekeeper, Strout, myself, and the police."

Downstairs, at that moment, the second porter was giving it to the head car washer in the hotel garage.

SO GILES JACLAND, the dramatic critic, aged fifty-two, was dead in a welter of blood that was darker than the red blocks of the Bokhara upon which he lay in the great living room of Suite 904. There was a moment of inactivity while the police photographer set his lenses.

"Them pajamas are the nuts," he remarked.

"Get that picture," Lieutenant Bone said.

"No kidding. If I busted out in a rash of nightdress like that the wife'd leave me flat."

Bone said, toneless, "Get done and scram." He had a dour, slab-cheeked face with high cheekbones and a chin like a doorknob. He stood paring his fingernails with a penknife.

Sergeant Raush was stocky and still worrying about the fifty bucks he'd lost on Schmelling. Strout, the house dick, stood near the windows, short and fat and white in dark clothes. The photographer got his picture, hummed, said, "O.K., Abe," to Bone and strode light-heartedly out of the apartment.

Strout said, "Did he begin life in a slaughter house?"

"No," Raush said seriously. "He used to be a barber upstate. He had political pull in the county and he used to get all the jobs shaving dead men."

"Carry her inside," Cardigan said. "It'll keep your arms occupied."

Bone suddenly went across to the telephone and made a call to headquarters. "I think maybe I ought to have a fingerprint man up here…. This is Abe Bone, on the Jacland kill, at the Saxony."

When he hung up, Raush said, "It must have been somebody Jacland knew."

"Maybe Cardigan'll know."

In Jacland's checkbook there was a stub showing that a check for $300 had been made out to the Cosmos Agency on the day before.

Bone said, sourly, "How about this guy's women, Strout?"

"Well, you know Jacland."

"If I knew him, I wouldn't be asking."

Strout shrugged. "He had the pick, I guess. He was a gay old bird and his women were usually young. No woman carved that throat, though."

"No. Some woman's boy friend, maybe."

The door opened and Cardigan loomed through, his battered felt in hand and his mop of black hair shaggier than ever.

Bone said, "Hello, Cardigan." He jerked his doorknob chin toward the body and added, "Get a load of it."

Cardigan looked. He came in, closed the door and leaned back against it. After a moment he looked back at Bone.

"That's tough," he said.

"What's the dope, Cardigan?"

"Dope on what?"

"This."

"Search me, Abe."

Bone sighed, strolled across the room and picked up the checkbook. "This guy was a client of yours. It began yesterday. Why was he a client?"

"It was his idea, not ours. He walked into our office yesterday morning, sat down and drew out his checkbook. He wrote a check for three hundred berries and said, 'There's a retainer. I may telephone at any time for a bodyguard, or for advice.' Like that—see?"

"Yeah. Now go on."

Cardigan shrugged, said, "That's all there was, Abe," and went across to the body.

"You mean to tell me," Bone dug in, "that this guy just planked down three hundred bucks and didn't give any details?"

Cardigan took his time in examining the body, then rose and said, absently, "Yes. We knew of him. A perfectly respectable citizen."

Bone chopped off, "I don't believe it!"

"Me, neither," agreed Raush.

"It does," Strout said, "sound crappy."

MEANWHILE Cardigan rolled across the room, disappeared into regions beyond—the bedroom, the bathroom, the dinette, the pantry. He reappeared in the living room plucking grapes from a bunch in his left hand and eating them. He blew the seeds into his right palm and deposited them in a tray on the desk. There were two newspapers on the desk. One was folded; the other lay flat. They were, otherwise, identical issues of the same newspaper—*The Press-Call.* On the desk, also, there were half a dozen pictures of as many beautiful women.

Cardigan pointed. "He was a good picker."

"Listen, you!" Bone snapped. "Why did Jacland hire you guys down at the agency?"

Cardigan disappeared again but returned in a moment with another bunch of grapes. "I told you, Abe," he said, unruffled. "I don't know. In times like these, when a guy walks in and signs his name to three hundred berries' worth of negotiable paper, what are we supposed to do, call him a dirty name?"

"You're lying, Cardigan!"

Cardigan indicated the body. "I'm lying, huh, when our client's been knifed to death? I'd give you a waltz-me-around, huh? Why, Abe? Why the hell should I? That looks like a head on your shoulders, boy—use it."

"I still don't believe you, Cardigan. I don't believe a guy would engage you birds, and pay for it, before he gave you a sound steer. It ain't being done. There's something crummy about it, and you know there is."

Cardigan ate grapes.

Raush said, "That's him, Abe; that's him all the time. Funny. Funny as hell. Maybe he knows who did it and maybe he figures on raking in a couple of grand from the right party for keeping his mouth shut."

"Hey, Abe," Cardigan said, "what's this crackpot's name?"

"Who—Raush?"

"Maybe that's what you call him."

Raush got up. "I don't like that, bozo."

Cardigan walked to the desk, dumped a handful of seeds, picked up the folded paper and pointed it at Raush. "That dirty crack you made, copper, is going to cost you a pinch. I told you guys the God's honest. Jacland came in and did just what I said. There was no explanation. He left the check because he knew it would bring prompt action when he needed us."

Bone broke in with, "Then you do know something."

"Who said so?"

"You just said Raush's crack would cost him a pinch."

"It will, honeybunch, if I land on the killer's tail."

He swung across the room, yanked open the door.

"Nuts, Cardigan," Raush said. "Lots of nuts."

Cardigan went right on out, slamming the door. A few minutes later the telephone rang and Bone answered it. "What?" he growled; and then, angrily, "Forget it!" He slammed the receiver into the hook.

"What's up?" Raush said.

"Room service," Bone growled, "said an order was just left for nuts for you. They wanted to know what kind."

SO GILES JACLAND was dead.... Dramatic critic extraordinary, raconteur, bachelor. Some said acid dripped from his pen and that he could make or break an actor. Merciless in his criticism, he was rarely satisfied with a performance. And once on the trail of an actor he considered bad, that actor thenceforth had little peace of mind.

But all that was done. Giles Jacland was dead and the crime lacked an exotic note. No woman's handkerchief left behind, no scarf, no scent of perfume. A knife had done it. A knife wielded, apparently, by a strong man's hand. Jacland had dabbled much in women; at fifty-two he had been a gay blade, lean, handsome, conceited, seen here and there at night clubs with a beautiful woman, but never the same one.

When Cardigan rolled into the agency office Pat Seaward was fixing her mouth with a lipstick and regarding the process in the mirror of a compact vanity case. She looked small, neat, trim in a summer dress of dark blue.

"Where's George?" Cardigan said.

"He just stepped out. For a drink. Every time Lieutenant Bone calls up, the boss has to go out an' get a drink." The vanity case snapped shut. "Bone was sore. So the boss is sore at you."

"Why me?"

"Said that since you won two hundred on that Sharkey-Schmelling adagio, there's no holding you. You walk up on the street and smack perfect strangers. You call nice little police officers names and things. In short, you're an old meany."

He gave her one of his dark, malignant looks—that really meant nothing—and swung across to the iced water cooler. He drew and drank two tall glasses. He said, "You're another one who's joined the razzberry bandwagon."

She turned and was suddenly sincere. "Gosh, chief, why don't you cut out riding people? Why get Bone mad?"

"Listen, duchess, I went into that apartment feeling swell. They asked me some questions. I answered truthfully. Then Abe started getting sarcastic and his busboy, Raush, pulled a crack I didn't stomach. So—" he slashed his hand down—"to hell with them. I—me—I, Pat, am going to find out who killed our late client. There's three hundred dollars' worth of finding out to be done, and this little choir boy is going to do it. Did Bone say I took anything out of that apartment?"

"No. Now you're not going to stand there and tell me you walked off with something right under their proboscides!"

He made a face. "You've been going in for deep books again." He drew a copy of *The Press-Call* from his pocket. "This, little bluestocking—this."

"A newspaper."

"Don't knock me over with those fast comebacks." He sat on the desk, unfolded the paper, which had been folded four times, and held it up. "Understand," he said, "when I found this paper, on the desk in Jacland's living room, it was folded just as I showed it to you. Before who ever had it, folded it, he'd been reading, as you see now, the dramatic page."

"Wouldn't Jacland read it?"

"There was another paper, just like this one, on his desk. Same issue, same everything—except that it had on it a little yellow slip saying: 'Good Morning! Compliments of the Hotel Saxony.' The hotel supplies one every morning to its guests. So why should Jacland order another sent up? He didn't. Even if he had, he wouldn't have folded it like this. You fold a paper this way only if you're carrying it on the street, either in your pocket or in your hand. Am I screwy?"

"No. It reasons."

"The guy that killed Jacland came in with this paper. You see this short column here?"

"Yes."

"What do you see? Don't read it, nosy; just tell me what first draws your attention."

"The paper's wrinkled right there, cracked a bit as if—as if—"

"As if," he took up, "some guy, while talking heatedly, kept jabbing it right there with his finger."

She looked at him. "Yes, chief."

HE GUSHED a great sigh of satisfaction through his teeth. "I'm glad to see I'm not entirely ga-ga. We are going to, in time, make a call on Rosalie Wayne."

"Rosalie Way—"

"Read that column," he cut in. "The last from the pen of Giles Jacland—aged fifty-two, a town rounder, an intellectual snob, a bum and, to borrow a crack you pull on me sometimes, a cad. Read it—and weep and I'll bop you."

Pat read it aloud.

"Last night these weary eyes beheld, this tired brain sought to absorb, the warp and woof of a play entitled *Sacrilege*. Why it was entitled *Sacrilege,* I do not know; unless perhaps the author, unwittingly, named it appropriately in its relation to the drama and what we like to believe the drama stands for. It was, indeed, a sacrilege—to make myself clearer—to thrust so infantile a potpourri into the laps of a much abused public.

"Yet more of a sacrilege to the Art of the Drama was the performance of Rosalie Wayne. Garbling her lines, throwing her arms about like a tree in a fall gale, but with less grace, she helped to make ludicrous a play that was already woebegone. Apparently devoid of talent, obviously lacking in subtlety, she tramped, wept, stumbled and clawed her way through three ungainly acts with the questionable agility of an elephant. She—"

"You get it?" Cardigan broke in.

Pat looked up and there was color in her face. "It's cruel!" she cried. "It's too personal, too unutterably bitter. It's malicious and horribly uncalled for!"

"You've got the language, kid."

"But," she hastened to say, "this would have no connection with

Jacland's death."

He grinned. "No?"

"Of course not! People—people like Rosalie Wayne—don't do that sort of thing."

He still grinned. "No?"

"It's unreasonable. It's not sense."

"Suppose," he said, "you hang around so you can be on hand to give me the horse laugh when I'm wrong."

He took the paper from her, folded it and thrust it into his coat pocket. He said, "I'll probably need you along—since there's a jane in it. I called her apartment but she's not in. The maid said she motored to Greenwich this morning—left at a quarter to nine; about three quarters of an hour after Jacland was bumped off. She'll be back in time for tonight's performance at the Rosemont. Afterwards, she sings one song at the Club Cordova—a kind of torch song. Wear the ice-blue rag that makes you look like a million."

She made a mock curtsey. "Yes, O Master."

The phone rang and Cardigan made a lazy sweep at it. "Hello.... This is Cardigan talking." He listened; then his eyes darkened, his mouth crowded the mouthpiece. "Oh, yeah?... Well, listen to me, mister— Hello, hello!" He juggled the hook. "Hello—" He whanged the receiver down. He stood holding the instrument and staring hard into space. Then he rasped out a short, contemptuous laugh and planked the phone down.

"Bone?" Pat dared to inquire.

"No. Some guy said, 'Cardigan, stay off the Jacland murder or you'll regret it.' And hung up."

She said, "Maybe Bone or Raush got somebody to call up and scare you. You know they hate like the devil to see you reach a case first."

He looked at her. "Maybe." He looked away and added, "Maybe not. Maybe it's the other side. If it is, there's only one way they'd know I'm on it. The maid. The maid in Rosalie Wayne's apartment." He smacked the paper in his pocket. "This rag is going to cause somebody a headache."

Pat sighed. "Heartache, maybe." And she didn't sound happy.

He said sharply, "Listen. You go up to Rosalie Wayne's apartment. Pass yourself off as a sob-sister from a daily tab. Get a load of the apartment and the maid. Especially the maid."

She said, "I've a feeling I'm not going to like this."

He was lighting a cigarette. "Don't be a sap. You work here, don't you? Scram."

CHAPTER TWO

NICE KNIFE WORK

THE PETREMONT PLAZA was an apartment house, tall, thin, white, off Park Avenue. Pat entered the dim, deftly lit lobby and was aware of quiet elegance. A black-and-chrome elevator lifted her noiselessly to the twelfth floor and she walked down a wide corridor on soft, plum-colored carpet. There was an ebony knocker on the door marked 1212. She used it.

A little plump woman in a black dress and an Eton collar opened the door. She wore old-fashioned spectacles and had a small, quaint face, a friendly but hesitant smile. Pat's heart sank, but she had a job to do.

"I'm Ann Walters from *The Daily Flash*. Could I have a few words with you?"

"Come right in, miss; come right in."

Friendly, Pat was sure; gray and dainty in an old halftone way.

"You're Miss Wayne's maid?"

"Yes, kind of."

The door was shut and the maid was indicating a chair. Pat sat down and the old woman took a chair nearby and let her hands lie in her lap.

"Well, Mrs.—"

"It's 'Miss,' please; Miss Leadley."

"How long have you been Miss Wayne's maid?"

"Many years."

It was tough going, but Pat went on. "Miss Wayne's a good actress, don't you think?"

"Yes." Her chin went up. "One of the best. And a good girl, miss. A very good girl."

"I like her myself. Some don't."

A shadow fell across the quaint old face. "Yes—some don't."

"Who, for instance?"

Miss Leadley looked up, startled. Then she said, "Oh, it doesn't matter, does it?"

Pat was quick: "I understand our great dramatic critic Giles Jacland—"

A hostile light shone in the old eyes. "Yes! But he will not—" She stopped short, flushed; went on, flustered. "He will not get anywhere with his bitterness."

"Why do you suppose he's so bitter?"

Miss Leadley sat back. "Miss, what is it you want to know?"

"I want to get an inside slant on Miss Wayne's life. I want to write a piece about her—from a human angle." She felt her face was going to flush any minute. "The human, heart-to-heart angle. I want to—"

A sharp sound, as if something had been knocked over, stopped her short. She swung around but there was no one else in the room. When she turned back, Miss Leadley had risen and was staring across the room. Pat followed her gaze toward a closed door. She stood up.

"There's someone in your apartment," she said.

"No—no, I think not."

"I heard something—in that room."

"It couldn't be."

Pat said, "You'd better call the superintendent. There have been apartment robberies in this neighborhood lately—"

"I—it must have been our imagination."

A door closed.

Pat went across the room swiftly, opened the connecting door and looked into a bedroom. On the farther side was a door, parallel with the one through which she had entered the apartment. She heard a sharp intake of breath behind her; turned and saw the maid, white-faced, with hands clenched. She looked into the bedroom again, then entered, stopped after she had taken a few steps and looked around.

The maid's exhaled breath was accompanied by, "See, we must have imagined it."

THE room was empty. The maid was peaceful, smiling again, but the white look ebbed slowly from her face. Pat felt she had played the fool. She shrugged and was turning away when she caught sight of a small, brocaded footstool—overturned. Her glance darted from it to the closed door. She sniffed. She smelled, she was sure, the odor of smoke—heavy, strong, the kind that a cigar leaves behind.

But she said nothing. She laughed. "I guess I was mistaken. You see, I'm used to living alone—and I'm kind of scary of prowlers."

The old woman beamed. "Yes, I know how it is.... Perhaps, Miss Walters, you'd better call again—when Miss Wayne is at home. Walters is the name, isn't it?"

Was there sly mockery in her tone as she said that name?

Pat felt uncomfortable. "I'd hoped," she said, "I would find her home. Thank you, Miss Leadley."

Red color did not flood her face until she was in the corridor. She waited a full minute before ringing for the elevator. In the lobby, she got beneath one of the lights and resorted to her vanity case. Snapping it shut, she went out into the street and walked west. She did not see a man step down from a doorway opposite and stare after her. She boarded a bus at Fifth Avenue and rode downtown as far as Forty-second Street. She got off, crossed the curb and spotted Cardigan in front of one of the library lions. He was always big in a crowd—big and a little shaggy.

"Well, Pat?" He searched her face with a dark scowl.

When she held her head level her eyes always rested on the knot of his tie. "I didn't find much, chief. The maid's an old woman—a dear, sweet old thing—"

"Did I send you up there to bring me a sob-story?"

Her eyes flashed up at him. He passed a hand across his mouth and made a face. "Sorry, kitten." But he didn't smile. "Well?" he said.

"She's been with Rosalie Wayne for many years."

"That means she's a good maid. Go on."

It came hard. "I think she suspected me."

"Why?"

"Well—I heard a noise in the other room behind a closed door and...." She related it briefly, ending with, "I guess I kind of fumbled it."

He stared west at a southbound elevated train. "The maid, then—she knows Jacland's dead. It's not in the papers yet, but she knows it. That's swell. See any pictures of Jacland?"

"No."

He caught hold of her arm. "Come on, kid. You did well. Could you stand an Old Fashion?"

She blew her nose quietly. "To be frank, I think I need one. Maybe two."

"You're going soft on me."

"I know," she said. "I'm a wash-out."

He chided roughly. "Yeah. Yes, you are."

THE Club Cordova was in East Fifty-seventh Street. You entered straight from the sidewalk beneath a dark-green marquee and a flunky in dark-green livery opened the big door and didn't bow as you passed in. The checkroom girl was small, dark, and she could smile, throw backchat, without looking you in the eye. Antonio, a Brooklyn dago with a marcel, met you in the foyer and did the gladhanding. He was a nice fellow who had found waiting on tables in a chop house beneath his ability. White, happy-faced, he treated names and nobodies alike.

"I have not seen you since—when, Mr. Cardigan?"

"Riddle me right away," Cardigan chaffed, and hooked his black fedora on the checkroom girl's hand. No matter how evening clothes smoothed down his bulk, his hair remained loose, shaggy, untamed, and the whiteness of his shirt front made his face look browner, bigger, in its rough masculine way. "This is Miss Seaward, Tony.... Pat, this is Antonio. A table for two, Tony, on the edge of the dance floor. We'll be in later.... Before me, Pat."

"Ah," said Antonio, "I will give you the royal box."

"Yeah. I heard that crack in Paris once. Look out for the copyright law, kid."

He piloted Pat into the bar. It was small, intimate, with few mirrors and lots of shiny woodwork, dark and impressive and paneled. There were high stools in front of the bar and the bartender, in a white jacket, vestlike but for the sleeves, was quiet, efficient and, carrying out the mode of the new era, properly self-effacing. It was exactly 11:00 P.M. and few people had come in.

Pat climbed onto a stool and Cardigan stood and said, "Name your weakness."

"You know it."

"Two Old Fashions," he told the bartender; and to Pat, sotto voce, "With the dress, Patrick, I myself could fall for you."

"Pouf!"

"Think—think of all the women who are mad about me?"

"That wouldn't call for much extended thought."

He sighed. "O.K. Maybe we'd better drink instead. Here's to you, duchess."

"Is it true that you once pulled stroke for Princeton?"

"What have you got against Princeton?"

She said, suddenly, "Oh-oh."

"Huh?"

"Father Bone, entering."

Abe Bone came up to the bar. "That cab you were in, Cardigan, should have been pinched for speeding."

"Hello, Abe. Have a drink. Did you tie Raush outside?"

"I'm on the wagon." He was dour, wrinkle-browed. "We got no fingerprints. There was a dead end. Whoever bumped off Jacland knew him, because nobody asked the desk for him; they knew his apartment number. I checked up on phone calls this morning, though. He got a phone call—early."

"Swell! You get a break then."

"Yeah. I get a break I find out you been two-timing on me."

Cardigan turned to Pat. "You better turn the other way, chicken. The Bone and I are headed for words."

Bone said under his breath, "You stay right here, Miss Seaward."

Cardigan faced him. "Spill it, Abe."

"What I want to know is, how did you find out Rosalie Wayne phoned Jacland a half hour before he got bumped off?"

"I didn't. Me—find out? You're crazy."

"That's a rumor you been tossing around town a long time. If you didn't know about the phone call, why did you send Miss Seaward to Rosalie Wayne's apartment this morning?"

Cardigan blinked. That was a fast one and he stalled, saying, "Who said she went there?"

"I got it from the maid there. She said a girl from *The Flash* dropped in. I called *The Flash*. No girl from their office went there. I asked the maid to describe her. She did it perfect. I got a hunch and I went to the taxi stand near your office. A guy remembered taking her from in front of your office right to the Petremont Plaza."

Cardigan said, "O.K. She did. Now what? You damned well know I'd have a hell of a time trying to get any dope out of the telephone exchange."

"That's just what I know. And now what I want to know is, how'd you find out about Rosalie Wayne? What did you pick up when you prowled through Jacland's apartment eating grapes?"

"Nothing."

Bone narrowed an eye. "I'm a tough baby, Cardigan. When a private dick bursts into an apartment I'm covering and walks off with some info, I'm tough. What did you find?"

"Nothing."

"Then how the hell did you get onto the Rosalie Wayne steer? Answer me that!"

Cardigan leaned back, looked down his nose. His face was not pleasant. "If I got onto that steer, Abe, I didn't find anything. And how did I get onto it? I use," he said softly, "a Ouija board."

"You can't pull that crap!" Bone muttered, grabbing Cardigan's arm.

"Take your hand off, Abe," Cardigan snapped. "You're not tough; you're just nasty. Take it off!" He wrenched free and a sullen look swept into his eyes. "If you found the Wayne steer, land on her—not me."

"I did," Bone said, slowly. "I quizzed her over at the theatre. She admitted calling Jacland, but she said she called him in a fit of temper—about something he wrote. I asked her if she was ever in his apartment. She said no. And that's why I tailed you here. What, Cardigan, what the hell did you lift out of that apartment?"

"I told you."

"The truth, I mean. You found some evidence there, damn you! You found something—a card, a case, something—that made you send Miss Seaward to the Wayne apartment!"

Cardigan patted Bone on the shoulder. "There, there, Abe. It's probably been your diet. You need a rest."

Bone flung the hand down. "I'm not kidding, bozo!"

"Neither am I!" Cardigan shot back at him, darkening. "If you want me to answer questions, get a subpoena, but for God's sake stop tailing me around town like a pup!" He turned. "Come on, Pat. We dine."

"You wait, Cardigan!" Bone cut in.

CARDIGAN ignored him. He handed Pat down from the stool, guided her across the bar and on into the dining room. A few people were at table and the orchestra was tuning up. Antonio led them to a table at the edge of the dance floor and a minute later Ken Strange, the owner, came over and bent over the table. "What's the matter with Bone, Cardigan?"

"He's got an idea, Ken; that's all."

"Listen, Cardigan. If he starts clowning around here I'm going to get in touch with Inspector Gross. I'm paying enough for peace in this scatter and I'm not going to have any dick raising a howl. I'll have him bounced out."

Cardigan laughed. "You don't hurt my feelings, boy. On second thought, Ken, I wouldn't do that. Abe's a nasty guy to cross. Especially in your business."

"I just ain't going to have him raise a disturbance!"

Cardigan shrugged and Strange turned on his heel and walked off.

Pat wasn't at ease. "Why didn't you try to humor Bone?"

"You ever try humoring a guy that's naturally bad-humored? Abe's a grifter. He's up a blind alley and for the sake of his face he's trying to shake me down for some dope."

The crowd began coming in. The jazz band began playing and couples swung out onto the floor. Cardigan danced with Pat, he could handle himself for a big man; and from time to time he caught sight of Bone beyond the entrance. There was consommé waiting when they returned to the table and Cardigan ordered some Chablis for the fish course. At 11:30 Rosalie Wayne came in with a tall, broad-shouldered young fellow and neither of them looked gay. They went to a table in a corner.

"She's lovely," Pat said.

"There's one thing about you I like, kid; you're no cat." He dropped his voice. "I think she's headed for the dressing room. Run along and get a close-up of her. See how she looks—how she feels. Hop!"

Pat left and Cardigan beckoned Antonio over. "Who's the guy just came in with Rosalie Wayne?"

Antonio leaned close. "Robert Drummond."

"That's a name. What's he do?"

"You haven't seen him in the play *The Backlands!*"

"No."

"Say, he's great. Leading man! And you know, he's come up. Yes, sure! And this play—I tell you, Mr. Cardigan, is the berries, like. Strong! For men! It is in the jungle, maybe Africa, I think. And in the last act—ah! In the last act, there is the jungle, dim and sinister, and the villain leaning in the girl's hut—the doorway, you understand.

He laughs. The girl inside cries out. Mr. Drummond appears from the wings. He makes one grand leap and with a knife kills the villain. I understand he studied for two months the use of the knife. Grand! Swell!"

"Thanks," said Cardigan. "See about that wine, will you?"

He got up and drifted into the bar, whence Robert Drummond had gone a moment before. He leaned on the bar beside Drummond and said, offhand, "I like your work in that play, Mr. Drummond."

Drummond turned. "Thanks. Thanks a lot."

"The knife work was swell. The way you leap across the stage and use that knife— You know how to use a knife, I'll tell you!"

"I—studied for the part."

Cardigan nodded, his eyes wandering. "It's a dangerous asset."

Drummond started. "I don't quite get you."

"Oh, nothing." Cardigan laughed. "I was just thinking of the Jacland case. Well—good luck!"

He turned away, taking with him an impression of the sudden white look that his words had brought to Drummond's face. He returned to his table, cocked an eye at the lemon-yellow Chablis. In a few minutes Rosalie Wayne returned to the table accompanied by Drummond. Cardigan began to get impatient when, with the lapse of five minutes, Pat did not put in an appearance. At the end of ten minutes he called Antonio.

"Send someone up to ask the maid in the dressing room if anything is wrong with Miss Seaward."

In three minutes Antonio was back, palms spread upward. "But she left the dressing room ten minutes ago—"

Cardigan was on his feet, a wicked look in his eyes.

CHAPTER THREE

IF THE CAP FITS

KEN STRANGE met Cardigan in a private room off the bar. "Look here, Cardigan, what the hell do you think—"

"Cut it, Ken!" His voice was low, thick, his eyes lowering. "I want to speak to that maid."

"But she said Miss Seaward—"

"Are you going to get the maid out of that dressing room or am I going to crash it and start a lot of female shrieks?"

Strange took a breath. "O.K. Come on."

They went up to the second floor, into a small, private dining room. "Wait here," Strange said.

He went out, reentered a moment later with a young woman dressed in black with a small white apron. She looked frightened.

Cardigan said, "Did any word pass between Miss Seaward and any other woman in there?"

"There was only one other woman—Rosalie Wayne."

"Well?"

"N-no. They didn't say anything—not to each other. Miss Wayne, I thought, at one time was crying. I can't be sure. I just thought so."

"Who went out first?"

"Miss Wayne. Miss Seaward left a moment later."

"O.K. You can go."

She went.

Cardigan turned to Strange. "Is there a back way down and out from this floor?"

"Yes."

"Where does it go?"

"A courtyard in the back. There's a through alley to the next street south."

"Where'd you last see Abe Bone?"

"In the bar. About fifteen minutes before you sent Antonio up here."

Cardigan turned, pulled open the door and went downstairs. Strange was at his heels saying, "Now for God's sake, Cardigan, don't start a rough-house!"

Cardigan strode into the bar, stopped short and turned on Strange. "Ask the bartender when he last saw Abe."

Strange shrugged and went to the bar, spoke for a minute or so, returned. "He said he saw Rosalie Wayne go through here to the back hall. Then the girl you came in with. He said Bone saw them too and went into the hall also. The men's room is at the back of the lower hall."

Cardigan went down the lower hall, took a look and returned. "The nigger in there said Bone wasn't in. Did anybody see Bone after he went into the hall?"

"He didn't come back here."

Cardigan jerked a thumb. "Go in and ask Rosalie Wayne if she saw a man hanging around the hall upstairs when she came out of the dressing room."

"Look here now, Cardigan—"

"If you don't, I will!"

Strange touched a handkerchief to his forehead and walked away. He returned in a moment shaking his head.

Cardigan said, "Now come with me, Ken, and show me every room in this place."

"Cardigan, I'm not going to have my place—"

"And me, Ken, I'm not going to have Pat Seaward drop out of sight in your joint. Get going."

"Hell, what a guy—what a guy! Come on."

They searched every room in the three-storied house, found nothing.

"There's no monkey-business goes on in my place," Strange said.

Cardigan grouched, "Hell, I've nothing against you, Ken. But I wanted to see. Listen. Get Pat's wrap from the chair and leave it in the checkroom, will you?"

"This kind of knocks me over, Cardigan."

"You should be knocked over!" Cardigan laughed grimly. "What about me?" He wheeled away. "I'll probably be back."

HE GOT his hat from the checkroom and rolled out the front door. He hailed a cruising cab and gave an address. He sat on the edge of the seat, the heel of his right hand grinding on his knee. He was too upset, too angry, to attempt to find solace in a smoke.

He snapped at the driver. "Listen, you! I've seen Broadway too many times. Get out of the traffic. Get over on the West Side."

"Geez, chief, I'm doin' me best!"

"For that meter of yours, yes. Hike west."

Ten minutes later the cab pulled up in front of a station-house's green lights. Cardigan heaved out and said, "Wait here."

He swung across the sidewalk, climbed steps and barged into the central room. A fat lieutenant at the desk was unimpressed by the noisy entrance.

Cardigan said, "Hey, Bromfield, where's Bone?"

"Bone?"

"Bone."

"He ain't called in lately. I don't know. Say, Cardigan, you think that Sharkey-Schmelling thing was fixed?"

"Where's Bone?"

"My, my, you got to take the roof off the house?"

Cardigan cursed and sailed on into the back room. Three plainclothesmen were sitting around, smoking.

One said, "Ask Cardigan, now. Go ahead. Hey, Cardigan, don't you think Sharkey beat hell out of—"

"Where's Abe Bone?"

"I mean, take it now like this: Sharkey boxed—he boxed, I say, and in the last round, why in the last round—"

"Where's Bone?"

The man gave it up in disgust. "I don't know," he growled.

Cardigan turned and went out of the room with slow, lagging steps. In the central room, he stood looking sourly at Broomfield, who was complacently eating an apple. He muttered and strode to the door, reached the curb by the taxi and stood there tapping his foot.

The driver stirred. "I see a lot of guys ain't satisfied with that there Sharkey-Schmelling decision. I—"

"You," bit off Cardigan, "start back for the Club Cordova."

He paid up in front of the green marquee. The flunky opened the door and Cardigan went into the foyer. The checkroom girl reached for his hat. It was in his hand, but he didn't see her. He ran into Ken Strange in the bar and he could tell by the look on Strange's face that something was up. Strange stopped him with a palm.

"Take it easy, Cardigan."

"What's on your mind?"

"Bone—"

"Where the hell is that bum?"

"Easy, Cardigan! For God's sake, easy! I may be in a jam, but so help me, it's not my fault! This way."

He led the way into the room off the bar. Bone was sitting in an easy chair, foggy-eyed. There was a welt on his forehead and his hair was tangled. He didn't seem to notice anything.

Strange was whispering. "We found him under the stair well in the hall upstairs. He was beaned—and out cold. For cripes' sake, look at the jam I'm in!"

Then Bone, seeing things, suddenly cried hoarsely, "You, Cardigan! You, damn you, you cracked me!"

Cardigan said to Strange, "Imagine!"

"You, Cardigan—" Bone heaved to his feet and clawed at his hip pocket. But he was sluggish.

Cardigan leaped, man-handled Bone back into the chair and took his gun away from him.

Strange rasped, "Damn it, Cardigan, don't do that!"

"You think I'm going to let him play cops and robbers with this rod?" He flung it on a table, spun on Bone. "Listen, Abe. I didn't crack you. I'm looking for the guy that did."

He wheeled about and with Bone's abuse still ringing in his ears he crossed the bar and was stopped by Antonio at the entrance to the dining room.

Cardigan said, "Get Miss Wayne—and her boy friend."

"But they left, Cardigan."

"Left! When?"

"Maybe half an hour ago. Miss Wayne, I think, did not feel well."

"Maybe," Cardigan said, pivoting, "she'll feel worse."

HE WENT upstairs, found the rear staircase and followed it down to a rear door. The door opened into a dark courtyard. He used a flashlight the size and shape of a fountain pen. Going round and round the courtyard, he covered every inch of brick with the small but thorough beam of light. Then he took the alley that cut between two stone buildings. The alley was a narrow strip of cement and he followed it with his flashlight. Halfway through, he picked up a crumpled handkerchief. Pat's initial was in the corner. She'd dropped it purposely, he guessed, to point the line of flight out to him.

Reaching the street, he caught a taxi and gave an address. In five minutes he alighted before the Petremont Plaza and strode long-legged through the lobby. The elevator whisked him upward and he went down the twelfth floor corridor looking very dark and malignant. He used the knocker of 1212.

Rosalie Wayne opened the door and Cardigan, dispensing with overtures, walked right in past her. She made a little startled outcry and Drummond, rising from a chair, rapped out: "Look here!"

Cardigan went toward him, patting down air with an open palm.

"I am, Drummond. Right here."

Drummond looked awestricken. "What in the name of thunder do you think you are doing?"

Cardigan swung around, shaggy-headed, brutal-eyed, and pointed at Rosalie Wayne. "Why did you phone Giles Jacland this morning?"

Drummond got between them. "Now look here, whoever you are—"

"My name's Cardigan, of the Cosmos Detective Agency."

"Oh!" quietly; and Drummond stepped back. "I see." Then he flared up again. "That still gives you no right to blunder in here and—"

"Blunder, is it?" Cardigan snapped.

"Please, please!" Rosalie Wayne cried.

Cardigan was hard at it. "Listen to me, you two! The girl I was with tonight disappeared from the Cordova. She was the same girl that came to this apartment this morning and spoke with your maid." He stopped short. "Where's that maid?"

"It's her night off," Rosalie Wayne said.

"Disappeared!" Drummond was echoing.

Cardigan turned on him savagely. "You heard me! Disappeared!" Then he was back at Rosalie Wayne, ripping out, "Why did you phone Giles Jacland just before his murder?"

She held hands to her face. "I—oh, it was nothing—nothing! It was stupid of me but—but I was angry, so—"

"Was Drummond here at the time? Did he go, then, directly to Jacland's apartment?"

"No! No!"

Drummond's voice shook with anger. "What the devil are you implying?"

"If the cap fits, wear it."

"Why, you dirty—"

"Wait!" Cardigan broke in, his voice low, held back. "Let that slide for the moment. All I'm interested in now is the disappearance of Miss Seaward. You two left the Cordova directly after she was kidnaped. She was up here this morning. There's got to be a connection. Now I don't want any dramatics or wisecracking repartee or third-act heroics or any other kind of bushwah. I want Miss Seaward. Get that. *I want Miss Seaward!*"

Rosalie Wayne drew herself erect. "I know nothing about her. I don't even know the girl. I'm sure Mr. Drummond doesn't."

"You?" Cardigan shot at Drummond.

"I know nothing."

CARDIGAN walked across to the telephone, picked it up and turned to face them. "I hate to do this, but I'm getting a couple of precinct detectives over."

Rosalie Wayne started. "But why?"

"They can get rough," he said, eyeing Drummond, "and they have the law to back them up. I haven't."

Drummond came across the room. "Please, Mr. Cardigan, wait, let us get this thing straight."

"Straight? This thing is about as straight as a roller-coaster. I tell you, I never run to the cops. I usually can settle my own troubles. But this time—my side-kick is in trouble and my hands are tied and nothing else matters and you're either going to come clean or play house with the precinct dicks. I'm not—"

The ringing of the phone cut him short. Rosalie started across the room but Cardigan answered it, said, "Hello." Then he looked up, pressed the mouthpiece against his chest. "This is your maid calling, Miss Wayne. I want you to tell her to come right home—as quick as she can. Understand?"

"Yes," she said, breathless.

"I want you to ask her where she is. I want the address."

"Yes."

He gave her the phone and she said, "Hello, Janie.... I know, I know; I thought you were out rather late.... But listen, Janie. I want you to come right home. It's imperative.... I'll explain later. And, Janie. Where are you?... You must tell me.... You must, Janie!... Oh. Oh, I see."

She hung up, said, "She said—a drug store."

Cardigan laughed shortly, unpleasantly. Then he said, "I'll be seeing you two later. The best way to get yourself into a pot of trouble is try leaving the city. You get that, Drummond?" he whipped off.

"I had no intention—"

But Cardigan was on his way to the door. He went out.

Standing in the doorway at the entrance to the Petremont Plaza, he was deep in shadows. The doorman had retired. Lights were low in the lobby behind and the street out front was dark, quiet. When he had been standing there for half an hour, a cab drew up to the curb.

A woman got out, paid the driver and the cab shoved off. The woman hurried toward the entrance.

Cardigan took hold of her arm. "Miss Leadley?"

"Yes— But see here."

She was small, quaint-looking in a quaint bonnet that sat high on her gray head.

"Mother," he said, "you and I are going places."

"Let me go! Let—"

"Yelling will bring only the police."

She stopped short, breathing hard. "But—but—"

"You don't really want to see the police: that's right. Come along with me."

"But I have to—"

He had no scruples. He showed her a gun. "I mean it! You're going to take me to the place you just came from!"

"I— No! No!"

"Madam, it's that or—" he moved the gun—"this." He lifted his head, called, "Taxi!"

CHAPTER FOUR

GUIDO

SHE HUDDLED in one corner of the rear seat, her hands tensely locked, her eyes wide behind her little old spectacles. She stared straight ahead. It was as if she dared not look at the man beside her. She had given an address.

"You know," Cardigan said, "you're a pretty old woman to get mixed up in a thing like this."

She bit her lips to keep words from issuing forth.

"Murder," he said, "and kidnaping are dangerous pastimes."

She muttered, "I murdered no one! I kidnaped no one!"

She began crying. The cab rolled on, heading west, its tires swishing through the dark, empty streets. The sound of her crying was hardly audible. Presently the cab stopped in front of a shabby brownstone house.

Cardigan said, "This it?"

"Yes," she sobbed.

He backed out, reached in and handed her to the curb. He paid the driver and the cab ground into gear, rolled off. He held the little woman's arm. She hung back. He tugged at the arm with his left hand. In his right was his gun—inside his pocket.

"Oh, please," she gasped weakly.

He lifted her bodily, under the armpits, and carried her up the brownstone stoop. He set her down in front of the vestibule and moved to one side.

He said, "Ring that bell."

She put her hand on the bell, her head on the hand, sobbing. He was touched by the hopelessness of her small, quaint figure, but he was also determined. He said nothing. Waiting, his hand was hard on the gun in his tuxedo pocket. He used his left hand to turn up the collar and drew together, as much as he could, the lapels. He regretted the low waistcoat, the expanse of boiled shirt.

The inner door clicked. Cardigan pressed close against the stone to one side of the vestibule. There was a pause, and then the vestibule door opened. The little woman swayed. Suddenly she let out a faint cry and collapsed.

A man pushed out of the vestibule and Cardigan said, "Up you!" quietly.

The man almost stumbled. In the darkness he looked tall, burly, had a bald head and what looked like white hair above the ears.

"Oh, yeah?" he said.

"Pick her up," Cardigan said. "It'll keep your arms occupied. Pick her up and carry her. I'll be behind you."

The burly man said, "I guess you got me," cheerfully, and lifted the old woman. She made a small package in his arms. Cardigan got behind him and they entered, Cardigan closing both doors.

The hall was lighted and at the head of the stairs stood the figure of a woman. She did not look young. She was plump and tall. The burly man carried the old woman up the stairway and Cardigan went behind him. The woman at the top could not see the gun in Cardigan's hand.

"What's the matter, Matt?"

The burly man's answer was in the nature of a short, guttural laugh. Brass strips on the steps clicked beneath his heels.

"It's Janie," the woman said.

"Yeah," the burly man said, hard humor still in his tone.

"Who's the man—" They were at the top and the woman caught sight of the gun. "Oh," she said, quietly.

She had a dowager look about her. Gray-white hair, piled high, and a black ribbon around her full throat. There were lines in her face, a double chin, growing hardness in eyes that were a queer shade of green. Majesty was in the straightness with which she held herself.

Matt said, "She fainted outside and this mug was there, waitin' with a rod."

"She fainted and— Oh, I see."

There was the sound of a piano, casually, softly played, in a room beyond. A door was part way open.

"Get going," Cardigan said.

THE woman turned and walked majestically toward the door and Matt followed. Cardigan crowded close behind them, entered the room with them. He remembered the drab outside of the house and was instantly struck by the splendor of a large living room containing scattered floor lamps. At a grand piano, a small, dark man was rippling his fingers over the keys. He seemed unaware that they had entered. Then he looked up—and stopped playing. Leaped to his feet and shot a hand toward his hip.

But Cardigan had him covered. "No you don't!" And to Matt: "Keep holding her, you!" He swung his voice back to the dark man: "Keep your hands up and come over here." The man came over. "Turn around." Cardigan removed a small automatic from the rear pocket.

There was in this room, about these people, a strange air that was oddly sinister. Cardigan sensed it vaguely but could not lay his finger on anything. The tall woman stood like a Tussaud figure, motionless; Matt stood holding the old woman and smiling with hard amusement; the dark man stood stonelike and stared fiercely, his eyes never blinking, at the floor. Cardigan moved until he could tap Matt's pockets. He withdrew a gun and stuffed it into the pocket where he had put the dark man's.

"Put her down," he said.

Matt laid Miss Leadley on a large divan. She muttered something and moved from side to side. Matt straightened and stared at Cardigan. The tall woman stared at him. The dark man stared fiercely at the floor. No one said anything.

Until Cardigan said, "I'm looking for Miss Seaward."

Matt and the tall woman looked at each other. Their glances showed nothing. They returned their stares to Cardigan and after a moment's silence the tall woman turned, walked leisurely to a straight-backed chair and sat down. She lit a cigarette, unhurried. Matt shrugged, took another chair and looked fixedly at his fingernails.

"Miss Seaward?" the tall woman said.

Suddenly the small dark man began crying. His shoulders shook and tears ran down his face. He returned to the piano stool, sat down, drew out a handkerchief and continued crying into it.

Cardigan looked exasperated. "Am I in a nut-house?"

The woman got up, crossed the room and patted the dark man on the shoulder. "There, there, Guido," she said. "There, there."

She returned to the high-backed chair and sat down. "So you want Miss Seaward, Mr. Cardigan."

"I'm glad you know my name."

She regarded her cigarette. "You are a very able detective. You are well known in the city and you wield a certain amount of power. So do I," she finished, sharply. "Do you know who I am?"

He shook his head. "I don't care. I told you what I want."

"You may as well put the gun aside, because it won't help you get Miss Seaward."

"I'll hold the gun while I can."

The little dark man was weeping into his handkerchief and rocking from side to side. Matt got up and rocked over and bent down. "Snap out of it, Guido. You got to snap out of it. Come on, be a pal and snap out of it." He rubbed Guido affectionately on the shoulder with an immense hand.

Cardigan said, "You, Matt, get over to that chair!"

"Me?" Matt chuckled hoarsely. "Sure."

Miss Leadley, only half conscious, was moaning. "O God, protect Rosalie! O God…." She trailed off into muttering.

The tall woman looked at her, then looked at Cardigan. She stood up and her head went back arrogantly, green flame moved in her eyes. "I will bargain with you, Mr. Cardigan! I have Miss Seaward in my possession and—"

"Get her," Cardigan chopped in.

TEETH, still fine and regular, shone between lips curving open in a smile of challenge. "The bargain, you remember." She went on swiftly. "I have her. I had her kidnaped right from under your nose in the Club Cordova tonight. I had to do it, you understand! And now—now, we shall bargain. Her life—against the thing I want."

"Spill it."

"You are to forget this address. You are to forget all and everything connected with the Jacland murder case. That is all."

He said roughly, "If you have her, what the hell can I do but say yes?"

"You can, afterwards," she reminded him, "double-cross me."

"Naturally, I could do that. I may have to. I'm not the only one mixed up in it. The cops are after me for what I already know. They're after Miss Seaward too. I can take it; I could talk them out of anything. But if they corner her, there's no telling."

"You're frank, at least."

"I'm frank even with killers. I'm telling you that, so far as I'm concerned, so far as things stand now, it's a bargain. It's tough to swallow, but it's a bargain. I'd be crummy to walk out on her." He was scowling, his face was dark and unpleasant and he was impatient. He growled, "Get her. Get her."

"First, put down that gun."

He gripped it hard. "I've got to see her first. I'll not put this rod down—not with that crying hyena there and this roughneck here. Get her! Get her in here and, so help me, I'll do nothing more than walk out with her!"

The tall woman folded her arms. "I, Mr. Cardigan, am making the terms of the bargain. You forget that."

Cardigan's eyes blazed. "Why, damn it, another crack like that and I'll get the police here! I'll phone them!"

"You will put your hands up, Mr. Cardigan."

Startled, he twisted his head around. Miss Leadley was sitting up, holding a gun in her hand. "Put them up, please. You forgot about me."

Matt heaved out of the chair and started toward Cardigan.

"You all forgot about me," another voice said. "Steady!"

Matt stopped in his tracks. Miss Leadley ducked her head. Pat came through a curtained doorway—small, trim, white-faced. There was a big gun in her hand.

She said, "Never bind a woman with plain rope. And never leave loaded guns around in bureau drawers.... O.K., chief. I guess that does it. The little dark gentleman there did it. He carries a knife in his right sock. I felt it in the cab with my ankle. You'd better get it."

Cardigan turned on Guido. "Shell out, you."

Guido wept again and, bending, drew a knife from his trousers leg. He laid it on the piano, sat down, put his face in his hands and began weeping hard.

Cardigan said to Pat, "You're telling me the Rosalie Wayne lead is all wrong? There's her maid."

Pat started. "I didn't recognize her!"

Matt's fists were clenched. "Listen, Cardigan," he growled passionately. "You can't drag Rosalie Wayne into this. You can't, you hear!"

"She's just as guilty—"

"She's not!" cried the tall woman, her eyes wide. "I tell you, she knows nothing about this! Nothing! She doesn't know me! Not even me! She doesn't know I'm alive! So help me God, she had no hand in this!" Suddenly she was out of breath, her face enflamed. "You can't ruin her, her career! You can't do what Giles Jacland tried to do! You can't!"

Cardigan was puzzled. He growled. "What do you know about Giles Jacland?"

"You ask me what I know? You don't know who I am. Well, Mr. Cardigan, I am Rose O'Day. I was—was Rose O'Day."

He said, "Rose O'Day was an actress who died—was drowned—when I was a kid. Fifteen years ago. I—" He stopped short. "You do," he said, his voice dropping, "resemble Rose O'Day."

She shook with emotion. "I am! I'm Rosalie Wayne's mother. Do you know who ruined me? Do you know who drove me to drink and then dope and who drove me from the boards?"

Matt was uneasy. He went to her.

"Rosie—calm, Rosie."

BUT no one could have stopped her.

She cried, "Giles Jacland ruined me! With his bitter criticism—his cruel, heartless satire. He ruined me! He made me lose faith in myself until I believed I was a rotten actress. And I went down. But going down—I thought of Rosalie. And I vanished. She was left with Janie

Leadley. Janie knew everything.

"And Giles Jacland was ruining Rosalie. He hated me—hated me always because I was one actress who never came to him. And he suspected I never died. And he somehow kept track of Rosalie through the years—even though her name was changed. And he tried to do with her what he never was able to do with me. But he didn't tell her he knew. He had a better way. His pen."

She spun around. "Just as he ruined Guido. Because one night, years ago, Guido got up in a restaurant and called him a fakir, a cad and a bounder. He ruined Guido—made him lose faith in himself just as I did. Matt caught me on the toboggan. Cured me of dope. Matt married me. Thank God for that!"

She dropped to the chair, wringing with perspiration, shaking all over. Matt stood behind her, his hands on her shoulders. There was a long moment of silence.

Then Guido snarled. "I killed him! Me! With my knife! No one told me to! But I—I went and killed him! For Rosalie's sake—but for mine also!"

Pat sighed. Her gun drooped. She said, "I felt, chief, it was something like this. Jacland was that way. A cad."

Cardigan was saying, with difficulty, "I know, I know, but Bone is on this. Bone is after you and me. Somebody has to take the rap for it. I'm not. I'm not going to let you."

She threw the gun on the divan. "I don't care, chief. I'm walking out of this. I hate murder, but there are times when you can't call it murder. I'm not a cop. I'm walking out."

She turned and went to the door.

He said, "Pat, wait!"

"Chief, you heard me. If you've any sense of decency in you, you'll come with me, you won't be a heel."

He felt his neck redden. His jaw hardened. "O.K., wisegirl. The cops'll come after us for a shake-down. I hope you can take it." He backed across the room. He said, "You, Rose O'Day—and the rest of you—take a heel's advice. Scram out of here—now, this minute. Pack like hell and lam. You hear me?"

"I got you," Matt said.

Cardigan said, "Because that operative of mine is only a woman. And cops are cops. And if they get rough with her—I tell everything—the whole works. Me they can rough-house and make me like it, when I get used to it. But—" he shook his head—"not her."

He backed swiftly to the door, backed out into the hall and closed it. Pat was waiting.

He clipped, "So I'm a heel, eh?"

She gripped his arm. "Chief, I didn't mean that. I know you were thinking of me. But, hell, if we turned them over, if we raked up Rosalie Wayne—I'd feel rotten for the rest of my days."

THEY reached the lower hall, opened the door and passed into the vestibule. Cardigan pulled the door shut. They went out of the vestibule, down the stairs.

A figure moved from the shadow of the stoop. "I've been waiting for you, Cardigan."

Pat's hand tightened on Cardigan's arm.

"Hello, Abe," Cardigan said. "I notice you waited outside—not in."

"Never mind that. I tailed you from the Cordova. I saw you get in a cab with a woman off Park Avenue and you come right here. So I've been waiting. It wasn't this jane you got on your arm now. What's in that house?"

"Rooms. Roomers, I suppose."

Bone made a jaw. "I'm not kidding, Cardigan!"

"The woman," Cardigan said, feeling his way, "was a stoolie of mine. I had her on this case. I had her planted out back of the Cordova. She saw Pat and the guy come through the alley and get a cab. She wasn't sure, but she followed the cab. She followed it to here.

"When I left the Cordova I called up the office and told them I was going to Rosalie Wayne's apartment. The stoolie phoned the office to find out where I was. They said I'd gone to the Wayne apartment. The stoolie called me there and I told her to meet me downstairs. A little woman, Abe? That's the one. She brought me here and rang the bell and a guy opened the door when he saw it was only a woman. I crashed in, taking the woman with me, but I sent her out the back way. I held the guy up, had my gun on him. I told him I'd kill him if he didn't turn over Pat. We went into a room and there was a lot of talk. He wouldn't turn over Patrick unless I let him go. What could I do, Abe?"

"You let him go?"

"I had to," Cardigan said. "He lit out the back way."

Bone said, "I don't believe you, Cardigan! You're a dirty Irish two-faced liar! You know what I'm going to do? I'm going to pinch this Jane! Why? For socking me in the Cordova. All right, you say she didn't. I say she did. I'm going to get some straight talk out of this if I have to break somebody's back!"

Cardigan was grave. "I told you the truth, Abe. You're not going to pinch Pat."

Her fingers dug into his arm. Was there a window open upstairs? She imagined she had caught a glimpse of a vague face. She gritted her teeth to keep them from chattering.

She cried, "I'll go, chief! He won't get anything! You must let me go!"

"No! Damn it, no!"

Suddenly the front door opened and a man started down the steps. Halfway down, he stopped. Pat let out a little cry. Cardigan, unable to figure this move out, stood rooted to the pavement. Bone whipped his gun out and leveled it at the man on the steps.

"Stick 'em up, you!"

The man walked down the steps, started to stop, then turned and began running. Bone fired. The sound of his gun banged in the silent street. The man pitched headlong and Bone prowled toward him, his gun raised.

The man turned over on his back and said. "All right, you shot me. It was a poor shot, though."

"I like 'em alive, guy."

"Not this one." Steel glinted in his hand. "You see this? It reached the throat of Giles Jacland, my mortal enemy, this morning. And so—"

"Stop that!"

But the blade was quick. It sank into Guido's chest and he gasped out and lay quietly on the pavement.

Pat was shaking. "Chief," she whispered, "he knew—he knew it couldn't be done! He heard Bone! He came down, giving the others time to get away by the rear! He— Poor Guido!"

Cardigan grimaced. Bitter-faced, he walked down the sidewalk, knelt, picked up the lifeless hand. He shook it and laid it down.

"What's the idea?" Bone crabbed.

"Just," Cardigan said, rising, "an idea."

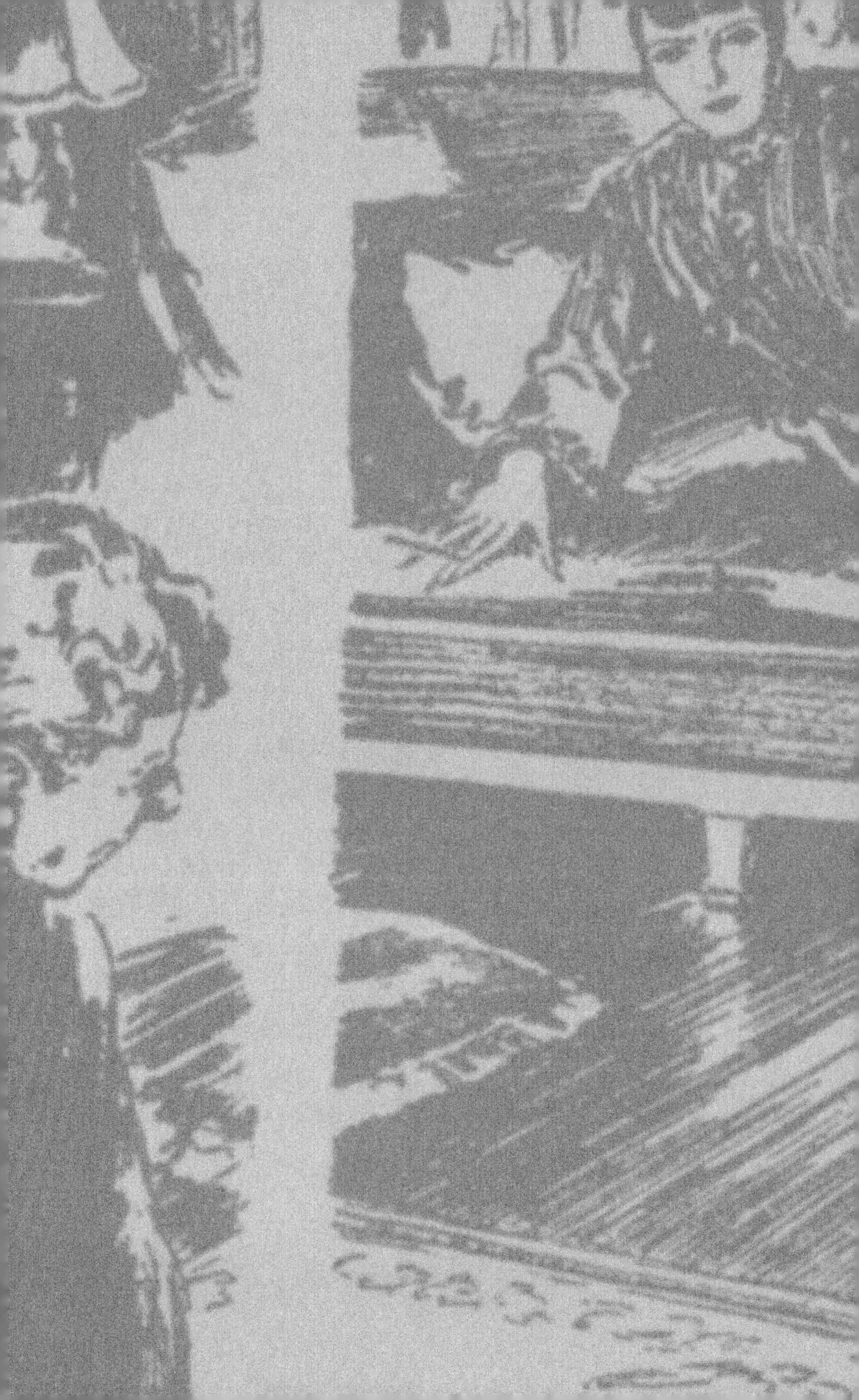

THE CANDY KILLER

CARDIGAN THOUGHT IT WAS A SWELL BREAK WHEN HE GOT SLATED TO HERD THE LOVELY MARTA DAHL AND HER $400,000 BACK TO POLAND. BUT THERE WAS MORE IN STORE FOR HIM THAN SWEET NOTHINGS AND KISSES ON THE BOAT DECK. MURDER, DOPE, AND A SUICIDE ALL HAD TO COME BEFORE "BON VOYAGE."

CHAPTER ONE

THE PEPPERMINT KILL

GEORGE HAMMERHORN, the head of the Cosmos Agency, was signing correspondence at five that afternoon when Cardigan pushed open the glass-paneled connecting door and came in. Cardigan, whistling a tune from *Show Boat,* sat down opposite Hammerhorn at the large double desk, jangled keys, unlocked a drawer, pulled out a bottle of Scotch and poured himself a neat jolt.

"George?"

"Nope."

Hammerhorn's pen scratched across paper. He said: "Ever get seasick, Jack?"

"Me? Once—on a troop ship. It wasn't something I drank." He raised the glass. "Mud in your eye."

"Bon voyage."

Cardigan chuckled.

Hammerhorn finished with the pen, laid it down, tossed the signed letters into a basket marked "Out" and leaned back. "Jack, you're going places."

"Tiarri's for ravioli and steak. Want to come?"

"You're going on a long journey, Jack."

"All right, be funny."

Hammerhorn scratched a match, lit a cigarette. "Poland."

"Now I'll tell one."

"Get your passport fixed up tomorrow and pay any bills you have around town. You'll travel on B Deck on the *Magnetic.* She sails day after tomorrow. You'll be gone three weeks and you don't have to send any postcards."

Cardigan sat back, laughed. "Rave on, George, rave on."

"Ever hear of Marta Dahl?"

"Ask me a hard one."

"You're going," Hammerhorn said, "as Marta Dahl's bodyguard. To Poland. Yesterday afternoon, as Marta Dahl walked from a taxicab to the entrance of her hotel, the Gallice, an umpchay broke out of the crowd and began calling her names. He was a bum, a tramp, with ideas. The essence of it is this: the umpchay thought it was an outrage because these foreign actresses come over, make a lot of dough and take it back to the fatherland. The guy got pretty rough and nasty and some guy took a swing at him. A cop comes up and grabs the umpchay and is going to run him in when Marta Dahl intercedes. She says, 'Let the man go, officer. It is nothing.' The cop swoons—who wouldn't?—and lets the bum go and Marta Dahl goes into her hotel. Catch on?"

"No."

Hammerhorn interlocked fingers behind his head. "About an hour ago her manager, a nice little old fat fellow by the name of Adam Baum, comes in here all hot and bothered. No, he's not worried particularly about the umpchay, but that helped. He wants a bodyguard to accompany Marta to Poland. Why? The umpchay? No. Tomorrow Marta Dahl will draw four hundred thousand dollars from a bank—in cash. Get that, sweetheart—in cash. She will lug four hundred thousand dollars in cash back to her native Poland."

He yanked hard and Sam went backward mightily.

"Why can't she transfer it?"

"Don't ask me why actresses do things. Baum tried to talk her out of it, but it was no go. The money's in a checking account and maybe she thinks that while she's on the water something might go wrong with the transfer. All that concerns us is that she's toting four hundred thousand dollars and you're to see that she and the dough get to Poland together. Our fee for this is one thousand berries, exclusive of your expenses. There is a Santa Claus."

"And I'm the goat, huh?"

"What the hell are you beefing about? An ocean voyage with the screen's hottest mama! I'd go myself, sweetheart, but the wife wasn't born yesterday."

He leaned forward, unhooked the telephone. "Get me the Hotel Gallice." He looked across at Cardigan. "Shuffle board, deck tennis, real liquor—"

"And a knife in the back."

"Do you expect everything for nothing? Think of the moonlight!" He ducked his head near the mouthpiece, spoke into the phone, waited, then said: "Mr. Baum?... This is Hammerhorn of the Cosmos Agency.... My ablest man will accompany Miss Dahl. His name is Cardigan."

"Suppose this dame falls for me and I don't come back?"

Hammerhorn hung up, made a sour face. "M-m-m, don't you hate yourself!

TIARRI'S was a noisy Village speak. It had a large, low dining room in which Tiarri had gone wild with plaster frescoes. The bar was better, though noisier; it did not look like a vain attempt to transplant an Italian alley to lower New York. Cardigan was rolling poker dice with Frank, the barman. One side of Frank's mustache was gone; he had promised to cut that side off if a local Dago boxer lost.

Angelo, a waiter, punched Cardigan in the ribs. "Ouch!" said Cardigan.

Angelo bowed. "Onna da tele-phono." He jerked an illustrative Sicilian thumb. "In-a da off-eece."

"Listen, Angelo," Cardigan said. "I'm not here."

"Uk-key, boss."

Angelo went away and Cardigan returned to the dice. But in a minute Angelo was back.

"Deesa gentelman say, 'Nuts to you, Dago. Tell-a dat gorill' to get-a hell on de tele-phono.'"

"Sounds like a pal," Cardigan said, and sloped off into the little cubbyhole behind the bar. He scooped up the phone there, said. "Who's a gorilla, you big stiff?... Oh, hello Garrity! How's your diabetes?" He stopped short, the laughter ebbed from his eyes. He said, after a minute: "O.K." And hung up.

He rolled out at the bar, lost, paid up. He went into the dining room, got hat and topcoat from a costumer, slapped the hat on his shaggy mop of hair and went out the front, up three steps out of the areaway and into a taxicab.

A man opened the taxi's door in front of the swank Hotel Gallice, on Park Avenue. The man looked like an Austrian general but was only the hotel doorman. Cardigan swung across the sidewalk, slapped his way through revolving doors and headed across the lobby. His coat was six years old and looked it and his lop-eared hat was faded from rain, sun and old age. His thick hair bunched around the ears.

A man headed him off.

"Hello, Yager," Cardigan clipped, and was on his way, long-legged.

But Yager caught up with him. "In my office a minute, Cardigan. I got a proposition." Yager was the house dick.

"Got no time. What suite?"

"Fourteen twelve. Now listen, Cardigan—my office—just a minute and—"

"While Rome burns?" Cardigan said and walked on into an open elevator.

Yager bounced in after him.

"Fourteen," Cardigan said. He stood on wide-planted feet, spinning his hat on a big forefinger while the elevator rose smoothly, noiselessly, to the fourteenth floor.

Yager got out with him. Yager was a pudgy short man with a bullet head, a squat hard neck and gimlet eyes. He said: "Now listen, Cardigan. There might be some dough in this for us. Baum, the dame's manager, said he'd pay five thousand dollars—"

Cardigan lengthened his stride, reached a door numbered 1412, knocked loudly. A cop opened it and said: "Hello, Cardigan."

"Hello, Swanson," Cardigan said; lifted his chin. "Hello, Garrity."

Yager pushed in behind him, looking abused and misunderstood. Captain Garrity, a bluff headquarters dick, was sitting on the arm of a chair swinging a foot.

"Thanks for coming, you roughneck."

A WOMAN sat on another chair. She was young and in black livery.

Her eyes were red-rimmed and she clasped a crumpled damp handkerchief in her hand. A short, rotund man in evening clothes was pacing up and down, his eyes glued wildly on the floor. He kept muttering to himself, shaking his head, rubbing his palms together.

Garrity clipped: "Mr. Baum, this is Cardigan."

The fat man stopped short, rushed across the room, bowed deeply, shook Cardigan's hand violently and then returned to pacing the floor. The maid broke out crying again.

"In here, Cardigan," Garrity said, and led the way into another room. He was a lean, hard-boned man with a good jaw, hard gray eyes. "What do you know about this dame, kid?"

"Not a thing, Pete. I'll give you the straight of it. The little fat guy dropped in on George this afternoon and hired a man to bodyguard the dame to Poland. She's drawing four hundred thousand dollars out of the bank tomorrow and lugging it home with her. George picked me to dry-nurse the dough home. Just what happened?"

Garrity scowled. "Well, a couple of cops heard shots in West Fifty-fourth Street at nine tonight. They legged it over and found a taxicab halfway across the curb. The driver was in the gutter with his belly all shot to hell. All they could get out of him for a while was 'Marta Dahl! Marta Dahl!' Like that—over and over again. They got an ambulance and went to a hospital with him. They didn't get much more out of him. Only that Marta Dahl was his fare. He must have recognized her. Who wouldn't? The cops tried to get out of him where he picked her up, but the poor guy was croaking fast. It gets down to this, near as I can figure it out. A guy crowded into the cab at a traffic stop and made the driver turn west. Another car followed. In West Fifty-fourth Street the guy in the cab made the driver stop. The other car drew up and they switched the jane over. Then the driver gets heroic and starts to fight. One of the eggs lets him have it in the guts. Now the taxi driver remembered one thing: he said he smelled the guy's breath—he smelled peppermint on the guy's breath. Why he remembered that, I don't know. He didn't get the pad numbers. So Marta Dahl is kidnaped. The old boy outside—this Baum lad—is all smashed up. I tried to stop him but right away he phones the papers and offers five thousand bucks reward."

Cardigan said: "That dough of hers is still in the bank. Has her manager got power of attorney?"

"No. Technically he's not her manager anymore. She's through with the screen. But the old guy's built her up and the way I get it, he kind of worships the ground she walks on. If these mugs call for ransom—if the call's in her handwriting—that can be fixed at the bank."

"How about that five thousand reward?"

"Well, I could use half of it."

"How about the other half?"

Garrity said. "What's the matter, you gorilla—can't you use half?"

Cardigan chuckled. "Pete, for a cop, I like you."

"Don't get me wrong, baby. A swell chance I'd have of grabbing the whole five grand with you waltzing around. So I'd rather have you with me than against me. Not that you faze me, Jack—but you have a habit of falling smack on your face into the breaks. This job is a tough one to crack. The jane walks out of the hotel at seven-thirty. The maid says she has a habit of taking these walks alone. The maid doesn't know where she went—only out. Ten to one she walked till she got tired, then snatched a cab."

CARDIGAN shook his head. "If these mugs tailed her from the hotel they would have nabbed her before she got in a cab. What I'd like to know, Pete, is where she went. She might have started out for a walk, but I'll bet you she changed her mind and went some place. Then she took the cab from that place. It was at that place that these mugs started to tail her. How about the cab?"

"I checked up on that. I thought the driver might have been on duty at a hack stand. He wasn't. I looked at his meter and from the fare on it he must have driven three and half miles. So start from that and tell me when you go nutty."

Cardigan said: "How about the umpchay called her names outside the hotel yesterday?"

"Yeah," Garrity chuckled, "I thought you'd come to that. No connection. Hackett, the cop collared him, says he's a hophead named 'Chink' Wiggins."

"Chinaman?"

"No. They just call him Chink. He thinks everything's wrong with the world. Every now and then they collar him for making goofy speeches on street corners."

"Listen, Pete. Collar that bird."

Garrity threw up his hands. "Nix. I'm not going to make myself a laughing stock by grabbing that sap. I'm out to grab some guys for the murder of Jacobs, that driver, and the kidnaping of Marta Dahl—"

"I tell you, Pete, grab him. We may be wrong, but what the hell!"

Garrity tossed his chin up. "Listen, Cardigan. I'm not asking you to think for me. I'm out to grab some killers, I tell you; not to make news by landing on any guy I happen to think of." He strode hard-heeled to the door, added: "Or that you think of."

Cardigan sighed out loud: "You cops, you cops! I think I find a cop with brains and what happens? Why, I find a Brooklyn Hibernian who's so proud of his record he never pinches a guy till the guy says, 'I did it, officer—with my little hatchet'."

"Oh, yeah?" Garrity took his hand off the doorknob and came toward Cardigan with a mean glint in his windy gray eyes. He punched Cardigan on the chest. "Listen, Jack, you bum: I'm one cop they can't hang anything on. I follow the line of my thinking. If that's wrong, it's my tough luck. But I let no guy make my decisions."

Cardigan laughed with rough good humor, threw his arm around Garrity's shoulder. "Good old Pete Garrity! O.K., Pete! If I need a battering ram some day I'll borrow your head."

He ducked a punch, yanked open the door and reentered the living room with a gust of laughter. Mr. Baum stopped pacing. He looked shocked. The maid, who had stopped crying, put her face in her hands and began again. Windy-eyed Captain Garrity stalked into the room, his chest out, his manner important.

Yager, the house dick, began crabbing: "O.K. I guess I see where I stand all right."

Garrity eyed him. "What's eating you?"

"Yeah, you and that big tramp going in a huddle behind the door and leaving me out of it."

Garrity twisted his neck and looked at Cardigan, jerked a thumb. "This house dick a friend of yours?"

"What's the idea of making a dirty crack like that?" Cardigan said, eating an apple he had taken from a fruit bowl.

Yager leveled an arm. "I've got as much right to that reward as anybody! Why leave me out in the cold?"

Cardigan assumed a mock-grave expression. "There you go again, Yager—thinking only of the money. Thought of that reward never entered my mind and I am sure—" he turned, bowed toward Garrity and lifted an eyebrow—"it never entered the captain's."

"Of course not!" Garrity said indignantly.

Yager reddened to his ears, spluttered, turned and thumped out of the room.

Mr. Baum raised his hands, shook with rage. "That foul person! Thinking only of money while my poor Marta is lost—lost!"

"And don't forget," Garrity pitched in, "the dead taxi driver. A wife and five kids in the Bronx."

CHAPTER TWO

HOPHEAD'S HIDEAWAY

WHEN CARDIGAN went through the hotel's revolving door into the street, a taxi was emptying. When the "Vacant" sign was raised he climbed in, gave an address, and leaned back. He was as Irish as Garrity was, and in his own way quite as stubborn. When he became obsessed with an idea, a hunch, he had to play it even though realizing, in great measure, the futility of it. The cab was heading south. At Grand Central it weaved through pedestrians. In the morning, Cardigan mused, these people would read of the disappearance of Marta Dahl. There would also be a parenthetical note about the death of one Jacobs, a taxi driver, who had attempted, apparently, to save her. But the death of a taxi driver is not news. The vanishing of a famous screen actress is news—a final fling for Marta Dahl at the headlines.

Leaving the cab, Cardigan said: "Hang around. I'll be right out."

He passed between two green lights and entered the station-house door. A lieutenant wheezed out a matter-of-fact greeting. Cardigan spoke through cigarette smoke, leaning comfortably with both arms on the desk. He got what he wanted and swung out to the taxicab, climbed in.

The city swallowed him and he turned up again, fifteen minutes later, on a downtown curb where an east wind pushed river smells up a dark street. When the taxi moved off, he dug his hands into his overcoat pockets and got under way. The street was not noisy. The sound of the departing taxi's engine echoed hollowly in the narrow street; and when it had died down the sound of a not distant El train crashed over the roof tops. After that there was only the sound of his footfalls, or a cough from an open window, or the squeal of cats.

Where two streets and a crooked alley wedged into a kind of triangular plaza, there was the distinct sound of pool balls striking. Cardigan, hitting the plaza on the north side, gave it the once-over. It was very dark, dismal—with a few window lights here and there looking like yellow moths. Across the plaza, at the mouth of the alley, was a gaunt brick house of five stories. From the street-level floor of this house issued the neat smacking of pool balls. The house itself was by way of being a beacon in an otherwise tattered, down-at-the-heel district. Crossing the cramped plaza, Cardigan could make out big letters on the broad plate-glass windows. The windows were painted a solid blue three fourths of the way up. The big letters said: "THE FRIENDLY CIRCLE ROOMING HOUSE AND RECREATIONAL PARLOR."

It was a dump.

Cardigan, opening the door, pushing in, prodding the door shut with his heel, was aware of noise, smells, and about two dozen arguments. There were many strata of tobacco smoke, lazy, sluggish, swamping drop lights that glared without benefit of shades. Two pool tables; round card tables and other tables; scarred oblong ones, littered with papers, magazines, the heels of men who reclined in battered chairs. There was dust. There was the smell of the unwashed. There were bromidic legends tacked on the leprous walls. There was a high pulpit-like desk at one side where a fat man with a pitted face and a nose like a Brussels sprout, sat beneath the only shaded light in the place. Behind him was a rack of keys. Above him was a big sign: "Beds—Ten Cents and Up. Rooms—Fifty Cents and Up."

A man in a rushing, passionate voice was explaining his ideas of government. He had greasy stubble on his face and looked like a phantom. Others listened, nodded, burning-eyed—wild-looking men, foreigners. Cardigan found that his entrance created no interest. He moved through the sluggish layers of smoke. Some of the men had blackened eyes, bruised jaws. He remembered there had been a riot at Union Square the other day. Cops had been stoned—and the cops had got tough. Cardigan reached the desk.

"Plainclothes?" asked the fat lump there, bilious-eyed.

"Guy named Wiggins. Where is he?"

"Ain't he here?"

Cardigan said: "Is he?"

"You cops take a chance dancing in this place alone."

Cardigan shrugged. He did not say he was not a cop. The fat man was craning his neck, roving his eyes around the crowd.

"I don't see Wiggins," he said. "He's got a room upstairs. Maybe he's upstairs."

"What's the room?"

"Three ten—third floor."

CARDIGAN turned and made his way through the crowd to the broad stairway. He climbed on worn boards. The first floor looked like a dormitory. There were cots in endless rows. A few men lay on them all dressed, without covers. He took the next stairway up. Three drop-lights made a dim glow in a long, bare corridor. He found a scarred door with tin numbers nailed on it. He palmed the knob and turned it and the door opened and he walked in, closed the door.

A man sat up on a cot that creaked. His face looked like yellow parchment and his hair was mouse-colored. He wore a flannel shirt, trousers, and his eyes were abnormally large, protuberant; his ears stuck out from his head and looked like dead shells.

He cried in a hoarse whisper: "Who're you?"

"You're Wiggins, aren't you?"

"What d'you want here? Get out of here!"

"What the hell are you scared about?"

Wiggins cringed. "I ain't scared! Just what right you got busting in here?"

"Where were you at nine tonight?"

Wiggins' fingers crept to a blue bruise on his jaw. He rasped: "Here! Downstairs!"

Cardigan gazed around the room. "What was the idea of making that grandstand play yesterday in front of the Hotel Gallice?"

The charred eyes blazed. "I'll do it again!" Wiggins cried. "I'm a citizen! I got rights! Them dames come over here, take all our dough—"

"Since when did you have dough? Did you ever do a stroke of work in your life?"

"*Ah-r-r*, you're one o' them too! I told her what I thought of her. I guess she'll remember it."

"She was good enough to ask the cop to let you go."

Wiggins jumped up, shaking. "What the hell do you want here?"

"I'm trying to piece together a puzzle. I'm trying to find a connection." He suddenly grabbed the man, tapped the man's pockets lightning-fast, tossed him away, picked up the coverless pillow, threw it down again. The man cowered in a corner.

"O.K.," Cardigan said. "I just wondered if you were heeled." He turned, twirling a broad blue garter on his forefinger. He had taken it from beneath the pillow. "Nice," he grinned.

"Gimme that!" cried Wiggins. He leaped like a cat, clawed at Cardigan's hands.

Cardigan bounced him onto the bed. "I'd like to meet the lady," he said. He tossed the garter back to Wiggins. He was groping in his mind, feeling his way, determined to leave no stone unturned. "Put your shirt on."

"I ain't going!"

Cardigan showed a row of dangerous teeth. "Get your shirt on, sap!" He towered, his eyes dark and threatening, his shadow massive on the wall behind. He leaned forward, showing a big brown fist.

Wiggins scampered off the bed, flew to a corner, shrank there. "I ain't!" he cried. "I ain't going!"

Cardigan took three slow, heavy steps, caught Wiggins by the throat, lifted him off his feet, held him up and shook him. Wiggins grinned at him. It was a crazy, maniacal grin—and in it Cardigan read a wild, fierce challenge. In that split minute Cardigan knew that this man would not obey. He unloosened his fingers. Wiggins fell to the floor and lay there making idiotic sounds. It was business Cardigan didn't like. He stood for a long minute, pondering, while the figure panted at his feet. He looked down.

"I'll find her," he said in a low voice. "I don't need you, Wiggins. I'll go out and find her myself."

He said no more. He turned and left the room, went downstairs and stopped at the pulpit-like desk.

"Was Wiggins in here at nine tonight?"

The fat man nodded. "Yeah." He pointed. "See that big bird over there with the red beard?"

Cardigan nodded.

The fat man said: "Him and Wiggins got in a fight. They were arguin' since about eight o'clock and then they got in a fight. Over the Roosian situation. They always argue. I been trying to figure out should I pitch 'em out."

"Thanks," Cardigan said.

HE WENT out into the street, crossed the dark deserted plaza and dropped down into a shallow areaway. It was damp and cold but from it he could watch the rooming house. A stray dog came down in search of scraps, yowled and scampered off when Cardigan moved. A few minutes later the door across the way opened; a figure slipped out and scurried past the alley in frantic haste. Cardigan gave it a head start, then rose out of the areaway, felt his way rapidly along the dark house fronts and caught a glimpse of the figure sloping beneath a pallid street light. He heard the frantic rap of heels. For seconds he followed this sound alone. Then there was a brief instant during which the figure sped past a lighted store window; then darkness again and then a momentary glimpse of the figure slanting beneath a street light. Alleys made shortcuts. Cardigan followed. He didn't bother with his gun. He somehow felt that this man was not a gunman. By profession perhaps a petty thief, a purse snatcher in crowds—stealing just enough to buy hop. A pitiful wisp of humanity. Maybe not even a petty purse-snatcher. Cardigan didn't know. The cops called him a nuisance. When he really got hopped up he criticized the government and created a disturbance, but he had no penal offense against him. Maybe he was a beggar.

In his haste, Wiggins fell. His heels rasped the pavement and he whined petulantly as he went down. But in a moment he was on his feet again—and running, skipping, through the dark streets, the back alleys. Until presently he fell against a wooden door and beat upon it with his fists. It opened and the house swallowed the man, and Cardigan, flattened in a nearby doorway, heard the echoes of the slammed door peter off in the silent street.

A minute later he walked on, spotted the house and counted the number of houses to the next corner. He went around the corner, found a board fence and scaled it, dropping into a yard. Moving through the darkness, he counted the houses and paused when he neared the rear of the house through whose front door Chink Wiggins had entered. It was three storied with a network of fire-escapes in back and the only light that glowed was one on the top floor, beyond a window whose shade was drawn down.

Cardigan put his hands on the rough metal of the fire-escape, took a few upward steps. He climbed in fits and starts, putting his feet down cautiously. He did not stop at the lighted window on the third floor. He went on up to the roof and then stood for a long moment among the dim shapes of chimney pots. The yard was a black well below and a damp breeze puffed from the river. Moving carefully, he found a roof entrance to the regions below—a door with a lock that answered to the fifth skeleton key he used.

Blackness yawned below, but he felt around with a foot, found a step. The narrow staircase was steep. He closed the door and went down slowly, making sure of each step before resting his weight on it. Then he was at the bottom. A door there opened at his touch and he found himself in a lightless corridor. The darkness enabled him, however, to place instantly the location of a door by the thin horizontal sliver of light visible where door did not meet flush with threshold.

Toward this Cardigan moved. For an instant he felt indecision of spirit, as though a large question mark had appeared in his brain to doubt, clerically, his movements. But he brushed it aside with a rough mental gesture. And then he asked himself why Chink Wiggins, yesterday, had chosen Marta Dahl as his particular target of abuse. A man who haunted the back alleys, the tawdry squares and shoddy streets of the lower city—why had he gone far afield, to Park Avenue, to abuse Marta Dahl in a public demonstration?

Cardigan stopped at the door. He heard the troubled whine of Chink Wiggins' voice. He noiselessly tried the doorknob and found that the door was locked. He waited until the whine abated a bit. Then he knocked. Instantly there was silence. Then a woman's voice, hushed, close to the panel. "Who is it?"

"A detective," he said in a low, casual voice. "Better open it, little one."

"W-what's the matter?"

"Open it, I said."

A bolt clanked. The woman opened the door on a crack but Cardigan punched it wide open and walked right in saying: "Now that's nice, that's nice, Chink!"

Wiggins almost fainted on the window sill. He had opened the rear window and now he crouched motionless in it.

Disgusted, angry, Cardigan snapped:

"Well, get in or out. If you go out, you won't have to walk down but you'll be a mess when you reach the yard."

Wiggins backed into the room. Cardigan strolled to the window, closed it with a bang and yanked down the shade. The woman had closed the door. She wore heavy red lounging pajamas—the blouse was Russian, with a stand-up black collar, embroidered in gold. She had hair black as jet, smooth as an otter's back, with straight bangs in front. Her eyes were black coals, her mouth a red gash in an oval face, her fingernails were lacquered red. She looked exotic, hard, cruel, beautiful.

UNLIKE the outside of the house, unlike the neighborhood, the room was large, spacious, with heavy Oriental rugs, teak-and-ivory statues and ivory figurines; bronze lamps with parchment shades, severe mirrors, a cloying odor of perfume—an air of luxury and lavishness without foundation, a kind of stage set, a rare nightmare in a lean-flanked, hungry fag-end of the great city.

Wiggins didn't like the silence. He began blubbering and his lips got wet but no words came out—only flip-flopping little sounds.

"Oh, cut it out," Cardigan growled.

He was making certain at the time, that broad sliding doors at the front end of the room were securely shut, and he did not look at Wiggins. Swift, silent, Wiggins palmed a heavy bronze paperweight. Fear, fright, drove him to it. He hurled the thing. But Cardigan's eye had beaten him to it. Cardigan raised his hand. The bronze weight made a loud slap in his palm, his fingers closed over it for an instant. Then he hefted it.

"Throwing things like that," he complained, and set the thing down on the long mahogany table. His grand unconcern struck terror to Wiggins' heart and Wiggins slumped into a chair like a balloon suddenly deflated.

The woman had not moved.

Cardigan eyed her. "I've walked into something that I get a swell kick out of."

Only her lips moved in a face that was like a mask. "What am I supposed to say to that?"

He picked up the paper-weight, grinned, said: "Catch!" as he tossed it lightly at her.

She twisted, raised her hands to cover her face. A small gun clattered to the floor from one of her broad blouse sleeves. She hissed, dived—but Cardigan's big foot landed on the weapon. He grabbed her, spun her away, picked up the gun, unloaded it.

He was grinning, but not pleasantly. "I thought so," he said.

She was mask-faced again, unemotional. Her voice was flat, toneless, measured. "What do you want?"

"I've found this out," Cardigan said. "That punk there lives at a cheap flophouse but he lives there only as a blind. A cheap punk wouldn't have an in to a place like this. I'm going to turn up something, little poker face, and you're going to help me. So is Mr. Wiggins."

"And what do you think you will turn up?"

"I've a strong suspicion that I'll turn up Marta Dahl."

Expressionless, the woman said: "You make riddles."

Cardigan went toward her with lowering brows. "When I told that bird over there that I was going out to find a woman, he left the flop-house like a bat out of hell and came straight here to warn you."

She mocked him with her flat voice. "Warn me about what?"

"That I was coming after you. Listen, sister; you can hand me all the crap you want, but I had this scatter figured out the minute I came in here. I've got you figured out. This place is lousy with hop. It's a hideout for the needle and the pipe and the sniffers. Wiggins is a contact man for the cheap trade. But this place right here—this room with all the fancy trappings—is a joy house for the swells."

"If all this is true," she said, calmly, "what connection has it with Marta Dahl?"

"That's a riddle you'll answer before you paint your lips again, honeybunch. There is a connection. I feel it in my bones. Wiggins didn't just wander up to Park Avenue yesterday. He—"

WIGGINS was on his feet, livid. He cried: "You leave her alone! You hear me, leave her alone! I went up there because I wanted to! I went up there to kill Marta Dahl!" He screamed it out; panted on: "But—but I didn't. So—so I got some friends—friends like me, that hate the rich, that hate these foreigners who come over here and take our dough back home. I got in a fight at the flophouse and Red hit me and I went to my room. But I didn't stay there. I had it all planned. I sneaked out, met my pals—" He stopped and shook an arm at Cardigan. "You leave this girl alone! I did it! Me and my pals! And you'll never know who them pals are! You won't!" he screamed.

He braced his arms on the table, his breath came hoarsely from his twitching mouth and his eyes rolled. Cardigan felt that he was looking at a madman, at a man whose brain was cracking, at a man whose brain was plagued by a dread disease.

He said: "Why did you come here?"

"To say good-by to—her. I knew you was after me. I wanted to say good-by. I—I killed that chauffeur. Me and my pals did away with Marta Dahl! I always hated her on the screen. She was rich, she took our money, hoarded it. Me—me—I did it!" He grimaced toward the woman. "I'm sorry I come here. But you was always good to me. I wanted—wanted to say good-by."

His eyes dropped from her face, bulged on space. He turned, sagging, and went toward the window. He pulled up the shade, opened the window. He turned and cackled.

"I'm going, mister. You know what to do."

Cardigan drew his gun. His brows were bent, his eyes glittering, his mouth tight.

Wiggins threw a leg over the window sill. His face was deathly gray but the crooked, unreal smile lingered. "I'm the guy you want, mister, but there ain't no cop taking me in for a shellacking—and I stick by my pals. Go ahead, shoot."

Cardigan was grim. "I'll give you till you get halfway down, Wiggins, to think it over."

Wiggins climbed out, disappeared. Cardigan, watching the woman, backed to the window, closed it, drew down the shade. "Now we can talk," he said.

"About what?"

"About who really killed that taxi driver and kidnaped Marta Dahl."

"You heard, didn't you?"

"I heard a poor little hophead. I saw a poor little hophead try to talk me into killing him. I'm not a killer, sister. The sap's in love with you. You've held him in the hollow of your hand. You've supplied him with hop, kidded him, fooled around with him till he's nuts—till he'd die for you. There are guys like that. But he didn't pull this job. He knows all about it because he knows you. No papers would have it yet. It's not news yet. But he knew the details. The sap, sister, was a fall-guy that I didn't let fall. I want Marta Dahl."

There was movement in her face now—slow anger, frustration. Jewels sparkled on her fingers as her hands clenched. There was the faint sound of her breath escaping.

Then there were footsteps in the hall; a moment later a knock on the door. Cardigan shoved his gun into his overcoat pocket but kept his hand on it. He went close to the woman.

"Open it—and one false move and you get hurt."

He backed up beyond the radius of the bronze lamps. The woman went slowly to the door and opened it.

CHAPTER THREE

"I HATE COPS!"

A MAN in evening clothes came in, said: "Nita—" and stopped short. She had turned from him with lowered eyes. He was tall, middle-aged, with white hair carefully combed. He stammered: "I—I beg your pardon."

"Come in," said Cardigan.

"No, thanks. I—I'll come back later and—"

"Get in." There was a whip in Cardigan's voice. "If you're a customer here, it's your tough luck. Close that door."

The woman closed the door. The man fidgeted with a black velours hat, bit his lip, turned and looked quizzically at the woman. She drifted past him with her head lowered, sat down, fitted a cigarette into a long ivory holder and lit up.

The white-haired man demanded: "What is this? What is this anyway?"

"It's a riddle," Cardigan said. "Sit down."

"But I tell you, sir—"

"Sit—down!"

The man sat down, his eyes wide and jerking from the woman to Cardigan.

Cardigan said: "I'm tailing down a little matter of murder. And kidnaping. I'm a private detective—"

The woman started.

Cardigan dipped his head toward her. "I forgot to tell you about the 'private' part.... Stay put!" he barked at the man. "Murder—and kidnaping. I was engaged by Marta Dahl's manager to escort her to Poland, but before I can start any escorting she's kidnaped. By dumb luck I land here—"

The man was on his feet. "I tell you, sir, I cannot afford to be mixed up with this. I came here for another purpose."

"I know what you came here for. You're a rich man with nerves and you need hop to keep you going. You crashed in here at a bad time but you're not leaving till I get things straight. The sooner this woman talks the quicker you go."

The woman said: "Of course, I am not talking."

The man said: "Oh, my God!" and patted his forehead with a handkerchief.

"There was a little sap in here," Cardigan said, "who tried to tell me he pulled the job. I had the choice of killing him or holding the woman. I held the woman."

The man raised his palms. "But why do you hold me? If you know what I came here for, and if it's not in connection with what you're after, why must I stay? Come, I can fix things with you. Surely a hundred-dollar bill—"

"Nothing doing."

The man groaned. "Then name your price!"

Somewhere a door banged. The woman started. The man with the white hair tensed.

"I've got to get out of here!" he cried.

He jumped up and made a blind dash for the door. Cardigan lunged after him. The man had his hand on the knob. He yanked open the door and spun around to strike Cardigan. Cardigan leaned with the blow and brought his gun down on the man's head. The man fell against him, a dead weight, slumping, and Cardigan tried to shove him off.

Something landed on the back of his head and he whirled around to find the woman there—her eyes staring fiercely, the bronze paperweight in her hand, upraised again. She struck and he caught hold of her descending arm, twisted it. There was a rush of feet behind him. The woman bit her lips, buckled downward.

Cardigan pivoted, his lip curling—to find three men covering him with leveled guns. Their faces were granite-hard. Their guns did not waver. The foremost moved wide lips.

"What the hell's going on here? Drop that rod, you!"

CARDIGAN scowled at them. His gun lowered and he stood on wide-planted feet, his hat knocked awry and a tuft of hair sticking out over his left ear. The woman was sitting on the floor behind him, rubbing her wrist. The white-haired man lay at his feet, unconscious.

It was the woman who spoke. "He's a private cop."

"Oh, he is, is he?" snarled the man who had spoken before. "So you're a private cop, are you? Well, I hate private cops!"

Cardigan was more angry than frightened. "Maybe you think I get a thrill out of heels like you."

The big man came forward; his gun muzzle stopped against Cardigan's stomach. "Take his rod, gang."

The two men moved. One took Cardigan's gun, examined it, said: "Nice hardware."

The big man hit Cardigan a punch in the jaw and Cardigan covered four feet backward and landed in an armchair. He rubbed his jaw.

"Geez, don't I hate private cops," said the big man.

The other two dragged the unconscious man from the doorway, closed the door and bolted it. They were quite young, wore snappy clothes, and seemed to enjoy the goings-on with a kind of satanic relish. They helped the woman to her feet and escorted her to a divan. She lay down. They propped pillows behind her head and she received these attentions matter-of-factly. She asked for a cigarette. One of the natty young men hastened to the table, brought back a box. She took a cigarette from it and the other young man was ready with a match. The big man who hated private cops turned and said: "Well, Nita—what went wrong?"

She inhaled, stared intently at Cardigan's profile for a long minute. Then she said: "This dick knows too much. Altogether too much. He fell on Chink Wiggins and it led here."

"Where's Chink?"

"He went out the back window some time ago."

The big man said: "Yeah?" He turned and stared at Cardigan. He hauled a paper bag from his pocket, drew out some flat, disc-shaped objects, shoved them in his mouth. He chewed industriously. He took two steps, leaned over Cardigan. "So you know too much, huh, baby?"

"I know more right now than when I came in here."

"Oh, you do! Ain't that just grand?"

"It's the nuts. Or should I say the peppermints? A big smart guy like you shouldn't go around bumping off taxicab drivers."

The big man straightened, looked around the room.

The woman said: "See?"

She rose, cool, composed, and let smoke dribble from her nostrils. "There's nothing else to do, Sam. This fellow knows too much and there is only one way out. You know what that way is. And see if you can do this job without bungling it."

The big man flushed. He started to retort, but the woman silenced him with a keen, steady look. She said: "And I want no arguments. If things had worked out the way we planned, I could have thrown Chink Wiggins to the cops. He would have taken it for me. The sap was dropped on his head when very young and he got an idea somehow that I was a goddess." She laughed coldly. "He was one guy would have taken the rap without a murmur. He took it tonight. But this cop was too wise. Well, mister private dick, you see what happens to wise coppers."

"You know," Cardigan said, "you're a dame I'd enjoy putting a bullet in."

"You should have done it when you had the chance."

"You're telling *me?*"

She turned to Sam. "I want you boys to take him out and polish him off somewhere." She indicated the man on the floor. "Take him in the other room."

SAM lugged the white-haired man into the room beyond the sliding doors. Returning, he closed the doors, ate more peppermints, looked at his watch. "We got to wait," he said.

"Wait!" snapped the woman. "I told you—"

"I know, Nita, but there's a cop comes through this street about now. We got to wait. Then we'll take him up in Harlem and let him have it. But I ain't lugging no guy when there's a cop around."

One of the natty young men picked up a banjo and began strumming it. The other hummed, kept time with his foot, rolled his eyes. The woman, seeming oblivious to the music, stared coldly, intently at Cardigan. Sam walked up and down heavily, munching peppermints. Every once in a while he took a punch at Cardigan's head and said: "Geez, ever since I was a kid, I hated cops!" He seemed to feel a little better after each punch.

Cardigan was perspiring. He didn't talk, he didn't look frightened. Every time Sam hit him he tried to roll with the punch. The strumming sound of the banjo, the humming of one of the natty young men, seemed unreal in the room. The dark, slitted eyes of the woman never left him. He wondered about Chink Wiggins. Where had the hophead gone? He had expected Chink to turn up again. It didn't matter, though. But he was glad he hadn't killed Chink. Though he wished he had killed the woman. Sam, after an especially hard punch, swung across the room and added his clogged bass to the banjo music and the humming tenor. The tenor broke off long enough to do a snappy soft-shoe dance. Through it all the woman remained remote, masklike, with her cruel eyes fixed on Cardigan.

Presently she said: "Well, Sam?"

The music stopped. Sam looked at his watch, scratched his head. He said: "Listen, Bertie, suppose now you take a run downstairs and see if that cop's in this street."

The banjo player laid down his banjo. "O.K., old boy, old boy," he said cheerfully and pranced out of the room.

Sam came over to stand spread-legged before Cardigan and said, grinning: "I'm gonna like this, baby."

"Can I make any kind of a deal?"

"What, for instance?"

"Well, I'd keep my mouth shut."

The woman laughed flatly. The tenor laughed. Sam roared and said to the others: "Ain't he funny!"

"Honest," Cardigan said, wiping sweat from his face. "I'd keep my mouth shut."

"Yeah," Sam said. "Till you got to the first cop, you would."

The woman said: "Nobody asked you to come into this, mister. You asked for what you're getting. These men do as I say. And you heard what I told them to do. You had a chance to grab Wiggins. It would have been a snap. He confessed. But no, you had to act exceptionally bright and now you're holding the bag."

He said grimly: "I knew Wiggins was lying. I knew he didn't have a hand in it."

"What you didn't know," she ground out, "was that I told Wiggins the other day he ought to tell Marta Dahl what he thought of her. His brain's not right. Ten minutes later he thought the idea was his own. So he went up to Park Avenue and told her. That was not an accident. I put the bug in his ear. For a reason. So that he would create a disturbance, the cops would pick him up, release him—*but remember him.* I was never afraid of Wiggins squealing on me. The poor little fool had a crush on me. He was simple as a kid. I figured the cops would land on him when Marta Dahl disappeared. I knew he was a sap they couldn't beat the truth out of. He'd die for me. I had him—" she held up her hand, closed it—"like that. I wanted a fall-guy if something went wrong with the snatch. Something did go wrong."

"And you didn't have a fall-guy," Cardigan said.

"So I've got to get rid of you."

"Hey," Sam said, looking at his watch, "where's Bertie?"

Nobody said anything. Sam went to the door, opened it and listened. "I don't hear him," he said.

The tenor said: "Maybe he went around for a drink."

"Geez, it would be like that guy to do that. Listen, Arch—you go see. Go get him and come right back."

"Sure thing, Sam."

CHAPTER FOUR

TICKETS TO POLAND

ARCH WENT out whistling lightly to himself and Sam closed the door again, took a mouthful of peppermints and sighted down along his gun. He twirled it carelessly in his hand, went over and sat on the edge of the table. He got restless there and stood up again, planting himself before Cardigan on one of the many small rugs that lay about the room. He regarded Cardigan after the manner of a butcher regarding a choice side of beef. He munched on peppermints.

"Have one," he said.

He tossed one and Cardigan reached for it, missed, and the peppermint fell to the floor. He bent over to pick it up. Sam laughed and took a lazy kick at his head. It might have been that that angered Cardigan beyond all endurance. It might have been the last straw, or the pain of the kick lancing his head might have snapped the idea to birth. But he followed out the idea.

His hand gripped the edge of the rug. He yanked hard. Sam went over backward mightily. Cardigan shot out of the chair as if a spring had driven him. The gun flew from Sam's hand, skated across the floor and disappeared beneath a divan. Cardigan's fist, traveling fast, crashed against Sam's jaw and banged his head back against the floor. Sam kicked up his legs and Cardigan went sailing over Sam's head.

The woman did not cry out. She dropped to her knees and tried to get the gun from beneath the divan. Cardigan bounced up from his knees, hurtled across the room. He got her by the back of the neck, swung her around and sent her flying away from the divan. She hit the table, knocked over one of the bronze lamps and tumbled to the floor.

She had not got the gun. Cardigan groped for it, but it was way back, and Sam was coming. Sam kicked out. His shoe grazed Cardigan's head and Cardigan caught the leg, rose with it and shoved Sam away. The woman leaped with a paper-cutter, a long, slim bronze blade. She was quick as a cat, but Cardigan had long arms. He laid the back of his hand across her mouth and this time she yelped and the paper-cutter spun across the room, flashing.

The sliding doors opened and the white-haired man teetered in like a man in a trance. He did not join the fight. He looked like a drunk who had entered the wrong house. He blinked, rubbed his eyes. A heavy book, flung at Cardigan by the woman, missed Cardigan and caught the white-haired man between the eyes. He fell back into the other room—patent-leather shoes flicking upward as his back struck the floor.

The hall door flung open and Arch appeared. For a moment he stood poised, then went for his gun. Cardigan leaped to the divan, hurtled over the back of it, landed on the floor. His hand closed on the gun that had disappeared. The room thundered and a slug, tearing through the back of the divan, buried itself in the wall. Cardigan gave the divan a shove that sent it scooting out across the floor. It struck Arch, who had bounded forward, and knocked him over. But he was up in a flash, his thin young face white and murderous.

"Kill him, Arch!" the woman screamed.

It was Cardigan's gun that spoke. Arch made a sickly face, turned and fell against Sam and Sam ripped the gun from his hand. The woman leaped with the agility of a cat, with the swift ruthlessness of something wilder—fell on Cardigan's gun arm. His gun went off, not aimed. A bullet drilled a hole in a mirror—bits of plaster fell from behind the mirror. Cardigan cursed and swung her around in front of him, his left arm locked under her chin.

Arch crumpled in a lop-sided heap and Sam, swinging his gun down, made a shuddering sound with his teeth and shook his head—because Cardigan was using the woman as a shield. And sweat stood out like blisters on Cardigan's face.

He snarled in the woman's ear: "You asked for this, you mascaraed heel—and if this punk of yours wants to get me he'll drill you first! Maybe one guy gets out of this shooting-gallery and I'm choosing myself—"

"Get from behind her, you!" Sam roared.

The woman choked, "Get—behind him—Sam. I've got his—gun hand—here—" With both hands she was gripping Cardigan's gun hand.

Arch, whom they all thought was dead on the floor, suddenly screamed. Then he died—rolling over. The scream seemed to shock Sam. He shivered.

The woman choked: "For God's sake—Sam—get behind—give this bird—" She kicked back at Cardigan's shins. He tightened his left arm. Her tongue stuck out, her eyes popped. Sam made a lunge across the room. Cardigan let the woman go and she slumped down, hacking.

The men's guns whipped toward each other. The two explosions interlocked. The wall shook. Plaster dribbled. A shot ricochetted and whanged into a porcelain vase and the vase went to pieces; flowers mushroomed upward and some fell on the back of Arch's neck. Sam flung backward with a look on his face that seemed like the beginning of an uproarious laugh. It might have been caused by the way the light and shadow networked the room. Sam's back hit the wall hard and then he stumbled forward. He fired with his gun pointing downward and a hole jumped magically into the carpet alongside Cardigan's foot. Sam went on stumbling and then began turning awkwardly, like a man turning around in a great gale. Sam seemed to be crying now. His left hand jammed against the table. He hiccupped, braced himself, raised his gun.

Cardigan, brown-faced, tight-lipped, shook his head slowly. His gun was leveled. His gaze was rooted on Sam. The woman reached up—like a cat's paw her hand struck at Cardigan's gun. He ducked as Sam's gun went off. The woman set teeth into Cardigan's gun hand. Sam lurched forward, coughing, raising his gun.

There was a terrific blast from the doorway. Sam went down like a felled tree.

"Hey, Cardigan," Garrity said, "what the hell do you think you're doing?"

THE skipper stood with a derby raked over one ear. His coat collar was up and there was a windy look in his eyes, a sidewise jut to his jaw. He snapped into the room after the manner of a man who knows his business.

"Hey, you gorilla, what are you doing to that woman?"

"Doing!" Cardigan exploded. "What am I doing! Don't I get a laugh out of that!"

Garrity went over, bent down. "Hey, lady, you're biting his hand! Don't do that!" He laid the flat of his hand across her face and she let go, flopped over. Garrity stood up, spread his palms in an explanatory gesture. "It's like you have to do to a drowning person."

Cardigan snapped his hand and blood flew from it. Garrity jumped back, clipped: "My new coat, damn you!"

Cardigan pointed. "Look out for that dame, Pete. She's a female Dracula."

"Listen, you. Who's that I handcuffed to the stairway downstairs? Listen. I met him coming out the front door before. He stopped and then he decided to go for a walk. So I walked with him and then I asked him if he always walked with his hand in his pocket. So he was warming a rod. So I waltzed him back to the door. Who is he?"

"A heel. They're all heels."

"Well, I'm glad I know. When I came in here, I didn't know whether to shoot you or this guy."

"My pal!"

"Who's this guy I shot?"

"His friends used to call him Sam. He bumped off that taxi driver."

"Listen, now after I save your life are you going to hand me a load of baloney like that?"

Cardigan pointed. "Hold that jane. When I say hold her, I mean hold her. Put your foot on her neck."

He gripped his gun in his left hand, pushed back the sliding doors, found lights, stepped over the white-haired man and put his shoulder through the next door. He brushed splinters from the shoulder, turned on lights, stopped short.

A woman lay on the bed. He saw her eyes rolling. She was bound and gagged. He tore off the gag.

"Oh!" she cried. "Are you the police department?"

"The police department is in the other room. You're Marta Dahl. Listen, don't tell me you're not!"

"I—I—am Marta—"

"Swell! I'm Cardigan. Glad to know you, Miss Dahl. Now don't get excited. We're going to Poland together."

"But I have a husband in Poland—"

"What the hell—I mean, I would get a break like that—I mean, sure, that's swell!"

"But please—these ropes—they're cutting me— Oh, I'm so hopeless—so horrified—so tired—"

He got the ropes off, said: "Now rest here. Just rest here a little while. Everything's all right. Only—" he nodded toward the rear of the house— "I wouldn't want you to see what's in the other room. Just rest here. There's no danger."

SHE nodded, put her hands to her eyes. He spun on his heel, strode long-legged through the next room, stepped over the white-haired man and entered the rear room. Garrity had laid the woman on the divan and was stroking his hard jaw. He sighed.

"Pretty, Cardigan, ain't she?"

"Now I'll tell one. What I'd like to know, Pete, is how the hell you turned up here."

Garrity scratched the underside of his chin. "It sounds nutty. Yager busts into headquarters a little while ago hauling this hophead Chink Wiggins. Yager is all smiles and yelling for the reward. He says he nabbed this egg on the back fire-escape of this address. What does the egg say? 'I killed the taxi driver. I kidnaped Marta Dahl.' And Yager says, 'You see!' like that."

Cardigan snapped. "That dirty bum Yager tailed me from the hotel and he's been tailing me—"

"Yeah, what I figured. So the newspaper guys flock in. Yager grins and sticks his chest out. The hophead says he killed Marta Dahl too. Yager don't say anything about you. But I begin to figure. I know he's a lousy dick. I figure he couldn't follow a clue even if it was hooked onto his nose. But I remember you had your mind set on this Chink Wiggins. I figure you tailed Chink and Yager tailed you. But I don't say anything. I slip out of headquarters and fandango over on my lonesome.... Oh, young lady, are you awake?"

The woman stared at them. "I guess I'm done for, huh?"

"I'll say you are," Cardigan said. "With Marta Dahl in the front room."

"What!" exclaimed Garrity.

"Resting, Pete. Sit down and wait. This jane here is the head of it. She got all these bums to kidnap Marta Dahl."

"Oh, yes?" the woman said and chuckled brittlely. "And who got me to get these bums to do it? I'll tell you. I won't burn, smart boy. Not me! Do you know who's behind it? I'll tell you." She leaned back. "Francis K. Braun. Who is he? Marta Dahl's banker. The head of a small uptown bank where a friend of a friend told her to put her money. When she wanted the four hundred thousand grand the bank was in a bad way but they didn't dare tell her she couldn't get it inside of two weeks. Braun had been fooling around with the funds. If he told her she couldn't have the money it would have raised a howl. Bank examiners. Ruination. Penitentiary. So he came to me. Knew me well. I supplied him with hop. Sure, he was a hophead too. So Marta Dahl was to be kidnaped, held until he could replace the money, and then released. That's all there was to it. It would have worked. Only Sam there went haywire. It was a neat plan. It would have worked swell but things happened."

Garrity was stunned. "You mean to tell me the head of a bank would do a thing like that!"

"Listen, copper, when a big shot gets in a jam he'll do anything. He invited Marta Dahl to his apartment this evening—"

Garrity got up, crossed the room and picked up the phone. "I'll have some men pick that guy up. I'll—"

The sound of a gun rocked the room. Garrity dropped the telephone. Cardigan bounded to his feet and lunged through the wide doorway to the other room.

The white-haired man was turning over on his stomach, groaning. A smoking gun slipped from his fingers. He stiffened and then there was a dark splotch growing on the old rose carpet.

Cardigan turned him over. He heard a faint outcry.

Marta Dahl was standing in the doorway that led from the front room. Her hands were pressed to her cheeks.

"That," she said, "that is my banker! That is Mr. Braun!"

Cardigan rose, turned and went back into the rear room.

Garrity was tearing a gun from the woman's hand.

He said: "By God, Jack, if she didn't try to put a bullet in your back!"

"She just doesn't like me," Cardigan said. "It must have been something I did."

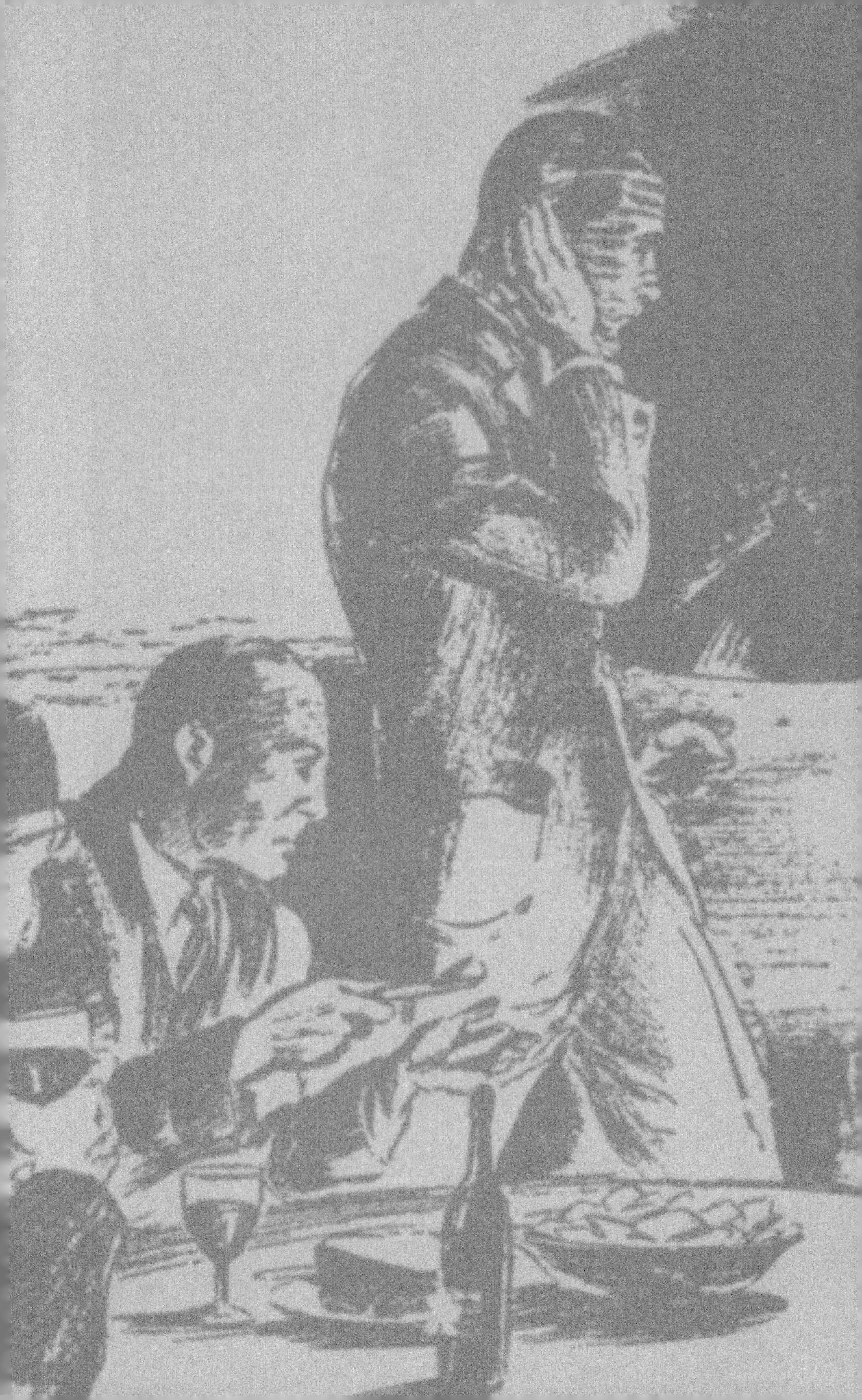

A TRUCK-LOAD OF DIAMONDS

CARDIGAN KNEW THAT FIFTY-GRAND DIAMOND NECKLACE HADN'T JUST MELTED AWAY—EVEN IF IT WAS HOT ICE. SOMEONE HAD THE LOOT AND HE WAS GOING TO FIND OUT WHO—IF HE HAD TO FILL THE MORGUE AND A COUPLE OF HOSPITALS TO DO IT.

CHAPTER ONE

THE HESITANT MR. MICAH

IT WAS something about a jewel theft in Thirty-seventh Street, over near Fifth Avenue....

Pat Seaward pronged the telephone receiver, sat back, killed a cigarette against the side of a corroded ashtray and read quickly the notes she had taken down.

Meantime she fooled with a lock of hair, near her left ear. It was late noon. She was the only one in the agency office—a trim, neat symphony of clothes, hairdress, good looks. She glanced up, reflected. Sunlight winked on the distant Chrysler spire.

Opening a desk drawer, she withdrew a dog-eared notebook, flipped the indexed pages to "C." At the head of the "Cs" was the name Cardigan; beneath it, in parenthesis, an explanatory line: "Addresses at which he might be found." There were twenty-one addresses. Alongside one of them was the word "home"; alongside eight, the word "girl"; to the other twelve addresses was appended the one word—"speakeasy." And there was also a footnote: "If not at any of the above, try police stations, jails, hospitals, or the city morgue."

She began using the telephone. The sixth call, ending in "Foggy Joe" Pomano's place, brought results, and Pat said: "Well, you vanishing American, it's about time."

His voice said: "You old nagger, you."

"Listen," she said. "Now listen. Traum and Fleer, the jewel people, just called up. Listen now, because they're one of our best clients. They've just had a sixty-thousand-dollar diamond bracelet snatched from their man Harold Micah, in East Thirty-seventh Street. They want you to look after their interests. The crowd's at the Twenty-fifth Precinct house. Are you able to ambulate?"

"Ever see me when I wasn't?"

He smiled innocently. Cardigan said: "What the hell?"

"Well, I shan't go into that. Will you go over?"

"O.K., precious. Soon as I finish this stud hand I'll take a tramp over."

She said: "Why take a tramp along?"

"You bring back my childhood," Cardigan said. "Haven't heard that one since I was six. Goom-by, chicken."

SO IT was something about a jewel theft in broad daylight, some minutes shy of high noon, four blocks from the Traum & Fleer establishment.

Cardigan, entering a large room of the precinct house, saw Captain Garrity, an H.Q. dick, sitting on a desk and spinning a coin in the air. Two precinct dicks leaned against the wall. Harold Micah, the jewel firm's man, sat in a swivel chair; he was small, plain, commonplace in looks and dress—and about fifty years of age. On another chair sat a tall, wiry, waspy man—cool, collected, with dark pool-like eyes. There was a blue bruise on the olive skin near his left cheekbone.

Garrity—hard, bluff, clean-boned and straight as a ruled line—Garrity said: "Did I hear you knock, Jack?"

"How come you're up in a white man's neighborhood, Pete?"

"Well, I guess that makes us even. I'll tell you, you gorilla. I just happened to be Johnny-on-the-spot…. This man is Mr. Micah. He was carrying the bracelet."

"We've met," Cardigan said.

"How do you do, Mr. Cardigan," said Micah. "I'm relieved to find you on the case."

Cardigan grinned at Garrity. "I guess that puts you in your place, Pete."

Garrity could take it. He grinned back with his hard bony face, then jerked a thumb, said: "This man says his name's Paul Kinnard. Have you met?"

"Haven't had the pleasure," Cardigan said.

Garrity said, "He was supposed to have snatched the bracelet."

"Yeah," said Kinnard. "I was supposed to have."

"Suppose now," Cardigan said, "instead of all this nice bright repartee—suppose I get some details."

Garrity flipped the coin, caught it, pocketed it. His voice was blunt, clipped. "At eleven-forty Mr. Micah left the establishment carrying the bracelet in a small case. The case was in his pocket. A man named Fitchman had telephoned them to send over the bracelet. Said he'd seen it in the window. The address was an office building on Broadway near Thirty-sixth. You've heard of Reuben Fitchman—the big silk man. The establishment was glad to send the bracelet over. We just checked up. Fitchman never phoned at all. It was a stall.

"Mr. Micah was jostled in a crowd in Thirty-seventh Street. He was tripped—accidentally maybe he fell; he says he was tripped. A man helped him up. He says this looks like the man. This man hurried off, west. Mr. Micah missed the case from his pocket and yelled. I was watching a safe being hoisted at the time. I got to him when he was running west. We saw Kinnard hiking it up the Thirty-eighth Street 'El' station. A northbound train was pulling in. It pulled out with Kinnard on board. We hustled into a cab.

"Traffic was at a standstill on Sixth Avenue. Some company was making a movie of a wild auto ride. We passed the outfit like a bat out of hell and reached the Forty-second Street station. We beat it up the stairs and got to the platform just as the train was stopping. I told a brakeman to keep the train stopped. We watched the people get off. Kinnard didn't get off. Then I gave orders to close all the doors. Mr. Micah and I went through the train. We found Kinnard on the rear end platform. I nailed him. He started to argue and I took a poke at him—"

"How the hell did I know you were a cop?" Kinnard said.

"I dragged him off the train," Garrity went on, "but he didn't have the bracelet. He claims he wasn't the guy helped Mr. Micah up. He claims he never swiped the bracelet."

Cardigan looked at Micah. "You're sure this is the man?"

"I'm pretty sure."

"You ought to be absolutely sure."

Micah looked uncomfortable. "I—I was a little upset when I fell. I didn't look squarely at the man who helped me up. But when I missed the bracelet, my instinct chose this man. There was something about his clothes—his walk. And when I yelled I thought I saw him walk faster. He didn't look around. And he ran toward the station—"

"Naturally," said Kinnard. "I saw the train coming. I wanted to catch it. Why shouldn't I run?" He scowled at Micah. "This guy's lying. He had to pick someone out. So he picked me. I'm the goat." He returned his dark gaze to Garrity. "You've got to get a little more to hold me, mister. I'll be no goat."

MICAH grimaced painfully. He wasn't sure, and this embarrassed him. Perspiration stood out on his face. Kinnard remained cool, dark, a little resentful, but unruffled. Garrity sighed. He motioned to Cardigan and they stepped outside the room.

"Jack..." Garrity paused, made a face, knuckled the hard slab of his jaw; then he looked up, puzzled but keen-eyed. "Jack, this case is punk. Either Micah's scared to come right out and say this bird robbed him, or he's not sure the bird did rob him. Maybe he just picked him at random. Hell, he had to save his face to some extent, didn't he? If he couldn't name anybody—if he said he just lost the ice, it'd look suspicious. Hey—" his voice dropped—"what do you know about Micah?"

"Been with the firm ten years. Lost his wife two years ago and collected ten thousand insurance. All alone now. Far as we know— steady, reliable, short on the brains side but that helps. A guy that messengers jewels around shouldn't have too much imagination. Think it's a frame?"

Garrity growled: "Hell, I was just thinking. Forget it. The guy seems kind of goofy. Why the hell didn't he come right out and say Kinnard was the guy? It'd make it easier."

"What about Kinnard?"

Garrity looked at a slip of paper in his hand. "He's living at the Hotel Gold on Lexington. I checked that up. He's played in a couple of movies—minor parts. Used to play a piano on the vaudeville stage for a while. Now he's a piano player and wit that hires out for swell parties, banquets, things like that. You see, Jack, things don't reason out. This bird has an address, a business. There's a fluke somewhere. If Micah don't come right out and identify him for sure, we can't hold him."

"If you let him go right away," Cardigan said, "you'll have the insurance people on your neck. You'd better stall around. Take him down to H.Q. See if he's got a record. If he swiped the ice, he could have passed it to a pal and steered you wrong."

"He's no sap. He'll want a lawyer and I wouldn't blame him."

Cardigan said: "Get Micah out here."

THEY took Micah to another room and Cardigan eyed him for a long minute. Micah's face looked pasty and he kept at it with his handkerchief.

"It's like this," Cardigan said. "You've got to know if this is the man. You've got to be pretty sure about it. You can't guess. You see, you work for a house that's got piles of dough. If you had this man arrested and filed the charge formally against him—and if it turned out he wasn't the guy, your firm might have a lawsuit on its hands."

Micah was troubled. "I—I should not like to have an innocent man arrested. I said I thought this was the man. I tell you I didn't look squarely at him—I was so shaken after the fall. I just said, 'Thanks,' brushed myself off and by that time he was gone. I suppose I just saw him, so to speak, out of the corner of my eye."

"Look here," Garrity chopped in, a little impatient. "I want to help you all I can. I've got a reputation I'm kind of proud of: I never pinch a guy just because I need a pinch. I won't do it now. I'll give you a break. If you swear outright that Kinnard's the man, I'll pinch him. Will you do that?"

"I—I—you see, an innocent man—I—"

"Oh, nuts!" Garrity growled. "Is this the guy or isn't he? Yes or no? Do you want to arrest him? I'm just a cop. This is up to you. You may not be certain, but if you just say you are, I'll arrest him. That plain?"

Micah inhaled deeply, stared at the floor. "I—I can't say for sure he's the man. I—I couldn't swear to it. There was, really, quite a crowd around me at the time. It might have been—I might have just thought...." He slumped, sighed hopelessly. "I don't knew. I'm all—all upset."

Garrity snorted. "O.K. So I'll let this guy go." He made a decisive gesture, swiveled, stalked to the door. His hand on the knob, he paused, turned around, then returned to face Micah. "Listen, Mr. Micah. I hate to do this. Can't you for cripes' sake know if this was the guy? Can't you say it was? Just so we can hold him. Huh?"

"No-o.... I can't. I—I'm sorry—"

Garrity barked: "Now you should be sorry! After I clown all over the street and bop a guy—now you're sorry! What the hell kind of a cop do you think I am?"

Micah made vague gestures.

"For crying out loud," Cardigan said, "don't be an old woman, Pete. Let the guy go. Be noble. But—listen, Pete—like an old pal, hold him for about fifteen minutes longer."

"Why should I?" crabbed Garrity.

"Now you wouldn't go cutting corners on a pal, would you?"

Garrity leveled an arm. "No longer, Jack—no longer than fifteen!" He jerked his chin toward Micah. "Come with me, Mr. Micah."

Micah and Garrity left the room. Cardigan scooped up a phone, leaned comfortably back on his heels, called the agency. George Hammerhorn answered.

Cardigan said: "This is Jack, George. Pat there?... No, I don't want to talk to her. Tell her to shoot right down to Thirty-fifth Street, near the Twenty-fifth Precinct house.... No, not in the house; near it. I'll walk out with a guy. She's to follow this guy and see if he meets anyone after I leave him.... Well, George, there's just something screwy here.... The guy's name is Kinnard."

CHAPTER TWO

THE GIRL IN THE GOLD

THE HOUSE was in the respectable West Eighties. Cardigan found the hall door open. The foyer was clean; an expensive but worn carpet padded the staircase. Once this house must have been the stronghold of the rich, but wealth had since migrated eastward, ramparted itself east of the Park, hard by the river. Renovations had not entirely wiped out the Georgian influence. The third floor was dim, cool; doors shone darkly. The door marked "33" was in the rear. It took Cardigan three minutes to find the proper master key.

The room was small. One window overlooked a courtyard. It was the modest room of a man of small means—neat, a little shabby, comfortable. Cardigan went to work. Clothes were hung orderly on hangars; two pairs of shoes, polished, stood side by side and rigid with shoetrees. Linen lay neatly in bureau drawers. Paper, writing materials, lay on a small desk. The desk drawer was locked, but Cardigan opened it. A packet of letters was held in shape by rubber bands. There was a checkbook showing a balance of $248.50. There was a savings-account book from which, over a period of fifteen months, a total of $8,000 had been withdrawn; the balance was for $100. Cardigan read the letters, frowned, shook his head. He hunted around for canceled checks, found none. Finally he replaced everything in order, stood for a moment immersed in thought, then left the room, locked the door.

He took a cab to the Traum & Fleer establishment on Fifth Avenue. Carl Traum, the senior partner, was a pale, distant man behind a tremendous mahogany desk. He did not rise when Cardigan entered. He did not stop writing. The office was silent but for the scratching of his pen. He did not look up.

"News?" he said in a dry, flat voice.

Cardigan said: "You satisfied as to the integrity of your man Micah?"

The pen scratched on. "Why do you ask?"

"Naturally I want to take all angles into consideration. I know that in two months he'll have been with you ten years."

"Not quite. That is, Micah finishes here the end of this month."

"Firing him?"

"Not because of this. He received notice the first of the month. Times are hard. We've had to cut down. I have utmost faith in Micah. This was indeed unfortunate. There has never been an irregularity in the house of Traum and Fleer. We could, you understand, hardly afford it. This was plainly a ruse, a daring daylight robbery. I can't understand why the police let that fellow go."

"You can't arrest a man when the victim can't identify him. I'm interested in Micah."

Traum laid down his pen, sat back, laid his fragile hands on the desk. Rimless spectacles glittered coldly beneath frosty white eyebrows; the thin, hueless face was bare of expression.

He said: "We have retained your agency for twelve years, Mr. Cardigan. It's your duty to keep, at all times, an eye on our men. Men do not turn thieves over night. Your regular reports on Micah have been such as to cause us no qualms. It is your business to warn us of any irregularity before an unpleasantness occurs. The house of Traum and Fleer can't afford a scandal. It has paid you well for protection against the unexpected."

Cardigan regarded him for a long moment in silence. "Do I understand I'm to drop this case?"

"Did I say so? No. You're to recover this bracelet, if possible, but you're not to choose a man at random merely because other channels might call for more work. Insurance companies are becoming pretty careful. I don't want rumors to get around that this was an inside job. Rumors are dangerous things. Only the facts must be used, my dear Mr. Cardigan. I value, you understand, the reputation of my firm. I believe—have I said this before?—that Micah is thoroughly honest."

He picked up his pen, returned to writing. Cardigan knew that the interview was over. His "Good-by" was hardly more than a husky whisper. He went out, nursing a peculiar feeling of frustration. The insurance company, he realized, would have to pay through the nose if the bracelet were not recovered. It was plain that Traum was more interested in the reputation of his firm than in the recovery of the bracelet. He wanted the bracelet but it would not please him if Micah turned out to be a thief.

CARDIGAN phoned the agency from a drug store booth. He was told that Pat had called up from a booth in the lobby of the Hotel Gold. She had tailed Kinnard there and was awaiting further instructions. Cardigan grabbed a cab and dropped off five minutes later in front of the Gold. He found Pat sitting in the lobby.

"So what?" he said.

"I picked him up when you left him at the corner of Fifth Avenue and Thirty-fifth Street. He took a cab and I took one and he came right here. He didn't stop to make any calls. I didn't hesitate about walking right in after him. He went to the desk for mail. There was none. See that big leather chair over there? There was a girl sitting in it. Nice. Did she know how to wear clothes! Kinnard spied her and went over to her. They talked for a few minutes. Then he went up in the elevator. The girl powdered her nose, watched the elevator door. When the elevator came down, she got up and went over and took it up. It stopped—I could tell by the indicator—it stopped at the ninth floor." Pat smiled. "That was the floor Kinnard stopped at."

"Two and two," mused Cardigan.

"Make four. Chief, she was a honey—and those clothes—"

"You women, you women! Forget clothes for a minute. Did she come down again?"

"No."

"Know what room he's in?"

"No."

Cardigan said: "Wait here. Stay right here and watch if she comes out—or if he comes out. I'll find the house dick."

He asked a bellhop. The house officer was in a small office beyond the desk. His name was Riordan and he was an old-timer. Cardigan showed credentials. "I want to do things right," he said.

"What do you call right?" asked Riordan.

"Well, how about ten dollars?"

"I couldn't think of it."

Cardigan said: "You don't have to think," and dropped a ten-dollar bill on the desk.

Riordan pocketed it. "This hurts me." He got up, left the office and reappeared in a couple of minutes. "It's an apartment—Number 909—one of those bed-living-rooms, with an in-a-door bed."

"What do you know about him?"

"Nothing. Never causes any trouble—quiet, apparently O.K. Has lady friends, but his apartment's on the residential side and so it's none of my business. If it's a pinch you want, you better get a cop."

"No pinch yet. Listen, Riordan. How far will you go if I need you?"

"It depends."

Cardigan stood up "O.K. You can put yourself in the way of some dough if you want to."

"It depends."

"Sure. I get you."

Cardigan returned to the lobby and Pat said: "No come down."

"Swell. Stay here." He dropped his voice. "I think the house dick's all right, so long as there's dough in it."

He took the elevator to the ninth floor, made his way slowly down the pale gray corridor. He used a bronze knocker on the door of 909. There was no response, and after a moment he knocked again. This time there was the sound of movement inside. The latch clicked, the door opened. Kinnard, immaculate in dark clothes, peered through a lazy column of cigarette smoke.

"You remember me?" Cardigan said.

Kinnard said: "Of course."

"I'd like to have a few words with you."

"Have them."

Cardigan made a wry face. "Kind of—well—you know—in the corridor...."

"Seems to me I've been subjected to enough nonsense for one day, Cardigan. I don't think I can help you. Mind if I ask you to go?"

Cardigan shrugged. "I won't take much of your time—"

"I'm sorry."

KINNARD stepped back, closed the door. But the door didn't quite close; it rebounded against Cardigan's foot and Cardigan walked in as it swung back. Kinnard tried to grab it, but by the time he had the knob in his hand Cardigan was in the room, his hands tranquilly in his pockets and his battered fedora shadowing his eyes. He looked about the room. The room was large, cozy, with two windows, a bath, and double doors of the kind that conceal an in-a-door bed.

Kinnard kicked the door. It banged shut. Color rose to his smooth olive skin and he said, irritably: "It's damned funny when a man can't have any privacy in his own home!"

Cardigan was softly whistling the refrain of a Broadway musical show. He took off his hat, sat down in a large armchair, hooked a leg over a knee. He was calm, unhurried. He kept looking around the room, tilting his head from side to side, whistling softly.

Kinnard seemed to have grown taller; he did grow darker, tightening his lips, bending his brows. He was a handsome man, with his well-cut clothes, his smooth black hair, his slightly arrogant air. Cigarette smoke spurted from his nostrils. "Well?" he snapped.

Cardigan stopped whistling. "You know, Mr. Kinnard, that diamond bracelet didn't vanish in thin air. It went somewhere. Micah's a fool—one of those men who doubt his own convictions. Micah wound up by being pretty certain you weren't the man who robbed him. That happens. If you tell a guy enough times that he killed a man, and if the guy's got a bum head, he'll wind up by believing that. I'm inclined to believe Micah's first impulse was sound. He picked the man who robbed him. When he began to think about it, when he tried to be rational about it, he got all balled up."

Kinnard did not become indignant. He chuckled drily. "Maybe if you work on me that way, I'll wind up by believing I robbed him. That would be swell. Why don't you try telling me I'm the man who built the Public Library?"

"Who cares about the Public Library? Suppose for the time being we leave the Public Library out of it. Let's stick to a diamond bracelet worth approximately sixty thousand dollars. You happened to fall into the hands of one of the whitest cops in New York. Garrity will never make a pinch unless he has a sound reason. As a matter of fact, he's so white that sometimes he's a fool."

Kinnard smiled ironically. "You—I suppose you are just brimming over with brains."

"It's not that. You see, Mr. Kinnard, you were shadowed from the moment you stepped out of the police station."

"Leading up to what?"

"A woman."

Kinnard's eyes narrowed but his ironic smile did not fade. He said: "Things I never knew till now."

"I think that crack's copyrighted by a famous columnist. Will you ask the woman to come out?"

Kinnard sighed heavily. "You're getting tiresome."

Cardigan stood up. "Get her out."

Kinnard's jaw set. He crossed the room, picked up the phone and said to the house operator: "Will you send up the house officer?… Yes, this is Mr. Kinnard." He hung up.

Cardigan was grinning.

"We'll see," Kinnard said, "what right you have to pull a song and dance in my apartment."

"We'll see," Cardigan said.

They waited ten minutes. Impatient, angry now, Kinnard returned to the telephone.

Cardigan said: "Don't waste your time. I saw the house officer before I came up here."

Kinnard pivoted from the telephone. "You've got a hell of a nerve!" He took four hard steps toward Cardigan. "You get the hell out of here before you get thrown out."

"Get hot," Cardigan said. "I like it."

"Get out!"

Cardigan was cool, hard. "Tell the woman to come out."

"Get out!"

Cardigan ducked, caught Kinnard's fist in his open right hand; gripped hard, twisted. Then he heaved. Kinnard hurtled backward, struck a chair, crashed down with it.

THE closet door opened. A woman stood there for a brief moment, then took a few steps into the room. She was tall, white-faced, exquisitely dressed. She was breathing rapidly, and her large, dark eyes kept darting from Kinnard to Cardigan. Kinnard got to his feet, brushed his clothes. His breath came hoarsely.

Cardigan said to the woman: "What's your name?"

"I—I don't care to tell."

"Oh, you don't!"

Kinnard rasped: "Don't pay any attention to him! By God, I'll see I get some justice in this town!"

Cardigan had not taken his eyes from the woman. "Where were you at noon today?"

"I was—I was downstairs—in the lobby."

"You can prove that, I suppose?"

She bit her lip and looked helplessly at Kinnard. "Paul, what is this, what is this?"

"I'd like to know," Kinnard said. "I'd certainly like to know about it myself."

"Never mind, you," Cardigan cut in; and then to the woman: "I suppose you can prove you were in the lobby?"

She held her breath. "I can—if I have to. I tell you I came in at a quarter to twelve."

"That's not proof."

"But why do I have to prove it?" she cried.

Kinnard said: "He's just a very smart person. I told you what happened. Some fool said I robbed him. This intelligent gentleman here has an idea, I suppose, that you were in the street at the time and that I passed the bracelet to you."

"To me?"

Kinnard laughed harshly. "He would think of something like that, you know."

"Can you," Cardigan hammered at the woman, "prove you were in the lobby?"

She nodded. "If I have to—yes. The little bookshop off the lobby—I was in there for at least half an hour—from a little before twelve until half-past. Looking at books. In fact, I discussed books with the girl who works there."

"What's your name?"

She colored. "If you don't mind, I'd rather not—" She looked confused. "This—this was a totally innocent visit, but if—if my name—" Her lip quivered.

Cardigan nodded. "Maybe I get you. O.K. Come downstairs with me and we'll see about the girl in the bookshop."

Cardigan and the woman went down in the elevator, crossed the lobby and entered the bookshop. The girl there smiled when she saw the woman. Cardigan's questions confused her, but she replied promptly. A moment later Cardigan and the woman went out into the lobby.

He said: "I'm sorry."

Her head was lowered. She walked away across the lobby, passed through the revolving doors into the street. Pat drifted up alongside Cardigan.

"Isn't she a knockout, chief?"

He said: "Listen, chicken. Tail her. Find out where she lives. Snap on it."

"What's the matter now?"

"Everything. This case gets nuttier and nuttier. Come on—shoo—get after her."

"I'm just crazy about the way she wears clothes—"

"Shoo, I tell you! Shoo! Scram! Get going!"

CHAPTER THREE

CARDIGAN CRASHES THE GATE

GEORGE HAMMERHORN, the agency head, was deep in the throes of a crossword puzzle when Cardigan entered the office. Hammerhorn did not look up. Cardigan unlocked a desk drawer, drew out a bottle of Scotch and poured himself a generous jolt.

"Say, Jack," Hammerhorn said, "what's an eight-letter word beginning with 'E,' that means greedy?"

"Who swiped the Traum and Fleer bracelet?"

Hammerhorn sat back. "Who did?"

"It occurred to me a little while ago that in all the hue and cry nobody searched Micah. The cops took his word for it that it had been stolen.

"I don't like to think he did. I like to think Kinnard did. I was just up to Kinnard's apartment and I let myself in for a nice lot of razzberry. Before I went there I frisked Micah's room. According to his books, he's almost broke. He's been doing things for a sick sister in California. I read some letters. In the past fifteen months he's spent about eight thousand on her. First of the month he loses his job. There's your motive. And yet, George, I can't forget Kinnard. I can't help feeling that Micah's instinct was right—that Kinnard was the man. I thought I had Kinnard where I wanted him. Pat tailed a woman to his apartment. I thought she'd be the pal Kinnard passed the ice to after he'd swiped it. But no. She was nowhere near the scene of the robbery."

The telephone rang and Cardigan picked it up. "Oh, hello, Pat.... I see. Good work, kid." He hung up, scribbled on a pad of paper. "That was Pat," he said. "She tailed the woman I was talking about. Woman lives at the Saborin, a swank apartment house in East Sixty-second Street."

"That's funny," Hammerhorn said. "You remember that when Micah left with the bracelet he was headed for Fitchman's office on Broadway."

"Sure. Fitchman was supposed to have called up. He didn't. That was a stall. The guy's got millions."

"I know. What's funny is this: Fitchman lives at the Saborin. I met him and his wife at a party once."

"What's she look like?"

"Tall—about five feet eight. A lulu to look at. A blonde. About twenty-eight or so. The kind you'd climb the highest mountain for. Fitchman's a little fat, a little old. He'd—you know—have a hard time climbing mountains."

Cardigan pointed. "It was puzzling me why the guy who phoned for that bracelet used Fitchman's name. Garrity had an idea he used it because it was a big name, one easily recognized. Fact is, I thought that too. It gets clearer now. Fitchman's bought several articles at Traum and Fleer's. There's your answer."

"Hell, Mrs. Fitchman wouldn't be mixed up in a robbery."

"Who's saying she would? But if she's the woman I saw in Kinnard's apartment, it would have been easy for Kinnard to have found out where Fitchman bought his jewelry. George, this guy's a heel." He corked the bottle, jammed it tight with the palm of his hand. "Untie that!"

CARDIGAN sailed out of the office, got in a taxicab and was driven to Times Square. He still had his doubts, still felt that he was stopped at the fork in the road. One way led toward Micah; the other led toward Kinnard. The razzing he had taken in Kinnard's apartment rankled, but did not impel him to run blindly. Swiftly he went, but with a narrowed eye.

He was known in several theatrical booking offices. Men there had good memories; and if these failed they had old books, old records. Here and there Cardigan gathered morsel on morsel of information, putting each down on paper, building up gradually a kind of composite picture of Kinnard's past. Kinnard had once been a gigolo in a Broadway cabaret. He had played bits in three motion pictures. He had been on the vaudeville stage as a piano player. Once he had taken the part of a footpad in a play. He had also been assistant, for two months, to a magician named Fogoro—a man famed for sleight-of-hand.

An old time theatrical man said to Cardigan: "After that, Kinnard studied magic and tried to put on an act of his own. He was pretty good—but not good enough. He became obsessed with magic, however. But the business was on the wane and there was no room for him. As the footpad in that play, he was good. I saw it. I could have sworn he never touched the fellow who was supposed to have been robbed—in the play. But he did. It was neat work."

It was half-past four when Cardigan climbed into a cab. He settled back, lit a cigarette, inhaled deeply and with relish. He gave the address of the Hotel Gold. As his cab was rolling up to the hotel entrance, he saw Kinnard swing out and get into a taxi that was waiting there. "Follow that one," Cardigan told the driver.

He sat on the edge of the seat. The possibility of Micah being guilty was out-balanced now by the information Cardigan had gathered concerning Kinnard. There was, Cardigan reasoned, another man, perhaps a woman. The police had searched Kinnard and found no bracelet. He must have passed it on to a confederate in the street.

Kinnard's taxi turned west at Forty-second Street. Traffic was heavy, loud with the hoots of auto horns, the clanging of crosstown trolleys. They passed beneath the Park Avenue ramp and continued west past the Public Library and Bryant Park. At Eighth Avenue Kinnard alighted and stood on the windy corner. Cardigan's cab crossed Eighth Avenue to the northwest corner. He got out here and saw Kinnard walking north on the east side of the street. He followed, but on the west sidewalk.

Farther north a corner had been razed. Here a new hotel was to rise. A board fence enclosed the now vacant lot on the west and north sides; below the level of the street the earth was raw; steam shovels were at work and trucks were being loaded with broken rock, earth, debris.

Kinnard was strolling. He paused at this corner, leaned on the wooden fence, watched the men and shovels at work. Cardigan leaned in the doorway of a cigar store. He looked at his watch. It was almost five o'clock. He saw Kinnard move on a few feet, then pause again. There was a crowd watching the business of excavating, but in a few minutes the steam shovels stopped, the day's work was done. The crowd moved off, and Kinnard, lighting a cigarette, continued to stroll north. Four blocks farther north he climbed into a taxi. Cardigan followed in another. Kinnard's cab moved slowly west on Fifty-third Street, stopped at the corner of Tenth Avenue. But Kinnard did not get out.

A minute later, however, the cab moved off, turned north into Tenth Avenue. The street was crowded and there were three trolley cars in a row, taxis hooting and speeding, trucks rumbling. At Sixty-second Street Kinnard alighted, stood on the corner, tapping a foot, drawing absently at a cigarette. Presently he turned and entered Sixty-second Street, heading east. The way was choked with traffic; children played and yelled in the street; women leaned from the windows of shabby tenement houses and shouted back and forth. Hard-looking men leaned in doorways, sat on stone stoops.

Cardigan followed his man with difficulty, and he began to feel a sensation of futility; for Kinnard had not the manner of a man destined for any definite objective. He strolled easily, casually. Finally, however, he stopped in front of a house, looked up at the doorway. Cardigan stopped, shifted behind a parked car. Several persons entered the house in front of which Kinnard lingered. The last of these was a roughly dressed man. Cardigan saw Kinnard's lips move. The last man paused halfway up the stoop, turned, scowled. Kinnard climbed the steps easily, stood gesturing casually; and presently the two entered the house.

AFTER a moment Cardigan moved past the house. A sign said "Rooms To Let." Cardigan went on, crossed the street, waited. In five minutes Kinnard reappeared. This time he walked rapidly toward Ninth Avenue. Cardigan followed him to Eighth Avenue, and here Kinnard boarded a taxi. Cardigan followed south. At Fortieth Street Kinnard dropped off, crossed Eighth Avenue and entered Fortieth. He walked a few yards, turned into a vestibule flush with the street, disappeared.

Cardigan knew the place: Cousino's, a speakeasy specializing in ravioli and steaks. He returned to the corner and waited, his eyes never leaving the dark vestibule. Half an hour passed. Several times Cardigan was on the point of entering the speakeasy, but each time he changed his mind. He had been on the corner for an hour when he saw a man get out of a cab at the corner and make his way into Fortieth Street. The man wore a blue overcoat and a derby. He was the man Cardigan had seen in rough clothing in front of the house in Sixty-second Street. The man entered the speak.

In a few minutes Kinnard and the man came out of the speakeasy. Cardigan ducked around the corner. The two entered a cab and headed south and Cardigan followed. He was becoming impatient, puzzled. Kinnard's cab turned east at Thirty-sixth Street, south into Seventh Avenue, went past the Penn Station and continued south; sped into Varick Street and then turned east into Canal and crossed the town to East Broadway. Street lights were glowing here. A surface car clanged and rattled south. Kinnard and the burly man got out of the cab and walked down East Broadway.

Cardigan went along in the shadow of house fronts, past blatant radio stores, cheap novelty shops, across iron gratings that rang beneath his feet. He saw Kinnard and the burly man pass into a narrow doorway hard by a dusty-windowed pawnshop. He heard the door slam shut. Stopping, he looked through the window of the pawnshop. A man was standing behind the counter, reading a newspaper, smoking a cigar. A rear door opened and a youth beckoned. The man laid down his paper and disappeared through the rear door, and the youth took his place behind the counter. Cardigan looked at the name on the window—S. Goldfarb.

He moved on, stopped, eyed the narrow doorway beside the store, put his hand on the knob. The door opened. He entered a dark hallway, closed the door, stood for a moment listening, blinded by the impenetrable darkness. After a moment he shook his head, turned, groped and found the doorknob, opened the door and returned to the street. He stood for a moment deliberating, flexing his lips. He had no wish to blunder in that dark hallway. His jaw tightened. He swung on his heel and walked into the pawnshop.

The pasty-faced youth looked up from the newspaper. Cardigan was in a hurry and inclined to be blunt and to the point. He reached over and plucked a handkerchief from the youth's breast pocket. "This," he said, "you'll stuff into your mouth."

The youth was sleepy. "Huh?"

"Cram it in your mouth." Cardigan leaned on the counter and hefted his gun absently in his right hand. "The handkerchief, little one—in the mouth."

The youth's eyes popped at sight of the gun. He grabbed the handkerchief and pushed it into his mouth. His cheeks, his eyes, bulged.

Cardigan said: "Say 'ah,' son."

The youth couldn't say anything.

"That's swell," Cardigan nodded. He drew out a pair of handcuffs, went behind the counter, made the youth bend down. He then manacled his hands to the leg of a work bench, took off the youth's tie and fastened it around his mouth so that the handkerchief could not be worked out. He knotted the tie at the back of the youth's neck.

Going to the door, he threw home the bolt. The youth on the floor behind the counter made no sound. Cardigan's gun was in his overcoat pocket; so was his hand, warming the butt. He opened the rear door and entered a small, cluttered stockroom. There was a door at the left, open, and a boxed-in staircase that rose abruptly toward regions above. Cardigan looked up. A door at the top was partway open and there was light beyond. He started up, placing his feet at the extreme sides of the steps to prevent them from creaking. There was no platform at the top; the staircase ended at the threshold of the upper room and Cardigan pushed the door wide open and stepped in.

He said: "Pardon my French."

CHAPTER FOUR

DIAMOND TRUCK-LOAD

IT WAS a cozy, comfortable scene—three men sitting around a table, a bottle of wine in the center, cigar smoke drifting slowly before their faces, clouding the shaded droplight that hung from the ceiling. Cheese and crackers in a convenient bowl. Mr. Goldfarb, putty-faced, fat and soft-bodied, with spectacles pushed up on his forehead. Kinnard with a glass of wine in his hand. His burly friend, shiny-faced from a recent shave, spreading cheese on a cracker.

"Ahem," said Mr. Goldfarb.

Kinnard's eyes narrowed for a brief instant. It seemed that he was about to rise, but he did not; he calmly took a drink of wine, set the glass down, reached for a cracker and nibbled off a small piece.

Cardigan said dully: "You've been doing an awful lot of chasing around, Kinnard."

"Any law against it?"

"I suppose Mr. Goldfarb is just a sick friend you're sitting up with. My, my—what a swell, domestic picture!"

The burly man's forehead was wrinkled. "Say, who's this here now mug?"

"A kind of busybody," Kinnard said.

Cardigan said: "You know what I've come for, Kinnard. You'll save a great big headache by coming across."

Kinnard laughed, explained to the others: "You see, this busybody thinks I have a diamond bracelet."

The burly man sat back and looked stupidly at Kinnard. Mr. Goldfarb wiggled his eyebrows and his spectacles dropped neatly to his nose. He looked shrewdly at Kinnard, at the burly man, at Cardigan. "A bracelet yet?" he said to Cardigan.

The burly man slapped the table and laughed roughly, good-humoredly. "Ain't that the nuts now!"

"I ask you!" Kinnard chuckled.

Cardigan's dark brows drew together, his lip lifted. "I'm being given the razz, huh?"

Kinnard tipped his chair back, put his tongue in his cheek. He looked very immaculate, very smooth and brown and self-contained, and very droll.

"You begin to get really funny, Cardigan. Honest, I get a great kick out of you."

Goldfarb said: "What about a bracelet? Who's got a bracelet yet? What's all this talk about a bracelet? Hey, Kinnard—you got a bracelet?"

Kinnard winked broadly. "Yeah. Want to buy it?"

"Sure. Where is it?"

"Ask—" Kinnard pointed— "ask Mr. Cardigan. He knows. He knows everything. Is he smart? Well, just ask him—just ask him!"

Cardigan looked somber. "I know, baby—I know."

"What did I tell you, Goldfarb? What did I tell you?"

Goldfarb looked peeved. "Go 'way, go 'way; you're only kidding yet, Kinnard, you old kidder, you!"

Kinnard chuckled with an air. The burly man laughed and slapped the table again. Goldfarb blinked, smiled, shook his head, said: "Yeah, you old kidder, you!" And the tobacco smoke moved sinuously around the droplight.

Cardigan looked from one to the other. His face was not pleasant. He towered in the room, his hair shaggy beneath his hat, sprouting alongside his ears.

His voice was low. "So I'm a monkey, huh?"

The men shook their heads, chuckled.

Then Cardigan's gun was in his hand. "I'm this kind of a monkey, sweethearts."

THEY stopped laughing. Goldfarb sat back in his chair and turned his head away but kept his eyes sidewise on the gun. The burly man looked suddenly stupid, and his big, gnarled, calloused hands plopped to the table, remained motionless there. Kinnard lifted his chin; a shadow passed across his face; his mouth warped.

"Put that gun down, you idiot!"

"So on top of being a monkey I'm an idiot. Open your ears, Kinnard—and you, Goldfarb—and you, roughneck: you know what I'm here for, all of you. You've jazzed too much, Kinnard. This roughneck is the guy you passed the bracelet to. That's the guy I've been looking for."

"Nobody passed no bracelet to me!" rumbled the burly man. "I ain't seen no bracelet."

"Of course he's seen no bracelet," Kinnard said.

"And this," Cardigan said, nodding to Goldfarb, "is your fence."

"And where," said Kinnard, "is the bracelet?"

"One of you three men has it."

Kinnard stood up, scowled. "I told you once before, Cardigan, that I'm getting tired of this clowning around. It's about time you found out you're up a wrong tree. There's no bracelet here. I never saw the bracelet you're beefing about. Damn it, search us if you want to!"

He held up his arms.

"Go ahead, begin with me. Stand up, boys. Once and for all, we'll get this thing over with. Come on, Cardigan, search me." He set his glass on the table and stepped back from it. "Come on, get it over with."

Cardigan eyed him for a long minute. He shrugged, but his gaze remained fixed on Kinnard. "Never mind, Kinnard. You're pretty smart, pretty smart. You've trumped an Irish dick's every move, but I still think you're a heel. See? Listen, baby—I've been in this business long enough to know a rat when I see one. You're a rat. I know who that woman in your apartment was. It was through her you found out the name of the jewel house Fitchman did business with. You're a sleight-of-hand artist. I know all about you. Your piano playing is not only a good blind—it's a good in. You get into swell homes and play for parties—and you find out things. It's a new racket, Kinnard, and a neat one. I know when I'm licked. Thing is, I'm not licked yet. You fooled a square cop named Garrity—you haven't fooled me."

Kinnard snapped: "You dumb Hibernian, you haven't got a thing on me—you haven't got a thing on anybody! I told you to search me. To search these two men here. No—you wouldn't! You know damned well you'd find nothing. There's not a thing you can do."

"No?"

"No!"

"How would you like me to tell the cops that the guy's name you used when you phoned for that bracelet was the husband of the woman I saw in your apartment?"

"I never phoned for any bracelet."

"It would," Cardigan said, viciously, "be a nice puzzle to explain how it happened the woman was in your apartment, how it happened her husband's name was used."

Kinnard snarled: "Like all dicks, you've got a big nose for tabloid scandal."

"Have I? If I had, you wisecracking lounge lizard, I'd have turned her up when I found her. I didn't. O.K.—but I can turn her up now. You think you're making a jackass out of me, don't you? I'll show you that when any guy tries to do that I can be dirty. I don't care what or who the woman is—if I've got to use her to get you pinched, I'll use her."

Kinnard's eyes glittered. "It won't get you any bracelet, Cardigan. Not a bit of it. Because I haven't got it and I never did have it. Turn her up, if you want to. Can I help it if she went soft on me? I'm leaving, Cardigan. Come on, Babe," he added to the burly man.

"You wait," Cardigan said.

"I'll wait my eye! If you want me to wait, call a cop. Make a jackass out of yourself. I don't have to try to make one out of you. I'm clean, Irish. Get the whole police department. Why, you big fat-head," he laughed, "you're a swift pain in the neck. You're last year's prize joke. There's a phone. Why don't you call the cops?"

CARDIGAN walked across the room and without stopping hung his left fist on Kinnard's jaw. Kinnard went down like a felled tree. Cardigan swiveled and aimed his gun at the burly man.

"Watch yourself, big boy." Cardigan's face was dull red; there was reddish color in his eyes. He said tautly: "I hate like hell to be razzed. This pal of yours thinks he's tough, but he's never been around."

Goldfarb flapped his arms. "Now, now, all this yet—all this fighting business yet! *Ach*, don't!"

Kinnard was coughing. He sat on the floor, shaking his head from side to side. He grabbed the edge of the table and got slowly to his feet. His eyes looked bloated. He stood leaning on the table, coughing, making faces. Then he straightened, his eyes shuttered.

"Thanks," he said, catching his breath.

"Please, now—please, now," Goldfarb said. "Don't fight. Like good guys, go out."

There was a moment of silence, broken only by the hoarse breathing of Kinnard. Then there were stumbling footfalls on a stairway. Cardigan's eyes jumped to a closed door across the room. He reasoned that beyond the door a stairway went down to the hall door. Next minute there was a knock on the door.

Goldfarb rolled his eyes. The burly man looked stupidly at the door and Kinnard's lips tightened.

"Open it," Cardigan said. "You, Goldfarb!"

Goldfarb shivered and stumbled to the door. He unlocked it and hurried back to his place at the table. A short fat man stood in the doorway. He wore a loud gray suit, a wild tie the color of burnt orange and a funny hat that sat on the very top of his head. His cheeks were like red apples. His grin was cherubic. He waved a hand.

"Ah, dere you are, Babe! Watcha t'ink—I damn near busta da head on de stairway, shoo! Dark as-a hell, shoo!" His grin faded and he looked puzzled. "Hey, Babe, whassa da mat'?"

The burly man was beginning to perspire. The little Italian came into the room, ducked his head comically, took off his quaint hat and rubbed it against the underside of his sleeve. Goldfarb rolled his eyes, picked up his glass, sipped it, patted the side of his head.

The Italian looked embarrassed. "Geez-a, Babe, dis-a no way to treat a pal, huh? What da hell—you call me on de telephono, tell-a me to come to dis watcha call him number on East-a Broadway."

The burly man made a sound something like *"Ahk"* and looked sickly, stupidly at Kinnard. Kinnard's eyes were glazed, his tightened mouth warped.

"You," Cardigan said to the Italian. "What are you doing here, huh?"

"I joosta say! Ain't I joosta say Babe call me on de telephono? What's all dis-a monkey-beezness?"

Cardigan said, "What did you come here for?"

The little Italian's hand went into his pocket. He withdrew a black leather case, snapped it open. A diamond bracelet glittered. He smiled, innocently.

Cardigan said: "What the hell?" He took a step, took the case and bracelet. He snapped the case shut, dropped it into his pocket. The little Italian looked mystified.

"Thank you very much," said Cardigan. "Where did you get this bracelet?"

The Italian laughed good-naturedly. "Was watcha call good joke on Babe! Ho-ho! Ask-a da Babe." He held his stomach and shook with honest mirth.

"Well, you?" Cardigan shot at the burly man.

Babe's face was mottled. His lip shook.

"Geez, guy, I didn't steal it. I'm a truck driver. I come up from the East Side today with an empty truck except for some picks—a half a dozen picks I had. We're on a job on Eight' Avenue—where the new Hotel Morris is goin' to go up. Well, I get there. Tony jumps up to the truck to chuck the picks out. When he jumps down that thing drops from his overalls and I ask him what it is. He says it's a gadget he got for his wife at dinnertime. There's a funny look on his mug, but I don't think much about it. Well, it turns out the thing was in my truck, just layin' there. Tony found it."

"How'd it get there?"

Babe looked uneasy. "Listen, mister—I ain't a crook, see. Neither is Tony. But, hell, when a thing like that drops out o' the sky—a thing worth a thousand bucks and a guy wants to give me and Tony two hundred a piece—gosh!"

Cardigan chuckled drily. "Two hundred, eh? You know how much it's worth, Babe?"

"Huh?"

"Fifty thousand dollars."

"Fifty thou—"

"Exactly."

THE burly man's face flamed. His eyes settled on Kinnard, then swung back to Cardigan. He said: "This guy said it was a thousand. I thought he was on the up-and-up because he said we'd all meet here at a jeweler's and the jeweler'd buy it for a thousand."

"He'd fixed it up with Goldfarb. How did the thing get in your truck?"

"I don't know. This guy follered me home from work and nailed me on the doorstep. I told him I didn't have it. He said he knew it was in my truck. Then I remembered Tony and I said maybe I could get it. I said I'd have to call a guy. I said I'd call the guy and then meet him later. He propositioned me. So I called Tony—he lives downtown—and Tony said he'd come across. Then I met this guy in a speak in Fortieth Street. I told him. We called Tony again and told him to come here."

"Where were you at noon today?"

"There was a traffic jam on Sixth Avenue. Some guys were takin' pictures I was tied up under the 'El' for about ten minutes—"

"Thanks," Cardigan cut in. He turned to Kinnard. "So, that was it, eh? You dropped it from the rear platform of the 'El' train when you saw you were cornered. You dropped it in this guy's truck. When Garrity hauled you down to the street you saw the truck—the number of it and the name of the construction company. You went up to Eighth Avenue this afternoon, just before quitting time. You saw the truck, you followed the driver home. Swell, Kinnard—very swell!"

Kinnard bit his lip to silence.

Cardigan said: "You guys—you, Babe—you, Tony—better scram out of this. You going to rat on these guys, Kinnard?"

"No. To hell with them. Let 'em go."

Cardigan nodded. "That's pretty white, Kinnard."

Babe grabbed his hat. "Come on, Tony. This ain't no place for us." He heaved across the room, yanked open the door. He reared backward with a hoarse outcry, fell against Tony. Both men toppled to the floor.

Cardigan had taken out the bracelet and was looking at it. His eyes darted upward. He saw Micah standing in the doorway—small, plain Micah. There was a gun in Micah's hand, a strained look on his face, a strange gleam in his eyes.

"You will put your hands up," he said. "Not a move out of anyone."

Cardigan blinked. It was hard to believe his eyes. But the man was Micah, and there was a gun in his hand. Entering swiftly, Micah closed the door.

"Now," he panted, "we'll see. Kinnard, you have a gun. Take it out. Help me cover these men. Take the bracelet from Cardigan. Quick! I listened. I heard. We'll have to hurry, Kinnard."

Kinnard did not move. He seemed shocked, rooted where he stood, at this pale, panting apparition of a man. Goldfarb groaned. Tony and Babe remained where they had fallen. Cardigan stood holding the bracelet in one hand, the case in the other.

He said: "Micah, you're mad. Put that gun down, man. I'm Cardigan. You're—"

"Oh, yes, oh, yes," Micah sing-songed. "I know who you are. Kinnard, will you hurry up! Don't stand there like a fool!"

Kinnard shook his head slowly. "I'm caught, Micah. There's no use. The job was a flop and I couldn't get away with it. I'll take my medicine. I'm not strong on gun work. Take my advice. Beat it."

Micah panted: "What! You're turning me down! You think I'm going to let this go? You've got to come, Kinnard. If you let yourself get arrested, you'll tell about me. One way or the other, they'll know about it—and we may as well have the bracelet. I've got to have my share. My sister—she needs more doctors—that damn firm is firing me—I need money. Don't you understand? Don't you see I've taken a step I can't undo? I've got to go through with it, I tell you! Money—doctor bills—my sister."

"I'm not going, Micah. I won't squeal on you. You better lam out of this."

Micah's voice strained: "But I have to have money! You said—you remember what you said—one third—"

"For God's sake, beat it!"

MICAH shook. The gun in his hand shook. His glazed eyes burned on Cardigan and he took a jerky step forward, held out his left hand. "The—the bracelet, Cardigan—give it to me."

Cardigan watched the gun's black muzzle come toward him. "Micah, you're out of your mind. You can't get away with this."

"Give—me—the—bracelet." The words ached out of his mouth. Anguish was scratched across his face. "I'll have to—kill—you—if you don't. Money—I need money—for my sister. Ten years with that firm—and they fire me—fire me."

"Micah—"

"Don't talk! God, don't make me kill you!"

Kinnard was leaning across the table. His hand rose. He switched out the light. There was the gun's roar—the stab of flame. Somewhere in the dark there was a choked cry.

Cardigan struck out. His fist collided with something that gave. He stumbled and fell on top of Micah. Micah's gun exploded a second time and glass broke. Cardigan got hold of the gun, ripped it from Micah's hand. "Lights!" he yelled.

There was stumbling in the dark. Then the droplight sprang to life. Goldfarb stepped back from it, stumbled, said: *"Ach!"* as he looked downward.

Kinnard was lying on the floor. His head was bleeding.

"Micah shot him!" Goldfarb cried.

Cardigan was holding Micah up. He dragged him across the floor and looked down at Kinnard.

"Accidents happen, huh?" Kinnard said, and grimaced.

"I—I didn't mean it!" cried Micah.

"Shut up," growled Cardigan. "Goldfarb, get a doctor. Hurt bad, Kinnard?"

"Yeah. I guess I'm going...."

Micah gibbered and Cardigan swung him around and shook him violently. "You fool! How did you get mixed up in this anyhow?"

"My sister—money—doctors. The firm was firing me. I did recognize Kinnard. I knew he was the man robbed me. But I began to think. I thought that if I said I wasn't sure, they'd let him go. Then I could go around to him later and tell him. I did that. I went around and told him. I wanted one third for my silence. The pay-off was to be here tonight. So I came—and then— You see, Cardigan, I needed money—lots of it—for my sister—and there was no way. I've been honest all my life. All my life. Until now. Ten years with the firm—and—and—" He covered his eyes.

Cardigan stepped away, shook his head. It was this sort of thing that often cropped up in his business—men down to bedrock, men who turned criminals over night for a reason that no law would recognize. Cardigan had read the letters in Micah's room. He knew.

Goldfarb was saying: "I call the doctor but—but"—he was pointing—"Kinnard won't need one yet—ever."

Kinnard was staring at the ceiling. His mouth was slack.

Cardigan said: "You, Goldfarb—go downstairs to the store. Tony, Babe—you too. The cops are there now."

Nightsticks were beating on the pawnshop door. The three men went down. Micah was staring at the man he had murdered. Cardigan took a breath, crossed the room, gave Micah back the gun he had ripped from his hand. He didn't say anything. He walked down the stairs slowly, listening. Reached the store. The thunder of the gun upstairs seemed to shake the building. Cardigan saw flakes of plaster dribble from the store ceiling.

"What was that?" Goldfarb choked.

Cardigan said: "Use your head."

THE Nebel LIBRARY

THE ENTIRE CARDIGAN SERIES BY
FREDERICK NEBEL FROM ALTUS PRESS:

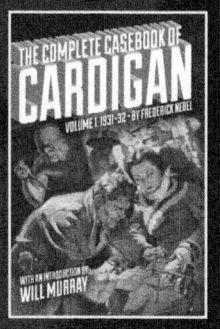

VOLUME 1: 1931-32

VOLUME 2: 1933

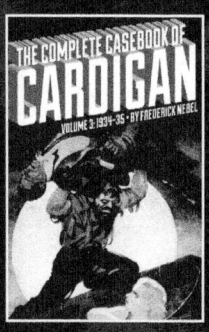

VOLUME 3: 1934-35

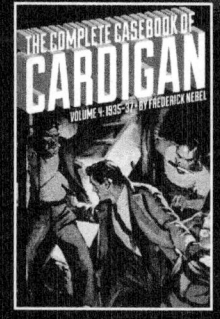

VOLUME 4: 1935-37

LOOK FOR ADDITIONAL NEBEL
LIBRARY TITLES AT ALTUSPRESS.COM

Printed in Great Britain
by Amazon